THE

Jefferson Parker is an ~~~~~ ~~~~
Orange County. His previous novels include *Black Water*,
Red Light, and *The Blue Hour*, featuring Merci Rayborn,
Silent Joe, winner of the Edgar Award and the *Los Angeles
Times* Best Mystery/Thriller Award, and *California Girl*,
another Edgar Award winner.

He lives in Laguna Beach, California. When not working
on his books, Parker spends his time with his family,
hiking, hunting, fishing and haunting the public tennis
courts.

www.tjeffersonparker.com

From the reviews of *The Blue Hour*:

'Parker has only one rival – Thomas Harris – when it
comes to averting the clichés of the serial killer book
by characterization . . . Parker excels at the multi-
faceted portraits of imperfect modern day heroes . . . If
you're seeking a thinking man's bestseller, Jefferson
Parker is the writer for you'   *Washington Post*

'Gripping . . . What distinguishes this moving book are
the finely defined characters, the author's accomplished
style . . . and the tale's unexpected twists. Contained
within this grim thriller is a surprising love story
between two people whose human quirks transcend
genre clichés'   *Wall Street Journal*

'A richly metaphoric and suspenseful ride to the end
. . . Parker on top form'   *Kirkus Reviews*

'Unpredictable and dynamic . . . far more gripping than
your average serial killer thriller . . . Sure-handed
Parker proves ever-surprising'   *Publishers Weekly*

'Parker's best work'   *San Francisco Examiner*

'Takes you where you've been and makes it seem like
the first time'   *Philadelphia Inquirer*

Also by Jefferson Parker

JEFFERSON PARKER

The Blue Hour

HARPER

Harper
An imprint of HarperCollins*Publishers*
77–85 Fulham Palace Road,
Hammersmith, London W6 8JB

www.harpercollins.co.uk

This paperback edition 2010

6

First published in Great Britain
by HarperCollins*Publishers* in 2000

A catalogue record for this book is
available from the British Library

ISBN: 978-0-00-651369-8

Set in Meridien by Palimpsest Book Production Limited,
Grangemouth, Stirlingshire

Printed and bound in Great Britain by
Clays Ltd, St Ives plc

Mixed Sources
Product group from well-managed
forests and other controlled sources
www.fsc.org Cert no. SW-COC-001806
© 1996 Forest Stewardship Council

FSC is a non-profit international organisation established
to promote the responsible management of the world's forests.
Products carrying the FSC label are independently certified
to assure consumers that they come from forests that are managed
to meet the social, economic and ecological needs
of present and future generations.

Find out more about HarperCollins and the environment at
www.harpercollins.co.uk/green

For Robert and Claudia Parker,
still showing the way.

ACKNOWLEDGMENTS

I would like to thank Robert Boettger, director of the Cypress College Mortuary Department, and Franklin Barr of Pacific View Memorial Park for their insights into the art of undertaking, sometimes known among its practitioners as the dismal trade. Thanks also to therapist Betsy Squires for her insights on the subject of chemical castration of sex offenders, and to Sherry Merryman for her helpful research into contemporary car theft and theft deterrents. Special thanks to Pam Berkson, R.N., of the UC Irvine Medical Center, for her help with chemotherapy. Finally, thanks to Larry Ragle, retired head of the Orange County crime lab, for his patient answers to my questions.

—TJP

The way to hunt is for as long as you live against as long as there is such and such an animal.

Ernest Hemingway,
Green Hills of Africa

1

That Sunday evening Tim Hess lumbered down the sidewalk to the snack stand at 15th Street. The skaters parted but paid him no attention. It was cool for August and the red flag on the lifeguard house pointed stiff to the east. The air smelled of the Pacific and ketchup.

Hess got coffee and headed across the sand. He sat down on the picnic bench and squinted out at the waves. A big south swell was coming and the sea looked lazy and dangerous.

A minute later Chuck Brighton joined him at the table. His tie flapped in the breeze and his white hair flared up on one side then lay down again. He set a briefcase onto the bench and sat down beside it facing Hess. He tore open a pack of sugar.

"Hello, boss," said Hess.

"Tim, how are you feeling?"

"I feel damned good, considering. Just look at me."

Brighton looked at him and said nothing. Then he leaned forward on his elbows. He was a big man and when he shifted his weight on the wooden bench Hess could feel the table move because the benches and the table were connected with steel pipe. Hess looked at the angry waves again. He had lived his childhood here in Newport Beach, well over half a century ago.

1

"You'll have to feel damn good for something like this. I haven't seen anything like it since Kraft. It would have to happen now, six months after my best detective retires."

Hess didn't acknowledge the compliment. Brighton had always been as generous with his praise as he was with his punishments. They'd worked together for over forty years and they were friends.

"We can put you back on payroll as a consultant. Full time, and you get all the medical. Forget the Medicare runaround."

"That's what I'm after."

Brighton smiled in a minor key. "I think you're after more than that, Tim. I think you need a way to stay busy, keep your hand in things."

"There is that."

"He's got to be some kind of psychopath. There really isn't much to go on yet. This kinda guy makes me sick."

Hess had suspected but now he knew. "The National Forest dumps."

"*Dump* isn't really the word. But you saw the news. They both went missing from shopping malls, at night. Cops waited the usual forty-eight to take the missing persons reports. The first was half a year ago, the Newport woman. We found her purse and the blood. That was a month after she bought nylons at Neiman-Marcus, walked out and disappeared forever."

Brighton squared his briefcase, fingered the latches, then sighed and folded his hands on it.

"Then yesterday late, the Laguna one. A week ago

2

she went to the Laguna Hills Mall and vanished from sight. Hikers found her purse. The ground near it was soaked in blood again—like the first. It'll hit the news tomorrow—repeat this, serial that. More mayhem on the Ortega Highway. Both the victims—apparent victims—were good people, Tim. Young, attractive, bright women. People loved them. One married, one not."

Hess remembered the newspaper picture. One of those women who seems to have it all, then has nothing at all.

He looked up the crowded sidewalk toward his apartment and drank more coffee. It made his teeth ache but his teeth ached most of the time now anyway.

"So, it's two sites off the Ortega in Cleveland National Forest, about a hundred yards apart. They're eight miles this side of the county line. Two patches of blood-stained ground. Blood-*drenched* is how the crime scene investigator described it. Scraps of human viscera likely at the second one. Lab's working up the specimens. No bodies. No clothing. No bones. Nothing. Just the purses left behind, with the credit cards still in them, no cash, no driver's licenses. Some kind of fetish or signature, I guess. They're half a year apart, but it's got to be the same guy."

"Everyday women's purses?"

"If bloodstained and chewed by animals is everyday."

"What kind of animals?"

"Hell, Tim. I don't know."

Hess didn't expect an answer. It was not the kind of

3

answer the sheriff-coroner of a county of 2.7 million needed to have. But he asked because scavengers have differing tastes and habits, and if you can establish what did the eating you can estimate how fresh it was. You could build a time line, confirm or dispute one. It was the kind of knowledge that you got from forty-two years as a deputy, thirty in homicide.

We are old men, Hess thought. The years have become hours and this is what we do with our lives.

He looked at the sheriff. Brighton wore the brown wool-mix off-the-rack sport coats that always make cops look like cops. Hess wore one too, though he was almost half a year off the force.

"Who's got it?" asked Hess.

"Well, Phil Kemp and Merci Rayborn got the call for the Newport Beach woman. Her name was Lael Jillson. That was back in February. So this should be theirs, too, but there's been some problems."

Hess knew something of the problems. "Kemp and Rayborn. I thought that was a bad combination."

"I know. We thought two opposites would make one whole, and we were wrong. I split them up a couple of months ago. Phil's fine with that. I wasn't sure who to put her with, to tell you the truth. Until now."

Hess knew something of Merci Rayborn. Her father was a longtime Sheriff Department investigator—burg/theft, fraud, then administration. Hess never knew him well. He had accepted a pink-labeled cigar when Merci was born, and he had followed her life through brief conversations with her father. To Hess she was more a topic than a person, in the way that children of co-workers often are.

4

At first she was a department favorite, but the novelty of a second-generation deputy wore off fast. There were a half dozen of them. Hess had found her to be aggressive, bright and a little arrogant. She'd told him she expected to run the homicide detail by age forty, the crimes against persons section by fifty, then be elected sheriff-coroner at fifty-eight. She was twenty-four at the time, working the jail as all Sheriff Department yearlings do. In the decade since then, she had not become widely liked. She seemed the opposite of her soft-spoken, modest father.

Hess thought it amusing how generations alternated traits so nimbly—he had seen it in his own nieces and nephews.

"Tim, she filed that lawsuit Friday afternoon. Went after Kemp for sexual harassment going back almost ten years. Physical stuff, she says. Well, by close of the workday two more female deputies had told the papers they were going to join in, file suits too. The lawyer's talking class action. So we've got a lot of deputies taking sides, the usual battle lines. I was sorry Rayborn did it, because basically she's a good investigator for being that young. I don't know what to make of those complaints. No one's ever complained about Phil before, except for him being Phil. Maybe that's enough these days. I don't know."

Hess saw the disappointment. For a public figure Brighton was a private man, and he bore his department's troubles as if they sprung from his own heart. He had always avoided conflict and wanted to be liked.

"I'll try to fly under all that."

"Good luck."

"What did the dogs find?" he asked.

"They worked a couple of trails between the sites and a fire road about a hundred yards south of the highway. The two trails were real close to each other—a hundred yards or so. He parked and carried them through the brush. Did whatever he does. Carried them back out, apparently. Besides that, nothing."

"How much blood?"

"We'll run saturation tests on soil from the new scene. Janet Kane was her name. With the first, most of it's dried up and decomposed. The lab might get some useful DNA. They're trying."

"I thought you'd find them buried out there."

"So did I. Dogs, methane probe, chopper, zip. A pea-sized part of my brain says they still might be alive."

Hess paused a moment to register his opinion on the subject of this hope. Then, "We might want to draw a bigger circle."

"That's up to you and Merci. Merci and you, to be exact. Her show, you know."

Hess turned and stared out at the riptides lacing the pale green ocean. He could feel Brighton's eyes on him.

"You do look good," said the sheriff. The breeze brought his words back toward Hess.

"I feel good."

"You're tougher than a boiled owl, Tim."

Hess could hear the sympathy in Brighton's voice. He knew that Brighton loved him but the tone pricked his pride and his anger, too.

The two men stood and shook hands.

"Thanks, Bright."

The sheriff opened his briefcase and handed Hess two green cardboard files secured by a thick rubber band. The top cover was stamped COPY in red.

"There's some real ugly in this one, Tim."

"Absolutely."

"Stop by Personnel soon as you can. Marge'll have the paperwork ready."

2

The sun had just come up over the hills of Ortega and invisible birds were chattering in the brush.

Hess stood under a large oak, near the place where Janet Kane's purse had been found. He looked down at the bloodstained earth. The crime scene investigator had dug out a patch that Hess now measured with his tape—twenty by twenty inches square and three deep. He scooped out the dead oak leaves and placed his palm against the earth, working it against the soil and debris. Then he held it up to the sunshine, trying to see if the blood had soaked down this far. No. His fingers smelled of oak and earth.

The tree itself marked the western edge of the blood spill. Hess hadn't realized how large the area was. It was roughly triangular, with the peak about six feet from the tree trunk and the sides spreading down the gentle decline caused by the roots beneath the ground. The sides were just under five feet long and the base measured at its widest exactly seventy-four inches across—as long as Hess was tall. The CSI had taken his baking-dish-sized sample way down at the base where the soil was looser and deeper and less involved with roots.

Turning slowly back through the pages of the file, Hess studied the deputy's first-call report and sketches. He compared them with the CSI's photographs, then, using fist-sized rocks, he marked the outline of the bloodstain, where the "unidentified body matter" and the purse were found. The bits of human insides had been scattered within a thirty-foot diameter of the tree, in all directions. Coyotes, he thought. Raccoons, skunks, twenty kinds of birds and a thousand insects. The steady buzz of flies filled the morning. Hess could not reconcile the idea that a fully grown human being had been here a week ago but now not a bone, not a tooth, not a single scrap of flesh or clothing was left. The contents of the victim's purse had been strewn about, according to a numbered legend on the CSI's site sketch.

The scene reminded him of something. He knew what it was but he put it out of his mind.

He set out to follow the trail the bloodhounds had worked. It led up a swale studded by small oaks and yellowed foxtails, then across a dirt road—old tire tracks, faint. Beyond the road was a gentle decline where the ground was softer, thick with cattails and pampas grass growing high and thick. He lowered his head and parted the stalks, pressing through. A moment later he could see the lagoon before him, a dark oval ringed by foliage and dappled with the rings of waterbugs. The air smelled sweet. He stood there for a moment, breathing hard and feeling the sweat run down his face. The dive boys have their work cut out, he thought: ten feet of mud to wade through before you hit the water, then two feet of visibility if you're lucky. It had been thirty years since he'd made dives himself. He'd always enjoyed them.

Back at the tree he took a knee and breathed hard. They weren't kidding about physical fatigue and weakness. The top two lobes of his left lung were gone as of two months ago.

He stood. The old oak had V-ed early in life and spread wide like oak trees will. The lower half of the trunk began only four feet off the ground. He set the files under the rock that marked the purse.

Hess climbed up and rested again, one foot braced on the main trunk and the other on the diverging limb. Slowly he walked it out toward the end, grabbing the sharp leaves overhead for balance. When he was over the place where Janet Kane had apparently been drained, he stopped and felt the branch above his head. His fingers found a smooth notch in the bark but it was hard to confirm what he felt without seeing it. In better days a simple pull-up would have gotten his chin over the branch and he could have seen what he needed to see.

One lousy pull-up, he thought. He remembered yanking off a hundred of them at the L.A. Sheriff Department Academy training course when he was a cadet. Then climbing a twenty-foot rope. Hess had begun to wonder lately if memory was supposed to be a comfort or torment.

He pulled himself up. Straining, he looked down on the notch in the bark and liked what he saw. It was just what he had imagined. The bark was worn about an inch across, all the way down to the pale living meat of the tree. His shoulder ached and his arms quivered.

Then the limb suddenly shot up past his eyes and

he was nowhere on earth for a moment. He lay flat on his back in the middle of the bloodstained ground.

Ten minutes later he was standing under the second tree, where Lael Jillson's purse had been found six months back. The big oak was part of a larger stand that blotted out the daylight and kept the ground in eternal shade. The trunk twisted up from the earth and the gnarled arms reached skyward.

He took his time making the climb. Using the foliage overhead for support, he walked out on a sturdy branch and found what he was hoping to find, the inch-wide abrasion where the bark had sloughed off. In the last six months scar tissue had formed and a surface of gray grain now covered the wound.

He saw her: ankles tied, head down, the rope looped over the branch. Hair swinging, fingertips a few inches from the dirt.

Hess trudged back to his car and got the folding shovel and two buckets from the trunk. It took him ten minutes and two rests to fill one bucket with unsoaked soil from near the Kane tree. It was important to get a control sample if you wanted to run a good saturation test. He finished, breathing fast. His palms burned like embers but when he looked down at them they were just a little red.

Then a quick sitting snooze during which he almost fell over. He finally filled the other bucket with clean soil from the clean side of Lael Jillson's tree.

When he got back to his car with the folding shovel balanced over one of the heavy buckets, he wondered if his fingers might actually break off. Dr. Cho had said nothing about loss of digits but that's what it felt like was happening. When he looked at them they were dented deeply by the bucket handles but otherwise fine.

The sun hurt his eyes and his kneecaps felt like they had rusted. He took another little nap—about two minutes—before heading back down the Ortega.

It was good to be working again.

3

Hess took the file to the hospital with him for his three o'clock appointment. Last month's program hadn't been so bad, although the cumulative effects by month number four could be devastating, depending on the patient. So said Dr. Cho.

He settled into the recliner, squared the file on his lap and listened to Liz the nurse talk about her new car. She slipped the big needle into the back of his wrist and Hess felt the stiff presence of steel in his vein. Liz taped it down and connected the intravenous drip line.

"How's that feel, Tim?"

"Foreign."

"Got some reading, there? Good. This is right here if you need it."

She rolled the wheeled table closer and lifted the little blue vomit trough. It was curved to fit around your chin, Hess had noted, but it didn't look wide or deep enough to accommodate a truly upset stomach. Maybe you were supposed to get too sick to puke right.

"You didn't even need this last time, did you?"

"I did okay."

"Good man."

"Blanket?"

13

"Please."

She lay it over his legs and feet.

"Try to relax now, and picture good things. I'll be in the next room."

Hess settled in. He looked down at the blanket. It was kind of like when he was a boy in his uncle's lodge up in Spirit Lake, Idaho, after the hunt. You were tired and fed, and the only thing you had to do through the long black night was read and sleep. The fireplace was so hot you had to move your sleeping bag to a cot on the far side of the room. Actually, this was nothing like the lodge at all.

Now, fifty-something years later, he could feel the cisplatin burning its way into his vein as he slid his free hand through the rubber band and opened the file on his lap.

Case # 99063375
Jillson, Lael

Detectives Kemp and Rayborn had procured two photographs of Lael Jillson: a snapshot taken out-of-doors, and a photocopied picture from her wedding. The snapshot showed her standing on a boulder with her arms crossed, dressed in shorts and hiking boots and a sleeveless denim blouse. She was smiling. Her blond hair was pulled back into a ponytail that shone in the sun. On her wedding day that same blond hair was swept up and detailed with tiny white flowers that looked like stars. Hess blinked and refocused on her. A slender face, a firm jawline, even white teeth and dark brown eyes. She was radiant. The picture

14

was black and white with a sepia overtone. It reminded him of his own mother's wedding picture, taken in 1928.

Of Lael Genevieve Jillson: age 31, 5'8", 130 lbs., blond/brown, Caucasian, married, born Orange, CA, maiden name Lawrence, distinguishing marks or characteristics—none.

None, thought Hess. As if being lovely was not distinguishing. Just another human female chewed up and spit into the dirt like a piece of gristle.

Most likely, he thought. Almost certainly, in spite of the pea-sized spot of hope in Chuck Brighton's brain.

Hess looked up at the mirror behind the counter in front of him. The chemotherapy room looked like a beauty salon, with four reclining chairs facing the mirror and the counter littered with jars and bottles. Televisions hung in two corners. The IV drip trolleys were pushed back against the wall. There were plastic curtains attached to the ceiling on runners, but none was in use. Hess was the only customer today.

In the mirror a pale man looked at him with steady blue eyes and a face that had not enjoyed a privileged passage through the years. It was sharp and unsentimental. The dark gray hair was brushed back like a World War II general's, with an upright peak in the front. The peak had gone to white years ago. Now the whole face was outlined in a shimmering line of red. Hess felt dizzy and he saw the head waver. He sighed and closed his eyes. He told himself he was too old for this, something men say only when they don't believe it.

15

You have work to do.

The Laguna Beach woman was reported missing six days ago, a Tuesday, from a shopping mall in Laguna Hills.

Case # 99075545
Kane, Janet

Age 32, 5'6", 120 lbs., brown/brown, Caucasian, single, born Syracuse, N.Y., orthoscopic surgery scar right knee.

Hess held up the photocopy of her picture. It was a studio portrait, the kind of picture you might have commissioned for a sweetheart, or your family. "Sanderville Studios" was visible in the lower right corner. Janet Kane was a genuine beauty, too: a good-humored smile, long dark hair with bangs parted over a high forehead, eyes that looked playful and assured. Her blouse was black and sleeveless, revealing graceful arms.

Beauty in both of them, Hess thought.

Lael Jillson, last seen in Neiman-Marcus, 8:10 P.M., according to the register receipt, purchasing panty-hose.

Janet Kane, last seen in a suburban mall, at approximately 8:45 P.M., according to a shoe salesman at Macy's, who had watched her walk out.

And their purses recovered in remote Cleveland National Forest sites accessible only by Ortega Highway or, less so, by a network of dirt roads that overlay the vast and rugged terrain. Lael Jillson's breath mints and birth control pills partially eaten by scavengers.

16

ATM, credit and insurance cards intact. No California driver's license. No cash recovered.

Who always takes your license?

A clerk. A cop.

And what would make a more concise and informative souvenir of someone you wanted to remember clearly?

A CDL. Vital stats and an image of her, collect them all.

Hess leafed through the files one page at a time. The detectives had included quadrants of a U.S. Government Survey topo map of the dump sites. Kemp/ Rayborn had marked the spots with red stars. Hess looked down at the swirling contours of the map. There was a freshwater lagoon—Laguna Mosquitoes —just a quarter mile to the west. He'd been there twenty-two years ago as part of the investigation into the killing of a second-tier drug supplier named Eddie Fowler, injected with a fatal dose of Mexican black and dumped by the highway side. The Ortega Highway—State 74—had been a popular place for body disposal for all of the five decades that Hess had been a deputy. Sixteen dumps, he thought, counting back. Yes, sixteen, counting Fowler. Kraft had used it. Suff had used it. Most of them unsolveds.

Hess had an infallible memory for such facts, though lately he had begun wondering if it was a good use of brain space. The older he got the more he understood the finite nature of things, the finite nature, in fact, of everything.

He felt a wave of nausea rise up. He breathed deeply. He closed his eyes for a moment and imagined the poison killing the cells. The bad cells only. Though he understood that the poison was killing good and bad cells, indiscriminately, like a gunman loose in a fast-food place. Liz had suggested the "positive mental imaging" before the first round while Dr. Cho had stood by in silence, smiling enigmatically.

He opened his eyes and forced his thoughts into order.

He looked at the topo map. The Ortega Highway was a long, winding road that led over the Santa Ana Mountains through two county jurisdictions, from San Juan Capistrano to Lake Elsinore. The curves were blind and people drove it fast. Traffic fatalities were commonplace. At one end was Capistrano, a quaint, sleepy little town marked by a Franciscan mission and expensive homes with acreage. Horse country: women in jodhpurs, Chevy Suburbans. Twenty-five miles away, at the other end of the Ortega, was the poor city of Lake Elsinore, built around its namesake lake. The water level used to rise and fall with the rains, which often left it little more than a polluted little slick of water with houses stranded back in dried mud. Bullthorns and ravens were what Hess thought of first, when he thought about Lake Elsinore. Then, hookers on Main, meth-racket bikers and coke-trade middlemen.

The highway ran between the cities, tethering the sunlight to the shade, the prosperity to the toil, connecting them in the way that such things are always connected, climbing past dark stands of oak, looping through miles of dense sage and chaparral, cutting along deep rock canyons and lazy spring-fed creeks

18

that nourished wildlife and sprayed the valleys with wildflowers every April. Hess had hiked and hunted it as a boy. He had always considered the Ortega to be a little haunted, and for this, he was drawn to it.

He turned the map and leafed through the pages of the files. It was frustrating how little information they had. He'd never seen thinner files on two assumed abduction/homicides where they had identified the victim so quickly. Of course, the complete lab work on Janet Kane would take time. And would add a few more pages. But nature's skill as a contaminator of crime scenes was considerable.

The cars were the key. If they were going to recover—or had already recovered—anything useful, it would be in the cars. Each was found parked and unlocked, miles from the stores where the women had shopped, on no likely route to their homes. The keys were still in the ignitions.

Then, the women had gotten into other vehicles.

Kemp and Rayborn had realized this, too. Hess read Kemp's notes. Then he turned to the CSI checklist of Lael Jillson's Infiniti Q45 and ran his finger down the page. The evidence techs had pulled up hair and fiber, of course, a fair amount of it. Human hair probably belonging to four or perhaps five different people. Based on specimens supplied by her husband, the lab had made likely matches with Lael and two family members—her husband and son. The fourth was Caucasian, dark brown, with some bend in it. The fifth was a red pubic hair that didn't fit with any of the others. Interesting, he thought.

But Hess knew the uncertainties of hair identification. Alone among the forensic sciences it was still practically unchanged in the latter half of the century. It was really done by eye, and was often inconclusive. The fact of the matter was that you could get a wide variety of colors and textures from one donor. And a hair could blow in from almost anywhere. Sometimes you'd get lucky with hair processing or pharmacological residue that would help narrow the players. Not often.

Hess read in Merci Rayborn's handwriting that Robbie Jillson had "purposely not washed the car" when his wife went missing because he immediately "knew" there was foul play, "whether you cops would take a missing person report or not." Good man, thought Hess. So the lab had gotten it in reasonably good condition, the inside at least.

Fingerprints were lifted from the interiors and exteriors of both cars. The lab had easily eliminated the victim and family members but a thumbprint in the Jillson Infiniti was still unidentified. The print had scored no hit from CAL-ID, the FBI or the regional registry in Tucson. The print results on Janet Kane's BMW were pending.

Soil specimens were taken from the interiors, good. Not taken from the exteriors, however. Bad.

Hess had once caught a creep because of decorative gravel caught in a tire tread. That was thirty years back. Since then he checked tire treads assiduously, because Hess believed that when something worked you did it again. And Lael and Janet had been *somewhere* between the time they left the shops and the time they pulled—or someone else pulled—their cars over for the last time. Sometimes tire treads had good memories.

Hess was disappointed to see that neither Kemp nor Rayborn had had the cars examined for basic mechanical problems. It was a rapist's trick old as the tire itself to let some of the air out, follow the driver and wait for her to pull over.

And no mention of the cars' alarm systems. Overridden, disabled or functional? It was an obvious question, and Hess had seen it left unasked a thousand times.

Always check the alarm.

Nowhere in the notes on the cars was there any mention or indication of a struggle.

On the back of the Kane Automobile Impound Order Hess wrote: *See dump sites, check Macy's clerk who saw Janet, check cars for window marks—alarms/problems, ASAP lab on Kane car and CSI results, check ATMs for cash withdraw post abducts, Kane purchase/how paid; where first contact made—in store, in lot, where vehicles found? Ways to get victim to trust/comply: badge, force, weapon, threat reprisal, security guard, impersonating PO, law enforce background or reject? Pure opportunity or victims chosen for specific reasons? Blood checked for drugs or specimen ruined?—How __much__ blood at each site? Saturation tests done with same soil or lab dirt? What viscera exactly? Creep/s organized, efficient . . . how finding, what doing between abduct and dump site, what doing at dump site, what doing after? Run bloodhounds in wider radius, drag or dive pond . . .*

*   *   *

That evening Hess watched the sunset from his deck. He snoozed through some of it, listening to the 13th Street surf rolling in and the voices of kids and tourists on the sidewalk below. He remembered what it was like to be a child and how he'd been mostly happy here, zooming through the alleys of the Newport peninsula on his bike, riding the waves with a pair of oversized swim fins that propelled him through the water like a dolphin.

His apartment was an upstairs unit with the garage underneath. It was big and furnished as a summer rental—turquoise Naugahyde couches sitting on bold black-and-white checked floors, a chrome dinette with a yellow tabletop stained by half a century of coffee cups. He liked the jarring cheapness of the place. When he came home at night and turned on the lights it seemed to jump at him. It was oceanfront and almost free for Hess because it was owned by a rich man he had helped once.

An uneaten plate of spaghetti lay on the table beside his patio chaise, an untouched tumbler of Scotch and melted ice beside it. They said he'd lose his appetite during the sessions and he did. They also said his hair would probably fall out and it hadn't. Hess felt a secret pride in this. The sessions were three days in a row, one session per month, for four months if you could take it. If it killed off too many blood cells you had to stop. Two sessions down as of today, two to go.

He left a message on Merci Rayborn's machine at work. He said he had started with the Kane site this morning, had some thoughts, hoped he could help her with the investigation. He wanted to get off on

22

the right foot, the fewer surprises the better. He wondered if Merci was still gunning for head of homicide by forty.

Then he called Robbie Jillson, who agreed to deliver his wife's car to the county impound yard at eight the next morning. He sounded drunk. According to the file, Janet Kane's car was still being worked over by the lab.

By nine he was in bed. It felt good to set the alarm for 5 A.M. and know you had a reason to get up for it. All Hess asked of life was to be required. He turned off the light.

He thought of his wives as he often did and realized that he wanted to say some things to them, a few things that needed saying. He listened to the ocean across the sand and wondered why waves can sound like cars but cars can never sound like waves.

The last thing he wondered was what the shoe clerk at Macy's was thinking while he watched Janet Kane leave his store.

4

"We need to get some ground rules straight," said Merci Rayborn. She walked half a step ahead of Hess, her hands on her hips and a pair of aviator shades on. This was their first time out of the building and earshot of other deputies.

They moved across the impound yard, past cars last driven by drunkards, thieves, batterers, killers or more moderate citizens who had simply neglected to pay traffic fines. The late morning sun was hot and the sky was dusted with smog. The dirty windshields held the sunlight in opaque planes.

"First of all, this is my case," she continued. Her voice was clear and certain but not loud. She was tall and big boned, dressed in chinos, a sport shirt and one of the ubiquitous black windbreakers of law enforcement, OCSD on the back in orange block letters. Black duty boots. Her hair was dark and pulled back.

She slowed a step and looked directly at Hess. "So I make the calls. If you've got a problem with that, you should probably excuse yourself from this one."

"I need the benefits."

"I heard."

She was just ahead of him again and they continued walking. Merci Rayborn's head turned and her gaze fixed on her new partner. Hess wondered if he'd lost half a step or if Merci was just fast. His neck was stiff from his fall out of the oak tree.

"Here's my wish list," she said. "One, don't smoke in my car. I quit again two months ago and I'm prone to recidivism. Two, don't bother asking me to lunch because I don't take lunch hours. I eat fast food in the car or cafeteria food at my desk. Don't talk to the media about Jillson or Kane. I'll handle all media, or else leave it to Wally the Weasel in press information. We're walking a tightrope here. You saw the *Journal* this morning so you know how it's going to be. 'The Purse Snatcher'—isn't that cute? They're on this and they'll stay on it until something better comes along. This is real middle-class fright-night stuff—not drive-bys in the barrio, not white trash, not narco. If women in this county stop going to malls it's going to ruin the local economy. So just let me control the temperature, okay?"

"Okay."

"If you have things to say, just say them. I'm a big girl. But I don't owe you any favors, no matter how many mastodons you slew with my father. I don't need any action behind my back, the way things are around here."

"That's concise. I understand."

She stopped and guided Hess to a halt with a hand on his shoulder. "Last, if you want to play grab-ass and titty-pinch I'll have your dick on a plate immediately. There, that's my wish list. Now, can we all just get along?"

Hess watched the small smile lines form at the corners of the woman's mouth, but with her eyes lost

25

behind the glasses he didn't know if they were born of humor or something else. The something else was what concerned him.

Hess understood now why Brighton had kept her on the case—a case that would surely get hot. He was trying to force either her triumph or her defeat. And his own role would be as witness to one or the other, depending on how it went.

She had to know it too. He nodded and shook her offered hand: dry, strong, smooth.

"I'm really not that hard to work with," she said. It sounded to Hess like something she wanted to believe.

They came into the high bay where the impounds are processed. An old Toyota being examined by one of the lab techs featured a bloody head-sized impression on its roof and two smaller ones high on the hood. Hess guessed kneecaps for the hood dents and guessed the impact speed at over 30 mph. A tech turned to them with no expression at all and a pair of tweezers clamped around a human tooth.

Janet Kane's BMW stood at the far end. It was still partially disassembled—doors off, side windows removed, seats pulled and now sitting against the bay wall. A loose tent of clear plastic had been taped over it.

Nearby was Lael Jillson's Infiniti, as promised by Robbie Jillson, shining black in the fluorescent light. The driver's door was open and one of the techs was lifting the window assembly from the side panel.

"What's this car doing here again?" she asked. "We did the processing months ago."

"I talked to her husband last night."

She moved between Hess and the cars, then turned to face him. She pulled off her glasses. Hess could see absolutely nothing patient or forgiving.

"No. Hess, no. *Do not* conduct interviews without clearing them with me first. *Do not* request impounds, lab procedures or anything else without clearing them with me first. *Do not* reexamine crime scenes without talking to me first. I am the lead investigator. You are a retired, part-time consultant. You do not follow hunches or make arrangements in private. We move forward as a team. Do you understand?"

"I think you forgot something."

"No, I did not."

"On the cars. We need to see the bottom of the window glass. All four panels. Both cars."

She was still standing in front of him with her head cocked just slightly to her right. She was surprisingly tall. Hess could see the anger in her eyes, and the suspicion.

"Kemp requested the car work," he said. Hess wasn't trying to blame Kemp on her behalf, but it sounded that way.

He watched as she forced her reason to override her emotion.

"Why dust the glass below the door line?" she asked. "Nobody can touch it down there unless the window's off to start with."

"Not for prints. For marks."

"From what?"

"A Slim Jim."

"Thieves quit using Slim Jims two decades ago."

"He's not a thief."

She turned and walked over to the BMW. She lifted away the plastic sheet. Hess helped her lift one of the heavy window assemblies and angle it into the overhead light. He looked down the gentle curve of the glass. The first two were clean.

Hess found what he was looking for on the third window—rear, driver's side. The jimmy tool had left three inches of dull scuff along the outer bend of the glass, near the bottom. It was the kind of shallow abrasion made by a steel tool as the operator moved it up and down, trying to hook the door release. You couldn't see it when the window was in the door. It looked to Hess like this one had taken a little time. He knew old-time car thieves who could hook a latch in five seconds or less, depending on the make and model. The rub was the alarm.

A few minutes later, Ike, one of the lab techs, got the rear driver's side window assembly out of Lael Jillson's black Infiniti. Black infinity, thought Hess, bending down to see the Jim marks low on the glass.

Rayborn brushed her fingertips against the mark and stood. "If he's forcing in with the Jim, then he has to shut off the antitheft alarms."

"That's first. If they're turned on to start with."

"I'll get Ike to tear them apart wire by wire. Find out how he's doing it."

Hess wondered how long a job Ike could make it, if you ordered him around like that. Cooperation in a bureaucracy was never free. It wasn't really Hess's business, but if something hurt the efficiency of the work, then it *was* his business. Merci Rayborn was his immediate supervisor, but the Purse Snatcher was running them both for now. He dropped the thought, something Hess was learning to do after sixty-seven years on the planet.

"It's all electronic now," he said. "On the later models."

Then Merci said something that surprised Hess. His own thoughts were moving in the same direction as hers, but she'd gotten there first.

"If he's not making them open up the cars," she said, "maybe he's already waiting for them when they get in. The backseat, behind the driver. That's why he's used outside parking lots, at night."

Hess looked down at the scratched window, then up at Rayborn, nodding.

"I hate this bastard," she said quietly. Then, over her shoulder, "Ike!"

29

5

Merci took Ike aside and told him to find out how the antitheft system had been overridden, and to find it out priority. She liked Ike because he was about her age—early thirties—and that meant he was the future of the department. Like she was. It was good to be one of the under-forties, knowing you would be running the place someday. At least some of them would. Ike seemed willing to work hard for her, so when she was in charge, she'd bump him up a pay level.

Ike smiled as she left. Merci gave him an informal little salute. Walking past Lael Jillson's car she imagined a man curled into the generous leg room of the backseat, hunched in the darkness. She imagined getting into her car at night, feeling secure and maybe a little tired from the long day, settling into the nice leather seat, interior light on, sliding the key into the ignition. Then what? She felt the hair on her neck rise.

Outside she slowed her pace to fit that of Tim Hess. Merci was a fast and determined walker and it irritated her to adjust. The fact that he was fighting cancer made everything twice as difficult as it should be. A murder investigation was no place for unwieldy sympathies. She glanced over at him, wondering how to project some kind of professional kinship with the new partner. She looked at his pale blue eyes and the

30

strong line of jaw, his thick short hair with the little crest of white that rose up like a wave in front. In his day, she thought, he must have been a decent-looking man.

"I'll eat my lunch in the car," she said, surprised at how abrupt it sounded. She was not socially graceful and she knew it. What she had meant was, I got five calls here at work from reporters yesterday, all wanting to talk about the lawsuit; and I had five more at home last night. She wondered if she should have just said that.

She looked back at him. His face looked intent. He seemed twice as large and vigorous as her father but she could see the tiredness in his eyes.

"This is how you're going to spend the next four hours," she said. "The ATM runs should be in from the banks. If he used her card for cash I'd like to know where. I want you to spend some time in their lives. If he chose them beforehand you might get lucky and stub your toe on him. I've got a call into the marketing and promotion departments for the two shopping malls, trying to see if this guy's drawn by some event, some common happening, some . . . you know, some bullshit they do to get business. When the lab work on the BMW is done we'll set it against the Infiniti and see what matches up. Gilliam told me noon on that. That's half an hour from now, and if he's good to his promise, get started without me. He said he'd know by early afternoon how much blood was lost at each site—using your samples. That's going to mean something to us. Last, one of us should run the bloodhounds in a bigger circle. If nothing pops, we'll have to dive or drag that lagoon. I know you used to dive for us, so I'm going to leave that choice to you—dive it or drag it. I also want you to see where the cars were found. That can wait, but not forever. How does all that sound to you?"

"Good."

Merci thought as she walked, not seeing the ground in front of her. "You're sure he's killed them, aren't you?"

"Yes."

"Where we found the blood?"

"I think so."

"Why?"

"There was so much of it. I didn't understand that until I saw it for myself."

"But no clothes. No flesh, no fiber, no bones. Nothing but blood and purses. The purses are for us and the CDLs are for him."

"Viscera, too."

"But did you read how much? The combined weight was less than a third of a gram. Gilliam's not even positive it's human."

"What else would it be?"

"Animals."

He didn't answer or look at her.

"What do you think he's doing with them out there?"

"Field dressing them."

She asked him what that meant and he told her. She felt the hair stand up on her neck again, and she imagined the draining body of a young woman dangling from the branch of an oak way back in the Ortega. She thought of steer carcasses, the way the extremities were clipped and tied off, everything truncated, no waste.

"Then why not more viscera, Hess, if he's disemboweling them?"

"Animals will eat almost every scrap of it. They're hungry now, a hot summer like this."

"Then we're not going to find anything in the lagoon or the woods around there," she said. "Because if he's going to that much trouble, he's not just going to abandon what's left of them."

"No. But you're right—we need to work the dogs in a bigger radius, then dive the lagoon."

Merci knew that to assume and be found wrong was the single worst thing an investigator could do. You spent a lot of time proving the obvious because you could never afford to be wrong. "Are you on good terms with McNally?"

Hess said they'd worked together.

"Line it out," she said, relieved she wouldn't have to talk to Mike right now herself.

"All right."

She saw the faint false frown on his face and felt the anger jump into her chest. Anger was a fast and powerful thing and she had not learned to control it well.

"You already have."

"That was before our ground-rules talk. Anyway, he's ready when you are."

"I wasn't kidding about any of that. None."

"It's a waste of time if I can't think a thought until you approve it."

33

"Hess, *all substantive decisions will be made by the lead investigator in counsel with his superiors and in keeping with the procedures of this manual and the policies of this department.*"

"I know. I wrote that section with Brighton, about a million years ago."

She refused to stumble. "I can tell by the pronoun it was quite some time back."

It seemed to take him a moment to figure that out.

"Well," he said. "I want both branches, where the rope burns are. There might be fiber to test. I'd have cut them off myself when I was out there, but I didn't have a saw."

"Fine. Good."

She gave him her cell phone number and told him not to use it unless he had to. "Calls are on my dime because the department's too cheap to give us our own phones. I put a fax machine in the car myself, too. Anyway, I'll take the lagoon and I'll get your branches. I need to see the dump sites again, too."

He looked at her with that hawk face and the sharp eyes and the jarhead haircut. This Hess was an odd one.

"When do you want McNally and the dogs?" he asked.

"Get them started now. I'll be there later."

"One more thing. Make the outside cut first. On the branches."

"I know."

She got a large coffee with a lid and drove the big Impala into Costa Mesa. She set her Heckler & Koch

34

9mm on the seat beside her because it poked the inside of her left arm when she drove. She liked to lower that arm to the rest and take the wheel at twelve o'clock with her right and guide the car around with the effortless power steering. She'd grown up watching her father drive the family car that way. The only difference was that her father drove slow and Merci drove fast.

The makeup girl's address turned out to be a nice little house on the west side, butted up against Newport Beach but still affordable for young people on small salaries. Her name was Kamala Petersen and she lived with two of the other cosmetic consultants she worked with. She'd been at the same mall the night Janet Kane vanished, and she'd seen someone who disturbed her. She'd come forward when Janet Kane was listed as missing. Merci had interviewed her two days ago, briefly, and found Kamala to be excitable, flighty, unable to focus. But there was something inside that Kamala Petersen wasn't letting out. Merci thought she knew what it was, and she was determined to get it.

Hypnosis was a trade-off because you could get good results, but hypnotized subjects can't testify in California criminal cases. Two of the district attorneys and the undersheriff had advised against the session. Merci had weighed the risks to her own satisfaction and decided that a suspect description outweighed the loss of a possible witness. There would be other witnesses; she would locate and subpoena them. She overruled. Merci mistrusted even the smallest of democracies, which was why she wanted to be sheriff someday.

Kamala was a big-bodied, unpretty girl, with brown tightly curled hair and a truly beautiful complexion. Rayborn thought she wouldn't mind having skin like that but the upkeep didn't interest her. Plus she had a ding in her forehead from a coffee table when she was three, and another one up by her hairline from falling off a fence when she was six. They weren't so bad but if she tried to make them over they just looked worse, in her opinion.

Kamala couldn't shake hands because her nail polish was drying. Merci said she'd rather not come in—they'd better get going.

"I'm kind of nervous," said the girl, moving her hands in front of her like she was playing an accordion.

"It's a snap."

"Last time I was hypnotized was at Magic Mountain and I thought I was Michael Jackson? The weird part was he hypnotized us to not remember any of it, so I didn't? My mom had to tell me what an idiot I made out of myself."

"No song and dance today, unless you feel compelled. Don't think about it. Pretend we're going to the beach or something. I want your brain fresh and uncluttered for Joan. Come on, let's go."

The medical towers were next to a big-screen theater. There were plenty of parking places and Merci steered the Chevy to take up two spots under a magnolia tree.

Dr. Joan Cash welcomed them into her consultation room—a hug for Merci and a handshake for Kamala. Merci had known Joan since college at

36

Fullerton and considered her a friend. She was a petite redhead with a spray of freckles across her nose and cheeks. Five years ago Merci had recommended her to the department for contract work, and the arrangement had been good for both parties: Joan got an occasional job and the county got a good psychiatrist.

Joan introduced Kamala to the sketch artist, Danielle Ruger. Merci had used her before and thought she was the best she'd ever seen. Merci shook Danielle's small, soft hand and smiled. It was nice to be doing work in a room with no men in it.

Merci thought very briefly of Phil Kemp's endless and asinine comments, his touches and gestures and jokes. It wasn't like she hadn't warned him a million times. It was simply that he wouldn't listen and she'd gotten tired of putting up with him. Tired of him getting away with it. It said right in the rules you couldn't do that. Now two other deputies—women she barely knew—had come forward with similar complaints. Had she started some ugly movement? Which was worse, putting up with Kemp or standing up to him? Merci willed away those thoughts because they were counterproductive and troubling. It was good to be here, where none of that mattered.

The doctor explained the procedure. Merci and Danielle would stay in the waiting room while Kamala was put into a deep hypnotic state. Then they would be allowed back in and Merci could take part in the conversation, make notes or tape-record it. Danielle would say nothing: more than two interlocutors might confuse Kamala, or even break down the hypnosis. Kamala would be brought out feeling relaxed and remembering what was said and done while she was under. It would take twenty to thirty minutes at the most.

Merci sat in the waiting room, made brief small talk with Danielle, then read through the last entries in the notebook where she kept a running log of her investigations. A lot of her initial-contact work was recorded in the little floppy books with the blue covers, and when she had a few minutes of down time she'd review, ruminate and brainstorm, hoping to chip something loose, see something she hadn't seen before, or see it in a new way. She liked that the notebook was not department issue, but rather a personal item she chose. She had twenty-six of them at home, filled with her writing. She always carried one in a right-side pocket—coat, shirt, even pants, it didn't matter—a companion to the Heckler & Koch so heavily invested on her left.

She took a minute to make notes on her conversation with Hess in the impound yard, following them with a sentence that she underlined: <u>Stubborn old guy and dying of cancer.</u> She looked at it and lined through it with the black pen, deciding that it wasn't up to her if he was dying or not, and it probably wasn't good policy to assume so.

She'd heard through the grapevine that he was doing chemo and radiation and that one of his lungs had been cut out. The last thing the old cop needed was his partner treating him like he was good as dead. Plus, Brighton had put him there to watch her as well as help her. Any fool could see that. Hess was

Brighton's eyes and ears, so why aggravate them any more than you had to?

Joan appeared in the doorway and waved them in. "She's down good and deep."

Merci followed her into the consultation room. The lights had been turned down and the blinds angled to admit little sun. There was a desk in one corner, bookshelves on two walls. In the middle of the room was a couch with three recliner chairs facing it across a coffee table. Kamala Petersen sat in the middle chair, tilted back like a man getting a shave, her hands crossed peacefully over her stomach, nails perfect, eyes closed. With her flawless makeup and attitude of repose she could be the newly dead, Merci thought.

"Kamala, Merci and Danielle are back with us now," said Joan Cash.

"Hi, guys," said Kamala, her voice faint but clear.

"Kamala and I were talking about waves just now. It didn't take us long to find out we both love waves. Long, gentle, never-ending Pacific waves. We've both bodysurfed."

"They scare the daylight out of me," said Merci.

"I think they're groovy," said the makeup artist.

"They can be very relaxing to contemplate," said Joan. "Ah, Merci . . . would you like to talk about a week ago? Last Tuesday night? That would be August third. Kamala, I'll be right here but you can go ahead and talk to Merci just like you were talking to me. Okay?"

"Sure."

Merci took out her notebook and pen. "Kamala,

you told me last Friday that you worked at the Laguna Hills Mall the week before. Why did you call me?"

"I saw on TV that a woman had disappeared from the mall? She disappeared the same night I was working there. It really like bothered me. And I remembered that I'd seen a . . . a . . . *rememberable* man the night she vanished. And that was why I called you."

Merci looked at Joan, who mouthed to her: *go slow* . . .

"So you saw this man Tuesday night of last week. Tell me why you thought of him when you learned that Janet Kane had disappeared."

A few seconds passed before Kamala spoke. "He was kind of . . . strange looking. I would use the word *startling*. He was standing in the parking lot when I left. It was dark but I saw him in my headlights. He was looking at his car in a very interesting way. Now, I saw him only for maybe two seconds or three? As long as it takes to see someone in your lights? And then again for maybe two seconds right when my car went by him. And he made an impression on me. But I forgot all that until I heard about the woman."

"What time did you see him?"

"It was about nine."

"All right. Now, you said this man was strange looking. You said he was startling. Describe him to me now, in as much detail as you can."

Kamala exhaled. "Blond hair, long. Golden. Goldilocks. Dark eyes. Mustache. Neither tall nor short. Average build. He was wearing a full-length coat, like

40

a duster. A light one, cotton, probably. Like a cowboy would wear."

Merci pictured the long-haired, long-coated man. A long beat. "Age."

"Twenties, maybe early thirties. And his eyes, when I got up closer? Because I could see them in the headlights? They looked wet and sad. He looked like a model. I mean a male model, not a female. He looked like a model, that was my first impression. I notice faces. And it seemed strange to me that I could notice this much about him when I was driving past him. But I think things happen for a reason, and so I noticed him for a reason."

Merci didn't comment on Kamala's cosmic outlook. To Merci, the only reasons things happened were the ones you supplied on your own. She also noted on her pad the apparent contradiction in Kamala Petersen's story: how could she see his "wet and sad" eyes when she was driving her car past him at night and he wasn't even looking at her? "So the strangeness was more in the way you reacted to him than the way he looked?"

"Well, maybe. Now that you put it that way, somewhat."

"What was startling about him?"

"It was partly his appearance. But it was something else." Kamala lay still and silent for a long minute. Then she exhaled rather loudly and shook her head. "This is just amazing. You guys aren't going to believe what I just thought of. What I just remembered. Oh my God."

I think I will, Merci thought. *Because I think you liked*

41

what you saw, and I think you had a moment with him, a
little something, a look, a glance, maybe even a word . . .

She glanced at Joan but the doctor was staring intently at her subject.

"You see, well . . . you know . . . I didn't realize it until just a minute ago, but the reason he seemed so strange and startling to me is because this wasn't the first time I saw him."

Merci thought holy shit and looked at Joan. The psychiatrist's eyebrows were raised and a smile was forming on her lips.

"I mean, like the first time was about a month before, at a mall in Brea. He was walking past the pet store. The girls and I were on our way to set up. And there he was, walking by alone, just like I saw him last week. He even had on the same coat. God . . . that's very weird I just thought of it now. This hypnosis is like really strong."

Merci's heart sped up at the word *mall* and she looked at Joan. The doctor was looking over her tented fingers at Kamala, and she lowered her expression for a long even stare at the detective. She mouthed, *wow!*

"You just brought a repressed memory into your conscious mind," said Joan, matter-of-factly. She was making notes in a book of her own now. "That memory was bothering you, and it was part of the reason you called Merci."

"I understand that now. You're right. God, this is weird."

"So, you had seen him before, Kamala," said Merci, betraying no enthusiasm in her voice. She had in her

42

heart a cold and efficient place from which to work, and she always knew where to find it. "Now, the first time you saw him, in Brea, was he just walking by?"

"By the pet store. He was walking slowly and he looked at me."

Of course he did, thought Merci. And you looked back. "Did he say anything?"

"No."

"What was his expression?"

"It was like he thought something was funny. Me."

The psychiatrist motioned Merci to silence. "Because of the way you looked at him?"

"That's right."

Joan looked at Merci and nodded.

"And how did you look at him?" Merci asked.

A pause. "I don't know, really. But I thought he was very handsome, like a model, and he must have seen this on my face. And thought it was funny."

"Did you turn around and look again, after you had passed each other?"

"Yes. And he did too, and he had the same look."

"But you didn't go up to him?"

"No."

Merci dug in. "Did any of your friends go up to him?"

"No."

"You're sure?"

"Way sure."

Merci considered. "Kamala, what was he doing the second time, when you saw him that Tuesday night? You said he was looking at his car in, quote: *a very interesting way*. What did you mean by that?"

43

"He had his hands on his hips and he was looking at the car like it had . . . misbehaved. Or like he was unhappy at it."

"Did you see any obvious problem with it? Like a flat tire or the emergency flashers on or the hood up?"

"No."

"What kind of car was it?"

"I think it was either a Mercedes or a BMW, but I'm not sure. It was white? Kind of square in the back?"

Merci made a note and thought for a moment. "How did you know it was his car?"

"I . . . don't. I didn't. I assumed it was, until just now. I guess it could have been anyone's. He was just looking at it like there was a problem he was trying to figure out."

Like whether or not it had an alarm.

Merci glanced at Joan, who was studying her with a grave expression.

"If we went back to the Laguna Hills Mall together, could you show me where he was, and where the white car was?"

"It was about in the middle of the lot, in front of the food court. But I could show you, sure."

Merci wrote and thought. "Kamala, did this man see you at Laguna Hills Mall, the second time you saw him?"

"No."

"You didn't slow down and roll down your window, ask if you could help, something like—"

"—I did *not.*"

Dr. Cash was shaking her head.

44

"Okay. Okay, Kamala. Now, could you help one of our artists draw a picture of this man?

"Yes. His face is mostly clear to me now. Anytime you want."

6

Matamoros Colesceau drove his pickup through the narrowing streets of Irvine until he reached the Quail Creek Apartment Homes. The buildings were tan stucco and wood slat, built around grassy knolls. The knolls had large decorative rocks arranged on them to suggest nature's balance and harmony. The units were not built in straight back-to-back rows, but arranged in wandering molecular-looking clusters that were supposed to promote a feeling of privacy. They were called apartment homes, not apartments. The place was like a gigantic beehive.

During his first two months here, some three years ago, Colesceau had gotten lost in his own complex four times. The many small streets all looked infuriatingly the same. There were four swimming pools designed exactly alike. The knolls were even similar, with like numbers and arrangements of stones. Now he could walk the grounds blindfolded and know exactly where he was. He lived in 12 Meadowlark, a two-level unit in the B building on the west side of the north quadrant of Quail Creek Apartment Homes.

His parole agent had already parked in the driveway, so Colesceau pulled his truck into a guest space. Now he would have to walk to his front door in broad daylight. In Colesceau's opinion Parole Agent Al Holtz was an inconsiderate pig, but he was generally amiable and unthreatening. He didn't carry a gun, although Colesceau knew he kept one in the glove compartment of his car.

He sat for a moment with the engine running. His truck was old and small, but the air conditioner worked well. He knew that what was about to happen was important to him and it made him sweat. He wanted to do well for himself. He closed his eyes and aimed the vent straight into his face.

Without any real choice in the matter, Colesceau had assented to meeting his PA, his psychologist, and maybe even a cop in his own home during his lunch hour from work. This was unnerving. But as a convicted felon and parolee he had no right to privacy, and the bureaucrats in charge of his life wanted to see him in what the psychologist called his "domestic environment" and the PA called his "pad." The ostensible reason for this meeting was his completion—in exactly eight days—of his parole. Two years at Pelican Bay State Prison, two in the Atascadero State Hospital, and then three on parole, ending at noon next Wednesday. But there was more to this meeting than just that.

He cut the engine, pulled hard on the parking brake and got out. The early August sun was bright and Colesceau shaded his eyes and leaned forward as he trotted toward the front door of 12 Meadowlark. He could feel the duct tape around his body, but he didn't think anyone else could see it through his Pratt Automotive shirt that said "Moros" over the pocket. The terms of his parole said nothing about duct tape.

He read the newspapers, however, and with the new applications of Megan's Law, cops were now telling people when "high risk" offenders were living in their neighborhoods. Here in Orange County they called it the SONAR program, for Sexual Offenders Notification and Registration. What it did was get you run out of your home if you had a history of sexual offenses and were considered "high risk" as opposed to "serious." He understood that this interview would help determine whether his neighbors were informed about his past.

Colesceau could think of no fate more humiliating than to be driven out of his apartment by squeaky clean blond people who did nothing more daring in life than cheat on their taxes.

Holtz was standing in his kitchen, drinking one of Colesceau's root beers. Holtz was fat with quick eyes and the habit of smiling when he gave you bad news. Colesceau had never once seen the lenses of his glasses clean. Holtz acted like a friend at times, but he wasn't.

"Moros! How are you?"

"Fine, Al."

"Hot one today."

"It is drastic."

"Carla should be here any minute."

Colesceau always saw himself from the outside when he was with other people. He always had, even as a boy. It was like watching a play he was in. The characters spoke, and he was one of them. He was a spectator and a participant. He had always assumed it had something to do with not being comfortable with the people around him. But you don't really choose your own company, he knew: especially in a family, a prison or a hospital.

So for a brief moment Colesceau saw himself standing there, talking to the fat man in his kitchen. Yes, that's me, he thought—short and pudgy, wearing a blue short-sleeve shirt with a patch and his name over the pocket. Mid-twenties. Hair medium length, black and wavy, complexion pale, lips pink and thick. Colesceau noted his own slightly enlarged breasts, courtesy of the hormone-altering drug Depo-Provera, which was part of his punishment. Treatment, he corrected himself: chemical castration is part of my *treatment*. And I'll be done with that treatment in eight days.

"Al, I have a new egg."

"Lay it on me."

Colesceau left the kitchen and walked into his darkened living room. He kept the blinds drawn tightly against daylight, especially in the infernal Southern California summer. The far side of the living room had three lawyer's bookcases against the wall—the kind with the glassed-in shelves and the interior lights so you could see your books.

He flipped on the lights in the middle case.

Colesceau: "Another emu egg. The blue one."

He pointed and Holtz leaned forward, his nose up close to the glass.

"Nice."

"She's producing more and more these days."

The egg producer was Colesceau's mother, Helena. Painting eggs was an old Romanian folk art and Helena had done hundreds in her life. Most of them

49

ended up here, in the lawyer's bookcases. They were painted in every color imaginable, and in many designs and patterns. The older ones were simple. The later ones featured lace, frill, bric-a-brac, bits of yarn and various textiles, and lately even plastic eyes with pupils that rolled around inside.

"Very nice."

"It's one of my favorites."

Colesceau always tried to endear himself to Holtz, who was a big proponent of what he called "family values." So Colesceau talked well of his mother whenever he could. In fact, Colesceau didn't care much for the hollow eggs his mother decorated. They were morbid and trite. If she hadn't paid for the three bookshelves he would have boxed them up and left them in the spare bedroom upstairs. But the display of eggs and his flattering words were a small price to pay for mollifying two of the most important people in his life. As one of his keepers at Atascadero always said, you catch more flies with honey, though Colesceau had wondered then—and still wondered now—why anybody would want to catch flies in the first place. The doorbell rang.

"Ah, that must be Carla!"

Colesceau went down the hallway and opened the door. Carla it was, tanned and blond and beaming as usual, with her prematurely wrinkled face and luminous teeth. Colesceau had never understood why California women so eagerly courted the damage of the sun.

"Hello, Moros."

"Hello, Dr. Fontana. You are free to come in."

50

She nodded, stepped inside and followed him back toward the living room. He could feel her behind him like a shadow. He watched her shake hands with Holtz, the PA eyeing her greedily through the dusty lenses of his glasses.

And then, like watching a play again, he found himself approaching the sofa, Dr. Fontana and Holtz settling into chairs equidistant from him. He watched himself curl into place on the couch. Colesceau considered himself catlike. He took off his shoes and pulled his feet under his legs as he sat.

Holtz held open a notebook that Colesceau had never once seen him write one letter in. Pen in fat right hand.

Dr. Fontana pulled a tape recorder from her purse and set it on the coffee table. She smiled at him with her halogen teeth.

Holtz looked at him.

Careful. Colesceau thought of the fog along the river Olt and the way it hid your thoughts.

It was Dr. Fontana who began. "I think we should start with your general outlook about things, Mr. Colesceau—*Moros*. Can you tell us how your job and family life are progressing, for instance?"

And it was Colesceau who answered as he watched and listened. "Yes. Very satisfactory to me. My job is retail, automotive parts and supplies. I spend many hours on the computer, to order and check availability. It's not difficult work, but it spends the hours rapidly."

Holtz: "He pretty much runs the place, Carla."

*   *   *

51

Carla Fontana listened to Colesceau's faint accent. His diction and syntax were a little off. Romanian, she knew. Colesceau came to the United States as a political refugee with his mother when he was eight. By age ten he'd killed six dogs in his Anaheim neighborhood, more suspected. He used Liva-Snaps to get them looking up, then an ice pick to lance their hearts. His mother caught him with the tails saved in a box taped to the frame of his bicycle.

Carla listened and questioned and listened and tried to do her job.

Her instinct was to pity him, but her job was to protect the citizens of Orange County from pathetic little monsters like Moros. Her heart told her he was harmless now, ready to begin a new life. But her brain buzzed with a high-pitched warning that said *he might be dangerous . . . we've got to tell his neighbors . . .*

Holtz tried to show no emotion as the interview went on, but all he could really feel for this guy was pity. God knew, he'd met the mother, Helena, and the woman was a hellish crone. No surprise that Matamoros was misshapen as a tumor. But what got to Holtz most was the fact that Helena's husband had been machine-gunned by Ceausescu's government police *while she and six-year-old Matamoros were forced to watch*. When the boy rushed to his father's body, the police dogs mauled him. Thus political asylum in the United States for Helena and her traumatized son.

Holtz listened and questioned and listened and tried to do his job.

52

His guts told him that Colesceau was harmless as a toadstool, so long as you left it in the forest. His head told him that this fungus had indeed done his time and paid his price. He would be a free man in a week and he ought to be treated that way. Maybe in Romania they let the dogs chew you, but here in America once you did your time, you walked.

Colesceau read their thoughts like skywriting—Fontana to convict, Holtz to acquit.

Now Holtz again, blathering on: "You still see your mother once a week or so, Moros?"

And Colesceau heard himself answer, "Yes. Invariably. She wants to live here, with me, but I'm not sure that would be healthful."

Now Fontana: "How do you feel about her living with you?"

Colesceau shrugged and sighed. Then he shrugged again. He wiped a dark curl from his forehead. "One must honor one's parents."

Holtz: "What you have to honor is yourself, Moros. You can't take care of everybody. Now, we've talked about this before. Your mother doesn't set your agenda."

Colesceau settled deeper into the sofa, feeling like a cat. Soft and flexible. Boneless.

Fontana: "What we're saying is you don't need added stressors just when you're concluding your parole term."

"No shit," Colesceau said quietly. Sometimes you had to be what Holtz called "candid."

He looked over at Fontana, and knew she'd have

53

him roasted in an American electric chair if she could. No, he corrected himself—she'd want lethal injection—it was neater and more modern and saved energy, which saved endangered species. And that was *after* she'd tried to ruin his manhood with her barbaric medications.

Fontana: "How is your libido, Moros?"

Colesceau saw the color rise in his own pale face. There would be no dignity in the coming minutes.

"It is still very removed by the medication—"

"—Removed or reduced?" she asked.

Colesceau looked at her again. "Reduced drastically."

Holtz: "Carla, we know that the Depo-Provera has been tested effective in 92 percent of subjects, with a 90 percent reduction in sexual drive. *Removal* isn't possible. Even with a full-on surgical castration the sex drive—"

"—I know," Fontana interrupted again. "Even with physical castration sexual drive can't be eliminated. Castrated men have raped."

Holtz: "Right."

Fontana: "Because rape isn't about sex, it's about anger."

Colesceau: "This is hard to imagine."

There was an odd silence, as if Colesceau had just shed unwanted light on their discussion of him.

"Why?" asked Dr. Fontana.

"Because of the reduction."

"Mr. Colesceau, just how big is the reduction in your libido?"

He imagined holding his hands about six inches

54

apart, then shrinking the distance to about a centimeter. But this wasn't the kind of humor that went over with government people, even in a democracy.

"Reduced more than you can understand."

Fontana: "How often do you experience physical sexual arousal, Moros?"

Colesceau looked down again. "Once at night I had dreams and it happened."

"Erection and ejaculation?"

He nodded. He felt his face turn redder.

Holtz: "When was that?"

"Last year. February."

Fontana: "And that's the only time, in three years of the medication?"

"Correct."

"That tracks with the better statistics," said Holtz.

Fontana: "I know the statistics."

Colesceau thought their rivalry was worse torture than their hormone treatment. Well, not exactly. You didn't have to tape down your breasts because of their rivalry.

Then Fontana, of course: "But when's the last time you saw an old lady and wanted to sexually assault her with a Coke bottle or your fist?"

He looked across at her. "I have no interest in that whatsoever."

The silence was thorough and artificially long. Like if it went on long enough he'd change his mind. These people were blunt as tongue depressors.

"And your neighbors are supposed to be comforted by that?"

"I've never hurt them. I haven't broken any law in

seven years. I'm a good neighbor. A man with tits. Just like you wanted me to be."

He saw his face again. It was red and heated and looked like shame and anger put together. Sometimes he just couldn't fake it.

Holtz: "Does that piss you off, Moros? The breast enlargement?"

"Of course it does, Al."

"Thank you for the brutal honesty."

"How do *you* know how honest it is?" asked Fontana.

Holtz shook his head sadly. "More pop, Moros?"

Colesceau unfurled from the chair, accepted Holtz's glass and left the room. The sound of their lowered voices followed him into the kitchen. He thought of the fog along the Olt and how it hid your own thoughts and kept other voices from getting in. He poured Holtz some more root beer and went back to the living room. With an almost courtly movement he handed the PA the glass, then sat down again.

He could tell it was over.

Holtz: "That's really all I have for Moros."

Fontana: "I'm finished, too. Just one question, however. Mr. Colesceau, can you give me one good reason why the people who live around here shouldn't know that you're a twice-convicted sexual predator?"

He looked at her and brushed the curl of hair off his forehead. "I can give you two. Number one, I am sorry for the things of my past. And number two, I will never do anything wrong again. I am a different man now."

7

By early morning the next day, both ATM searches had come up empty. Hess wasn't surprised because this guy didn't seem to have money on his mind. Other than the cash in the purses, which was gone of course. But even that could be used to establish special circumstances for the death penalty, if things got that far.

The soil percolation test wasn't finished, so Hess helped Ike examine the antitheft systems of the Kane and Jillson cars. In Janet Kane's car there was no alarm at all. A sticker on the inside of each rear window proclaimed the car was protected by "Electronic Engine Lock and Radio." All it meant was you couldn't drive the car away without the key, or if you pulled out the radio it wouldn't work again without entering a code. You could smash out a window and climb in without setting anything off.

The Jillson Infiniti was another story. It had a keyless entry and a loud horn that went off if the door handles were pulled. The alarm worked well and hadn't been physically tampered with, unless someone had taken the time to replace the cut wires, which would have to be replaced or repaired before the ignition would work again. There was no reason to do that, then abandon the car.

Ike held up a small component bristling with pins and connectors. He was bright eyed and his thin blond hair fell onto his forehead like a boy's. Hess wished he was Ike's age again.

"This is the wiring harness and the logic module from the Q, sir. There's a deactivate switch right here—yellow wire to pin five. That's the positive input disarm wire for the keyless entry. The brown pin is driver door, the gray is passenger doors, the black is ground."

"And?"

"The unit is working perfectly. Relays, switches, resistors, perfect. Which means a couple of things. One, he could have gotten her key, opened the locks, then got it *back* to her before she got in her car. Easy enough for a parking valet to do—but he wouldn't need a Slim Jim to get in, then, so why the scratches on the windows? Good call on that, by the way. It's low tech, so no one thinks of it anymore."

"I'm low tech, too."

"I'm glad you are. So, easy for a valet, but not so easy for anybody else. Or, he could have bought a spare keyless unit to fit her car—but that means he'd have to have her picked out way in advance. See, this system is awfully hard to beat. It's designed to defeat the old code grabbers, keep them from grinding their own keys from the vehicle identification or serial numbers. This has got rolling codes that change every time the key is used. If he had his own keyless unit, I don't understand why he would deactivate the alarm but not open the doors. I don't understand why one and not the other."

Hess nodded and didn't understand either. "Then he must not have had a keyless entry device. Not one that was working."

Ike shrugged. "Well, he didn't override the alarm mechanically—the good thieves can pop the hood and cut the system before it sounds more than once or twice. They usually work in pairs. But that's messy and there's no sign of forced entry at all, other than the Slim Jim abrasions. This guy beat the alarm system electronically, then used the Slim Jim. That would be his only chance, out in a mall parking lot. People around, security. Two things cancel all our bets, though: if she never turned on the security system. Or if she knew him."

Hess sighed. His vision blurred for just a second, then sharpened again. "Amazing what people forget to do."

"Amen to that."

Hess had already cross-checked the Jillson and Kane lists. Both were still growing, but so far, no friends in common. No shared business associates, retailers or service companies except for gas and electric. They belonged to no common organizations unless you counted the auto club, which had millions of members in the state. But he understood that the observers of a person's life can be many and easily overlooked. And that finding the shared point could be very difficult. He needed to stand in the middle of Lael Jillson and Janet Kane's lives and look out from there. See what he could see.

"We're looking," he said. "Could he make his own? Some kind of universal override device? Something that would work on a lot of different makes and models?"

Ike's eyebrows and shoulders raised and lowered. "The creeps are always finding a way. That's what creeps do. You'd have to be pretty darned good with this kind of stuff."

Ike set the module on the floor, straightened and snapped his head left to get the hair off his face. "I'll work the interiors again for the usual evidence, Lieutenant."

"Hit the space behind the driver's seat extra hard."

"Yes, sir."

Hess looked at Janet Kane's disassembled BMW.

"Lieutenant Hess? I just want to wish you all the good luck in the world, with what you're going through. It's good to have a low-tech guy around."

Hess smiled. The chemotherapy made his lips feel too small and his teeth feel huge.

"Thanks, Ike. It's good to be around."

He parked in front of Janet Kane's Laguna Beach cottage. It was slat construction circa 1930 and painted white with gray trim. There was a shaded front porch with beds of flowers in front of it. Two adirondack chairs by the door. The garden hose was coiled on a crank stand and ended with a sprinkler spiked into the ground. The walkway across the lawn was bordered by river rocks with purple lobelia and white alyssum sprouting up between them.

Hess took the two missing persons files and got out. The air smelled of flowers. On the way up the steps he stopped and looked down at the flower beds. They were dry and dying in the warm August sun. He turned on the water and collected the mail before letting himself into the house.

Inside he confronted the personal surroundings of Janet Kane. Hardwood floors and pale green walls. Rich-looking red French furniture with curvy legs, but not a lot of it. Paintings, sculptures, stacks of art books on the shelves. A red plastic TV with a seven-inch screen. The kitchen was small but light, with big squares of alternating white-and-black tile, just like his. Hess noted that there was a painting in the kitchen of her living room and a painting in the living room of her kitchen. Her file said she was a sales representative for a New York publisher of art books.

He pushed the message button on her answering machine and turned up the volume all the way:

Janet, this is Dale. We just got a 1,500-copy order from Borders for the Cézanne and a lot of that is thanks to you. Just wanted you to be the first to know. See you at pre-sales.

It angered Hess that whoever had taken Janet Kane out to the Ortega probably had no idea that she was artistic and joyful and a little bit unconventional. He probably knew nothing about her except the way she looked. He probably didn't know her name until late in the process. Hess looked at her picture in a frame on the bookshelf—Janet Kane and two girlfriends about her age standing three across at a party of some kind. An art opening, Hess speculated, a reception. She was in the middle. She would be the brave one of her group, Hess thought, the one quick to laugh, chide, take a stand or take a chance.

Hi, Jan, this is Pete again. Just checking in. Hope we're

61

still on for dinner Friday. Looking forward to it. Keep in touch, now.

The bedroom smelled of woman. It remained cool and dark at the back of the house with the shades drawn. Her bed was unmade and there was a coffee cup on the nightstand by the clock. Something on the ceiling caught his eye. Hess turned on the light, then turned it off. To the ceiling plaster Janet Kane had affixed luminescent stars of plastic, the kind made for children's rooms. Children, he thought, or anyone who had a sense of humor left.

Hi Candy Cane, this is Sue-Happy, you home? Pick up. Piiick uuup . . . okay, look—let's have a late one at the Zoolo Cafe tonight. I've got to tell you about last Sunday and I want to hear about Pete the Peeve. Cheerio, ding-dong . . .

Hi, Jan, this is Pete. It's Thursday and I know you're working hard but give me a call. I want to get Friday nailed down or not—got some things I'd like to talk about. 'Bye for now.

Jan, Pete again. I'm at 555-4459 today. Later!

Rayborn had interviewed Pete Carter. According to her notes he was saddened, shocked and not to be suspected. He'd claimed to have been out in local bars the night she died and Rayborn had already confirmed it. He was a popular guy—people here knew him. Hess heard sincerity in his voice—maybe a little too much of it, maybe that's why she hadn't called him back to begin with.

Hess turned on the light again, then sat on the bed and looked through Janet Kane's mail. Bills. Junk. Invites to art events. A card-sized envelope with a return address for "P. Carter" scribbled on the back.

He remembered from Rayborn's notes that Kane's mother and father had arrived here the day after the missing person report was filed by Kane's friend, Sue Herlihy. Kane owned the home. Hess wondered idly if she was intestate but assumed that either way, her folks would be around for a few more days.

A pea-sized part of my brain says they still might be alive.

Hess tried hard to think of a way this might be possible. He couldn't reconcile the amount of blood he saw under the oak tree with the continuation of human life. But maybe the crime lab would come up with different results in the saturation test. The Jillson site was too old for a reliable estimate. The Kane site would be their gold standard.

Janet, this is Sandy at Prima Printers. Your cards are finished and ready to be picked up. Bye.

Janet Kane? This is Brian at Len's Wine Cite. The Brunello you liked came in today. Steve said it's the best he's had. We'll hold a case for you if you're still interested. Thanks.

Hess slid open the closet. A soft puff of perfume and leather. Half her clothes were still wrapped in plastic from the cleaners. Suits and trousers, dress blouses and casual ones. Lots of blue jeans. Toward the back was a black leather bodice of some kind, with big stainless zippers. There was a hanging shoe rack with each compartment occupied. A hamper held the things you would wash at home. In the bathroom he found her prescription medicine: an outdated antibiotic for cough and some ointment for a rash. He looked in the shower at her soaps and hair care products. Under the sink he found the bulk-sized bottles she refilled them with. Frugal, he thought. Organized. Efficient. Good at living alone.

End of messages.

He found her banking statements and canceled checks in a cardboard file in the spare bedroom. It was more or less an office, with a bed for guests. Her checking account had just over $3,000 in it. A savings account had $15,500 and her KEOGH was just over $65,000. Doing all right, he thought, especially for thirty-two. Living well. Drinking Brunello. Saving some. Friends. Good job. Going to the mall late for a new CD and makeup remover.

He went through her cleared checks and wrote down the names of the garage where she took her car, all service people—hair stylist, landscape maintenance, plumber—and a few others that caught his eye for reasons he neither understood nor questioned.

Hess read the Macy's shoe clerk's description of Janet Kane as she left his store, the last known person to see her alive: "Average height and weight, dark hair worn up, a black skirt and white blouse and two-inch heels." He would know the height of the heels, wouldn't he? That was 8:43 P.M. She was dressed nicely. She was alone. The clerk saw a thousand women walk through his store that night but he identified her from a picture.

He found a description of Lael Jillson supplied by her husband, who had been at home with the children when Lael went to South Coast Plaza for hosiery. She had been wearing a blue woolen dress from Nordstrom. White shoes and the white purse.

Hair up in a white plastic clip, a white woolen jacket with her but not on her when she got in the car.

Her hair was up, too, thought Hess.

He replaced the bills and checks and put the accordion file back where he'd found it. He put her mail on the kitchen table, beside a stack of *Publishers Weekly* and a black-and-white ceramic cow creamer, a cow sugar bowl and cow salt and pepper shakers.

Kitsch.

Art.

Bulk beauty aids.

High heels and her hair up.

Hess went into the living room and sat down on the big red sofa. He put his head in his hands and thought about Janet Kane, then dozed a moment, then thought about Janet Kane again. The fact that she had black-and-white checked linoleum made him feel irrationally bad.

For a moment he thought about himself, picturing the dead cells dying, the good ones multiplying by the millions. The doctor had said he was in a battle for his life and that's how it felt.

A few minutes later he got up and locked the door behind him. He turned off the garden water and walked past the white and purple flowers to his car.

"We were closing," said the Macy's men's shoes clerk. His name was Drew Allen and he was twenty-two years old, a student at a local junior college. "And I'd pretty much finished up, just had to run the vacuum. She came down the center of the store there, because it leads to the exit. She was just beautiful. A beautiful face. She looked over and she knew I was watching her and she smiled. That doesn't happen much. Most women catch you looking they don't like it. Anyway, when someone that beautiful smiles at you, you remember. At least I remember. I looked at my watch and it was exactly 8:43. Tuesday. You make kind of an event out of some things. On a job like this. I remember thinking I'd watch that walkway at 8:42 every night from then on out. I started dreaming up ways to find out if she was married, maybe ask her out, but I couldn't come up with anything good. No point in that now, right?"

No suspicious men.

Nothing unusual.

Except for Janet Kane, just another boring night.

Robbie Jillson answered the door in shorts and a T-shirt and acknowledged Hess with a tired nod. He was a handsome young man with a surfer's bowlish haircut and the first touches of gray appearing just above his sideburns. Hess noted the big knots built up on the tops of his feet by years of lying on a surfboard. Part owner of a beachwear company, Hess remembered, "Pure Risk" or "Risk All" or something like that. Had the brains to leave his wife's car undisturbed because he knew she'd been taken.

"The kids are at camp until six," he said.

Hess was pleased but not surprised that Robbie Jillson had gotten together the things he'd asked him to. Robbie showed him into the library. It had a view of the hillsides to the east. There were high bookshelves with ladders to get to them and a very large burnished desk. On the desk were pictures of Robbie and Lael Jillson and their children. It was the prettiest family Hess had ever seen. He thought they were just the kind of people you'd expect to find in this house. It was a good family until the mother got careless and thought she could go shopping alone.

Robbie brought Hess a fruit drink and closed the door behind him. Hess could feel the waft of the air conditioner on his scalp, and the drink made his teeth feel like they were being squeezed. He ran through the cleared checks and listed the same kinds of parties he'd listed in Janet Kane's house. He'd hoped for some connection between the two cars, but there was none he could find. Nothing popped. There was an overlap in bottled water service—Mountain High Springs—but a call to the company confirmed that the delivery routes were different. Yes, Hess elicited from the district delivery manager, it was possible that a fill-in driver could have delivered at both residences. Yes, all new drivers started as fill-ins, to get experience. But the manager said it was impossible to check back for a year, even six months, because every quarter the weekly route schedules went back to corporate. Hess would have to take it up with them and she gave him the number. He thanked her because patience was the linchpin of any investigation and of Hess's soul.

He was surprised to find Lael Jillson's diary included in the box full of personal, medical and financial information that he had requested. There was a gummed yellow tag on it that said, "I've never looked at this, but you can if it will help—RJ."

He opened to the last entry and read in Lael's graceful hand:

June 2—A rare afternoon alone in the house here. Robbie and the kids gone surfing at Old Man's but I didn't want to go this time. Too much sun these days, feel like I'm drying up. Sometimes I like it just like this: me and the mansion and the air conditioner off and the windows open and a giant G&T or two, and just me. No talk, no noise, no nothing. For about an hour, maybe, then I start missing them. Sometimes I think there's not quite enough of me to entertain me for long. It's a problem, I know, but I've chosen to raise children rather than develop myself. Robbie says children shouldn't be an excuse. But then Robbie has never complained about my lack of a me, either. Sometimes I don't know why he loves me. Sometimes, like today, when I look around me I see all this bounty I don't deserve and I wonder if it's like they say—what goes around comes around and karma and all that stuff—and someday everything you don't deserve in the first place will be taken away and then some. Because if you have so much more than you deserve to have what's to keep you from losing more than you deserve to lose? Oh well, too much G&T and quality skunk weed. One more puff on the pipe and I'll sign off. 'Til next time, thank you Lord for this embarrassment of riches I call my life. I love it!

Hess closed the book and tapped his thick fingers on the leather cover. His desire for a cigarette was suddenly strong, but he'd had to stop them when they took out the upper two-thirds of his lung. The first two weeks without the smokes had been almost intolerable but he'd been pretty much alone so he hadn't taken it out on anyone. Every time he wanted a smoke he touched the scar running from the back of his shoulder to the bottom of his ribs. Fifty years of cigarettes were enough—Hess had started when he was fifteen because his older brothers did. He knew that if he'd stopped thirty years ago it might have saved him some considerable pain and maybe some years of life, but there was no profit in this knowledge, no one to pass it along to.

Hess felt the scar through his shirt and looked at Lael Jillson's picture in front of him. He saw her hanging upside down from a rope slung over the branch of the Ortega oak. He saw the slow twist of her body. At first her arms dangled down, then he saw them tied up behind the small of her back. He saw the blood running from her neck and pooling on the ground. Hess wondered if they had been chosen with their hair up to save someone the trouble of doing it himself. No, he wanted these particular women more than that. He wanted them very badly. The hair up meant something else. Hess saw a similar scene with Janet Kane. He saw the scenes again.

Terrible sights. Hess had learned to forgive himself for them. Sometimes it made him sad to know he was like this. It was part of what made him good at what he did—the detective's version of the athlete's positive imaging. But he never got to see home runs or three-pointers. And he could never unimagine what he saw. The memory was part of the price he paid for a skill he had purposefully worked to develop, a useful part of his portfolio.

In the larger sense Hess believed that most of life's givens were just that—given. He had yet to meet a man who had created himself, and this is why he thought he understood the nature of evil.

Robbie showed Hess into his bedroom. It was half the upper floor, with magnificent views to the west and south. The wall opposite the windows was mirrored glass, which offered the same view, inverted. Hess saw Catalina Island far offshore caught on Robbie Jillson's wall.

"You want to know her, don't you?" asked Robbie. "But I can't contain her for you. I can't, like, present her in a few words or with a few pictures and give you an idea of what she is."

Is, thought Hess: her husband still hasn't accepted it. Hess supposed that if he were in Robbie Jillson's position he wouldn't either. He would love to be wrong about her and Janet Kane.

They stood outside on a deck off the bedroom. Hess felt the afternoon breeze in his bones.

"I'm trying to see how your wife's life might overlap with the Laguna woman. Janet Kane. Why they were chosen."

"It's because they're beautiful."

"How, specifically?"

"Her face. Her posture."

"What about inside?"

"Her happiness. She . . . was a happy person, and it showed. She was a happy woman, Lieutenant. I mean I was really lucky. She was like that when I met her. It's just the way she . . . was. She loved her life, and if you were around her it made you appreciate your life, too. She always knew it would end, though. She wasn't shallow or stupid. But she wasn't morbid and

70

she wasn't cynical and she didn't look for the dark side of things. If there was something good or joyful to be found, she'd find it."

Hess thought about this. He watched Robbie looking out the window. Six months and the man still couldn't decide whether to speak of his wife in the past or present tense. It was the uncertainty that broke people down, he thought, and he'd seen it happen a lot. When you had a body you had the end, and people could work with endings. But without a body all you have is a mystery that eats the soul like acid.

Jillson turned and looked at Hess. The expression on his face didn't match the face—it was like a guy in a surfboard ad ready to shoot somebody.

"I smelled him."

Hess's heart seemed to speed up a beat.

"I didn't tell the other cops because the other cops didn't ask. Some guy named Kemp? He's the reason some people hate cops. Anyway, Lael disappeared on a Thursday night. Friday morning her car was found and towed I was called to get it out of hock. When I let myself in to drive it away, I could smell him."

"And?"

"Faint. Cologne or aftershave maybe. Real faint. But I smelled him. If I ever see him I'll kill him."

Hess nodded. There wasn't much you could say to that, except to be practical. "I'd like to, too. But don't. You wouldn't like prison very much."

"It would be worth it, just to punch a few holes in his face with my magnum."

"It's a better thing to dream about than do."

71

Hess looked out to the west. There were other mansions, acres of rolling yellow foothills, clean asphalt roads and the sharp blue Pacific rising up to the sky. Robbie was still stuck in paradise, his Eve departed.

Hess could say it wasn't fair but he'd already said it a million times in his life. In spite of its truth, the idea counted far less than it should.

8

Colesceau sat on his stool behind the counter and looked out the dusty window. He read the words Pratt Automotive off the glass for the billionth time in his life and looked at his watch. Twenty minutes. He could hear Pratt and Garry out back with the Shelby Cobra, and the occasional cackle of Pratt's wife, Lydia. Every day, half an hour before closing they'd start drinking beer and Colesceau would hear the rising pitch of their conversation punctuated by the *cchht, cchht, cchht* of the cans popping open. All Pratt and Garry talked about was cars and the body parts of women.

His job was to count and bag the money at closing, so he counted and bagged it. There was $14 in cash and $220 in checks. He noted the amounts and check numbers on the deposit slip and added the subtotals twice before writing down the total.

"Hey, hey, Matty."

It was Lydia, sneaking up behind him again, hanging her hand over his shoulder like they were on the same football team or something. She took liberties with his first name, which he had clearly explained was *Matamoros* or *Moros* for short. But Lydia was always playing with words and had called him *Matamata* for a while. According to a library encyclopedia

73

that Colesceau had consulted, the matamata was a "grotesque" river turtle of South America that caught prey by distending its huge lower jaw and sucking unwary animals down its gullet along with the water. He had asked her not to call him that any longer and she had not.

"How did your interview go?"

"Very well."

"They're not going to rat you out to your neighbors, are they?"

"I don't think so."

"Well," she said, hand resting on his shoulder again, "I hope they don't. It's hard enough to get on in this life without the cops stirring up the water every place a man tries to go."

He wondered if this water metaphor was a veiled reference to the grotesque matamata, but with Lydia you couldn't say for sure. "I hope for the best."

"You're an optimist. I admire that. You carry the weight for yourself. You're the only one around here isn't always complaining."

"You don't."

She rolled her eyes and shook her head. "I can keep my own counsel."

With Lydia, it was always between you and her. She would be vague and playful, then pointed and prying, all in one minute. But she had never betrayed a confidence to her husband or Garry, at least Colesceau had never caught her at it. She had this way of pairing off, of making you think that somehow she was in this with you.

She stood beside him now. With him sitting on the

74

stool they were the same height. Her breasts were heavy and low in the tank tops she always wore and she had a way of brushing them against his back when she did this teammate thing. She ran her fingers over the duct tape he wore around his body, casually scratching it through his shirt, like it itched her as much as it itched him.

Months ago she had gotten him to admit that he wore the tape to hold down his budding breasts. That he folded squares of toilet paper to go over his nipples so they wouldn't get pulled when he removed the tape.

He had been livid at her lack of manners and at himself for making such an admission, and at Holtz and Pratt for their big gossiping mouths, but to his surprise Lydia had never made reference to the tape or his breasts again. Other than the light fingernail scratch she offered without comment every time she let her hand rest on his body.

"You let me and Pratt know if we can testify or anything," she said.

She always called her husband by his last name instead of his first, which was Marvis. She always wanted to help. Like a mechanic/ex-car-thief/beer guzzler or his wife were going to make you look good to the parole board, he thought. She had a thin dark body and lank dark hair with ears that showed through it and a little nose that stuck more up than out.

"Yes."

"How'd we do today, Matty?"

He told her. It surprised him that for such a dusty,

poorly stocked, out-of-the-way place, Pratt Automotive managed to take in close to two thousand a week. And the heart of the business was the custom work that Marvis and Garry did in the back. That made some bigger money and he never saw so much as a dollar of it. It was a cash thing between car lovers and he was told from the first that there were really two "operations"—the store and the custom work—and Colesceau was to mind the store. Only. He knew that Pratt was in cozy with Al Holtz, which is why he was offered the job here. And Pratt was also in cozy with a lot of custom car and biker types and Colesceau wondered if part of Pratt's deal with Holtz was an occasional betrayal.

"Why don't you go ahead and split," she said. "I'll take the bag to the bank."

This was no surprise because Colesceau, though trusted with the handling of cash and checks during his workday, was never asked to make the nightly deposit. He assumed this was some furtive directive passed from his PA to his boss. Colesceau had long since lost his amusement over how Holtz demanded his trust but wouldn't trust him back.

He thanked her and went to the back to say goodbye to his boss. Pratt stood in the high bay behind the office, his arms crossed, looking down at the brilliant yellow Cobra with the black hood and the chrome roll bar and headers. It was an $80,000 car, Colesceau had heard. Four hundred fifty horses, top speed up near 180 mph. You had to register it in Nevada because it wasn't quite legal in California. Colesceau had a brief vision of himself at the wheel and his lover beside him, peeling across the lawless American desert at top speed, outrunning the world. Garry came from the refrigerator with two more beers. *Cchht. Cchht.*

"Next week we'll crack one for you," said Pratt.

"I haven't had alcohol in seven years."

"All finished up next week, aren't you?" asked Garry, though Colesceau knew he already knew the answer. Garry was a man who pretended to be stupid. He believed that you would tell him things because of that. But Colesceau had been around him enough to understand that he was as quick and self-serving as a dog.

"Yes, next week."

"Here's to you, my friend."

Garry tipped his beer at Colesceau and took a sip.

"Five hundred and four dollars today, Mr. Pratt. And the Ford dealership says the EGR module for the Bronco will be here tomorrow morning."

"Thanks, man."

Back in the store he saw that Lydia was outside smoking. In spite of the strong smell of machined metal, motor oil and solvent, Marvis Pratt forbade his wife to smoke inside the establishment. She'd put a wrought-iron patio table and two chairs out there, her smoking area. Pratt had donated a ground-out piston head for an ashtray, but the piston head was full and the ground was littered with her butts.

Colesceau searched under the counter for his lunch box but remembered he'd left it in the back. He was going through the short hallway that connected the retail store to the work bay when he heard Garry say something about tits, then the low-pitched, wicked chuckles.

Colesceau pretended he hadn't heard, and grabbed his lunch box off the counter above which hung the centerfolds of beautiful women in bathing suit bottoms and no tops. Today he'd put his lunch under a brunette with a gorgeous smile. His heart was beating hard and he could feel it against the tape. There was a heavy, clumsy silence as he nodded to the men and headed out again.

He stopped in his driveway at 12 Meadowlark in the Quail Creek Apartment Homes and used the remote to open his garage door. The faded little pickup truck chugged at idle while he waited. A moment later he was inside the cool of the garage and the door was coming down.

Inside the apartment Colesceau moved in the dim light. Lights off, drapes drawn. He was a pale man who preferred a little shade with his sunlight, a little dampness with his day.

The California sunshine didn't want you to have secrets like that: just look at what those people had done to him yesterday. *How is your libido . . . erection and ejaculation . . . physical sexual arousal . . . do her with a Coke bottle or your fist?*

Amazing, he thought, just what people in the government would do to a man. Humiliation. Control. Chemical castration. No better than the state police who had executed his father, really, just different methods, slower rates of extermination. And no dogs, so far.

On the way past the bookcases he glanced at the scores of eggshells, his mother's treasures. Most of them were pastels—baby blue and pink and pale yellow. Sickening, infantile shades he thought. The ones with the little skirts of lace and bric-a-brac and lace were by far the worst. In his mother's hands, egg painting wasn't so much a noble Romanian folk art as a garish display of inner imbalances too acute for Colesceau to ponder.

He didn't linger on the eggs however, because he knew that a twenty-six-year-old man must have more to think about than his mother. Not for the first time he wished she lived just a little farther away. The idea that she might move in with him was distressing.

He went into the kitchen. Colesceau knew for a fact that if the police exposed him and the neighbors rallied to have him removed, then his mother would move in to protect him. It would be her duty. She would fight them like a bulldog. He shivered and felt the tape up tight against his breasts. Thank God he'd looked ahead, seen the possibilities, made arrangements.

He made a very strong Bloody Mary. The vodka was in the freezer and the mix was in his refrigerator. He loved his drinks cold. But he liked them hot, too. So he ground half a teaspoon of black pepper, shook four jets of Tabasco and three of Worcestershire sauce into the jar, then broke off a stalk of celery and stirred it. It cooled and heated his lips at the same time. Nice.

After dinner and two more drinks Colesceau dialed Al Holtz's office number. He knew the fat PA would be

79

home by now, but he thought he might sum up his case for mercy with a brief message on Holtz's machine. He always saved a little bit of old-world formality for law enforcement:

"Yes, hello Mr. Holtz, this is Matamoros Colesceau. Moros. I want to say thank you for the interview of yesterday. I will successfully satisfy my parole next week. I hope that you will allow me to maintain my life and privacy here on Meadowlark. I will continue to live up to my obligations as in the past I have done. I will never again harm any person. Thank you very much. I look forward to talking with you. Good-bye."

When Colesceau hung up he was already brooding about women and his sexual capacity and he could feel the faint stirrings of desire down in his pants. It was difficult for him that his thoughts about sex were linked to his thoughts about castration, but the two went everywhere together, like twins, one beautiful and one ugly. *Castration.* The word sent a chill through his nervous system. It was one of the few English words with the power to do that.

Colesceau had done his research into chemical castration. In fact, he liked to think of himself as a detective who went and found things out. Depo-Provera was a brand name for medroxyprogesterone acetate, a chemical reproduction of the female hormone progesterone. Injected into males it was a hormone inhibitor, and it affected people differently. In some males it nearly eliminated the sex drive; in others it diminished it; in still others it seemed to have little or no effect. Recidivism rates were between 3 and 8 percent, depending on who you believed. It encouraged breast growth, hair loss and a loss of overall energy and strength.

Only some of this was disclosed in the State of California Department of Health protocol agreement between Atascadero State Hospital for the Criminally Insane and committed patient Matamoros Colesceau.

Since he'd been released three years ago, they'd injected the stuff into him at the end of his counseling appointment every week. What a strange feeling to sit there and watch that swarthy female nurse jab the needle into his arm and make small talk about sports or the weather while she pushed the plunger down: all this to remove from Matamoros the keen fury that brought such pain to women and such pleasure to himself.

What he discovered was that the people giving him this drug had no firm idea of what it would do to him. Which was why he got a special deal for joining the protocol—a slightly early release from Atascadero and parole terms rather lenient for a twice-convicted violent sex offender. The privileges of the lab rat, he had thought.

But the larger reason he was chemically castrated was because there was no more space in the mental hospitals, because his prison term was satisfied, because he needed—according to current budget-tightening policy—to be "re-integrated into the community." So they'd given him a choice of castrations: chemical or surgical. The chemical was temporary; the other permanent.

Now that was funny. Which one would you take?

81

Infuriating, too.

In the upstairs spare bedroom he took off his shirt. He hated the way the silver duct tape cut red furrows into his side. He hated the way the edges became slippery after only a few minutes—sweat and adhesive oozing down his ribs. He hated the smell. He'd actually tried a corset but it made him feel more female.

But what he hated even more was the way his breasts stuck out after just six months on the Depo-Provera, and the way his complexion became smoother. He couldn't do much about his skin, but he *could* do something about the tits.

Three full wraps, all the way around. Through his shirts, you couldn't even tell, he was pretty sure.

But he could certainly tell now, as he pulled off the tape and watched his skin peel away and then sag back, reddened, to his body. As the tissue fell to the floor, his pubescent girl's breasts jiggled into view. He knew there was something not completely usual about this thing he was forced to call himself.

In fact, there was something drastically not usual about it.

He saw all this and he thought about what had been done to him and it made him even more furious than he'd been to start with.

Colesceau had learned one more thing about Depo-Provera as a castrator. It might be 92% effective 100% of the time, or 100% effective 92% of the time. But it wasn't all effective all the time. Because sometimes, although not often, his rage and his lust would join fists like in the old days. Every couple of months, say.

Sometimes it would only last ten seconds. Sometimes a few minutes. Nothing like before, when he could sustain himself at peak levels for hours at a time then go again with only a little rest.

But that was all right, because Wednesday he'd be through with this hell on earth and on to the next destination, whatever that might be.

9

Merci could hear the dogs yapping in the distance, deep in the Ortega brush. She pictured Mike McNally in hot pursuit like some flummoxed jockey in charge of three horses at the same time. By the sound of the dogs they were half a mile away from the Kane site.

She looked at the hole in the ground where Hess had taken out his bucket of earth. She pictured Janet Kane dangling from the oak branch as Hess had described.

How did he see that *before* discovering the notch marks on the tree? She meant to find out and learn to do it herself.

It took her a few minutes to get positioned for a good view of the branch and she almost fell off for her trouble. But she found what the old man was talking about, the shallow groove worn through the bark into the softer pulp of the living tree, eroded away by rope—or perhaps chain. She hadn't done a pull-up since the Academy.

She had also forgotten how tiring it is to operate a handsaw. Standing on her toes she huffed away at the first branch, realizing she'd probably bought the wrong kind of tool. Wasn't this big flat-bladed thing for boards? It had run her $18 at the hardware store— still another expense she'd be hassled over by Payroll.

There was already the car fax. And the good body armor. And the "Italian" stiletto made in China she carried in her purse. And the dozens of swap-meet admission fees she accumulated on Saturday and Sunday mornings when she roamed for bargains and stolen merchandise rather than develop what Joan Cash would call a meaningful social life.

The new saw seemed to cut about one-one-thousandth of an inch deeper with every labored cycle of her arm. Five minutes later her coat was on the ground, her rolled-up shirtsleeves were collecting pulp dust, her hair was stuck to her face with sweat and she was still less than halfway through.

By the time it cracked and splintered and finally crashed to the ground, Merci had the idea that she could barely handle the Heckler & Koch right now, let alone shoot a tight group at fifty feet in less than ten seconds.

She looked down at the branch and realized with some anger that she'd made the cut nearest the trunk first, instead of the cut farthest from it. Now, in order to cut the section she needed, she'd have to climb down and try to hold the branch still with one hand, or stand on the damn thing, while sawing it with the other. Unless she wanted to bring the entire twenty-foot branch to the lab with her.

That's what Hess was talking about, you stupid bitch.

Things like this—little things like this—revealed to Merci her true character. *Your stupidity could fill volumes.* It made her wish she could change everything about herself, totally reinvent her personality, her IQ,

85

her looks, her voice, her name. Her only consolation now was that nobody—especially wiseass McNally or the old fart Hess or her quietly disapproving father—was here to see this act of *total, unconscionable and absolute stupidity.*

"You will do dumber things than this in your life," she muttered. "If you're lucky."

She dropped to the ground on the uphill side, her duty boots sinking into the bouncy layer of leaves.

And that was when the sunshine jumped off something in front of her. Stepping forward and bending, she saw a shiny disc apparently dislodged from the leaves by her crashing, ill-cut branch.

It sat balanced against the limb now, as if placed there. Nothing, really. Just a metal jar lid, made of a common alloy of some type, gold hued, the kind with the red rubber gasket built within the threaded circumference.

For pickling. Preserving. Storing over time.

Lost in the sharp oak leaves; found by stupidity.

She got down on her hands and knees and hovered over it like an entomologist over a bug. She stabbed her hair back behind her ears. The dry oak leaves bit into her knees and forearms. The metal was not oxidized. The rubber was not cracked.

Seeing this object sent a wild little shiver up her back because the best feeling in the world to Merci was finding evidence she could use. Because it was always evidence of more than just a crime. It was evidence of herself, too. It let her know she was good, lucky and prepared. It showed that she was not so stupid after all.

She went to her coat and got out a paper bag. She knelt and pushed in the lid with her pen.

She worked out concentrically from the log, bag in hand, kicking through the prickly detritus and soil and stiff roots.

Ants. Acorns. A thin layer of mulch. Hornets buzzed nearby and the sun was low enough to shine through the oak branches and paint the ground with spots of light and shadow. She kept waiting for her toe to hit something hard but hollow, for a ray of sunlight to bounce off glass and into her eyes.

She didn't find the jar the lid fit and she hadn't expected to. You could lose a lid in the leaves at night, under pressure, in a hurry. Not a whole jar. But what, exactly, in the *hell* would you be doing with it in the first place? In the woods? While a beautiful young woman dangled dead (and naked?) in the tree and her blood flooded downhill like something released from a dam?

She had imagined Janet Kane's throat laid open ear-to-ear when Hess had told her what field dressing was. It sickened her a little and made her angry. It frightened her too, to be so close to where he had been. Where he had done what he did. Because she was the kind of person—she was just thinking generally of her appearance now—that he would truss up and hang from a branch just like he did to Janet Kane. If he could.

One of the many advantages, she thought, of a nine millimeter at your side and a two-shot .40 cal derringer and fake Italian stiletto in your purse. As long as you have the nerve and skill to use them.

You could learn those things—the skill more easily than the nerve—and she had.

Still, she would slide into her car seat like any other person . . .

She wouldn't look in the seat behind her, nor into the space behind her seat. She wouldn't have her hand near the butt of the H&K—in fact, she'd probably be holding the keys in her right hand. *Check handedness for Kane and Jillson.* She would already have unslung the purse and set it on the passenger seat. So the derringer and knife were useless. She might even have lifted her eyes into the rearview for a quick vanity check—not that she was likely to do this, but a lot of women did: she'd seen them. And yes, to be honest, she herself had done it more than once.

Then what? How was he subduing them? Choking? A gun to the skull? Some kind of drug or stun gun?

A cool tingle issued across her scalp as she thought about how easily he had taken them. She stood under the tree now and looked up into the sun-shot branches. She realized that their field dresser might not have had anything to do with a jar lid at all.

But if he was the one who lost it, he wouldn't have wiped off his fingerprints first, now would he?

Pray for prints.

Praying, Merci Rayborn sawed her heart out for the next ten minutes. Done. It took another twenty to find the Jillson site, get arranged on the tree and make the two cuts—*outside cut first*—then load the branches into the trunk of her car. She examined the abraded notches with a magnifying glass. She could see the orange and black fibers attached to the broken edges of the bark and to the meatier fiber beneath it. She taped some newspaper over the notches. Gilliam, she thought: I'm bringing you the bacon and you're going to fry it.

The sun was almost behind the hills and the evening was cool and pink on the water. She stood on the shore of the lagoon and watched the bubbles of the divers mark their slow paths across the bottom. One by one the men surfaced on the far side and struggled through the cattails to the black muddy shore. They waved at her in their absurd gear, shaking their heads, wobbling on their swimfins.

She heard one of their voices carry across the water:

Sorry, Sergeant—all we found was mud!

We mucked up!

Mucking fud all over the place!

And mucking fosquito larvas!

She shouted back: *Hey, you tucking fried!*

She watched as one of them got pushed into the water by his buddies, then struggled up and dragged another down with him. Their laughing and curses came off the surface at her and she wondered why men could so easily become friends with each other, whereas they distrusted most women while still wanting to fuck them.

I just don't get you guys. But sometimes it looks like a lot of fun.

She waved again and turned back toward the dirt road. Halfway to her car she saw Mike McNally trudging toward her with a bag in his hand. His handlers were around him with their dogs dragging tongues in the dust. For a mean-spirited moment she hoped that McNally hadn't found anything useful so she wouldn't have to thank him for it or seem impressed. Then she hoped he'd found the Purse Snatcher's severed penis and testicles and had collected them in his Food for Less bag.

She fell in with them because it was clear this army of tired men and panting dogs was not going to come to an easy stop even though she outranked them all but McNally, who was her level. He was tall and square jawed and had the plain good looks of a surfer without the simpleton cool.

"Same as last time," he said.

"We had to check," she said.

"Three terminuses—the two sites and the place on the road where they lost the scent. It's where his car was. Has to be."

She knew the Purse Snatcher wasn't going to this much trouble to leave his kills in shallow graves. It didn't take Hess to convince her of that.

"Wish they could track a car scent on command."

She wasn't trying to be hurtful, but such was the tone of Merci Rayborn's voice, the history of her attempts at light comedy.

She saw the anger in his face. "They can. But it's too goddamned dusty for that here."

Last year McNally testified that one of his dogs had followed the trail of a kid who was picked up in a park, transported in a car to another site, molested, then let go. His dog had followed the in-car part of the trail for two and a half miles. As it turned out the dog had been exactly on trail, but the defense attorney had sunk McNally in court because he couldn't explain exactly *how* the dog had done it. They'd canned the perv anyway, but McNally had been embarrassed and bitter. He wasn't good on the stand because Mike wasn't a people person, he was a dog person.

A month later a judge had thrown out evidence that McNally had gotten with a "scent box" that one of his teachers invented. They used the box to pull a suspect's scent from a shirt that had been in a refrigerator for three years. The dog had trailed the scent straight to their murder suspect, and the jury had bought this one—explanation or not. But this time, it was the judge who'd overturned McNally and his dogs.

All this at a time when Mike was trying to get more budget for the scent dogs—a program he administered above and beyond his usual duties on vice. Two high-profile convictions would have helped, but he got neither.

She thought he might be over it, but she should have known that McNally tended not to get over things very quickly, if at all. He was stubborn and sensitive at the same time, possessed of an ego both huge and brittle, something Merci had decided was common to the male sex. He was a second-generation deputy, too, and Merci wondered how much of Mike's energy came from trying to outdo his father.

"Thanks, Mike."

"Welcome, Sergeant."

"What's in the bag?"

Without breaking stride he opened the bag and held it down. A little brown-and-white banded snake lay on the bottom, vibrating with McNally's footsteps.

"For Danny."

"He'll love it, Mike."

"He'll probably be scared of it."

Danny was McNally's five-year-old. He was moody and glum and intensely serious about all things. She'd always secretly liked him. Liked him the same way you'd like an exquisite little pet, maybe, or a tremendously valuable classic automobile. Liking him wasn't the problem. But how did you *show* it? How did you *touch* something like that, so small and fragile and utterly priceless? What did you say to it?

The kid had actively reviled her, which she understood, but it made things kind of tough. Not my mother, not my mother, *you're not my mother!* Yeah, yeah, *yeah*.

A few months later she had stopped sleeping with Mike but wouldn't have minded seeing him some more. Just slow things down, unstick a little. He said all or nothing. The mandate was his and she'd known it was coming. She'd slept with a man out of a sense of obligation before, but that was back in college when the world was simpler and less permanent. She'd lost a friend and gained nothing.

Mike had acted caustic and amused. Some angry crap about her being a control freak, afraid to let go. It really didn't surprise her—that was his way. Then she heard the dyke quip one day in the cafeteria and it hurt her in a place she never knew was vulnerable. It had flabbergasted her to be thought of in that way.

It made her wonder about men, too, how they'd indulge an instinct for cruelty they should have outgrown in high school.

So she had sued for a truce, but with no definite result. She hadn't heard any fresh talk about herself for a while, so maybe that was her answer. He'd talked to her about it just once, something about the humiliation of being dropped like a hot match in front of all the people he worked with, something about keeping him in the loop, something about treating people the same way you'd want them to treat you. Incredibly, something about taking little Danny's heart. It was a bad fight. It was one of those arguments that blew truth into little bits, then scattered it all over the place like a round of exploding ammunition. When you were done, there was nothing illuminated or resolved, no clarity, just a lot of shrapnel stuck in your face.

Now Kemp. She'd either survive Kemp or she wouldn't. She put it out of her mind.

"What's in *your* bag?" he asked.

She showed him the lid and explained how she found it. He nodded but said nothing.

Merci turned to behold Daisy, a 100-pound female, her favorite. The heavy thing waddled along with her teammates, ears and tongue out, jowls loose, saliva dangling. Merci knew better than to try to touch her right now—the hounds were always temperamental, more so when they were tired.

Mike's cohorts stopped to look at a hawk eating a rabbit atop a huge sycamore.

"I hear Hess is your new partner."

93

"Until I get a permanent one."

"He was my favorite, of the old farts. Phil Kemp didn't deserve you."

"So far, so good."

"You've got in almost eight full hours together."

"About that."

"He'll try to get you between the sheets, you know. He was married something like four times."

She looked at his face and saw his smile. Hard with him to tell an authentic one from a mean one. But one of the things she liked about McNally was that he walked fast like she did, so you didn't have to keep adjusting your speed.

"I'll just turn down his pacemaker," she said.

"Yeah, pull the plug on him if he doesn't mind himself."

She nodded, feeling bad about dissing Hess behind his back, uncertain how far she should take a joke with Mike NcNally anyway. Because if he wanted to let it out that Merci was talking about her new partner's pacemaker, that would make things tough with Hess. On the other hand, a joke is just a joke, right? Hess was a big boy, she thought; she just wasn't sure if Mike was.

McNally looked at her, then away. "What do you think about those other women filing suit? Kemp's got it coming from four directions now."

"Four?"

"Well, Stratmeyer in records was talking to some reporters this morning. What I heard was, she's accused Kemp of raping her. At his house."

"Oh, Christ, I hadn't heard that."

"Ugly stuff. I never had Kemp measured as that big an asshole."

Merci kept up her brisk pace beside McNally. She shook her head and felt that tightness in her chest. She willed away the tightness, willed away thoughts of Kemp and Stratmeyer.

Mike seemed to know what she was doing, because he changed the topic completely.

"So, he's bled at least two women out here. Then what? How come there's nothing else left of them?"

"We think the animals have . . . cleaned up."

"Maybe they're still alive."

"If Gilliam ever finishes the saturation test, we'll have a better idea if that's even possible."

"Well, they're not around here anywhere, except for those three points and the lines in between. What about the lagoon?"

"The dive team is finishing up. We won't find them in the lagoon."

They continued down the dusty road. She could hear the others catching up.

"We should talk about things sometime, Merci."

"Can't we just not?"

"Fine. Hey, why knock my head against your wall?"

"Please stop. It doesn't help either of us."

"Okay. Sure. I'll just see you around."

He sped up. Merci stepped to the side of the dirt road and let the handlers and their panting bloodhounds shuffle past.

10

"First off, the canning jar lid didn't hold any prints. We've got smudges consistent with fingers inside rubber or latex gloves, but no prints."

It was early Thursday morning, two days after Hess had found the Slim Jim marks on the car windows. He stood in the crime lab and felt the tips of his fingers burning. Next to him was Merci Rayborn, with her hair back in a ponytail and a tight set of lines at each side of her mouth.

James Gilliam, the director of Forensic Services, looked at her, then at Hess. To Hess he looked un-customarily perplexed.

"Now, based on the stain size and the perc rates I can tell you that at least two liters of blood went onto that ground. I can't tell you how much ran off. An adult human female contains just over four liters. So the chances are excellent that whoever lost this blood is dead. Given the circumstances, the chances are overwhelmingly good. I don't think our victim was in the presence of a lifesaver, a do-gooder or an ER nurse."

They were looking down at a bench on which sat a collection of plastic pet litter boxes and plastic food containers filled with earth. Gilliam had aerated the boxes with a narrow-bit drill to replicate natural porosity before adding the soil. The food containers had the original dump site earth, collected by the CSIs. He had gotten plenty of older, soon-to-be-discarded blood units from the UCI Medical Center to see what the blood would do in the dirt.

"You answered what we needed answered," said Merci.

Hess watched Gilliam peer toward her over the top of his reading glasses. The lab director was a soft-spoken, deliberate man who took his time and never forgot the difference between a scientist and a cop. You couldn't hook him into seeing what wasn't there. He was almost a head shorter than Merci Rayborn.

"I found something else," he said. "Kind of interesting, really."

Hess's pulse rose a blip—he knew from experience that "kind of interesting, really," was James Gilliam's way of saying hold onto your hat.

Merci knew it, too.

Gilliam said, "Those soil samples you brought me in the buckets, Tim—good thing. That was the only way to replicate the conditions in Ortega closely. But you brought me more than just soil samples. I'll bet you didn't know that."

Hess shook his head.

"I set a little from each bucket aside, just as a precaution. When the perc tests worked out I thought I'd run the extra through the mass spec, just have a look. I tried the Kane soil first and got unusually high amounts of some unusual things—trioxane, formic acid, methanol, and CH_2O. When I ran the Jillson dirt I got nothing like that."

Gilliam stopped here, as Hess knew he would. The man was a scientist and saw no reason to explain his own punch lines.

"Well, Jim, what is it?" Hess prompted.

"Oh, sorry. Formaldehyde—simplest of the aldehydes, highly reactive. In the soil samples, it was dehydrating to form the trioxane, oxidizing to make the formic acid and reducing to simple methanol. But it started as formaldehyde—there was enough of the unreacted CH_2O left to determine that. Actually it was probably formalin, which is formaldehyde in a 37 percent aqueous solution. Pure formaldehyde is just a gas."

"How did it get there?" asked Merci.

He looked at Hess but he answered Rayborn: "Someone put it there. Or, more likely maybe—spilled it."

"Just the Kane site?"

"Just the Kane site. But remember, six months of weather and rain would have washed out the Jillson ground."

Hess had already pulled down *Remington's Practice of Pharmacy* from one of the crime lab shelves. It was a large book and punishingly heavy—he'd never noticed how heavy until today. It was the same 1961 edition, priced then at $22.95. Hess had used it a hundred times over the decades to look up answers that Gilliam had in his head. There was something of the educator in James Gilliam and Hess had never minded it.

He glanced at Merci and saw the quick look of irritation she gave the lab director. Gilliam missed it, lost as he was to the mass spectrometer. He hovered over the machine, bent at the waist with his hands behind his back like a helpful valet.

"Uh, James?" she asked. "Maybe you could spare us some heavy lifting here and tell us what formalin is used for. I mean, all I know is that's what the frogs were pickled in for biology class."

Gilliam was still bent over his machine. "Usage: a preservative. A solvent. A tanning agent for leather. Mix it with ammonia and you get a urinary tract antiseptic. It's a big part of two different and powerful explosives—cyclonite and PETN. It combines eagerly, so it's used to make everything from resins and disinfectants to embalming agents, plastics to polyvinyls. It's also used as a soil sterilant. Which is interesting, since that's exactly where Tim found it."

"A preservative," said Merci. "And the lid of a pickling jar. Do the jar and the formalin go together?"

Gilliam straightened and rubbed his chin. He sighed. His pale eyes were turned up to Merci but looked to Hess like they were focused somewhere past her head. A little odd, Hess thought: Gilliam distracted, Gilliam nervous, Gilliam not looking the woman in the face. It took Hess another moment to get it: she's attractive to him and he doesn't know how to act.

"They don't have to go together, though I see what you're getting at," Gilliam said quietly. "Formalin will evaporate quickly, but you can transport it in any jar, really. And, maybe he didn't bring the jar. We only found the lid. I guess the larger question is—"

"—Yeah—what the hell is he dumping formalin into the ground for in the first place?"

"Yes, of course."

"While a body hangs from a tree, eviscerated and bleeding," she said.

A moment of silence while three imaginations tugged at their respective tethers.

Until Gilliam cleared his throat. "I had a case where a rape-killer would wash off his victim with isopropyl alcohol before he . . . coupled with her. Something about germs and religion gone pathological, is what the prosecution said. He had to have her pure, clean, clinically . . . worthy."

Rayborn was nodding. "I had one where the prick washed her out with bleach *after* he raped her. He wanted his seminal fluid destroyed."

"Maybe he's preserving *parts* of her," said the director.

"As keepsakes," said Merci. "Eyes. Hearts. Whatever in God's name turns him on."

"And when the meat hits the jar, the formalin spills out."

Quiet again.

Another meditative pause.

Merci next: "If formalin is used in tanning leather, you could use it to tan human skin, right?"

"I guess you could. But if all he wants is their skin, where's the rest of them? Even the coyotes and vultures can't completely consume a full human skeleton in one week."

Hess reentered the room after a brief mental departure. He was still looking down at *The Practice of Pharmacy*.

"Maybe he's preserving the bodies," he said. He set

the *Remington's* back on the shelf. "Taking the whole woman."

Merci and Gilliam both looked at him—two mouths slightly open, four eyes intent.

Hess continued, "It would account for us finding nothing but lots of blood, scraps of innards, and the primary ingredient of embalming fluid. He's taking everything but fluids and viscera with him."

"Okay," said Merci. "Then what about the canning jar?"

"Maybe he was just using it for the obvious."

"And what's that, Tim?" asked Gilliam.

"To carry something to eat. All that work must make him hungry."

"He ought to apply for a job here with the ME," said Merci, with a small smile for Gilliam. "If he can eat while he carves."

Gilliam smiled too but looked away from her. Then he was moving toward the door. "I found some other things from the cars. Kind of interesting, really."

Merci held open the door for the director and looked over his head at Hess.

"I *love* this part of the job," she said.

The comparison scopes were ready. Gilliam's voice carried through the hush of the Hair & Fiber room as Hess and Rayborn looked at two different hairs magnified one thousand times by the phase contrast microscope. Then they traded places.

"We were able to get the Jillson hair because her husband knew something was very wrong," said the director. "So when he got Lael's car out of impound he kept it exactly like it was. It sat under a cover in his garage for a month before we saw it. Never washed, never vacuumed. Sharp guy, Mr. Jillson. He was stubborn enough to leave the car untouched again *after* we examined it, in case we wanted a second look. We did. And I'm glad we did.

"The hair on the left is likely from a Caucasian. It's blond, long, with some wave to it. We found it in the Jillson car yesterday. It was caught on the lap belt buckle—the plastic housing that the tongue goes into. I don't know why they didn't find it the first time. I don't care, so long as it isn't Ike's or one of his workers'—which it's not. And it's not a likely match with the victim or anyone in her family. We've eliminated them as donors, too, based on their scale counts and pigmentation. They all used the same hair conditioner as the victim. This hair wasn't washed or conditioned with the same product. We found completely different pharmacological traces on it. Nothing we can identify yet, by the way. But the scale count is higher than any of the Jillson clan we tested. I'm going to say it's possible, very possible, that this hair came from your man."

"Which seat?" asked Merci.

"The one behind the driver."

"I think he waits there."

"That's very interesting. Now, on the right-hand scope is a hair that very likely came from the same person as the hair I just showed you. We pulled it from the Kane car yesterday morning. It was caught up in a mesh netting attached to the back of the driver's seat. You know, one of those things to secure

102

personal items in a car—maps, tissue, maybe a flashlight or magazines for a long trip. This certainly suggests that the hair's owner was behind the front seat himself. Maybe even crouching down at some point, resting his head against the back of the seat and the mesh. Waiting for her? Who knows? You both do know that *match* is a bad word in hair analysis—we can't say it in court—but what we have here is as close to a match as two hairs are likely to come."

"I smell the creep," said Merci.

"There's more," said Gilliam.

He led them around the microscope stations to a counter that ran along the wall. Hess followed. Sunlight came through the narrow vertical slots of the windows. The slots had always made him think of hidden archers. The heavy book had left a scalding outline on his thighs.

Gilliam brought a small plastic box from one drawer of an old steel tool chest that sat on the counter. He opened it, snugged the lid onto the bottom and handed it to Hess.

The old man looked down, then reached in with a thick fingertip and poked the item in question. It was a standard 20-amp automotive fuse, the kind you'd find by the dozen under any dashboard. The color of the glass was good and Hess could see no break in the filament inside.

"I already checked, and it's good," said Gilliam. "More to the point, there's no fuse like it used anywhere in Janet Kane's BMW. The car is only seven months old, so all the German-made factory fuses are still in it. They're a different design. This one must

103

have come from somewhere else, been *intended* for use somewhere else. Some other car. Some other piece of equipment. I don't know. But I'd like to know what it was doing in Janet Kane's car."

Rayborn asked him exactly where they'd found it and Hess asked if they'd printed it, at the same time.

Gilliam looked from one to the other.

"Behind the driver's seat. Sitting right in the middle of the floor. And yes, Tim, there was a print on the glass of it. Just a partial but we've got some ridge endings and bifurcations to work with. I eliminated Janet Kane myself. I've made up an AFIS card for CAL-ID and WIN, but the specifying parameters will be up to you two. If he's got a thumb on file, we've got a shot at him."

"Write up the parameters, Tim," said Merci.

"I want to talk to Dalton Page first. And to an old rapist I busted. They know what we're looking for."

Merci ignored him, looking instead at Gilliam with what Hess was beginning to think of as her customary suspicion. "Anything else, Mr. Gilliam?"

"That's the bulk of it."

"Good work." Then she turned her dark, adamant eyes on Hess. "Tim, go see your profiler and your rapist now. Because I want those parameters ready by the end of the workday and I want those prints on their way."

"You'll have them. I can talk to Dalton alone. But I think you should see the creep with me."

"I'll consider it."

Hess turned and started across the room. He heard the conversation without seeing it and wondered if that's how it was when you were dead, hearing things without seeing them, aware of a world going on without you. He looked back at them with something like longing.

"What about my oak branches, Mr. Gilliam?" asked Merci. "I sawed hard to get them. Outside cut first."

She looked over at him with a humored expression and Hess realized she'd cut the branch the hard way.

"Oh, standard nylon rope, Sergeant. Safety orange in color—something you might find in a camping or hunting or surplus store. Judging from the depth of the notches and the strands that wore through and stayed for us to see, it was bearing some weight. The same rope—or very similar—used on each tree."

11

Dr. Dalton Page asked Hess to meet him at his home. They had talked there, on his patio, several times over the years. The house was up on Harbor Ridge in Newport, an older tract in the city, where rambling ranch-style homes sat on terraces in the hills with views of the ocean. If you stood on the beach at sunset and looked up at them, a hillside of orange reflections looked back at you.

Driving out Hess recalled that Page had bought the place twenty years ago, anticipating retirement from the faculty of Johns Hopkins medical school. Hess had asked his help the first summer Page came to vacation in California, and they had kept in touch after that. Friends at the FBI had recommended Page as one of the best forensic psychiatrists in the country. He lectured at the Bureau regularly and had testified often as an expert witness.

Hess had helped organize a little party—mostly law enforcement and DA officers—to welcome Dalton and Wynn Page to Orange County. That was a decade ago, when the doctor retired and they moved here year round. Wynn had grown up in Newport and Hess remembered her seeming happy to be back home. Page himself had been wry about living in la-la land, but he had quite a suntan. After that the Pages had made little effort to include Hess in their social world, but he knew from department talk that they kept an extremely busy, bicoastal lecture and appearance schedule. Page had written a bestseller about criminal personality types.

The back patio was bathed in sunshine and looked out over the bright blue Pacific. Dr. Page sat at a glass table in the perforated shade of a lattice awning. Mandevilla vines snaked their way through the lattice and the pink blooms hung in the air.

He was wearing tennis whites and a white vest, which set off the darkness of his skin. His face was taut from surgery. There was a box of small weights and a jump rope sitting off under a Norfolk Island pine. Hess shook his hand and his grip was strong and dry.

Wynn brought them iced tea and set her hand on Hess's shoulder as she poured his.

"Carry on, crimebusters," she said, then headed back into the darkness of the house.

Not for the first time in his life Hess wished he was still married to his first wife, Barbara. It was a hypothetical longing based on what he thought he saw in some long marriages: trust, comfort, mutual respect. Two hearts seemed to beat slower than one. Couples like the Pages made him feel it. He guessed if he was still married to Barbara he'd have a lot less to worry about. He wouldn't be broke, for one thing. Children would have given him a firmer grip on the future. A grip, he just now realized, that would have been easier to relinquish when it was time.

Beat this tumor and you've got ten more years, he

107

thought, possibly fifteen. You can turn around a lot of things with that much time.

"The Ortega sites, Tim?"

"I brought the files. We don't have a lot to go on, but we've got a partial print. If you and I can get the parameters right we might get lucky with it. If not, we'll wait until he does it again and hope he gets careless."

"Um," said Page. It was between a grunt and something more thoughtful.

Hess knew Page was already disagreeing with him, and that was fine. That was why he was here.

Page looked through the glossies of the dump sites. He wore a homely pair of black reading glasses. Hess remembered Page bragging he had 20/15 vision because that's what Hess had.

Hess listened to the swish of the photographs and the mockingbird in the pine.

"Tim, tell me what you know about the victims. While I read through this."

Hess told Dr. Page about beautiful, confident and occasionally lonely Janet Kane. Then about the very spoiled though very decent Lael Jillson.

"The pictures in there don't capture how beautiful they both were," he offered.

Dr. Page, with a curious smile: "And what have you seen that does?"

"Other pictures. Family. How they lived."

"How was that?"

He told the doctor about Janet Kane's bulk hair products and Lael Jillson's enthusiasm for private hours without her husband and children around. He

108

mentioned Kane's interest in art and Jillson's thoughtful diary. He didn't say anything about the leather playthings in Janet Kane's closet or Lael Jillson's weakness for marijuana and gin. As he talked about the two women he'd never seen Hess felt protective of them, like he owed their memories a simple kindness that their bodies, at the end, were not offered.

"That print on the fuse may be your miracle," said the doctor. "Because you're right, Tim—if that's what you were assuming, anyway—he's been printed before. He's got a sheet and he's spooked and he knows what pressure feels like. You've run across him somewhere. Could be way upstream in juvenile court, but somewhere he's felt the lash."

"That's why he's careful."

"You're damned right it is. But what an ego. I mean, what an astonishing arrogance by leaving those purses."

"Do you think they're more for us or more for the public?"

"For you. Funny, the media calls him the Purse Snatcher, but he's the opposite of a purse snatcher. He leaves the purse and takes everything else. It's all he leaves. That and the blood."

Page looked up at the sky like it might have something to say. Hess liked the way Page could draw sense out of something that seemed only evil. Hess took the pieces and made his own picture.

"It would be easy for him to take the purses," Hess said. "But if he did, we'd have to keep the women in the missing persons' files forever. In an investigative sense, there would be no murder."

"He needs someone to hear the tree fall—you."

"He's experienced, isn't he?"

"He's *practiced*, but not necessarily experienced. From the time and distance between the dumps I'd say Jillson and Kane were his first actual homicides. Plenty of time to let the first one blow over, but not enough confidence to vary the routine very much. Nobody starts with something of this magnitude. You work up to it. If nothing else, you work up to the *how* of it. And like most builders he's never really satisfied with what he makes. It's always got to get bigger, better, more elaborate. Riskier. More complex. So, you may have two purses sitting in evidence right now, but when he goes again, he might just *give* you more to work with. It's part of escalating the risk, and the risk is a major stimulant to him."

"He'll go again."

"Absolutely. He's abducted and murdered twice. And we understand that this is a sex killing, of course. So, there won't be any more half measures for the Purse Snatcher. No more of the things that he practiced, the scenarios he created to get him to this point. He's graduated. He's big time. He might move halfway across the country, he might win the lottery, but he won't stop."

"Any chance at all that he's keeping them alive?"

"None whatsoever."

"Why?"

"For one, it's totally impractical. But more importantly, he prefers them dead, Tim."

"How do you know that?"

Dr. Page smiled, a little ashamedly, thought Hess.

"Tim, he's *taking them with him*. His fantasy doesn't climax in a rape-kill scenario. It *begins* with one. What is interesting to this man—what is essential about him—happens after he's killed and raped them. Note the order there—not rape and kill."

Hess thought about this.

"How old is he?"

"Twenty-five to thirty. That's enough time to see his vision and learn his methods. But not enough to leave twenty or thirty women dead behind him— because that's how many you'll have ten years from now if you don't catch him. Actually, I'd guess he'd leave the area before he got that many. Any hits through VICAP?"

"Nothing hot. I talked to Lyle Hazlitt back in Washington early this morning. He says there's a Michigan case open, two women kept in a cabin after they were killed. Wife and mother-in-law, though. They're chasing the husband down in south Florida now."

"No," said Dr. Page.

"There's a guy breaking into funeral homes in New Orleans, taking the corpses. They don't know where or why."

"No. But that's an interesting case. That kind of protracted necrophilia is extremely rare. There's very little even written on it."

"Maybe he's holding the corpses for ransom, wait- ing for the furor to die down before he calls their families."

Page smiled. "You're such a Pollyanna sometimes."

They laughed at this.

"I'd love to interview this guy, Tim."

"I'd like to stop him."

Page nodded and looked through the photographs again.

"He thinks he's repellent to women, so he blitzes them. But if he was truly physically hideous someone would remember him hanging around the malls. No, he sees himself as unworthy of engaging a live woman. Takes the whole woman. A corpse is reusable, Tim. Look for a freezer or a large cooler, possibly in a storage unit somewhere close to where he lives. It's possible he's cut them into refrigerator-sized parts, but I don't think so. No evidence of flesh rent or bones sawed, no easy way to use power tools out in those woods . . . no. I think they're whole. The formalin near the bleeding ground makes me think of embalming or preserving, too. I see from your notes here that you thought of that, already. The question is why would he lug embalming fluid and the requisite needles and tubes around with him if he could just do that all at his place a little later? He takes tremendous risk out there in the Ortega."

"Efficiency. Blood out, fluid in. Done."

"I guess. Nothing to hose off. Interesting how neat he is, isn't it? Hang and bleed them like deer. Now, that's a direction you can go if you want to."

"I want to."

"It's too obvious to ignore. A hunter. Someone with experience dressing animals in the field. An outdoorsman. Likewise a butcher or slaughterhouse employee. Certainly someone with the rudiments of human biology and a knack for the mechanical. I mean, he's

112

getting into those cars without tripping the alarms—
that isn't easy. So, throw some electronics know-how
into the profile. He's also got to be pretty strong, to
hoist them up like that with the rope. White male, of
course. I don't have to say that. How do you think
he's subduing them, Tim?"

"I have no idea."

"He may strangle them right there in their cars.
Dark parking lots. It could be over pretty quick if he's
strong."

"True. But wouldn't he want to damage them as
little as possible?"

"Correct. Just like plums in the market."

"And if he can get them to the woods under their
own power, it saves a lot of hard work," said Hess.
Lately, he had become acutely aware of what it was to
be tired and to save energy. It was hard for him to
imagine carrying a human body even the hundred
feet or so from the dirt road to the oak trees. Not to
mention hoisting them up with a rope. Check the
hunting and camping stores, he thought: see what
new gadgets they've got for hanging a carcass.

"Of course," said Dr. Page, "he has to drive a vehicle
large enough to carry a body in. Trunk, most likely.
Maybe a van or a pickup truck with a camper on
it."

"Physically, what can we look for?"

"Compact and muscular. He wouldn't even think
about waiting in the backseat of a car if he was large.
Note, however, that he's picked out fairly spacious
cars."

"What else can I use for parameters? That partial

113

print is all we've really got. I want to send it through CAL-ID with all the blessings we can give it."

Page nodded curtly, folded his fingers under his chin and shut his eyes. The sunshine came through the lattice in little rectangles and landed on his face. Hess saw the Mandevilla blossoms nodding in the breeze like they were talking to each other. Between the doctor's elbows were photographs of ground soaked in at least two quarts of human female blood and the words of a young man currently employed in the shoe department of a major department store: *anyway, when someone that beautiful smiles at you, you remember. At least I remember* . . .

"Tim, a man who has reached this level of specialization has had a long and . . . thorough journey to this point. Look for a juvenile record of academic failure, truancy, exposure, peeping, breaking and entering to take underwear or other fetish items, or perhaps a masturbator, urinator, defecator. Fire setting, of course. If he's got the sheet I think he does, look at the sex crimes. No matter how far off the mark they might seem, remember that he's grown, changed. Anything but pedophilia, that's its own world. I honestly believe you will have run across him before. You, meaning law enforcement. His need for risk will be his undoing, if you get him. He'll have to give you more and more. And forget your stooges and snitches and jailhouse songbirds—the Purse Snatcher will have told exactly nobody on earth about his deeds. That's why he has to tell *you* about them. That's why he left the purses."

Dr. Page set his hands on the table top. His fingers looked seventy and his face looked fifty. He was staring down at the pictures still lying between his arms.

"No one's had a look at this guy? Not one single eyewitness at the malls? Someone lurking, following, checking out the cars, anything out of the ordinary?"

Hess considered. "Rumor has it we've got some kind of witness. I guess I'm not supposed to know. Rayborn hypnotized her for the sketch artist, but I haven't seen the results."

"Then a witness is what you don't have. In court."

"Right. Dalton, do you see the Purse Snatcher trying to get himself close to the investigation?"

"I doubt it. He's not that naive. He would be more likely to send you a body part, UPS."

"Something from the inside, though."

"Correct. Something from the inside. He doesn't want to spoil her appearance."

12

It angered her to pose for a rapist but she knew Hess was right: if Izma got interested he might talk to impress her.

Hess talked to the manager while Merci stood in the lobby and read the LA PALOMA HOTEL RULES sign:

1. No checks
2. No overnight guests
3. No loud music after 10 P.M.
4. No hot plates
5. No solicitors
6. No kidding!

"Three-o-seven," said Hess.

"How come I haven't seen this creep's name on the SONAR lists?"

"He's not considered high risk."

"A low-risk rape-kidnapper."

"That's what they say."

They took the stairs to the third floor and walked down the hall. Merci touched the gun that was snugged against her ribs the way a Catholic might touch a medallion of St. Christopher. It was for luck and for something more than luck: it was for peace. Her last qualifier was her best in ten years, putting her fifteenth overall in a big department that had a lot of good shots.

Mercy had drawn down only once in her life and didn't have to fire, but she was steady on target in a Weaver stance and would have hit him clean if she'd pulled. She liked what she'd said to the creep, something unrehearsed, something that just came out and worked real well, at least on this guy: *Hey Jack, you gonna be just another dead asshole?*

That had done it. Luck. Peace. The nine.

Before they got to the door Hess said, "Let me lead it. I know a little about him."

"Just stand there and look my best?"

Hess stopped outside 307 and turned to her. "It would be better if you sat. He liked them small and helpless."

"I'm five-eleven."

"He's six-ten."

When Ed Izma opened the door Merci's heart gave a startled flutter, then settled uncomfortably. Part of the reason was the size of the man, his head coming almost to the top of the seven-foot door frame. She leaned back reflexively to look up at him. She could feel the willingness of her right hand to move up under her coat, so she made a point to keep it at her side.

He was not an ugly man at all, in fact his face had an economy of line that was interesting, and his eyes were a placid and unthreatening gray. He was smiling and his teeth were large and even. Merci thought his head looked small.

"Sorry to upset you," he said. "But nice to meet you. I'm Ed."

He offered his hand. Merci took it and understood instantly that he had her now, could easily force her any direction he wanted, or snap her into the room and right out the third-story window if he wanted. It seemed an awful long way to his eyes or balls, and she doubted she had the speed and strength to damage them.

"Sergeant Rayborn, OCSD."

He smiled down on her and let her hand go. His eyes had light in them. "You know, I haven't committed one serious crime in the last thirty-five years, Hess. In fact, I've only committed one serious crime in my entire life."

"It was kind of a whopper."

Merci, in the center of the room now, turning to her left, saw Ed Izma's gaze bearing down on her. Hess had told her Izma raped his victim a dozen times in the two days he had her. The cold of the freezer had actually helped keep her alive; that and Izma constantly putting her in and yanking her right back out for various reasons. She'd had the luck to be put in an old freezer with bad wiring, a poorly fitting top and a shot gasket. She'd needed a blood transfusion when they got her to the hospital.

"By today's standards? I don't think so. I never took another life."

"One that we know about, anyway," said Hess.

Merci was suddenly aware of multiple facts: hot room, thick air, useless air freshener, a fan oscillating to her right; Hess and Izma to her left, five hundred plus pounds of antagonistic male bulk. There was a large bed that took up most of the room. It was made.

118

She felt like she was looking at things through a hot fog. Dizzying. Another room behind: bath and bedroom but too small for the bed? She was aware of being stared at. Didn't the room smell like air freshener and semen? Where was the real air in here, anyway?

"Something to drink, Merci?"

"Water. Ice if you have it."

"I'm sorry, I don't have either."

"What do you have?"

"Nothing, actually."

"Thanks anyway, shitbird."

"I really dislike foul language from a woman."

"She doesn't care what you like, Ed. She doesn't want to date you."

Merci, breathing deeply and letting the anger clear her head, caught the flash of meanness and pride in Ed Izma's gray eyes.

"Something like that, though—right, Hess? A little temptation?"

"She's my partner."

"You're a lucky man, then. Sit. Please. I wiped these chairs off just for you."

The chairs in question were two white plastic patio chairs. Merci looked hard at the seat, wondering what the giant had had to wipe off.

Izma lumbered into the other room and she heard the suck of air and gasket, then water running. Tricky bastard, she thought. He wore a white singlet and a pair of very tight shorts, a swimsuit probably, that made him seem even bigger than he was. The swimsuit was yellow with white piping. His legs were

119

trunklike and pale and mostly smooth, with an occasional patch of very dark hair. His feet looked enormous. He wore the kind of cheap rubber thongs that click when they hit the bottom of a heel.

Merci felt the hair on her neck rise.

Luck. Peace. The nine.

She took a deep breath, then another.

Hess was seated well away from her but close to the huge bed that sat against the wall. He was looking at the bed. His legs were crossed and his hands were folded over one knee, and Merci saw him for the first time as a calm and strong man, a man you wouldn't want to mess with, and she was happy to see him this way. He looked at her but said nothing and his eyes asked the same of her.

She felt trapped in the dismal room and her palms were still damp but she could feel her reason coming back. Hess's level stare helped. She nodded, gazed around. There were indentations on the carpet at the midway point along each wall. They looked to Merci about twenty by twenty inches, the size a TV set might make, or a small nightstand, or a file cabinet. They were a darker shade of yellow than the carpet around them—no sun on them.

What had been there, and why had Izma moved them?

The light diminished as a body darkened the doorway and moved toward her with a glass of ice water.

"Just kidding," he said.

"You're a crack-up." She took the glass.

He chuckled quietly and moved away. He sat at the foot of his bed.

Then he arched his back and hiked up his feet and walked himself backward across the bedspread on feet and hands. His legs were spread and his hips raised high. His genitals slopped out from behind the mesh liner of his bathing suit, and he smiled at her over his groin—a bloated, four-legged, upside-down spider dragging melons across a web.

It only took about three seconds. It was the single most vulgar thing Merci Rayborn had witnessed in her thirty-four years. She had no idea if Hess saw it because she refused to look anywhere but back into Ed Izma's happy gray eyes.

"Now," he said. "What can I do for law enforcement?"

He was sitting cross-legged on the mattress with the pillows behind his back and his back against the wall. His hands were in his lap and Merci could see that he could move his trunks aside and flash her whenever he wanted.

She looked to Hess in appeal. He was already looking at her, with a bland, admonishing expression on his face.

Up both of yours, she thought.

"We've got a guy who's taken two women, Ed. He's got them somewhere—home on ice, preserved in a storage unit—we're not sure where."

Izma's head angled to Hess. "Preserved how?"

"We don't know that yet, either. But we found chemical."

"The Ortega Highway women. They were nice-looking babes, from the TV pictures."

"Nice women, Ed."

121

Izma said nothing. Merci watched his small still head and wondered what was arcing between the poles of his brain. Then he was looking at her. She could see his hands doing something down in his lap but she wouldn't offer him the satisfaction of discovering what.

"Ed, put your hands to your side."

She had never heard this tone of voice from Hess. There was a threat in it and it was a threat that she would have taken seriously. But it was calm. Izma was staring at him.

"But I'm not—"

"—Hands at your side or I'll hurt you."

The big arms flopped to the bed.

"There. There you go."

The giant sighed and his head pivoted and he gave Merci a look of contempt.

"Keep them there, Izma," said Hess, his voice still flat with latent violence. Merci wished she could get a tone like that, although, *Hey Jack, you gonna be just another dead asshole?* had worked just fine.

"So, Ed," Hess continued, "we got to thinking about this guy out in Ortega. He seems to like women, like you did. He's keeping them with him, like you did. He's probably making sure they're in good shape, like you tried to. So I thought to myself: Ed Izma might be able to tell us something about him. Ed's a bright guy, tested in at just under genius. Maybe he understands this guy, can help us understand him too."

Izma sighed and seemed to relax. His hands moved from the mattress onto his lap again. He looked down

122

at them, then put them back on the bedspread. He looked at Merci, then to Hess.

"The difference is, he's not man enough to deal with them alive. Like I did. I always wanted Lorraine to be alive. I wanted Lorraine alive and happy. But I needed her in every sexual way, constantly. I was quite a virile young man back then."

"She had come to your door selling . . . what was it?"

"Cutlery. TrimCo. *I'm Lorraine Dulak with TrimCo?* is what she said. And sometimes, well, everything just comes together for a man. Inside a man. You know what I mean. I had to invite her in. The DA didn't believe I could truly love a woman after knowing her less than two minutes. I disagree. I mean look at what happened. You don't do something like that to a woman you don't love."

Merci looked down and she wondered again what had left the square dents in the carpet, and why Ed Izma had removed them from her view. She looked at these things and knew the whole time that Izma was looking at her. She disliked being held captive in someone else's thoughts, someone this close and this hateful. It was like being fucked by his imagination.

Hess's voice seemed to rescue her. "Okay. This guy isn't man enough to deal with them alive. I think you're right. But now what?"

"He wants them lifelike. So, maybe a freezer. Not parts, though. *Whole*. A guy who would cut a woman into parts to freeze her isn't a real man at all."

"Why keep them? Why not just use them and let them go?"

123

"Because that would be just like letting them run away. This is about love, Hess, not just sex. He really loves them. That's why he wants to be with them. This is all about keeping your true love from running away from you. You don't just discard it. I mean, when you get right down to it, us special types are awfully sentimental."

Merci felt her throat tighten and her stomach shift. "Especially vile and disgusting, is what you are," she said.

"You could have her de-barked."

Hess's lethal voice again. "Look at me, Izma. Not the woman. What's he looking for in them? Why take one but let another go?"

"It's just his needs. They're different for all of us, what makes things come together for us. I noticed the faces on the TV. They're both very beautiful women."

"But what *else*, Ed? What's he see that makes things come together for him?"

"Well, they were both extremely sophisticated, you could tell. They had intelligent faces. Now to me, when I see a woman that intelligent and educated, with that kind of look on her face, I want to smash it. I prefer humble women. I like women who work with their hands. I like no-frills women, but they've got to be pretty. Blue collar. Peasant stock. Like Lorraine. Or Merci."

She returned Ed Izma's stare.

Merci saw the giant's pelvis start to move. His hands were still on the bed. His head was small and distant, like a remote controller left on top of the set.

124

Hess stood. "I'm going to show her what's in your closet, Ed."

"Don't touch, please."

Merci felt the blood rush from her head as she stood. "Keep your balls in your shorts, pinhead. I'll be right back."

She followed Hess into the back room.

Hess gestured toward the open closet. At first Merci was startled, then it made some kind of sense, then she was just chilled. There were five of them in there, standing along the wall of the closet, looking at her.

"These are what made the carpet impressions you were looking at. He had some of these sweethearts back when he took Lorraine Dulak."

Four were mannequins dressed like tradeswomen —construction worker, a Post Office employee, a mechanic or plumber, a cop. The fifth wore a smart little skirt and had a head of luxuriant black hair that suggested to Merci her own. This last one held a card in her hand. Merci leaned in and read it: *Lorraine Dulak, TrimCo.* The mannequin bases were square.

"I should have puked when I first got here, gotten it over with."

"I'm sure he does the hair and makeup himself. Probably changes them around, buys different clothes. I don't know why he wanted to hide them from us. Maybe he thought I'd be envious. Or you'd be jealous. Or maybe he thought he was being a bad boy."

She saw his small dry smile and shook her head. "Let's get the hell out of here, Hess. I mean, what did he really tell us?"

"He doesn't understand himself well enough to help us on purpose. But I thought we might see something in him that we could apply."

"Well, did you?"

"I think the Purse Snatcher loved Janet Kane and Lael Jillson the same way Izma loved Lorraine. I think the Purse Snatcher is a collector. He's collecting them like Izma does mannequins and pictures of mannequins. This is all about keeping your true love from running away from you."

"It makes me want to vomit."

"Why?"

"Because it's a lie. And I'm sick of creeps who try to justify what they do by calling it love."

"It doesn't matter what they call it. It's only a lie to us. To guys like Izma and the Purse Snatcher, it's the truth."

"*Fuck* guys like Izma and the Purse Snatcher. You spend an hour with this guy to find out that?"

"It was worth it. We've been here exactly thirty-two minutes. I learned something about our man and you got a chance to understand something you don't understand yet."

"Yeah? *What.*"

"That other people don't think like you. So you have to think like them. They don't feel like you. So you have to empathize. They don't behave like you, so you have to get a feel for what they're going to do next. That goes for creeps, so you can catch them, and everybody else, so you can get along with them."

"And what if I just decide not to?"

"Then you won't make sheriff by sixty."

The rage hit her heart like a shot of speed. "Fifty-eight. And that's not a joke to me."

"I'm not joking. And you could handle that job, so long as you understood that the only person in the world who thinks like you is you. Being a good hunter isn't about being in touch with your feelings, Rayborn. It's about being in touch with everyone else's. That's how you find the people you need, no matter what you plan on doing to them. Creeps or husbands, you find them the same way."

"I don't *want* a husband. And you picked a helluva time for a lecture on feelings."

"It was important."

"I'm not convinced. Now, can we just get the hell out of this room? I've had enough. And if I spend another two minutes with that . . . *gentleman* out there who thinks and behaves differently than me, I'm going to draw my cheap Chinese Italian stiletto, cut off his tiny gonad-sized *head* and flush it down the nearest toilet. Can you understand *me* and *my* feelings now?"

He shut the closet door. "I don't feel that great either."

13

That afternoon after work Tim Hess received his first treatment of thoracic radiation. The stifling atmosphere of Ed Izma's room was still within him as he lay back and the technician aimed the contraption at his chest. Hess wondered if the radiation could kill the sickness of Izma's soul that had surely gotten into him. The doctors had told Hess it was intended to "clean up" any small cell carcinomas residing in his lymph system. If they'd found any there during his operation, they'd have sewed him shut and he'd be dead in half a year. They'd found nothing, but the radiation came heavily recommended.

It was painless and took about thirty seconds. But the radiologist told Hess that the side effects—fatigue, hair loss, appetite drop, insomnia, gastrointestinal upset—built up over time and he'd feel a whole lot worse after six weeks of daily treatments than he did right now.

"If you guys don't kill me I don't see how a little cancer will," he said.

The radiologist smiled serenely. "We're doing everything we can, Detective."

To kill me or save me, Hess wondered as he made his way back through the waiting room.

*   *   *

Back home he called Barbara, certain that he wanted to say things, uncertain what they were.

"How are you, Tim?"

"I feel strong."

"Do you really? Or are you just being strong?"

"It hasn't been bad. Thanks for the letter and the flowers."

"I felt helpless."

"I didn't call because I was kind of out of it."

A lifetime of booze and cigarettes had caught up with Hess after the surgery. Delirium tremens, nicotine withdrawal, three days of mostly unremembered paranoid lunacy that he pieced together afterward from doctors, nurses and friends. At one point he had fled the IC unit, popping IV lines and catheters on his way to freedom. Three orderlies had brought him down.

He heard her breath catch. "I was so worried."

"Come on, Barb, cut it out," he said gently.

"I can't help it. I'm just so sentimental about you, Tim. I know it's ridiculous. But I can't talk to you without feeling like I'm sixteen again. That's so trite but it's so true. First love, and all that. I feel like I let it get away."

"We had different things to do, Barbara. It's okay we did them."

"Yeah, I guess."

He pictured her like she was when they'd met, bright and pretty, with a smile that would stand up to the decades. And her feet always on the ground.

"I just wanted you to know I was okay, not to worry. You hear things, rumors get started."

There was a long silence then, which Hess felt obligated to fill.

"To tell you the truth, though, I've been . . . thinking some thoughts I never thought before. I mean, forty-odd years as a deputy and I never worried about dying. I never really thought about it. I had guns pointed at me and knives thrown and plenty of threats from unhappy creeps. Then, I get a routine scan as part of a physical and there's a spot on my lung the size of a pencil eraser. And that scared the hell out of me. I've got as good a chance as anybody else, Barb, but it can take you down pretty fast. And if it does, I want you to know that of all the people I've known in my life you're the best. You're the best human I ran across on earth. Not that I was in the kind of business where you run across a lot of really good ones. I didn't mean that like . . . you know how I meant it. Anyway. True story."

"Oh, Tim . . ."

He could see the tears filling Barbara's dark eyes with diamonds.

"If you need some TLC, Tim—you know, anything at all—you can get it here. I still like to cook. I spend a lot of time with the kids and grandkids, but that leaves me lots of time alone, too. I'd like the company."

"I'll take you up on that."

"No, you won't. I thought about it a lot, Tim. After we broke up. I thought about why it happened. And what I came up with was this: you were afraid to slow down. You were afraid to take a few less units at school, take a few less patrol shifts, and just be. Be with yourself. Be with me. Be in the world. And you're still that way now, you're still afraid if you slow down you'll miss something."

"I'm afraid if I slow down I'll die."

"I didn't mean it like that."

"But you're exactly right."

"It's not true. If you slow down, you'll be happier. You'll understand more. People will mean more to you. And you'll mean more to them. It's not so bad, Tim. It's just a matter of sitting still. Being you. Just being."

"It's a flaw in my character, Barb."

"Well, you know what they say about smelling the roses. Or the coffee. They change it every few years. If I were you, I'd slow down and smell the ocean on my skin when I'm out riding those spooky waves at the Wedge. You still do that?"

"I did last summer. Not since the surgery."

"I can remember when you loved those waves almost as much as you loved me. And I can remember when you loved them more, too."

For all her optimism and refusal to engage her darker side, Barbara was, Hess knew, a clear seer.

"Maybe that could give you something to slow down for."

She blew her nose. Hess remembered teasing her about crying over anything—TV reruns, radio ads, newspaper articles. He had actually found it irritating once that Barbara had been decent enough to cry over things he would only crack wise about—tough cop that he was, enforcer of the law, prince of the suburbs, badass with a gun. I have been a fool, he thought. So many times. And what am I now but a hollow old man filled with poison on the off chance it can save my life?

"If you ever need me I'll be here, Tim."

His heart was a gathering storm and all he could say was thank you.

He tried to believe what she said. That evening he stood on the sand at the Wedge and watched the mountainous waves form on the jetty rocks, lunge toward shore and finally break in hollow caverns that huffed spray out the barrels like breath from a dragon. It was big enough to keep the crowds down, and Hess recognized a few faces out there in the turbulent soup between sets. Mostly kids now, he saw, which is what he was when he first braved this wild and unpredictable break, a wave that no other wave on earth could prepare you for. He could feel the reverberations coming up through the sand into his feet.

The evening had gone gray and humid and there was little breeze so the water was smooth. The spectators on the sand were all standing. Plenty of cameras on tripods, huge lenses. When it was big like this the waves spat enough spray into the air to make a salty mist over the water and the immediate beach. The lifeguard boat bobbed just outside the breakers. Hess could see another set of waves starting to form on the distant rocks and thought the rescue boat was in a perilous place. They rarely bothered with the Wedge—it was either big enough to capsize the boat or not breaking at all. Hess wondered what had brought them here this evening.

The water was surprisingly warm around his ankles

as he stood there and waited for a lull in the waves. He was aware of people looking at him because he was old, and maybe because of the scar. When the last wave of the set had broken Hess waded in backward up to his knees then turned and dove flat into the receding brine and rode the backwash out into the deep Wedge bowl.

It always impressed Hess about the Wedge, how close you were to the beach while ten-foot waves picked you up and charged toward shore with you. Up on top of one was a scary place to be until the speed replaced the fright. Then you had the barrel covering you and the touchy problem of getting out before it snapped your neck on the bottom. But you couldn't try to bail out too soon, either, because then you faced a long drop before the power of the wave was dissipated and that's how you got tangled up in the heart of the fury and held under for longer than you could stand. Hess didn't know exactly how many necks, backs and shoulders the Wedge had broken, but he knew it was a lot.

There were five people in the water around Hess and they all started swimming out at once. A jolt of adrenaline went through him as he followed, feeling his legs stretching out behind him, the weight of the big fins on his feet, the movement of his arms through the water. It had been a year.

The first wave lurched up and peaked and Hess watched a scrawny kid shoot across the face, tucked up high, skipping across the water on his hands like a waterbug. Hess dove under and felt the powerful tug on his fins.

A stocky young man Hess had seen before caught the second wave of the set, but he took it late, too close to the peak, and the whole thing just collapsed on him like a dynamited building. Hess glided under it. He knew it was the kind of wipeout that you couldn't slide out of, it would take plenty of air to ride out the white-water roller coaster to shore. He wondered if a lung and a third would do it, then figured it would have to.

When the next wave rose before him Hess realized he was exactly where he needed to be to catch it. Two of the other guys made for it too, then cleared out in a rare act of respect. Hess let the rising water draw him up the face, let his fins float up over his head. At the last second he turned toward shore, kicked once hard and leaned his back into the wave as it took him. A vertiginous lift. A surge of speed. Tiny people below. Beach towels as postage stamps. Rooftops in the distance. It had him completely, tons of charging water eager to possess him. He dropped his left hand, palm down, and planed along. This was the real magic of it for Hess, the part that was never quite fully believable—how a 200-pound man could ride the bottom of his own hand like this, feel the water resisting, feel it rushing beneath his fingers, feel the wake spraying off the heel of it. A tiny portable surfboard, connected to one's self. Then he could see the lip far above him starting to crest and he bent his right shoulder back hard to keep himself locked in as long as he could. Spray in his face, he glanced down at the people on the beach and at the jetty behind him and the harbor beyond the jetty and the sky above the harbor. Then the roaring cylinder broke over him and the sky was replaced by rifling water and he was deep inside for a second or two, still happily gliding along on the palm of his hand until the wave finally caught him and drove him down toward the sand.

A moment later he found himself in the soft white-water, being deposited on the shore. He sat there for a moment in the sand like an infant while the water receded around him. Some of the people on the beach were clapping.

He took off his fins and stood. He smiled back at the crowd—what a strange feeling to smile—and knew he could do it, he could beat this thing inside him with a little luck, a little applause, a little nod from God on high.

His heart was pounding strong and his lung and a third were full of good salt air.

Big Bill Wayne, erect in the captain's chair of the panel van, steered through the great master-planned community of Irvine toward Interstate 5.

He looked out at the identical homes, the clean streets, the streetlamps glowing in the dusky summer evening. Orange County, *California*, he thought: home to the Happiest Place on Earth, a baseball team called the Angels, an ocean called the Pacific and over two and a half million people, many of whom are beautiful women who need the company of men.

And I'm a part of this place.

I, Big Bill Wayne—alluring blond bachelor and lover of women.

First he cruised the parking lot of a giant entertainment complex known as the Big One. It had twenty-one screens and a bunch of restaurants. The parking lot was large, outdoors and not well lit. He parked and followed a couple of nice-looking women toward the complex, aware of their perfumes trailing back to him, attuned to the click of their shoes on the asphalt. Like most women together they talked incessantly and paid him no attention whatsoever. He got into one of the long lines behind them and moved closer.

His knees felt weak and his heart was pounding as he tried to strike up a conversation about movies. One of the girls had brown eyes that shone like candle-light. The conversation seemed to be going well until one of them made a joke he didn't hear, then they both laughed and turned their backs on him. And that, he thought, is the essence of what I hate most about women: the way they can change their minds so fast. He felt the white cold fury rise up inside him. He knew it would come because it always had and it always did. It grabbed his heart and made his muscles ready and brought a very sly smile to his face.

Bill followed a crowded walkway to a bar called Sloppy Joe's, which was advertised as a replica of Hemingway's favorite bar from Key West. The hostess was lovely.

He paced slowly along the bar, hands held behind his back and head slightly down like a man with heavy ideas. In the mirror behind the bar he admired his long coat and vest, his golden flowing hair and thick mustache.

He looked at the women's faces, too. So challenging, their eyes, so haughty. He toured the perimeter of the place, analyzing pictures of the handsome writer—many with women—and wondered if writing a book would help him form relationships.

But it troubled Bill that writers needed to have a conscience to write good books, because he knew for a fact he had no such thing. He'd heard about it all his life—the way you were supposed to have feelings that guided you, helped you decide if what you did was right or wrong. Conscience.

It was easy to understand what you were supposed to feel. Parents and teachers, priests and cops, doctors and judges, TV and movies were all eager to tell you how to feel. But if you never actually felt it, if your actions generated absolutely no clear sense of either right or wrong, if those ideas were simply not present inside you, the way that some people are born without certain organs, then all you could do was fake it. And sometimes it was difficult, manufacturing the illusion of those emotions upon your face for someone to read correctly. Well, no use feeling sorry for yourself.

A few minutes later he cornered the hostess against one of the empty tables and tried to ask some questions about Ernest but she got away by leaning into a chair that slid away with a bark and she disappeared into a door marked Employees Only. A moment later a hefty young man came through the same door and glared at him.

Bill swept from the room, hands behind his back again and head forward, imagining what it would feel like to pump a round into the man's heart and watch the expression of disbelief on his stupid face. Watch his eyes roll around like the last two olives in a jar.

Back up the freeway then to more familiar ground, better hunting actually in the indoor malls where women fearlessly wandered alone and were always so distracted by merchandise you could hover about undetected and think anything you wanted about them. His kit, shopping bag, bedsheet, the Deer Sleigh'R, Pandora's Box and three purses were all back there, everything but the Deer Sleigh'R locked in two large metal toolboxes. He'd imagined more than once just what a policeman would think if he saw his things. But no officer could search his van without probable cause and Bill was not about to offer them anything remotely like probable cause to search his vehicle. He was clean. If pulled over routinely, or caught in a CHP sobriety checkpoint, his fake CDL from the counterfeiter in Little Saigon was a good one, descended from the high-quality false passports so indispensable in the early days after the war.

But thank God for the American Constitution's Bill of Rights, Bill mused, because without it, his Deer Sleigh'R—advertised as "a great way to protect your trophy's meat and hide from dirt and damage caused by rough, jagged ground"—would send your average cop into fits of suspicion. The purses would sink him. And what would they make of Pandora's Box, he thought: it was a prototype, unique and one of a kind, just the sort of thing that would alarm a low-IQ policeman. An explanation would be demanded.

He remembered that it was about time to go see the box's maker again, get the thing repaired. It wouldn't even turn on the last time he tried it. Like the battery was dead, or a fuse blown or something. Luckily, he hadn't needed it. But the inventor could figure it out and fix it—he'd created the damned thing in the first place.

So he drove through the exhaust-fragrant night to a newly remodeled mall called the Main Place. He cruised the lot once to get a feel for whether it was hot or cold. He liked the Main Place because it was small and seemed kind of homey, for a mall. In order to harvest he'd have to park safely away from the

Main Place, in a construction zone he'd scouted months earlier where he could make the transfer from car to van. Where he parked the van was critical because it had to be safe for the transfer but not too long a walk or bus ride to the parking lot.

But he wasn't in good enough spirits to collect tonight. No. Tonight was a night for tasting, for preparation, for inspiration. A night to be a scout, like the great Kit Carson.

Bill spotted a very attractive woman walking toward the Nordstrom entrance but her shorts and T-shirt disappointed him. Summer was always a time when women dressed down, it seemed, definitely harder to find one wearing good fashionable clothing.

The positive side was that many liked to wear their hair up against the heat, and hair up always signified to Bill breeding, class, education, sophistication and ungovernable carnal appetites. But this one had her hair down and wore unflattering flat-soled sandals and didn't even roll up the sleeves of her T-shirt to expose the deliciousness of the upper female arm.

White trash, he thought: common as sparrows and about as interesting.

A blond woman in a red dress and red shoes: too flabby.

A lanky Negress: too young.

A Central American woman: rich and dark as coffee but what do you say to her?

A stubby little clerical type with a hop in her step and a face like a frog: um, sorry, ma'am.

But then out of the blue came a very interesting possibility, getting into her beat-up old sedan now, so

140

Bill brought his van to a stop behind her and off to one side as if wanting her parking spot. She was tall with curly dark hair and an intelligent forehead and shapely legs. Her skirt wasn't short except when she lowered herself into the car, but her shoes were high enough and her blouse was rich purple and sleeveless. She knew how beautiful her arms were. He imagined her face captured by photography on her driver's license, and her physical characteristics listed beside the picture, in plain black and white. It was really something to have so many facts about a woman contained on a concise, durable, stackable card. You never forgot a birthday. And there was more truth on a CDL than most women would tell you in a lifetime.

He rolled down his window to give her a good look at his handsomeness. He motioned her out when she turned and looked through her window at him. She smiled and waved. Lovely teeth.

She backed out her long, boatlike American car and Big Bill waited, judging how well he would fit behind her seat. She made the half turn and shifted into drive but now, rather than nosing into her place, Bill backed his van into her path and all she could do was wait and look up at him, imperially seated in his captain's chair. He was proud of the new silver paint job he'd given his vehicle. He smiled down at her and felt the cold white anger blooming inside him.

She rolled her window down to just below her mouth. "Thanks for waiting," she said.

"You're very welcome, ma'am."

"Well, thanks. But now you're kind of in my way."

"I was just wondering if you'd like to have a drink."

141

She was still smiling. He couldn't believe it. In fact he *didn't* believe it because he knew how fast things could change with a woman. In that second she measured him, he knew, making difficult decisions faster than any computer, assessing his threat and attractiveness, calculating his likely gifts and his potential dangers, judging both the safety and the profitability of his company.

"Look," she said. "I work here, at Goldsmith's Jewelry? Come in some night and say hi. Maybe we could get coffee. I'm Ronnie."

"They call me Bill."

"Cool! Nice to meet you."

"Have a nice evening, Ronnie."

He bowed his head in what he thought of as an Old West manner, then eased his van forward and into the place.

A moment later he looked to see Ronnie's one-tail-lighted heap of a car wobble around a corner and out of the lot. He wrote down her license plate number just in case she didn't work at Goldsmith's Jewelry. Bill didn't mind research. Research was part of scouting. And nothing on earth infuriated him more than being lied to by a woman he trusted.

The parking spot turned out to be a pretty good one—facing one of the main entrances, no cars in front of it to obscure his view of the crosswalk. He cut the engine and sat back. Ronnie's car vanished onto the boulevard. The only reason he could tell it was hers was because of the broken light. What a smile. Bill felt a little stirring down there south of the belt line.

Bill watched a couple of teenage girls walk toward the entrance, but they didn't interest him. He was a mature man with mature tastes. He believed that young people deserved a chance, and who knew, maybe one of them would grow into a woman he could enjoy someday. Bill then entertained himself with a recurring daydream: sailing down the highway in a fast car with a couple of his girls in the back with their hair blowing free, another in the front next to him with her hand on his crotch. Tape player up loud, that Springsteen song where the guy wants to get the electric chair with his girl on his lap. Heading for Vegas. Ninety miles an hour and a vintage 9mm Luger under his thigh. *Oh, really, officer? B-LAM!*

It was pleasant enough to imagine this, but a little absurd. He didn't like to gamble and he had no desire to die at the hands of law enforcement. He didn't quite understand martyrdom of any kind. There was no glamour in it.

He pivoted in his captain's chair and stepped into the back of the van. He gloved up with fresh latex and took out the purses by their straps, stashing them behind his seat.

He started up the van and backed out of the spot. Out of the lot, down the boulevard where Ronnie had gone—she was almost certainly a lying, scheming witch—then back onto the freeway bound for the master-planned community of Irvine and the sanctuary of his home.

He felt behind him and brought out the purses, setting them all on the big console beside the driver's station. Each had its own smell. He lifted and sniffed and enjoyed them one at a time. His program hadn't been worked out for the first three—he didn't know how to do what he wanted to do with them. He knew he had to keep something from each of the women he loved—why bother if you just dumped them forever, treated them like they didn't matter?

He tapped to the radio on his steering wheel, wondering what he'd do if he could do anything in the world he wanted to.

One thing he'd do was develop that conscience. It seemed like life would be easier with such a thing. He'd know the difference between right and wrong.

And if you knew, you could easily pick the one that was best for you.

He'd also get that job at Saddleback's, the one advertised on the sign in the window last week. The pay was decent, and he would be surrounded by boots, hats, dusters, thick belts with enormous buckles and genuine feed and tack. The place smelled of hay and leather. Either that, or get a job as one of the costumed gunslingers at Knott's Berry Farm, blasting away while women in bonnets admired his gunplay.

Big Bill remembered the first time he actually saw John Wayne's house—*former* house, to be exact. It was just over the hills there, on an island in Newport Harbor. He'd stood for hours, contemplating it. And gone back a dozen times, at least. That had naturally led to a dinner cruise aboard the Duke's former boat, *Wild Goose*. The cruise had set him back $50 but Bill would never forget the majesty of the enormous wooden bar where John Wayne had drank and gambled, the master stateroom or the little berths set up for his kids. Standing on that ship while it hummed around the harbor Bill had felt like he was stationed in the very heart of the American West.

Now the West was mostly suburbia, but that was okay, because the suburbs thrived on the illusion of tranquillity.

Bill checked his speed and thought of the old detective they'd brought back to catch the Purse Snatcher —Hess was his name. He was in the papers this morning, a picture and everything. He looked like an Old West sheriff, all the lines in his face and those cold eyes. Obviously a man with a conscience.

Naturally, however, the cop in charge of his case was a woman. She'd clucked on in the article about what a privilege it was to work with the foul old investigator. In the newspaper picture, she looked about half the age of her new partner. Bill liked that idea: an old corpse of a guy and a perfectly preserved, young, fresh woman, trying to catch a criminal genius.

Give them something to think about. He reached into his shirt pocket, took out the folded paper and stuffed it into one of the purses—his very first, actually, the brown-and-black one.

He checked his mirror, then reached over, swung all three purses across his body and dangled them out over the carpool lane. The wind ripped them from his hand. He watched them in the sideview mirror, bouncing like heads along the asphalt.

15

"We got a hit from CAL-ID, Hess," said Merci Rayborn. "Those must have been some damned good parameters you and the witch doctor worked up."

She couldn't control the excitement in her voice. "Creep named Lee LaLonde, car thief, meth freak, nice healthy sheet—mostly Riverside County. Get this, he lives out in Elsinore now, just off the Ortega. I let Riverside know we're coming in. I'll pick you up in half an hour."

She could hear a lamp click on, then the sound of the old man breathing. Her bedside clock said 4:56.

"Get some backup?" he asked in a calm, clear voice.

"No. The shitbird's still on parole. We can do what we want with him. Don't worry."

She felt presumptuous telling a superior officer not to worry but Hess wasn't superior anymore, she reminded herself. It made her feel powerful. The adrenaline was jumping through her now and she couldn't stop it if she wanted to. She didn't want to.

This was what it was all about, life made vivid and death made close by force of arms. It was better than being in love.

He gave her directions to his apartment, told her he'd be out front, and hung up.

Merci had already hit the coffee maker, which she

146

set up before bed each night in case something like this broke. Hot cup now in hand, heart pounding good and solid but not too fast, she went back to the bedroom where she turned the radio on her dresser to the news and the radio in the bathroom to a rock station.

She tied her hair back in a scrunchie, pulled on trousers and boots, cinched her SpectraFlex Point Blank armor vest over a T-shirt and holstered up. The old shoulder rig fit like silk but the snap came loose sometimes: time for a visit to the leathersmith, or maybe to get a new one. The Point Blank was a composite formulated to take multiple hits, angled impacts and high-velocity ammo. Five pounds, black. It ran her $650 from a catalog because the county wouldn't spring for anything but the old Kevlar IIs. Another beef with accounting, she thought, damned bean counters anyway. No Sig-alerts according to the news from the dresser—good. The bathroom radio was playing something fast and brainless. Her dad had always played jazz. She tossed one extra clip on the bed and put the other in the front pocket of her pants. Badge holder in the rear right. Flashlight, handcuffs and mace onto the duty belt. Finished off with the Sheriff Department windbreaker. She got the clip off the bed and put it in the left jacket pocket. She made sure the double-barreled .40 caliber derringer in her purse was loaded, even though she wouldn't carry the purse into Lee LaLonde's domicile. She realized she needed a calf holster for the little cannon, made a note to price them at a store where she could find hunter's cleaning kits, ropes, pulleys for sale. She made sure the stiletto was in her purse, too, for reasons no more clear in her mind than general notions of security and excitement.

Purse Snatcher, dirtbag, shitbird, she thought: try getting this stuff away from *me*.

Eight minutes and fifteen seconds from the time the call came through. Down from her last one, which was just over nine, but that had just been her weekly drill to stay loose.

She left on the radios and living room light and slammed the front door behind her.

One single thought about Phil Kemp entered her mind and she banished it like a sick dog.

Hess got in with two mugs of coffee and shut the door without spilling any. With the interior light on she could see his hair was brushed back as always with the little white wave out front and she wondered if it just grew that way. His face looked old and lined and tired. But the blue eyes, which he trained on her for the first time as he quietly closed the door with his right hand while offering her a cup of coffee with the other, were clear and bright as the moon.

"My heart's really going," she said.

"Mine, too. This is great."

Merci gunned the car down the empty avenue and heard the tires swish through a sprinkler slick.

"You still feel that way, Hess? That this is great?"

"Absolutely."

She hit sixty and looked for a speed sign: thirty-five, the coffee jacking her up a notch, Hess telling her to make a U-turn at the next stop.

"What about the ferry?"

"It quit running five hours ago."

"Right. Hey, I'll settle in, don't worry. I know this old guy named Francisco? Used to live near me. I mean, he's really old. When I look at him I realize I shouldn't get all worked up like I do. I should try to step back and settle in. Just *go* with it."

"I'll drive if you want."

She looked at him in the passing bars of light cast by the streetlamps. "I'll drive."

"Stay inside."

"Inside what?"

"Yourself."

She looked at him with a little more offense than she actually took, but he wasn't looking at her so it didn't matter.

"Hess, I don't need pithy aphorisms all the time. How to drive my car. How to feel what goddamned Ed Izma is feeling. I mean, I appreciate it, but I'm really not a six-year-old."

"Ignore me. I mean that."

"I know you're coming from the right place."

"It's just part of getting old. I want to blab everything I think I know to someone I think might use it. Like giving away your hunting gun or your first baseball mitt or something. You'll do it too someday."

"I hope so," she muttered, feeling the V-8 downshift and gather force as she guided them down the Newport peninsula. When she got past city hall she flogged it and set the flasher up on the hood. She had never given her life expectancy more than a moment's thought, and she didn't feel like giving it any more than that now.

It was after five-thirty and the first blush of light was in the sky. When she got onto the freeway she used the carpool lane and held the Impala at ninety. The airport whizzed by then the strawberry fields covered with plastic that shone like water then the Santa Ana Mountains then the marine base. She felt just exactly right at this moment, speeding forward through the blue hour in her unmarked with a good partner beside her and a suspect to engage.

"Yeah, okay, Hess. I'm going to stay inside myself."

"I told you to ignore me and I meant it."

"No, I wasn't chewing on you. *I* meant it—and thanks for a good word. I may be kind of a bitch sometimes but I'm not too dumb to take good advice."

She was aware of him studying her. She glanced up at the rearview to change lanes and could see his face in the periphery.

"You say what's on your mind and that's mostly good."

"But?"

"Nice to hide your cards sometimes."

"It's more cunning, I know."

"Well, it gives you more time to figure things out. Like yesterday, if you'd have kept cool at Izma he'd have heated up more. He might have given us something. He needed to get a rise out of you. And you knew it. But you gave it to him too easy."

"It goes against my principles to watch some gigantic moron drag his balls all over the room and try to make me watch."

"Leave your principles at home."

Even with guys like Kemp? "You don't."

"I do. A lot. It works."

"Explain that one."

"Let other people do the talking. Then, when you understand what they're doing, take them down. Or out. Or up, or any place you want to take them."

"Thanks, *dad*."

"It's like . . ." Hess lifted both his hands out in front of him, one with the coffee cup still hooked on a finger, the other with the fingers open in a gesture of emphasis.

Merci looked at him. She'd never seen him animated before. His raptor's face had something puzzled in it.

". . . It's like you're a fort," he continued, "and your head's the tower and your eyes are the holes for sharpshooters and your ears are where the spies live. You're this . . . this . . . living . . . "

"*Fort?*"

"Yeah. See? You stay inside yourself and look out of yourself, like looking out of a fort."

"I can see it. If I look real hard."

"You're right. That's not very good. Cancel it."

She could feel the coffee and adrenaline working to make an odd joy in her heart. "I do see it, though. It's not exactly elegant, but I see it."

"I'll shut up. I'm feeling pretty good right now, for being full of chemicals and radiation."

She made the Ortega Highway turnoff and headed inland. She looked in the rearview again and noted

151

that Hess was staring out the window while the gas station lights colored his face.

Then he turned to her and she wondered if he knew she was looking at him in the mirror.

"Tell me about Lee LaLonde," he said.

"A speed freak and a car thief," she said. "Down twice for grand theft auto, twice for selling stolen parts. Four years, two bounces—Honor Farm and Riverside County. Released and paroled two years ago."

"A thief, not a carjacker?"

"Just a thief, so far."

"No sex crimes?"

"None."

Hess said nothing.

"He's a little creep of a guy—perfect size for the backseat of a car. Five-eight, one-twenty, blond and blue. Twenty-five years old. Last scrape with Riverside Sheriffs was a year ago—questioned in a burglary of a plant where he worked. Nothing filed. They fired him."

"What's the plant make?"

"Irrigation supplies. Cloudburst is the name of the outfit. His jacket says he runs his own business now—retail sales at the weekly swap meet here at the lake."

"Sales of what?"

"Doesn't even say what. Anyway, that's the last thing in his file. He's got a barb-wire chain tattooed around his left biceps and knife puncture scar on his stomach. Grew up in Northern California, Oakland."

They were past the city and the big houses now and

152

the highway was dark and beginning to climb. The traffic was light now, still early for the commuters who worked in Riverside County.

"Who stabbed him?" Hess asked.

"His dad."

When she looked at him he was already nodding, as if he'd expected the answer. Maybe he saw it ahead of time, Merci thought. She was about to ask him how he saw things in advance, but she didn't and she didn't know why.

She reached into the folder on the seat and handed Hess the artist's sketch. Hess took it and angled the lamp on the dash over, clicking it on.

"It's lifelike," he said.

"Whose life is the question."

"How come you waited so long to show it to me?"

"I not sure how solid it is. See, this Kamala Petersen lives on TV and fashion magazines. Everybody looks like somebody she's seen before. I had to hypnotize her to cut through all her bullshit. And get a load of this—she's seen the guy *twice*. Once the night Janet Kane disappeared, and once the week before, *at a mall, walking around, checking things out.*"

"Checking out Kamala?"

"Correct. She'd stuffed that down deep. That's what we got through to."

"This is valuable. This is good."

"Unfortunately, I lost a court witness. Hess, I'm praying it's worth the trade. I spent the last two days worrying about that sketch. Is it close? Is Kamala reliable? I'm not going to go public with something that's way off—gets people confused. But I'm going to release it to Press Information when I go in today. I took the gamble, now I'm going to stick with it. I'm trusting me."

Hess continued to stare down at the paper. Merci saw the light in his face, the uncluttered intensity of his gaze.

Hess, again: "LaLonde doesn't fit the profile. Page says he'll be a known sex offender."

"So. What's a profile really mean anyway?" she asked.

"Dalton's good. What do you think of them?"

"I've only had first-hand experience with two. One was right on, the other was pretty far off. Dalton did the one that was off. The Bureau did the one that worked. In general, I prefer evidence that's actual evidence. I don't like trying to figure out if something applies or not."

"Well, we'd all take a blood sample or a fingerprint over a piece of speculative thinking."

"You asked what I thought."

No reply. She guided the Impala up the grade and through the swerving turns of the Ortega. She thought of all the wrecks on this highway, a bloody stretch of road if there ever was one. A prime dump site, too—the Purse Snatcher wasn't the first creep to bring his victims out here. She looked out at the sycamores now just barely visible on the hillsides, the way their branches jagged out like dislocated arms and gave the trees a look of eternal agony.

They were near the top of the grade now and Merci could see the oaks in profile against the blue-black sky.

"I always thought this was a spooky old highway," she said.

She looked at his face in the rearview again and thought it looked pale, but maybe it was just the parsimonious light offered by the east. He looked old and tired, but that's exactly what he was. She wondered what it felt like to sit there with cancer growing in your lung, watching the sky get light. She had no idea because she wasn't used to figuring what other people were thinking. Hess was right about that. So she tried to feel what he might feel, pretending she had the cancer too and she was heading down into Lake Elsinore to interview a speed freak who might be a murderer. But it was hard to feel what Hess felt because what she felt was already there. It was right in the way. So she sent her thoughts out around her own feelings, like birds flying around trees.

What she came up with was, if she was in the same position, every waking moment would scare the living piss out of her.

"Me too," he said. "A spooky old highway."

16

The sun was low over the hills when they dropped down into Lake Elsinore. The water was plated in bronze. Merci gave Hess the paper with the address on it and Hess got the map out of the console.

"Take Main south to Pine," he said. "East to Lakeview."

At the corner was the entrance to Elsinore Shores trailer park. Merci sized up the place as she made the turn: old trailers, failed dreams and broken lives. It was the kind of place she used to see as a kid and feel afraid that was where she'd end up.

Until she realized, many years later, how powerful she was, how she could make things go the way she wanted simply by using her will. *Will.* She had created that power herself, bit by bit and over time, but it still astonished her to know how large it was. Once she had understood it, she knew she'd *never* end up in a spot like this. But it still made her think of all the people who didn't have the juice to get what they needed out of the world. A lot of them ended up taking it away from someone else and those were the kind of people she threw in jail, which is where they belonged.

Hess aimed a thick finger to the right. "That's his building, there. He must live in his shop."

She slowed and studied the little complex as she drove past. Two long cinder-block buildings faced each other across a concrete alleyway. The buildings were divided into workshops. Their doors were all the same aqua blue color, the kind that slide up, wide and high enough to get a small truck in or out.

She came back around and parked a block short of the entrance. She took the H&K nine off the seat and holstered it.

The blue door to Lee LaLonde's space 12 was closed all the way down. Merci glanced at Hess, then rapped the backs of her knuckles against the metal. She waited a moment and did it again, harder.

"Second," said a thin voice. "Comin'. Who is it?"

"Deputies Rayborn and Hess. Open the door, Lee."

"All right."

"You alone in there?"

"Yeah. Second. The runner on the door's rusty."

There was a moment of quiet, but none of the drug addict's usual scuffle to hide stash, Merci thought. Nowhere for him to go but out the window. Then the clang of metal on metal inside. A padlock. The door began its screeching way up. Merci got her badge holder ready in her left hand and rested the other inside her jacket, on the butt of the nine.

LaLonde manifested, bottom to top. Bare white feet. Baggy, dirty jeans slung low enough to fall off. The bunched elastic of boxer shorts sprouted just above the waistband. Flat stomach with a knife scar on it, narrow chest, thin arms. His face was odd but not particularly unpleasant. His hair long, blond, wavy.

157

She badged him quickly. *"Step back from the door, please. Now."*

"Okay, lady. I'm steppin'."

"Stop right where you are and turn around," said Merci. He started his turn. When his back was to her she stopped him with a strong take of his right wrist, a firm twist to bring his arm out with the elbow down. She stepped up behind him and braced the back of his shoulder with her left hand so it was easy to see down the extended arm or to break the elbow. She felt him comply because he'd complied a thousand times before.

"Staying off the meth, Lee?"

She ran her fingers over the veins in his forearm, snapped her nails against them, then angled his elbow into the weak light for a view down the muscles.

"I never did shoot it," he said slowly.

"Just smoked it by the ton."

"Yeah."

"I can tell. It kills brain cells."

LaLonde stood back. He was shorter and thinner than she'd expected. Speed freaks tend to stay skinny in life and LaLonde looked the part. His long blond hair hung over his forehead. His face was narrow and all of its features seemed crowded down into the lower half. Big mouth, goofy teeth.

"Lead the way." She let ten feet open up behind him, then followed. The shop was big—sixty feet deep and thirty wide, she guessed. It was lit by fluorescent tubes hung from the ceiling by chains.

There were workbenches along each of the two side walls. Vices. Spools of wire. Indeterminate projects in indeterminate stages of completion or repair. Bench vices, an electric grinder and polisher, a benchtop drill press. Toolboxes. More tools were neatly hung on the Peg-Boarded wall behind the benches.

Merci walked and studied. In the right back corner was a sleeping area, and behind that a bathroom. There was a counter, a two-burner stove and a small refrigerator. LaLonde stood beside a dilapidated plaid couch and gestured for Merci to sit.

"I'll stand. You'll sit. Tim, make yourself comfortable."

Hess waited for LaLonde to take one end of the couch, then he sat in the middle. Merci crossed her arms and stared down at LaLonde without comment. LaLonde looked at his hands. She let a long moment pass.

"Lee, look at me," she said. He did. She thought he looked like a parrot fish. She remained standing a few feet away from him, leaving some slack to take up if she needed to.

"Janet Kane was murdered week before last. We know you knew her. We got your prints out of the back of the BMW. Those are facts. Now, we can talk about her here or we can take you back to Orange County with us. If we talk here and you lie to me I'll have you cuffed and stuffed in about thirty seconds."

He looked at Merci, then at Hess, then at Merci again. She watched his face hard because that first denial was sometimes the hardest one a creep would make. Half the fuckers couldn't even lie right. They giggled or blushed or started crying. The better ones

159

broke a sweat or their faces twitched and if you saw it you had them. The rest could tell you a lie you might believe the rest of your life if you didn't know better. She saw no trace of guilt or dishonesty in LaLonde's face yet.

"I got no idea what you're talking about."

"Get one."

"If I knew a woman who'd let me in her BMW, I'd marry her, not kill her."

He grinned, lips spreading tight, teeth amok.

"What were you doing in her car?" she asked.

"I don't even know her."

"I don't care if you knew her. I care if you killed her."

"I didn't."

"Where were you last Tuesday night? Don't think, just tell me."

"My girlfriend was here."

"What did you do?"

"Watched TV. Ate. She drank some beers."

"Name and address."

LaLonde gave her name; didn't know her address.

"Then what about the fuse—the little 20-amp auto fuse that had your thumb and index prints on it? The one we found in Janet Kane's car."

He looked at her with deep suspicion and his eyes gave him away. Something wrong. Scrolling back. A hit. He looked away with a nonchalant shrug and she knew she had him. Hess glanced up at her with a questioning expression on his face. He missed it, she thought—but I didn't.

"I've worked with fuses in my life, Sergeant. I use

160

them in my inventions sometimes. I used to do some electrical stuff down at the marina here. Yeah, I've worked with 20-amp fuses, but I never killed anybody."

"When's the last time you touched one?"

"The *last* time? I wouldn't know the last time exactly."

"When? When's the last time you personally touched an automobile fuse, that you can remember, Lee?"

"That would have been about . . . maybe . . . three months ago."

He was ad-libbing now, and she knew it.

"You're shittin' me, Lee. You sit there and think about what lockup's going to feel like again. All the boyfriends you can make. Maybe think of a way to stay out of it. I'm going to take a tour of this shitheap you call a shop."

She looked over the kitchen and little bathroom, checking the magazine rack by the head because she'd found an automatic in a rack once before, hidden between the curling covers of nudie magazines. *Hobby Magazine. Arts & Crafts. American Inventor.* No automatic. LaLonde didn't strike her as violent and his sheet wasn't violent, but that didn't mean a thing to Rayborn because there was a first time for everything and a creep was a creep pure and simple.

She toured the workbenches. The closer she studied what she found on them, the less sense they made. For instance: umbrellas with inverted domes and hollow tubing that led to detachable plastic bags. A collection of mouthpieces with rubber teeth protruding.

And an odd contraption involving a small gyroscope and a large outdoor patio lamp. A set of large concave plastic circles, like giant contact lenses, connected with what looked like a headband. And a collection of wooden cigar boxes with metal antenna protruding from their backs. She opened one and looked at the bird's nest of batteries and chips and solder and circuitry inside. No fuses that she could see.

"What are these for?" She waved one of the cigar boxes.

"Those are for jamming eavesdroppers on a cell phone."

She turned and studied him. From a distance he looked less like a fish and more like a regular guy with a not-very-good face.

"You can buy 'em new for a hundred bucks," she said.

"Mine go for twenty-five. I do okay with them."

"Where is it that you do okay with them?"

"Swap meet out here. Sundays, at the Marina Park."

"Where did you learn electronics?"

"High school. My dad was an engineer. I've got a knack."

"Got a knack for stealing cars?"

"Cars are easy."

"What about the alarm systems?"

She turned and looked at him again. LaLonde shrugged.

"I didn't mess with those. If you work with a partner you can pry and clip pretty quick, or use a code cutter."

162

"Well, did you or did you not work with a god-damned partner?"

"Right. No. I worked alone, used a slapper."

She set the cigar box down.

"What do these upside-down umbrellas do?"

"Collect rainwater. It runs down the line into the bag. You clip the bag on your belt or pants."

Merci picked up an inverted umbrella and looked at the way Lee LaLonde had reconfigured the ribs and nylon. She looked back at him again. "What, because we live in a desert or something?"

"Yeah," said LaLonde. "We're supposed to get less water from the Colorado River soon."

"They say that same goddamned thing every year."

He shrugged.

She picked up a tooth-studded mouthpiece. The gums were soft and the teeth were firm. "What's with the mouthpieces?"

"Protect the teeth while eating. Abrasion wears out more enamel than cavities."

"You chew with these things on?"

"That idea started out as a way to make your own false teeth. Cheap. Different styles. You know, so you could change them around like clothes. Like, different teeth for different occasions. I called them Occasional Smiles. It was one of those good ideas that aren't so good when you do them."

She looked at LaLonde, considered his dentition, then dropped the rubbery gums to the bench.

"You're a real loser, Lee."

LaLonde said nothing.

"Where's Janet Kane's body?"

"I don't know. I honestly don't."

"We know about Lael Jillson, too."

"I don't."

She nodded. "Tim, please handcuff this dirtbag."

Hess looked at her, then stood and helped LaLonde off the couch. Merci watched as he handcuffed LaLonde's wrists behind his back. Hess guided him back down to the couch.

"Thank you," said Merci. "Lieutenant Hess, why don't you step outside, pull that door shut behind you. Have a look around out there."

She waited by the bench as Hess plodded across the shop. He looked at her once on his way past but she couldn't read the expression. He pulled the door down behind him and Merci listened to the metallic echo.

"Sounds like lockup," she said.

"It don't sound like lockup when you can open it anytime you want."

"They treat you bad inside?"

"What do you expect, a guy like me?"

"I expect bad."

He nodded, not looking at her.

"You're always working on something, aren't you?"

He nodded again. She could feel his irritation rising, just what she expected in the absence of Hess.

"I don't think you killed her."

"I didn't."

"Get up."

He stood and Merci turned him around by one shoulder. She was surprised how light he was. With her arm extended she guided him into the bathroom with the tip of her left index finger.

164

"Kneel down in front of the toilet. Do it."

LaLonde knelt and looked back and up at her. Merci looked inside the bowl: pretty bad. The lid was already up.

"Stick your head inside and put your neck on the lip."

He did.

"Knees together."

He did that, too.

"Here's the deal, Lee. You seem like a pretty nice guy to me. I'd hate to arrest you for the murder of Janet Kane, but with your prints on that fuse I don't have much choice. So spill it—tell me how your prints got on that little glass tube and how the tube got into Janet's BMW. The reason you're looking at the toilet is because I want you to think about spending the rest of your life in one. That's exactly where you'll be in about one hour if I don't get the answers I want."

His head shook back and forth. "I can't explain it."

"Broaden your horizons."

She squatted and used her weight to push his face into the water. He sucked in before he went under, then tried to wait her out. He lasted about half a minute then struggled. She actually imagined Kemp's head in there, almost smiled. She let him up for one breath then pushed his face back in.

"Lee, you got to tell what you know. I know you're lying because it was written all over your face."

He shook his head again then tried to back out. She used his hair this time, a good wad of it, sitting forward and sitting down hard on him. She wanted to flush it but couldn't without letting go. When she felt the panic of drowning hit him, she let him up again.

He gulped down a big swallow of air. Then another. But no words.

Down again. She kept her knees pushed up tight against his shoulders and her arms extended and her hands locked hard on his neck. It was easy to keep her weight forward and down.

Next came a long one. His neck was wiry and hot. She felt the panic in him, and the strength the panic gave him. Then she let him up.

He was gasping now. The big overlapping breaths came too fast for a full lungful of air to get in. When they started coming one at a time she waited for him to say something and when he didn't she drove him back under again.

"Next air's about sixty miles down the road, Lee."

He writhed hard but her weight was up over his shoulders and she wasn't about to let go of his neck. He tried to splay his knees and slide out under her, but her legs kept his arms pinned close and the cuffs kept the wrists tight. His voice echoed up from the water but it was just a kind of scream and no words. She looked back and saw his fingers reaching up for her like a hand in a horror movie. It felt good to dominate a creep this totally.

When she let him up he drew a huge breath and blew it out and took another, then another. *"I was at. At the swap meet. Marina Park. This guy said could I. Could I build him a thing. A thing that got around car alarms. Because I had. I had the cigar boxes. For the phones. I said I could. Probably. Figure that out. I made him one. Used two*

20-amps. He came two weeks. Later and picked it up. Don't send me back. Back to prison for his. Lady. Lady, I don't know what he did with. With it. But he came back again about three. Or four months ago. To see me at the swap meet. I'll tell you what. He looks like. And I'll help you get him. Just lemme breathe and don't send me back."

Merci let go of him and stepped away. Lee LaLonde slumped to the dirty tile.

She went outside and found Hess leaning against the cinder block.

"Interesting sound effects," he said.

"Maybe there's an award in it for me."

From the car she retrieved the artist's sketch of Kamala Petersen's heartthrob at the mall.

Back in LaLonde's bathroom the young man was sitting on the floor, dazed. Hess stood with one foot braced against the wall and his arms crossed, looking down.

She showed LaLonde the drawing. He stared at it for a long moment. Hess looked at it, then at her, and she saw the look of disappointment cross his sharp face.

LaLonde nodded. "That's him."

"Name, Lee."

"Bill Something. He never said his last name."

"Clean up," said Merci. "You smell like a sewer. Then we'll have a talk. Then I'm going to trash this place and find your little gadget. Because I don't think you made it for some guy named Bill. I think you made it for you."

Hess helped him up.

* * *

Three hours later Merci called off the search. She'd found out more than she wanted to know about Lee LaLonde—his work, his diet, his old clothes, his piles of magazines about inventing.

The mystery girlfriend even came over, un-announced, at 10 A.M., and unhesitatingly repeated LaLonde's story about them being together, right here, the night Janet Kane left the living. She gave Merci her sister's number because her sister sat with the kid while Mom was over here.

Hess ran a sheet on her while Merci interrogated her: two pops for drug possession, two drunk-in-publics, one prostitution charge she pled down to loitering.

He took her aside. "The girlfriend's got narco and prostitution."

"I'll get Riverside to surveil them."

"Merci, if that fuse is really the one our boy used, what's that tell us?"

"Tells us the gadget isn't working."

Merci went back to the inventor and his girlfriend, now seated side by side on the old couch.

"I'm going to leave you here for now," Merci told him. "You see Bill, you call me. You remember any-thing about Bill, you call me. You dream about Bill, you call me. Bill shows up here, wanting you to fix his toy, you call me faster than you've ever called anyone in your life. That goes for you too, hot pants."

She wrote her home and cell phone numbers on the back of a business card and set it on one of the benches.

"I expect to hear from you, Jack."

17

That afternoon Hess sat in an empty conference room at Sheriff headquarters and studied the pages in the fat blue binders, comparing the mugs with Merci's sketch. She had already gone through the registry once, then asked Hess to do it, separately. Something about "comparing independent data," which was fine with Hess. He felt an odd roiling in his blood, like it was hot, like it was starting to bubble inside.

Of the 3,700 sex offenders then registered in Orange County, 335 lived in areas patrolled by the Sheriff Department. Some 259 were considered "serious," 11 others, "high risk." High risk is three or more violent sexual attacks. Serious is two or less. Sex Offenders Notification and Registration—SONAR—was instituted to keep track of them all.

He'd already eliminated the 11 high-risk offenders. He was now at "D" in the serious category. He was surprised that a two-time rapist, recently released at the age of thirty-six, for instance, could be considered less than high risk.

D'Amato. Darcet. Davis. Deckard.

Too fat. No. Too old. No.

According to the sign-out sheet, four of the thirty-five binders were checked out to the SONAR team, who were transferring most of the information onto compact disc for public release. New state law required that agencies make their sex offender registries available to the public in areas of high population. SONAR was deleting addresses—but not zip codes—from the files before making them public so as not to encourage trouble from neighbors. The SONAR deputies were finishing up the last three books, "T" through "Z", and also a supplemental registry for the criminally insane.

He studied the artist's drawing again. Kamala Petersen's man was mustachioed. Wavy blond hair. He'd never seen a composite wearing a coat and a vest. The artist had given something sad—perhaps even something damp—to the man's eyes. Or was it Kamala's "hyperromantic vision," as Rayborn had put it?

An interesting face, Hess thought: handsome, groomed, unusual. Unusual in what way? Not typically Southern Californian. Mustaches are out. Long hair is out. The appearance wasn't simple or casual, or offhand. It was formal. Created. A "look." A look of *what*? What are you supposed to be? A model, like Kamala said? Actor? Celebrity? Quick now, describe him in three words: intelligent, secretive, regretful.

Regretful. In forty years of law enforcement Hess couldn't remember describing a sketched suspect as regretful. Later, in court, maybe. Maybe.

Could be way upstream in juvenile court, but somewhere he's felt the lash.

Regret, thought Hess. You regret what you've done. You regret who you are. Or is that *part* of your look—the appearance of sorrow?

Personally, thought Hess, if I had taken two people from their cars, hung them in trees and bled them, I would feel sorrow indeed. But not everyone would, and that was what made the worst people in the world different from the rest of us—no regret, no remorse, no feeling for anyone but themselves, no conscience. The tricky part was that Hess knew a lot of people like that who weren't criminal. Some of them were cops and deputies. Some were accountants and mechanics. Some were teachers and housewives, though if the truth be told, most of them were men.

Delano. Dickerson. Diderot.

No. No. No.

Then there was Eichrod. Hess popped open the rings and worked it out. Eichrod, Kurt; 32 years old; 5'10", 185, brown and brown. Hair long and wavy. Mustache. Possession of obscene material; solicitation; indecent acts; peeping; battery; assault with intent to rape. Two of the sexual assault raps got him a total of four years served. Released on parole in 1995, parole satisfied late last year.

Hess set Merci's sketch beside the binder page and considered. They were close but not close, alike but different. Something more in the attitude than the physical.

What disturbed Hess was Eichrod's rising line of intensity, from porn to sexual assault in a six-year span.

You don't just go out and start with something of this magnitude. You work up to it. If nothing else, you work up to the how *of it.*

The *how* of it, Hess thought: hunter, butcher, packing-house worker? Embalmer?

Eichrod's jacket would tell. He set aside the binder page to copy later.

Gilbert. Greers. Gustin. Gutierrez.

No.

It was amazing how many sexual criminals were out there. And these were only the ones who had been caught, convicted and registered. Police scientists said the realistic number would be more like quadruple what the registry held. Hess was ashamed of some of his gender for failing to mate legitimately, then turning furtive or brutal. Desire for sex was at the center of almost everything that went wrong in a guy's head. That, and desire for money.

He turned to Ed Izma's page and looked at the picture of the huge man. Reduced to a three-by-four image, Izma lost all of his panoramic menace.

Jackson. James. Jerrol.

Mickler, Mondessa, Mumford.

No. No. No.

Then there was Pule, Ronald E. Abductor, rapist, torturer. A user of pliers. Fourteen years back in Georgia. That was ten years ago. His only offense. High risk, due to special circumstances—abduction and forcible sodomy. He was forty years old, which put him out of Dr. Page's profile age. He wasn't a builder, apparently. He just exploded on the scene, skilled beyond his years, fully formed. He was big and probably strong enough to hoist a full grown woman over the branch of a tree: 6'3'', 220 lbs. Too big for the backseat of a car? Maybe. Long blond-brown hair, mustache. And there was that something different in his eyes, too, the thing that Merci's artist had tried to capture. Remorse? Self-pity?

Hess put Pule on top of Eichrod and continued.

An hour later he was at his desk in the investigators' bullpen with the arrest files for Eichrod and Pule. It was almost seven and Hess was the only one there. He looked at his watch and saw that it was Friday, the thirteenth. He had already photocopied their registry sheets and made a note to get "S" through "Z" and the supplemental volume from the SONAR team when they came to work the next day, first thing. He realized now that the next workday was three days off. As a young investigator it had angered him that people could be hard to get on weekends. It threatened to anger him now, but he sighed and told himself that "T" through "Z" and all the psychopaths would just have to wait.

There was nothing in either file that suggested Eichrod or Pule were experienced as meat cutters, packinghouse workers or embalmers, anyway. Hess hadn't expected anything.

He stared at Ronald Pule's registry picture again, then compared it to the sketch. Promising. But his arrest mugs didn't look like the sketch at all—his face was wider, his eyes smaller, his tight mouth nothing like the full-lipped man that had stirred Kamala Petersen's interest.

Of course, Kamala had probably exaggerated his virtues.

Hess watched Rayborn come toward him with thick blue notebooks under both arms and a newspaper propped across the top of each armful. With her hair loose it framed her face. She looked intent as always.

She set one stack of binders on his desk, then the other, saving the two papers for herself.

" 'T' through 'Z', and the crazies?" he asked.

"I got them from Carla Fontana, the shrink for the SONAR team."

She plopped the newspapers onto the desk beside Hess's, and swung herself into the swivel chair. "Let me guess—you picked out Eichrod and Pule."

He smiled faintly and tapped the photocopies with his knuckles. The skin across the bone felt like it leaped into flames and Hess actually looked down at his hand.

She picked up one of the papers, stripped off the plastic string and looked down at the front page.

Hess started in on the "T's."

Tabling. Tanaha. Tenerife.

No. No. No.

For just a second he was back inside that big churning cathedral of water at the Wedge, gliding through it on his palms like a waterbug while the tonnage roared over. Then he had Barbara over the dryer with her skirt up in the laundry room of their first apartment with the windows fogged from humidity while outside it poured rain at 3 A.M., the moment being one of those delicious chances neither one of them could pass up for the first five years they knew each other.

"What?" asked Merci.

He looked up from the Sex Offenders Registry.

"You groaned," she said.

174

"Oh. Thinking about dinner."

"I thought chemo and radiation killed the appetite."

"It was supposed to make my hair fall out, too. I'm really not that hungry."

"But hungry enough to groan? Maybe you should eat."

It didn't take long to finish the regular volumes, because the last six letters of the language don't begin many names. The registry of recently released mental patients with histories of sex offenses was fairly brief.

None of them looked even generally similar to Merci's drawing. Hess thought that one had the weepy dark eyes that Kamala had described, the look of remorse, but that was a real long shot. Nothing else about him seemed right.

"Colesceau," he said. "Matamoros Colesceau."

Rayborn didn't look up. "No. He likes older women, the real helpless ones. The eyes are interesting, but there's no other facial similarities I can see. Plus, he's castrated."

"Castrated?"

"Yeah, snipped him under AB 3339, Chapter 596. He won't be hard to keep track of, either," said Merci. When Hess looked over she was standing by his desk. She was smiling. She set a paper down in front of him.

There was this Colesceau fellow, front page above the fold, looking not much like he did in the mug, his hair thinner and shorter, his face wider and less defined. He was wearing a short-sleeve shirt with his name over the pocket. It appeared that he was leaving a vehicle and caught by surprise. His hand was on its way up—to cover his face, Hess figured—and it made him look pathetic. Hess was disappointed, because he still didn't look anything like Kamala Petersen's mystery man. Eyes, maybe. But with a wig and a mustache . . . Well, with a wig and mustache a lot of guys could look like Kamala's weepy boulevardier— blonds, redheads or the completely bald, for that matter.

"We'll know every move he makes now," Merci said. "The crazy, nutless sonofabitch. Actually, they leave the nuts on. And the effects of the hormone wear off when they stop shooting him with it, so the whole punishment is only temporary."

Hess read the headline:

CASTRATED RAPIST BRINGS
TURMOIL TO OC COMMUNITY

While Hess read the article he was aware of Merci dialing out on the desk phone. He read that Colesceau would satisfy the terms of his parole the following Wednesday, at which time his chemical castration would end. The SONAR team had decided to notify his neighbors, thus the turmoil and the article. The neighbors were already protesting.

Kamala, this is Merci over at . . .

He read Sheriff Department spokesman Wallace Houston's statement that the sheriffs "didn't reveal this felon's whereabouts in order to run him out of town. It was a matter of protecting the public safety. We believe people should know who he is and what he's done, but we want them, basically, to leave the man alone."

176

Fat chance of that, Wally, thought Hess. Wally the Weasel. There was a picture of protest organizer Trudy Powers. She was blond and quite beautiful. The sign she held said RAPISTS MAKE BAD NEIGHBORS.

. . . wanted to know if the picture in today's Times *resembles the man you saw at the mall . . .*

Hess read that the soon-to-be-free Colesceau had a full-time job in Costa Mesa and had lived in the apartment at 12 Meadowlark for all of his three years since release from Atascadero. He'd volunteered for the Depo-Provera treatment—one of only twelve mental patients included in the protocol. He was injected and interviewed every week. Depo-Provera was the brand name for the female hormone medroxyprogesterone acetate, which causes breast enlargement, hair loss and genital shrinkage when taken by males.

Then, a week before completing his sentence we rat him out to his neighbors, Hess thought. I thought I had problems.

. . . so, what are you saying, Kamala, that it could be him, but probably not? Is that what you're saying?

Hess read that Romanian-born Colesceau had been arrested and prosecuted in Los Angeles County. It wasn't uncommon to release sex offenders into different jurisdictions because of the controversy created if they were discovered. He made a note to get the jacket from Sex Crimes and see if this pudgy, chemically castrated man had a background involving hunting, meatpacking or embalming.

. . . realize that a person can add a mustache or change clothes any time he wants . . .

In fact, he'd have trudged over to Records right

then and asked the clerk for Colesceau's file but they were closed by now. Hess suddenly felt as if he was part of the chair he sat on. Like he'd painlessly melted to it and couldn't get out. Stuck. He sat back and crossed his hands behind his head to mask the dizziness. Knuckles on fire again, dipped in acid.

. . . and we'll run two others past you. Sunday morning is good for me . . .

Hess wondered if it was the radiation that had gotten him feeling so weird. He wasn't supposed to feel the damage until later.

"Kamala doesn't think so," said Merci. "She saw the paper. A whole different look. She pointed out that her man was wearing fashionable-looking clothes, which tells you something about Kamala. Anyway, she says no to this guy. We'll show her Eichrod and Pule on Sunday morning."

He was aware of her looking at him, setting back the phone. She stared at him frankly now, nothing covert about it. Nothing like her glances in the rearview on their way to Elsinore.

"Hess, what do you think about when you stare at nothing?"

He shrugged. He felt sick now, all the way down to the marrow of his bones, which was where, the doctors had told him, the chemotherapy was most damaging. Because bone marrow made white blood cells. And if you interfered with that production your cell count could drop. You could become anemic. You could die from that. Or from a thousand diseases that were easy to catch when your white cells got low. That's why they did the blood work once a week, to keep the chemicals from doing to you certainly what the cancer only might accomplish.

"Is that when you're seeing things? Like the women hanging from the tree before you saw the rope marks on the branch?"

"Well, no."

"I still want to know how you . . . "

She either didn't finish or he didn't hear it. There was a big silver passenger train bellowing through his eardrums now. He could feel the tracks shaking in the bones of his legs. Then a blast of hot steam against his face. Everything so goddamned loud.

Then quiet.

His heart was racing and his face was still hot and when he looked at Merci she was outlined in shimmering red.

"You put everything out of your head, first," he said.

"You all right?"

"You forget what you think you know. All your assumptions. They get in the way."

"Yeah. Let's get into it some other time, okay?"

"You start off with what you know for sure. Out on the Ortega, when I was looking down at the ground, I saw how neat the blood was. It wasn't splashed out in a struggle. It didn't spurt out in a fight. It came out slowly, and the source wasn't moving much, if at all. So, she's restricted somehow as she bleeds. Okay. You know what I saw first? A woman in a cocoon. Then I saw a woman in a spider web. Stillness. Immobilization. I'm still wondering if he's poisoning them somehow. Anyway, I know I've got a dead woman, bleeding. Then I see what's left of her when he's

179

done—nothing. Because he's taken her with him. That requires a lot of work and energy and planning. I saw him walking back to his car with a suitcase in each hand. Hard luggage, made out of plastic. Washable. Waterproof. Round edges, gray. But that didn't make sense because she was too big and too heavy, And according to what we found, he didn't cut her up. He took her. Because he values her. He knows he values her. So, he'd planned to take her from the start—and he didn't want to mess her up. He didn't want to spoil her but he wanted her blood drained and he wanted her body? Why, of all the millions of spots along the Ortega, did he bring her *here*? I looked up and saw the branch—low enough but strong. I remembered a deer hanging, bleeding, after my father shot him out at my uncle's place in Idaho. So I climbed up and found the notches."

She said nothing. Hess wasn't sure if she'd heard. His voice sounded like it was coming from a canyon twenty miles away.

Hess unlocked his fingers from behind his head and picked up the newspaper again. He wanted to appear strong and well. He tossed the newspaper aside as if it annoyed him and folded his hands over his lap. His hands were shaky but he could feel his heart slowing down now and Merci was no longer silhouetted in red neon. His face still felt warm but the burning of his knuckles was over. He breathed in deeply and it felt right.

"It's easy to understand, on paper," she said. "But when I went out there and tried it, all I saw was what you had seen."

"You need to do it alone."

"It's hard, eliminating the things you assume, because you need to assume *some* things. Like with the tree, you had to assume that the body was there. When in fact, he could have bled her somewhere else, contained the blood and just poured it out where we found it. Right? You assumed the body and the blood were together."

"There's some of that, yes."

He could feel the cadence of his heartbeat slowing and his vision coming clear again. But it was still like he had melted to the chair and he couldn't imagine getting out of it.

"Do you ever see things that are wrong?"

"They're not as clear as the right ones."

"I don't see pictures. I see video, and it's blurred."

He looked at her. She was sitting backward in the swivel chair, leaning forward, her feet spread. Her arms were along the top of the backrest and she was resting her chin on her wrist.

"Seeing a lot of bad stuff helps. The older you get, the more of it you see."

Hess expected some comment like *I don't need these pithy aphorisms all the time*, and he really didn't blame her. Instead she was quiet for a long beat.

"I've worked thirty-eight homicide cases. How about you?"

"Eight hundred and fourteen."

"Bigger library."

"Forty-three years' worth. Plus Korea."

"How come people who have been in wars always mention it?"

"We're proud."

"Just in the obvious ways?"

"Yeah, they're obvious. Like coming out alive."

"I'll never be in a war."

"That's not a bad thing."

"It is, if I'm building the library."

Hess thought about that. It was a delicious feeling to get a clear thought, after his body had rebelled like it just did.

"About that library—you're a lifetime cardholder. The things you see don't go away. All the clichés and stories about burnout and booze and depression and suicide. Well, they're true."

"But they don't always have to be true."

He looked at her and smiled. It was half because he enjoyed her optimism and half to portray a heartiness that he didn't feel. She was quiet again. Her chin was still on her wrist and she was looking at him with an expression of frank thoughtfulness and curiosity, like a boy might examine a new green bug found under the porch light.

"This is a hard one, Hess."

"They're the worst. A guy who doesn't regret it in the morning. Just starts planning the next one."

"But isn't that a weird look in the sketch? In his eyes, like he's sorry or sad or something?"

He nodded. He was proud of her in that moment and wished there was a way to say so without making her feel small.

"I've never seen a look like that," she said. "I wonder if Kamala Petersen might have added it."

She stood then and slid the chair under the desk

with a push of her foot. She put her hands on her hips and looked down at him uncertainly. "Well, it's Friday evening, Lieutenant. Want to get something to eat?"

Hess said fine with me before reminding himself that it was going to take considerable effort to leave his chair.

Too late now, he thought. He lay his arms along the rests and set his feet squarely and looked at Merci again to see if she was registering his weakness. She was standing close by with one of her large hands out and he took it before he realized everything that taking it would mean.

He glided upward on her strength.

18

Colesceau sat in his darkened living room at 12 Meadowlark and listened to the chanting of the crowd on the street outside. The blinds were closed and the lights were off. He stared openly at the images on the TV screen but his attention was outside with the mob. His heart felt heavy enough to stop beating. Five *days* before the nightmare would end, and this is what they do to you. He felt a rage so overwhelming his arms trembled with the power and urgency of it. He felt the weight of ice picks in his hands.

When the chanting stopped he went over and worked the blinds open just a crack so he could see out. But as soon as they saw the plastic louvers move they started yelling again. It had gone like this for two straight hours now, and six hours yesterday after work. It amazed him how a news story in yesterday's morning paper hatched a crowd so instantly. One day he had privacy; the next he had these . . . concerned citizens howling for his blood. And photographers bushwacking him as he got out of his little red truck.

But he looked through the thin crack anyway, at the outraged and outrageously beautiful face of Trudy Powers contorted into a mask of purest hatred. She raised and lowered a sign in rhythm to the chant:

MAKE OUR NEIGHBORHOOD
SAFE for the CHILDREN!
MAKE OUR NEIGHBORHOOD
SAFE for the CHILDREN!

Her sign said RAPISTS MAKE BAD NEIGHBORS and Trudy waved it up and down like a fan at a soccer game.

Jesus, thought Colesceau, I don't exactly love children but I've never even considered hurting one. He wondered what the police had told these people. Did they know his convictions were only for attempted rape of very old, pathetically ugly and helpless women, *not* the glowingly healthy children of people like Trudy Powers? Did they know he was pumped full of female hormone and quite harmless? He was astonished. He touched his crotch—a bag of dumplings.

The reporters were still there, too. They were different ones but you could tell what they were—cameras and microphones and grim, hungry faces. There were two big news vans parked on the other side of the street. One of them was from the channel he was watching!

Five more days. Now this. Thank you, Holtz. Thank you, Carla. Thank you, fucking police. At least in Romania they just shoot you and get it over with.

He twisted the blinds shut all the way again and went into the kitchen. He made a big Bloody Mary with the mix from the fridge and the vodka from the freezer and about a tablespoon of hot sauce.

MAKE OUR NEIGHBORHOOD
SAFE for the CHILDREN!

His phone rang again. Holtz had called once yesterday and once today. Kaufman, the ACLU lawyer, had called twice today and promised to call again. Sure enough:

Mr. Colesceau, this is Seth Kaufman of the American Civil Liberties Union again. I just wanted to make it clear that we're concerned about you and your rights. We think we can help you and we're willing to do so. I'll leave my number again and encourage you to call. We can't help you if you won't help us help you. My home number is . . .

Colesceau felt a rush of anger surge through him and he picked up the phone.

"This is Matamoros."

"Good, great. I'm glad you picked up. Now, how are you holding up?"

"It is difficult. I feel like an animal."

"They're treating you worse than an animal. I hear something in the background. Are those your neighbors?"

"They chant like monks, hours at a time. I feel like it may cause me to lose my mind."

"Can I come over? Like right now? I think we can get a court order to desist against them, or at least move them back to the nearest public place. You live in an apartment complex, correct?"

"The Quail Creek Apartment Homes in Irvine."

"Well, that's private property. Do you have a back door into your unit?"

"None."

"All right. Look, there are a lot of people out there

who are on your side. And we can convince a lot of others, if you're willing to stand your ground and speak your piece. We'll talk about our options. Would you mind making a statement on-camera? It could go a long way to getting some public sympathy coming our direction."

"I have nothing to hide. But I don't like cameras."

"No cameras, then. Until we meet, don't say anything to anybody. Don't open the door. Don't say anything to those people. I'll be coming down from L.A. so let's say exactly one hour from now. I can get you out of there, we can go get some coffee or dinner if you want. Or I'll bring some takeout."

"That would be welcome. I need to go out."

"Do you have a copy of the medical protocol you signed when they released you from the hospital?"

"I have it."

"Perfect. Give me your address."

Kaufman brought an overcoat that Colesceau pulled on over his own before they walked through the front door and into the jeers of the crowd. Even with his face buried down in the big coat he could see the bright jolts of light from the photographers' flash attachments, and he could feel the white brightness of the lights set up for the video shooters. And the chant tripled in volume as he moved toward the driveway and Kaufman's car.

. . . get out of Irvine . . . miserable creep . . . pack your bags . . . the fuck out . . . rapist, raper, human swine . . . don't come back . . . keep on going . . . filthy animal . . . don't sleep or we'll burn your place down with you in it . . .

187

"Middle America snarls," whispered Kaufman as he swung open his car door and guided Colesceau in. "You're just this week's entertainment."

A moment later Colesceau's head pitched forward as Kaufman backed out of the driveway and swung wide, then shifted into drive and gunned it down the street.

Kaufman suggested a family-style restaurant on a busy boulevard up in Costa Mesa. He spoke to the waitresses by name and seemed expected. Colesceau was shocked to be introduced and not see them recoil in disgust. Pratt and his sneaky sidekick Garry had told all their customers about him before he even started work there, apparently, and rarely did he meet someone who failed to register morbid interest. You could see it in their eyes.

The booth was back in the corner by the rest room hallway. It was large and private and upholstered in vinyl. Plastic ferns hung above it from thin chains. There was a bus tray piled high with dirty dishes across the aisle from the table in front of them, but other than that the table was fine.

He studied the lawyer for the first time: a pretty man of perhaps thirty, physically fit, sandy brown hair and very blue eyes. Pretty in the sense that he was so vibrantly groomed: teeth and gums sparkling, fingernails coated with clear polish, casually perfect hair. Colesceau, no stranger to fine menswear—at least as a window shopper—priced out Kaufman's tie at $80. It made absolute sense to him to be represented by a lawyer who was successful.

First Kaufman told him what the ACLU was, how it

188

stood for protecting individual constitutional rights, often from those very agencies that were supposed to guarantee them—government, law enforcement, the courts of law, and so on. There was no charge for their representation. All ACLU attorneys were paid an annual salary, modest at best. They had been behind some of the biggest decisions ever made in this country, and had successfully defended men and women from small civil courtrooms to the Supreme Court in Washington, D.C. Kaufman personally saw his organization as the best and final weapon a citizen could use against the powers of the state. A weapon against fascism, racism, the abridgment of personal liberties. A sort of David to the state's Goliath.

Kaufman spit all this out in a hurry, and Colesceau had the impression he'd said it a million times before. The waitress took their orders.

"Are you willing to speak to me frankly?" Kaufman asked when she was gone.

"I have nothing to hide."

The lawyer studied him with his cool blue eyes. "Did you bring the protocol for the hormone treatment?"

Colesceau withdrew the document from his coat pocket and handed it to Kaufman.

Kaufman unfolded it and smoothed it out against the tabletop. "Have you had all the injections, every week?"

"Every week."

"What's it feel like? To have that hormone in you."

Colesceau looked hard at the lawyer, then out toward the bus tray of dirty dishes still sitting in the aisle, then to the stout redhaired waitress busying herself under the flickering fluorescent light behind the counter. She glanced at him with exaggerated indifference.

"Don't answer that if you're uncomfortable. I just remember reading the Assembly floor analysis of AB 3339—the chemical castration bill—and thinking what a goddamned barbaric thing it was."

Colesceau almost liked this man. "It feels terrible. It turns you into a woman very slowly. But not all the way. I have gained weight and my genitals got small. My breasts have grown unnaturally. The hair on my face turned to fuzz. I'm irritable and emotional in a way I never was before. I feel like my soul has been asked to change. I feel like I am being forced to become a person different than the one I was born."

Kaufman had produced a narrow notebook and was writing in it now. "What's it done to your sex drive? Do you get erections?"

"Almost never."

Colesceau looked at the lawyer. This lawyer is really no different than anybody else, he thought: he's nosy, impudent, disrespectful and gleefully fascinated by the plight of my testicles. Colesceau imagined his own right arm in a short, chopping motion, totally unexpected, delivering an ice pick straight through the expensive cotton shirt and through the attorney's stunned heart.

What's it feel like? To have that pick in you?

"Can you describe to me what it *feels* like to be chemically castrated, then to see attractive women, or to be around them?"

190

At this point the soft drinks arrived and Colesceau went into that strange state in which he both observed and participated. He watched himself sitting there, as if he were looking in from the other side of the window. He saw the top of Kaufman's head, as if he were a bird perched in the fake fern above them. He heard himself chattering away now, laying it on thick for Kaufman, being as humble and misunderstood and innocently wronged as possible.

". . . and you can understand the great disappointment of my mother. Without her love and attention, without her support, I truly think I might die."

He was careful to use the word *support* because Americans loved to use it so much, as if friends and family were actual structural elements that held them in place, as if they were so physically fat and mentally weak they'd collapse without *support*.

"We've been very close since the murder of my father by fascist state police in 1979."

"You were actually forced to watch as trained attack dogs mauled your father to death, Moros?"

"No. He was shot by fascist police. The dogs attacked me when I ran to him after."

I actually enjoyed every second of it, Seth. The man was a drunken pig except when he was asleep. I was the one who made it possible. I listened to his conversations. I made reports by a secret phone in the cooperative leader's barn. I spoke creatively, as a child would. I added more subversive material when I needed impact. I stole his letters and put them back before he knew they were gone. I put the guns in our barn. When they finally murdered him it meant more coffee for me in the morning and nothing more. Stupid to rush to his side as if I cared. That was to throw my mother off my trail. She knew he had no guns. But what are a few hundred stitches compared to living years on end with that cruel, stupid hog?

"Do you relive that moment still? Do you ever *see* what they did to him, or what the dogs did to you?"

"Yes. Every morning in the mirror I see what the dogs did to me. What the police did to my father is a thing I can't remember without tears. For a boy, some horrors never die. The scars on my body are nothing compared to the scars on my heart."

"Amazing."

The lawyer was staring at him now like one of Pratt's or Lydia's friends, friends who were trying to act like they knew nothing about him. He had seen the same expression on hundreds of TV audience members during the daytime talk shows he sometimes viewed when work was slow at the auto parts store. Of course Lydia was constantly tuned in. It was a look that made him think of hungry cows. Purposeful. Intent. But lacking any means to satisfy themselves except for the passive ingestion of whatever the host or guest would say next. Such insatiable appetites for accounts of calamity, misfortune, ruination, perversion, violence, death.

For them it was just entertainment.

"Is it true, as it states in the protocol here, that your breasts have swollen?"

"I already told you that they did."

Kaufman pursed his lips and shook his head. He made a note in his book and sighed.

"Well, here comes dinner. After we eat, would you

192

mind talking about your rape convictions? I'll need to know about them. I'm interested particularly in your state of mind during the acts. Anger, sexual drive, your thoughts and feelings. What was going through your head. Why you chose older women. It might help us toward an overrule at some point. I'm thinking of the Circuit Courts of Appeal."

Colesceau looked at the lawyer. Then he explained briefly that he needed to be loved and in his confusion he thought he could force his victims to love him. He said, in a confession that surprised him, that his penis felt like an extension of his heart, which was actually quite true.

Seth looked slack-jawed at this.

"But those events are past. My punishment was supposed to end Wednesday, so long as I obeyed the rules. I obeyed every rule. I allowed myself to be poisoned and polluted with unnatural substances. Every week, into my veins, with needles. Now I have crowds outside my door. I have been evicted. I will probably lose my job. A drastic injustice has been done."

"That's why I'm here. But my ammunition has to come from you."

"So, I will talk about these things if you need to know. Even though they shame me."

"It's going to help us, Moros. Everything you can tell me is going to help us."

19

Less than twenty-four hours later, on Saturday, Colesceau was shocked to see Seth Kaufman again.

But this time Seth was on the TV that Colesceau was idly watching while the crowd chanted outside his apartment home. And this time his name was Grant Major, of County News Bureau.

He was in his studio, telling a fellow TV reporter about his exclusive interview with the castrated rapist Matamoros Colesceau. He looked even prettier than he'd looked in the family-style restaurant. The other reporter, whom Colesceau recognized, said that this seven o'clock "special report" from CNB's "newest investigative star" would be "bone chilling."

Next, on CNB.

He saw himself on the screen, leaving the apartment home wrapped in Seth Kaufman's long coat, leaning forward through the crowd of reporters and neighbors.

Then he was sitting in the restaurant, talking to the man he had genuinely believed was a lawyer from the ACLU.

Colesceau could tell that the camera had been hidden in the tray of dirty dishes.

He understood why the waitresses had been expecting them.

He felt his heart growing hard and cold again, but it beat fast, like a good machine.

He watched himself explain what went through his mind as he tried to rape the two old women—the anger, the confusion, the feelings of helplessness in the world, especially with women his own age.

He listened to his tales of hormone treatment—the swelling breasts and shrinking genitals. On TV it sounded like he was whining, ready to weep.

He sat and watched in helplessness as he explained the death of his father at the hands of the police. He couldn't understand why Grant had edited out the part where he told how difficult it still was for him, how he still thought about his father, how the scars on his heart were worse than the scars on his body.

He made me look bad, Colesceau thought. And through his rage all he could think about was hurting Grant Major in a terrible way.

A chorus of boos erupted outside. He went to the window and cracked the blinds.

Trudy Powers stood at the forefront of the mob, her hair lifted away from her face by the breeze. Her brow furrowed as she glanced up at the sky. In that moment she looked like a saint in stained glass, Colesceau thought, or one of those Agony of St. Somebody paintings, maybe the one with all the arrows in him.

He let go of the blind string, stepped to his front door and opened it. The voices hit him like a gust of wind. Without the glass between them Colesceau could feel the heft of their presence, and sense that their forward thrust was held in check only by the

195

restraining hand of human law. Without that, they'd hang him Western style, then drag his body through the streets of Irvine behind a Saab convertible.

Then the crowd hushed. He looked at Trudy Powers and the happy, shiny suburbanites and the news people scurrying toward him with all manner of cameras and contraptions. They came to a stop not ten feet away and knelt as if he was shooting at *them*. It was one of the strangest sensations he'd felt in a life of strange sensations—the world before him and at his feet as he stood firm as the pope and looked them over. He glanced down at the Bloody Mary still fresh in his hand, then back out to the mob.

"I am not a monster," he said. "I have tried to be a good neighbor. I have paid for my crimes and want to be left alone now to live my life."

Go live it somewhere else.

"I have received eviction. I have twenty-nine days."

We'll be watching you every second, scumbucket!

MAKE OUR NEIGHborhood
SAFE for the CHILdren!

Colesceau raised his hand. He was utterly dumbfounded when the crowd stopped the chant. All he could hear then was the whir and click of the equipment aimed up at him from the sidewalk ten feet away.

"Ummm . . . I've never hurt a child in my life. Never."

Yeah, just old women who can't protect themselves! Get back inside you cockface or I'm going to yank your head off and stuff it down your fuckin' neck!

He looked at the yeller, a burly long-haired man with a can of beer in his hand.

"Carl, you're worse than him when you talk like that."

Trudy Powers's voice hung in the still air. She stepped forward from the crowd.

"We understand your problems, Mr. Colesceau. But we have rights, too. And we want this neighborhood safe for our children, our seniors. We don't want trouble, either."

"Then why do this?"

Ah, fuck you.

Trudy's face turned in a flash of blond hair, then came back to Colesceau.

"We think you could find a more appropriate neighborhood."

In the fuckin' nuthouse you came from!

Trudy lifted one of her arms up without looking back.

"Sean, we're dialoguing! Listen, Mr. Colesceau. We intend to keep this vigil every day until you find more appropriate lodging. We're citizens with rights and we intend to exercise them. We'll keep our demonstrations peaceful. But we're going to have to watch you until you go. We won't trespass or harm your property in any way."

Colesceau stood with his drink in one hand and the mob stilled in front of him and the cameras executing him from ten feet away.

"I live here. I go to work. That's all I do."

He watched Trudy's golden hair catch the light and the breeze. She was wearing denim short shorts that

197

showed off her long girlish legs, white tennies and socks and a brief white blouse with a scalloped neckline. Her tall and feeble-looking husband had stepped up beside her now and Colesceau saw the sunlight condensed in his glasses. He was bearded and thin-necked. Colesceau had seen him driving a huge expensive vehicle that had stickers all over the back window asking you to save just about every animal you could imagine.

"We're dead serious," he said.

"Dead? What do you mean?"

"God, Jonathan," said Trudy.

"It means you'll see us every day for the rest of your life here. We'll know exactly where you are, *every second of your life.*"

"I have no objection to this at all. I am an innocent man. And to show my innocence, I want to give you something. Please, wait here."

No problem there, dude!

Colesceau went back inside his apartment and picked out one of his mother's most preposterous painted eggs. It was a lavender ostrich egg with gold bric-a-brac and a little bunched-up skirt of lace around the middle of it.

He took the egg back outside and resumed his place in front of the TV shooters.

"This represents all the goodness I possess on earth. I offer this as a pledge of my perfect behavior for the next twenty-nine days."

He held out the egg with both hands, elbows tucked and head slightly bowed, as if his posture could increase its value.

"For you, Mrs. Powers. For all of you."

The cameramen inched closer. They emanated an instinctive fear that Colesceau respected. They were used to being hated.

But not Trudy Powers. Trudy, he clearly understood, was used to being adored and loved and deferred to because of her high value as a sex partner. So she came forward with a kind of gliding step, eyeing Colesceau with an expression of self-confidence and self-respect. You could tell she saw herself as an ambassador from one world to another, from the world of the good to the world of the damned. And her willingness to approach the damned pleased her deeply. She was going to accept a handful of feces from the devil himself, smile and be gracious about it.

My evil stimulates her, thought Colesceau. I am titillation. I fortify what she believes is her soul.

She came around the camera people, stepping over a thick bundle of cable with a jiggle of inner thigh, her eyes locked on Colesceau's. There was pageantry in them.

Colesceau proffered the egg. She reached out with both hands, and a firm but forgiving expression on her face. She looks like Mary on the outdoor fresco at Voronet, he thought, pious and blank and immovable all at the same time. He trailed her palms with the tips of his fingernails as he laid the gift in her hands.

Then he stepped back and looked past her to the crowd. He bowed very slightly and strode back inside 12 Meadowlark.

20

Freedom. Velocity. Interstate 5. Windows down, air blasting through the van. Bill felt the rage filling him now, moving throughout his body. Like boiling water removed from the burner, it settled and filled the shape of its container. Bill Wayne, he thought: vessel of retribution, bucket of hate. Witness this.

He found Ronnie's beat-up old four-door in the Main Place parking lot, near the entrance closest to Goldsmith's Jewelry. So she hadn't lied. All the more reason to get to know her. The mall shops closed at nine tonight, which gave him almost an hour, just right.

So he drove away and into the cluttered construction zone he'd scouted earlier, just .85 miles from the mall according to the van odometer. The mess had something to do with CalTrans and the I-5. He found the bumpy turnoff and drove along the beaten chain-link fence, past the scaffolding and the water trucks. The gate was closed but not locked. He drove inside with his headlights off and parked, hidden between two big Cats. He cut the engine and sat there a moment. The moon was just a faint face risen prematurely in the eastern sky. It looked alone and embarrassed. Perfect—just two blocks from a stop for the

OCTA bus, which would take him straight into the mall when he was ready.

Bill slipped to the back of the vehicle and opened the toolbox. He wouldn't need Pandora's Box because Ronnie's car was almost certainly too old and cheap to have a comprehensive antitheft alarm wired in. Good. Less to carry, less to depend on. No fuses to slip out of place and end up who-knew-where? That meant he'd only need the knockout cloth in the heavy-duty freezer bags, his shopping bag and his trusty Slim Jim. Traveling light.

He got the gas bag out from his instrument kit. It sat atop his surgical "sharps"—the scalpels, dissecting scissors, retractors, forceps, needles and catheters used for the preliminary veinous removal of blood and arterial introduction of fluid.

Holding his breath, he gave the chloroform cloth a heavy fresh dose from the 50mm bottle he'd stolen from the body and paint shop where he'd briefly worked, Saturdays only, over two years ago. He had been a prep man and gofer, tasked sometimes with the unpleasant job of mixing chloroform and alcohol for use as a solvent. The liquid was heavy and smelled kind of pleasant, he thought. When he'd tried it out on a near helpless drunk one night up on Harbor, he had been surprised how quickly it worked.

Bill sealed up the bag very thoroughly and waved his hand in front of his face before breathing in. It was wonderful stuff—fast acting, quickly metabolized out of the system and only occasionally responsible for heart failure and strokes in people and animals who had breathed a little too much of it.

201

He slipped the plastic bag inside another one, sealed it, and set the thin package into the shopping bag. The shopping bag was black, large and strong, featuring thick twine handles and the name of a department store in gold script. His book and bedsheet were already in it. New latex gloves, too. He added the Slim Jim. It extended a few inches from one end so Bill used the sheet to cover the top of it, disguising it as a mysterious purchase, or perhaps something to return. The sweet, ethereal smell of the gas lingered as he went back to the driver's seat.

His last piece of working gear was the micro .32 derringer that he now took from the glove box and slipped into his coat pocket.

Bill always brought reading material for his short bus rides. In this case, *Fodor's Los Angeles*, to suggest he was just visiting. He sat near the front of the bus, on the right side, glancing out the window only occasionally and otherwise engrossed in the book. In fact he was picturing Ronnie: her shapely legs, dark curly hair and high, intelligent forehead. Tall and young. Wouldn't it be something if she'd worn her hair up today?

He disembarked at the north side of the Main Place, then walked around the parking lot to where Ronnie's car was still waiting on the south side.

The light wasn't particularly good where Ronnie had parked: perfect. He walked past her car and noted it was a Chevrolet. He looked around, saw no one nearby, then went back to the car, set the bag down and acted like he was getting out his keys. Instead he bent down and got the Slim Jim, leaned up close to

202

the old sedan and slid the tool down between the window glass and the door. He kept his head up, his eyes alert. It was a matter of feel at this point, and Bill had plenty of that. He'd practiced on hundreds and hundreds of cars so that this part of his job would go smoothly. And it did. On his third pass with the Jim he caught the lock arm and he pulled it up. He heard the tinny report of the lock opening and saw the little black plastic rod stand up inside the glass like a soldier at attention. Then he opened the door, set his bag on the passenger's seat, sat down and slammed the door shut.

A moment later he was in the backseat on the driver's side, slumped down and head back like a dozing airline passenger, keeping his eyes on the mall exit.

The black shopping bag with the *Fodor's* and Slim Jim was tucked behind the passenger's seat. The gas bag was on his lap. It was important to have that in a convenient place when you needed it, because if you opened it too soon they might smell something funny and whirl around and ruin the whole capture.

That hadn't happened, yet. The closest was Irene Hulet—his third—who had sneezed one second before he was going to clamp his hand over her mouth and apply the chloroform cloth. That had left him with the cloth already out, spreading its deadly fumes into the closed car.

Luckily, the sneeze had left her without breath for a few nice seconds, as sneezes often do. So by the time she was ready to breathe again, Bill had his left hand tight against her mouth and his right cupping the cloth over her nose. About seven seconds. The reason it worked so well was that people inhaled abruptly and deeply when they were surprised and frightened, then needed to do it again quickly when they got mostly gas. That, plenty of $CHCl_3$, and a little muscle. It helped if the headrests were solid rather than adjustable, so you could clamp your forearms around each side for purchase as you pulled back.

Bill slid down a little further for comfort, but kept his eyes open. His heart was beating hard and fast. He wanted to hurt someone badly while he felt good. Real good. He was angry, and getting angrier the longer he waited. He could almost smell the anger inside him, like a bad wire smoldering deep within its bundle. He worked his hands into the gloves.

Then he saw Ronnie come through the door.

He melted down into the floor space behind the driver's seat, unlocking the outside gas bag and positioning his thumbs and index fingers on the lips of the inside one. The closing of the car door would be his cue to open it.

He heard her keys in the lock, then the door opening. Her purse clunked to the passenger's seat. When he felt her weight settle and heard the door slam he rose behind the seat and clenched his open left hand over her mouth. A split second later his right snugged the damp rag over her nose and Bill pulled back, hard, like a rower going for speed.

"Evenin', honey."

Ronnie was a strong one. One. Two. She felt like a big wild animal. Three. Four. But Bill was stronger. This part of it was like a cowboy trying to stay on a bucking bronco. Five, while her feet kicked the pedals and her knees banged the underside of the dash. Six. She dropped the keys. Seven.

Then it was over. He felt her head go loose on her neck and he wrenched her down and to the right, out of sight. He slid up onto the seat, resealing the cloth and tossing it into his shopping bag. Bracing his feet on the front seat he pulled Ronnie toward him like a spider gathering in a huge moth. Head and shoulders. Butt. Legs and feet. One shoe had fallen off somewhere.

She whimpered. The sweet smell of the chloroform lingered in the car.

He was breathing hard as he got her laid out across the back and squeezed himself into the front of the car. He pulled the sheet out and covered her, tucking it just under her chin like she was asleep. The keys had landed right in the middle of the floor mat, as if she'd placed them there just for him.

Three minutes later he was slipping the big Chevy in between the towering earth movers, up next to his van. The fury was at bay now and he could feel the deeply meaningful sensation of affection stirring again down there. He looked out at the moon, then back at the unconscious woman.

He imagined cruising into his garage and having the door shut automatically behind him, then getting things set up. Preparation was sacred. He imagined the candlelit garage with Ronnie on the table and the Porti-Boy pulsing rhythmically as the fluid ran in. He could feel his hands massaging the fluid deep into her thirsty tissues, bringing her body to life again, to a rosy glow that began its bloom at the jugular in her clavicle and spread down, throughout her system and finally back to her angelic face. She would bloom beneath his touch like a flower. He could see her eyelids flutter as they awoke to the fluid of eternity. And he could see himself restored, too, gradually, as he worked the spirit back into Ronnie's tired body. Yes, slowly it would come to him—the feeling worth any price, the feeling that was the spark of his dreams and the flame of his humanity. He would caress her with the expensive scented oils, perfume and dress her in the silk and satin lingerie, dry and style her hair while he grew powerful in his desires. He imagined carrying her upstairs to bed, whispering in her ear. And then he'd really find out how much she wanted him. It was the best thing this short, sad life had to offer, for both of them.

21

Hess stood beside Merci near the CAT D6 and looked at the tire tracks left by the vehicle that had carried Veronica "Ronnie" Stevens's body into the night.

Kneeling and pointing with his pen, he commented on the tracks of the mismatched tires. They were some of the best tire prints he'd seen at a crime scene because of the soil here in the construction yard—oily, damp and loosely packed.

Hess had been awakened by Merci's call at 6 A.M. He was a little groggy then, but unfettered by chemotherapy, radiation and the stout scotches he'd drunk before bed. Now his mind felt sharp and clear, though his fingers were oddly heavy, like saps at the ends of his hands.

"I hate this man," said Merci, quietly, slowly. "I want to commit mayhem on him."

This was one of the most dismal scenes Hess had ever run across: the big slick of blood that had spread over soil that was already oil stained and packed by heavy machinery; the splash of it against the CAT track; the forlorn Chevrolet with the keys still in the ignition and the purse sitting upright and open on the hood, overflowing with multicolored vitals that spilled out and sent up heat waves from the paint.

Hess had never seen such a gruesome thing. He had

stood there for a moment in the early sunlight in disbelief.

Merci had stared in silence with him.

He'd be more likely to send you something UPS.

After that, as always, work to do.

"He must not know," he said. Hess had been wondering if the Purse Snatcher knew about his tires and now had to guess he didn't. Either doesn't know or doesn't care, he thought: and so far he's been very careful. He slipped the pen back in his pocket, his fingers thick and imprecise. He glanced at Merci but she was still looking at the bloody ground.

"Not know how much I hate him?"

"That he's riding on two different tires."

"He'd change them."

"He hasn't."

"He thinks we're as stupid as I feel. I wish I had one of those drinks from dinner right now."

She'd insisted on joining him in Scotch at dinner on Friday. This had not surprised Hess. They had gone to Cancún, a deputy's hangout in Santa Ana. The food was good and cheap and they made the drinks strong if you appreciated them that way. He could feel the disdain when they walked into the place and he knew it was for Merci and not for himself. Kemp was there, unfortunately, with a table of his friends, and the drunken tension in him had leaked into the atmosphere like a gas. It had been too late to back out and go someplace else, so Merci had downed the drinks.

"It wouldn't do you any good, Merci."

"This girl was nineteen years old, Tim. That's just

unforgivable. There ought to be special circumstances for victims under twenty-one. You do somebody under twenty-one, any reason, you get the fucking guillotine."

The patrolmen had taped off the scene and kept the construction workers out of the yard as best they could. A foreman had found the car and purse, seen the blood and guts and called it in. He'd heard about the Purse Snatcher, seen Merci on TV, knew what he was looking at. He got her to autograph a piece of paper for his kid.

Hess watched the CSIs working the purse and the door handles of the car. The hood was smeared and murky where the innards and purse had been. Goddamned flies. He wondered if the Purse Snatcher had picked a woman in an older, alarmless car because Lee LaLonde's electronic override box had lost a fuse in Janet Kane's BMW and failed. Maybe he just liked her. Maybe she had her hair up. Two hunts in two weeks.

Building. Growing. Speeding up.

Would he get his alarm override back to LaLonde for repair?

Hess recalled the statement. LaLonde was selling his inventions at the Marina Park swap meet in Elsinore on a Sunday in late August of last year. A medium-height, medium-build male Caucasian, blond/ brown, had approached his table. Around thirty years old. "Bill" wore his hair long. Bill asked how LaLonde knew electronics; LaLonde told him of father, school-ing, aptitude. Suspect asked if LaLonde knew how to build a small device that would override the alarm system on cars. LaLonde said there were too many combinations on door locks and keyless entry chips to make a universal unlock device feasible—it would be too slow and possibly too large. Suspect then said he didn't care about the locks, he cared about the *alarms*. LaLonde said that both the lock and the disarm combinations were frequencies digitally registered by a microchip in the keyless entry module—and constantly emitted by the alarm system of a vehicle. He told Bill he could configure a universal override if he had the manufacturer's specs on the frequencies. The suspect had shown him several sheets of paper that "looked like computer printouts" by nine of the major carmakers, containing the information. The suspect said he had a friend in the business. Three weeks later, LaLonde had sold Bill a working override device housed in a cell phone body, for $3,000, and given Bill back the printouts.

With the fear that Merci had put into LaLonde, Hess bet the young man would call them if his customer contacted him for a repair. Then again, he might not, because the override box could convict them both. Merci had made this clear, that LaLonde was staring at a murder conspiracy rap if he didn't cooperate. It was hard to know which way a person would lean.

LaLonde had sketched his device for them, and Hess now turned to the drawing and noted where the fuse would go.

But you lost it in Janet Kane's car, thought Hess. You opened the cell phone body and the fuse fell out and you didn't notice in the dark. And the override hasn't worked since. Why open it? Was it failing? Unreliable? Did it open accidentally?

Thus a 1978 Chevrolet Malibu belonging to Veronica Stevens of Orange, California.

Hess could see the wavy-haired, mustached suspect wheeling a vehicle with mismatched tires into this yard in the dark last night, pulling up between the CATs. He knows this place because he scouted it early. Ditto the last two places he's used to hide the van and later transfer the woman.

He could see Ronnie Stevens inverted from a rope tied to the top of the CAT's hydraulic blade—about seven feet off the ground. Like the oak branches, strong, but easier to get to.

But, question: How does he get from where he parks to where he hunts?

Hess cursed himself for not thinking of this before. Then he searched his memory for the pertinent distances: between the Jillson abduction site and where her car was found—5.3 miles. Between the Kane abduction site and where her car was found—3.3 miles. Between the Stevens abduction site—if it was indeed the nearby mall—and where her car was found, well, how far was the mall from here, maybe a mile?

You don't walk five miles unless you have to. Or three. Or even one.

Then how does he get from where he leaves the van or truck or station wagon to where he hunts the women?

A bike? Too clumsy and hard to handle. Hard to stash in the victim's car.

211

A friend? Hess had hoped that they weren't up against a pair. You didn't see it much in sex crimes, but two were twice as hard to catch, not twice as easy. None of their evidence, until now, had suggested that possibility. For the time being, he let it go.

Hitchhike? Too conspicuous.

Taxi? The same.

The OCTA bus? Well, he thought, check the routes. Should have done that two days ago. Goddamnit, anyway.

Merci was talking to the foreman again. He pointed to the car, then, presumably, to the route he'd driven in.

Hess walked the mismatched tread tracks until they came to an end near Main Street. The ground trembled from the vibrations of the freeway the same way the beach trembled from the waves at the Wedge.

The van had gone right, which was the shortest way back to I-5. This part of Main was light commercial and residential, or had been at one time. Now the buildings were either razed or awaiting demolition to make room for a new bend in the interstate and a fat new on-and-off ramp. Hess trudged back to his car and got out some plastic bags, into which he spooned soil samples from every twenty yards or so of the dirt drive. He spread the samples against the insides of the bags. He knew that all the various oils and fuels and sand and gravel dropped to the dirt and ground in by construction machinery might help an analyst match up samples taken from the tires of any given van. He wiped his forehead with his shirtsleeve. Give me the truck or van, he thought. Give me the truck or van with the odd tire.

Back at the Chevy he watched the CSIs dusting the window exteriors. The purse was already gone, bagged up and secure inside the CSI van. Hess stepped over the crime scene tape and looked through the dust on the driver's side window.

"Are you done with the door handle?" he asked.

"Yes, sir, Lieutenant."

"I'm going to open it."

"It's all yours, sir."

Hess swung open the door, bent over and put his hands on his knees, looking in. The interior was alive compared to the Jillson and Kane cars, he thought: recent players; recent events. It was just a feeling. He thought he smelled something sweet and not unpleasant—Ronnie's perfume, perhaps. Or maybe a man's cologne. He remembered what Robbie Jillson had told him about smelling his wife's tormentor when he got into her Infiniti a *full day* after she went missing. How did he describe it? *Faint. Cologne or aftershave maybe. Real faint. But I smelled him.*

He leaned further in, hoping for a more definitive whiff but getting none. A woman's scent lay underneath it all, he thought, but something else?

A woman's shoe lay on the floor, down by the pedals. It was a black sandal with a thick sole like the young people were wearing these days. Hess leaned in and confirmed that the shoe came up fairly high—above the ankle—and that it fastened with a buckle at the top. The buckle was burst open and the perforated length of leather, bent from hours of use, had sprung free of the broken buckle. He could see her fighting. He looked back up toward the headrest of her seat. One long dark hair caught in the stitching of the pad. Because you were being pulled back? Because he's behind you with, what? A cord? A club? Just his strong hands? No chance, really, with him coming from behind in the dark. You could have a .45 in your purse but it wouldn't help. It wouldn't help *you*, anyway. No warning. No purchase. Nothing but your fists and your nails. He could see her unlocking the door, swinging her purse in, dropping herself to the seat and closing the door at the same time. She's just about to put the keys in the ignition when he moves. After the door closes; before the engine starts. Keys still in her hand.

Keys. We always say to use the keys as a weapon.

Hess saw that they were still in the ignition, a fat bunch and a small flashlight on a ring. The flashlight had a good surface for prints. The Snatcher had touched at least one of those keys, for certain. Hess used his pen and a pocketknife to guide the ignition key almost free but keep it from falling out. In the smoggy morning light he did not see what he hoped he'd see: darkened blood in the slot and on the teeth of the key. He saw nothing but the clean old metal of well-used metal.

It made him angry and Hess thought, Sonofa*bitch*, I'm going to find you. And if Merci Rayborn takes target practice on your face I might look the other way.

It was easy to get worked up about what had happened to a young woman like this, when you were close enough in time and space to smell her.

Hess backed out, gently shut the front door and opened the rear one. There you were, he thought. Your place. Not much room, really. Hess wondered if he just sat on the seat, unmoving and dressed in dark clothing—maybe a dark ski mask pulled down—and let darkness, reflections on glass and people's general inattentiveness be his cover. Maybe.

You find the woman and you know her car, which means you must have seen her in it. You are on foot now, in the parking lot, where Kamala Petersen first saw you. You walk purposefully and deliberately: a gentleman going to or from the mall, to or from his car. Alert. Observant.

You override her alarm if she has one; jimmy the door lock; get in. You carry the Jim where? Down your pants? In a bag or box? Along with the "cell phone" override? Along with your choke cord or sap?

You wait in the back; overpower; take the keys and drive away.

Hess tried to picture the Purse Snatcher slugging his victims unconscious with a sap or a club. But he couldn't see it happening—the headrests kept getting in the way.

He shut the back door and looked at one of the CSIs. "Do your best."

The CSI nodded. "We've already got a lot of prints, sir. But cars are traps—you know that. Can I mention something? Did you notice a smell in the car?"

"Yeah, I can't place it."

"I think I can. My cat was operated on a few months ago. They let me watch because the vet's an old family friend. Typically they put the animal under with a ketamine and Valium shot, then keep it down with halothane gas. But last time, my cat got real sick with either the ketamine, the Valium or the halothane. He's old. Almost died. Anyway, they tried chloroform. The vet's an old guy—he used it decades ago and he was good with it. But I got that same smell, sweet and kind of nice, when I opened the door of this car."

It made the kind of sense that sent a little shiver of recognition to Hess's heart.

"It knocked out that cat in about two seconds. And you know how uptight and nervous a cat at the vet is?"

22

They found Ronnie Stevens's Santa Ana address and parked right out front. It was a fifties' suburban home in a tract that looked well tended and peaceful. A big acacia tree bloomed purple in the middle of the front yard. An older Chevy—a model once driven by Sheriff Department deputies, Hess noted—sat in the driveway.

"I hate these," Merci said. "Maybe you can do the talking."

Ronnie Stevens's mother was tall and dark-haired, an aging beauty, Hess saw. He wondered that a sixty-seven-year-old man with ten-pound fingers would consider a fifty-year-old woman aging. She'd been cleaning the house.

Hess stumbled through his lines as best he could. He felt his face flushing and heard his voice crack as he told her that her daughter was missing and presumed dead. He hated these moments, too: tragedy revealed, and irrefutable evidence of his own failure. Of the failure of his entire profession.

Eve Stevens received the news with a small nod, an uncertain wobble of chin and eyes filling quickly with tears.

"We're going to get this guy, Mrs. Stevens," Merci said.

Eve Stevens excused herself and left the living room. Merci was standing by a cabinet that housed family photographs and mementos. Hess saw the eager shine of trophies and the twinkle of keepsakes.

"Brothers," said Merci. "Baseball and archery. The girl, Veronica, she was a swimmer."

Hess heard a toilet flush. He heard the low keening from the bathroom, then the toilet flush again. When Eve returned her face was a sagging mask of tragedy and her eyes looked like they'd been burned.

Eve could only talk about Ronnie for a few minutes. She sobbed steadily the whole time, but Hess was impressed by her courage. Ronnie was a conscientious young woman, had been a good student and reliable worker since she was sixteen. She had graduated from high school a semester early to go full time at the jewelry store. She had no ambitions other than to travel and see some of the world. She saved her money, had a few friends, stayed out late on Fridays and Saturdays. No steady guys. Eve didn't think Ronnie had much interest in drugs, had never found any or seen her intoxicated or overheard her talking about them with friends.

Then she stood, and Hess knew the expression on her face.

"May I?" she asked.

"Please."

With this, Hess went to her and hugged her, very lightly, almost formally, and not for very long. He let her break it off when she wanted to.

"Thank you," she said.

Hess just nodded, then handed her the sketch of the

Purse Snatcher suspect. He watched her tears hit the paper.

"No. She liked the clean-cut type. At least, I think she did."

Hess asked if Veronica had remarked anything unusual about a man lately—any man—a stranger, an acquaintance, a customer, a new or old friend.

Eve nodded. "Two nights ago, Thursday, we talked when she came home from work. We talked late. We talked about men, how funny they could act. Because this man had blocked her from getting out of the parking lot, then asked her for a date. Odd."

Merci exhaled with some disgust. "This guy's odd for more reasons than that."

Hess looked at her but it was too late. Rayborn was thick as a post sometimes. "Did she describe him?"

"No."

"He just parked his car right behind her?" he asked, anything to get Merci's last implication out of the air.

"His van. Ronnie said it was a silver panel van."

The OCTA bus driver on the Saturday evening route recognized the sketch immediately. It had taken Hess about two minutes and the transit district schedule to see that there were bus routes proximate to all three sites where the cars had been abandoned.

"Last night, late, after eight-thirty," he said. "He got on at Main and 17th, got off at the Main Place Mall. What did he do?"

"We think he killed a woman," said Merci.

The driver looked at Hess, then back to Merci. "He sat on the right, up near the front of the bus. I remember that he wore cologne. Kind of a funny smell. Strong. Had a shopping bag—the ones with the handles on them. He had a book out. *Fodor's Los Angeles.* So I thought he was a tourist. Nice clothes, country and western style. Long coat. Mustache and long hair, like the picture. But some guys, they've got this thing about them, you notice it."

"What thing?" asked Hess.

The driver thought a moment. He was wiry and middle aged, looked to Hess to be of Latin American blood. "They're fake. They're not real."

"Maybe the mustache is fake," said Merci.

"I didn't notice that," the driver said. "It's more to do with attitude. The whole look. It seemed false. There's something else I noticed about him, too. I look at my riders a lot. I talk to them."

"And?" asked Hess.

"He was the kind of guy who is always alone. There's no one in the world you can picture with him. No one to be around him. Just a feeling, that's all."

Merci left him her card with her cell and work phones on it, and carefully told the driver how critical it was to call if he ever saw this man again, or remembered anything more about him.

At his desk, Hess listened to his messages while Merci showed the Sex Offenders Registry mugs of Pule and Eichrod to Kamala Petersen. It was late Sunday morning by then and headquarters was dead. Hess looked over to see Kamala looking down at a picture on Merci's desk, shaking her head.

Barbara had called to wish him well and tell him it

was good to talk to him. She wanted something, he could tell, but he had no idea what.

Dr. Ramsinghani, the radiation specialist, had called to inquire about his general feeling after the first thoracic scorching. The doctor reminded him that the second treatment would be Monday, same time and place.

Hess listened, wishing that he wasn't the center of his own universe. Like you'd forget a date like that. It would be nice to just blend in and be.

An old contact of his at the DMV had been kind enough to return his call promptly, and with good news: Hess's 1028 request for a list of panel vans registered in Orange County would be coming through by Monday morning. Too bad DMV in California didn't track vehicles by color. How many, he wondered. Two hundred, or fifteen? But how many with mismatched tires? That was the wild card.

Word from Riverside Sheriffs, too: LaLonde surveilled, no unusual activities, would continue another forty-eight hours.

The phone rang. It was Arnie Pickering of Arnie's Outdoors, following up on Hess's request of earlier in the week. He was proud to announce that he had found in his computer files just the kind of purchase record that Hess had asked him to find. The talkative Arnie chattered on but finally got out the basic facts: a sale was made in February, the off-season for deer hunting, Hess knew, but the month that Lael Jillson was field dressed off the Ortega. The Arnie's Outdoors customer had bought a device known as a Deer Sleigh'R, a gambrel for securing game, a hoist for

221

lifting it, two lengths of nylon rope, and an electric lantern.

"Can you find the clerk who rang it up?"

"It was Big Matt, here at the Fountain Valley store. He's here right now if you want to talk to him."

"Give me the fax number there. I'm going to send over a sketch I want him to look at. See if he can put the face with the sale."

Hess took the number and faxed the artist's sketch to Big Matt at Arnie's Outdoors in Fountain Valley.

He collected the picture as it groaned haltingly through the fax machine, then looked over at Merci. She was just coming back into the room after escorting Kamala Petersen to the exit. She shook her head disgustedly and came to his desk. She looked around, then leaned forward toward him. He could see the anger on her face, in the hard set of her jaw and in her cold brown eyes.

"Eichrod, Pule and Colesceau all just flunked the Kamala Petersen romantic-vision test. None of them has sad enough eyes. None is Mr. Remorse. She also let it drop that she'd had three margaritas the first time she saw the sonofabitch, up in Brea. When they *communicated unspoken language* with their eyes."

Hess thought about it. "But the bus driver and Lee LaLonde all said the drawing was good. Kamala saw our man, the genuine article, in person. If we haven't shown her his picture yet, then we haven't shown her his picture yet. Maybe we don't have it. Maybe Dalton Page is wrong. Maybe he's never even had a parking ticket."

Hess's phone rang. He put his finger up to hold

222

Merci in place, then picked it up. Big Matt from Arnie's Outdoors said that the out-of-season purchase was his, he remembered it. It was raining hard that day, and business was slow. But he remembered the buyer because he was dressed up in a kind of gun-slinger's outfit—vest and long coat—with long blond hair and a mustache, not a typical Arnie's Outdoors customer at all. The buyer looked similar to the guy in the sketch that he was looking at.

"He asked me something odd," Matt said. "He asked me how the gambrel held the ankles of the deer. I showed him how the hooks go through the ankle tendons. He said he didn't want his deer messed up. I said the gambrel just made a little hole in the ankles. So he asks me if we sell pads to keep that from happening. I said we didn't, nobody cared if the deer had little holes in its ankle because the feet get cut off and thrown away anyhow. You know, unless you're going to save a foot for a trophy or something. He was real certain about not damaging his deer, though. So I showed him a cinch gambrel and he bought that."

Hess thought about this. "It's got loops for a cord instead of hooks? The cord cinches over the animal's feet?"

"That's right."

He wasn't sure why, but this news didn't surprise him. Maybe something to do with his memories of how difficult a deer hunt could be. He and his father and uncle packing big bucks out of the deep country around Spirit Lake. It was hard work. If you were hunting for the meat, you protected that meat. If you were hunting for something else—whatever it might be—you'd protect it as best you could. No holes in the body. It made sense. If the Purse Snatcher used some padding between the gambrel cinch and the flesh, there wouldn't be any bruising or abrasion, either. Especially if he worked fast.

"The Deer Sleigh'R is a carcass sled?"

"Yeah, it's got a rope to secure the game on it, then you use the rope to pull it."

Hess tried to picture the Deer Sleigh'R in the back of the Purse Snatcher's silver panel van. "So, there's no wheels on it—it's stiff and flat?"

"It's flat, but it rolls up. That's one of the marketing things they're proud of. You can roll it up like a sleeping bag. Doesn't take up much room. And it's light, too, in case you're packing in."

"No skinning knives, cleaning tools?"

"Nothing like that. Just something to move a body and something to hang it with."

Hess thanked Matt and hung up. He looked at Merci. She was still hovering over his desk. He could see the malice bumping around behind her clear brown eyes.

"A clerk at Arnie's recognized the man in the sketch," he said. "He bought some hunting equipment out of season. February—nine days before Lael Jillson disappeared. Things you move bodies with. Hang them up with. Cash, of course."

The anger and the stubborn resolve were still on her face. "I should have had this picture out there sooner. I should have had this asshole two days ago, when Ronnie Stevens was still drawing breath."

"You didn't kill Ronnie Stevens. Be kinder to your-

224

self, Rayborn. You're stuck with you for about another fifty years."

A very young uniformed deputy worked his way through the pen toward them, a large cardboard box in his arms. The look on his face said he had interesting bad news.

The deputy nodded at Merci, then at Hess, setting the box down on Hess's desk. His mustache was mostly fuzz.

"Excuse me, Sergeant Rayborn, but CalTrans found these on I-5 in Irvine about an hour and a half ago. CHP got the call. I just pulled over because I was driving by, wanted to see what was going on. When I saw these, I thought of you-know-what. They got handled pretty good by the road guys and the patrolmen. But who knows?"

Hess looked down into the box at the three purses.

"One of them must have broken open on the freeway," said the deputy. "The other two, they've got ID, credit cards, personal items. No CDLs. No cash."

Merci looked at the young man.

"Good work, Casik."

"Sergeant, I want to work with you in homicide someday. So I took the liberty of running the two names through our missing persons files. Both of them vanished without leaving any trace we could find. One had car problems on the 55, her car broke down and she apparently went for help. That was twenty-six months ago. The other was shopping at a mall here in Orange County, three months later. Riverside County Sheriffs found her car in Lake Matthews a week after she disappeared. I've got no idea where these purses have been since then, but I've got a hunch."

"I see you do."

"And also, the CalTrans guys shuffled through the purses a little, let some stuff fall out. Then they just threw everything in this box. I couldn't help but notice the newspaper clipping you'll find near the top of the black one."

Hess watched Merci use her pen to lift the top of the stiff black purse, and he saw the folded newsprint. He lifted it out with a couple of paper clips, then set it on the desk and pried it open enough to see inside.

It was the article and photos from the Orange County *Journal*, six days ago, when Hess was brought back to help on the Purse Snatcher case. Mugs of Merci and Hess, standard issue from Press Information, and apparently in the *Journal* photo file. Hess hated it when they ran pictures of him.

In the shots, both his and Merci's eyes were burned out, the paper browned around the holes like a kid's pirate map.

23

Hess was still at his desk late that evening, on the phone with the head of the mortuary sciences department of a local college, fishing for something he couldn't articulate yet. Something to do with Deer Sleigh'R, formalin and missing women.

Brighton, who rarely came in on Sundays, appeared in the bullpen and waved him over. Hess made the appointment with the mortuary sciences director, then hung up and followed Brighton down a short hallway into his office. Brighton waited for him, then shut the door.

"*Three* more?"

"Two look real likely. The third, probable."

"He's been at this for two years?"

"Just over. The first went missing twenty-six months ago. Car trouble. The next was last seen, guess where—at a mall."

"Oh, good Christ. No break this morning? Nothing?" He pointed to a chair in front of his desk.

"No." Hess sat.

"He's thorough and careful, isn't he?"

"I think he's using chloroform to put them out. One of the CSIs recognized the smell from his vet. It makes sense. There's been some struggle in the cars. But not a huge amount. No blood."

227

"Can Gilliam verify the gas?"

"Not with the blood we've found. Chloroform metabolizes out real quick. But we think he's driving a silver panel van with a set of mismatched tires. It's the best thing we've got."

"Jesus, Tim. *Six*."

Brighton sat back and crossed his arms. He was a big man with a rural face and a cool intelligence in his eyes. Hess had always liked the way Brighton made ambition for power look easy and natural. He shared the spoils. He wasn't the kind of man always looking around corners at you.

Then again, Hess had little idea what the sheriff did with his spare time, though he did know that like a lot of ranking law enforcement people in Southern California, Brighton owned a house and property somewhere in Wyoming or Montana. Hess had rarely visited Brighton's home, never dined there or associated with the sheriff outside of department functions, never learned the names of his children. Those intimacies had been shared over the decades with more family-oriented men and women on the force—the ones who, like Brighton, had kids to raise. Children and the raising of them seemed to adhere the parents to each other in ways that didn't stick to Hess and his childless marriages, ugly divorces and the long stretches of aloneness that separated them.

Hess was drawn to people more like himself: on the make for something they might understand but often didn't, either recovering from or searching out the next romantic disaster. It always seemed to work out that way, but it was never how he planned it. He saw that you needed to put aside that selfishness if you wanted to fit in with the department pack, otherwise you were perceived as a danger at some point. A family made you understandable, declared your values and your willingness to sacrifice.

Hess hadn't wanted children with Barbara—who was willing—because he was young and hogging his liberties. The world seemed huge then, though his place in it with Barbara—who was insecure and jealous as time went on—seemed constricted. He was stupid to leave her but only realized it later. His guilty conscience had left everything of value to her and to this day he was thankful for that.

He was willing and interested with Lottie when he was in his thirties, but she was young and enjoying *her* liberties. They drifted away from each other in the classic fashion and parted with minimum drama and no rancor. What amazed Hess more than the divorce was the way a decade could come and go so quickly.

Children hardly seemed to matter until he was halfway through his forties and married to Joanna. His paternal instincts crept up on him like a big cat: a bold but calm desire to guide his blood into the world, to give life. He actually began looking at other people's babies, thinking of names he liked, picturing himself with an infant in his arms. Doted on his nephews and nieces. Thought a lot about his father. And his mother. Something inside him was changing for the good.

Joanna was younger than him by fifteen years, quite beautiful and willing to have a family. These were three of the reasons he married her. Hess suspected a child would help keep them together because they actually shared little in common outside the bed. After five years of trying and failing to conceive, countless consultations and tests, then three increasingly heartbreaking miscarriages, Joanna gave up on doctors, children and Hess. On the dismal March night of his fifty-first birthday, both of them drinking at high velocity, Joanna surprised him with a tearful confession that she was in love with another man. With one of the doctors who had failed to help her, in fact. It was with extreme and surprising anger that Hess imagined this man with Joanna on his examination table. She said he had his own children and with him she felt less like a failed breeder and more like a successful woman. She took half of everything and dropped all contact with Hess. He rented a room to a young deputy so he could keep the house.

By the time he realized he had pretty much missed his chance to be a father Hess was three times divorced and pushing fifty-three years old. Did everyone know he was a fuckup? He felt like an ostrich with nowhere to hide his head.

Now, sitting in Chuck Brighton's office, Hess considered all of this to be nothing more than the ancient history of an everyday life. His. And this is where it had led him—semi-retired and sixty-seven years of age, alone again, afflicted by cancer and by treatments for cancer, shadowing a murdering phantom through what could have been one of Hess's golden years. So you don't always get what you want. But grace grows in the cracks sometimes.

You have work to do.

"That must have been bad this morning."

"I've never seen anything quite like it, Bright. I mean, it was so . . . deliberate. Deliberate and disgusting and just really mean. All at the same time. This guy's got some snakes in his head."

"He'll make a big mistake. You know that."

"When, is what bothers me."

"Tell me about Rayborn, Tim."

"There's not much to tell. I think she's doing well."

"Good, good. Do you get along with her?"

"She's honest and to the point."

"Like you."

Brighton could be obtuse and Hess figured it was his right.

"What about that sketch of hers?"

Hess shrugged. "The witness needed to be hypnotized. Merci got good results."

Brighton nodded. Old news.

"It was her call, Bright. That sketch is getting hits."

"What, the bus driver, that car thief out in Elsinore?"

"And a sporting goods store clerk said it looked like a guy who bought some hunting supplies out of season."

"The question is, why'd she wait so long to get it done—hypnosis or not?"

"Some time to consult with the DA. A day to do the hypnosis and the sketch. She thought it over, wanted to make the right move. More time to get copies, get them out to Press Information."

Hess understood that what kept Merci from acting quickly on the sketch was her doubt about Kamala

Petersen's reliability. She'd hesitated on instinct. The margaritas seemed to have justified that doubt, but Hess said nothing. The booze was going to make Merci look bad.

"And Merci paid out of her own pocket for that psychiatrist to hypnotize her, didn't she?"

"I really don't know. But she told me she bought some Point Blank body armor with her own money."

"What's wrong with our PACAs? They're rated to threat-level Two-A."

"I guess she thinks they could get her killed."

Brighton raised his eyebrows. "She lost a potential witness."

"Yeah, she knows that. She knows it was a gamble."

Hess suddenly felt his tiredness slap up against him. It was like a big wave of cold water that sucked the warmth right out of you. It usually happened when he was sitting down. Like Friday, when Merci had to help him out of the chair. Maybe the secret of life was to keep moving. Hop 'til you drop.

"How did she miss those Jim marks on the car windows?"

"Well, they were below the door frame."

"That's absolutely not what I was asking."

"In that case, it was Kemp who missed them."

"I'd taken Kemp off the case by then, Tim. You were on it."

"The damage was done. She couldn't redo every bit of his work. Ike would have found them sooner or later. Or she'd have thought it through and had a look for herself. Really, Bright, that wasn't the kind of thing you'd think of unless you'd run across it before."

Brighton nodded, unconvinced. "It's basic car theft, is what it is."

"Well, she's Homicide."

"Maybe that's what worries me. Besides, it took you about thirty seconds."

"I'm old."

"Tim, I'd like you to document what you think of her performance on this case so far, just something brief, in writing."

"What about it?"

"How she's handled it—the privately funded hypnosis, not taking the DA's advice about the legal fallout. The car windows—whose decision it was to remove the glass and have a real thorough, old-fashioned look at it. Just a note for my files, nothing elaborate. A quick and dirty."

Interesting use of words, thought Hess. "I'm sure she'll put all that in her report," he said.

"Her reports are evasive, partial and uninformative."

"The kind I always wrote."

"Those were different days, Tim. We were small and tight and we hung together. Anyway, I want your angle on it."

"That wasn't exactly in my job description, Bright."

"It is now."

Hess said nothing.

"Is this LaLonde creep a suspect or not?"

"Riverside is watching him for us. So far, nothing unusual. My guts tell me no."

233

"How did Merci handle him?"

"Well. He built this override device for our man. It works on most car alarms, or so LaLonde says. He can ID our guy if we can deliver him."

"Nice work."

"Rayborn called the shots. I just held up a wall."

"She really carry a switchblade in her purse?"

Hess looked at the sheriff, then slowly shook his head. "I don't know," he said quietly.

"I'd be curious. Look, Tim, I've got some problems here. Merci's lawsuit accuses Phil of potty-mouth and grab-ass, but it accuses me—between the lines—of looking the other way. In fact, if she wants some kind of monetary damages, she'll eventually have to name the department, and probably me."

"Then she must not want money, Chuck."

"You know me, Tim. I don't *look* the other way. I've worked hard to make this a good place for men, women, the best sheriff department in the state. Now Merci files this suit out of the blue and three more women have come forward, talking to the press, getting their own suits ready, I assume. One says Kemp raped her. Merci opened the floodgates."

"Damn it, Bright. Maybe you should be glad she spoke up. If you've got house to clean, you've got house to clean."

"And I'll clean it. But I feel like I got a gun to my head. And she never *once* came to me about any of this."

A long silence then.

"What does she want?" Brighton finally asked.

"How would I know? She hasn't said one word about Phil Kemp to me."

"Find out."

"That in my job description now, too?"

"Absolutely. Find out what she *wants*, Tim. I'll accommodate her if I can get this snowball stopped."

Hess nodded. He felt exhausted.

"Ever heard of a friend of hers named Francisco?"

"She mentioned him."

A long pause then, during which Hess deduced he was supposed to make something of this friend. He sensed the amount of brainpower necessary for such a formulation would be a lot more than he wanted to spend.

"McNally told me she'd mentioned a guy, is all. Never introduced them. I'm curious if she might be sleeping with this man."

"I'm not."

"Find out about it and let me know. You can add that and the switchblade to your job description too, if you want to. Help me, Tim. I'm helping you."

Hess looked at him.

Brighton sat back. Hess felt the resentment stirring inside—resentment that his own stupid cigarette addictions had led him to this position, and resentment that Chuck Brighton had allowed peevishness to bloom in his old age. I got cancer and Bright got petty.

"How are you feeling, Tim?"

"Strong as an ox. A little tired now and then."

"I admire you."

"Thanks."

"And that has nothing to do with feeling sorry for you."

"I hope not," said Hess, but in fact he knew it did, and it broke his heart in a minor way to hear it from an old friend who was ordering him to piss on a fellow deputy half his age.

Hess stood and shook Brighton's hand.

24

Merci studied the two missing persons files that Casik had bird-dogged for her, then hovered around the unbelievably slow clerk who processed the purses into evidence. She estimated the guy had an IQ of about 50.

Six, she thought. Six. The idea made her furious.

By the time she got to the gym she was even more furious. And livid at Kamala for drinking on the night in question—then not admitting it until later.

But Merci knew she was primarily angry at herself for not hurrying up the hypnosis and the release of the sketch. If it had been all over the newspapers and TV two days ago, like it should have been, Ronnie Stevens might be working at Goldsmith's today. It was a grinding guilt she felt, tangible, right there in her throat. And now, by the looks of it, three more women had been taken by the Purse Snatcher. *Six.* Time to work off the rage.

The weight room was empty on Sunday. She looked at herself in the mirror when she walked in— face in a scowl, sweats disheveled, arms up, big hands twisting her hair into a wad and applying an elastic band and thought: *Loser. You are a large dark-haired loser who belongs in Traffic.*

She humped the stationary cycle for thirty minutes

with the resistance up almost all the way. She was dripping sweat and standing on the pedals to make them move after eight minutes and the final twenty-two were actual torture. Blister time. *Good,* she thought. Let the pain bring the gain. She got off the bike and wobbled to the ab cruncher on legs that felt like petrified wood. Good again: hurt to learn, learn to hurt.

She ran the Nautilus circuit once light and once heavy, resting five seconds between each of the three sets and thirty seconds between each station. Her heart was beating fast and light as a bird's, fast as that wren's that was blown from its nest in a Santa Ana wind one year. She'd found it in the grass and cradled it home in her hands while its heart beat like some overcharged machine against the inside of her middle finger. The bird had died overnight and Merci prepared a tissue box to bury it, but her mother flushed it down the toilet. She'd never had luck with animals: her dog chewed the hair off its own body; her cats ran away; her parakeets died quick; her hamster bit her. Merci catalogued these failures as she struggled on the chin-up bar—twelve was more than she could do so she set her sights on fourteen and slid to a gasping heap on the ground after thirteen.

Up, loser. You have work to do.

Time for the free weights. She had just settled under the bench press bar when she heard some commotion near the door. She turned her head to the mirrored wall and watched in the distorting glass as Mike McNally and three of his deputy friends swaggered in, all muscles and mustaches and towels over

238

their necks, smiles merry to the point of insanity. The atmosphere of the room changed instantly. Suddenly she was aware of herself, her body, her clothes, her sweat, what she might look like, what they might do. It was like having 30 percent of your energy sucked down some useless hole. Fucking great.

She did her best to will them out of her universe, turning to look up at the rusted bar above her nose, spreading her hands wide for a pec burn on her beginning weight of eighty pounds, digging the leather palms of her gloves against the worn checkering of the grip.

"Hi, Merci!"

"Hi, guys!"

"Need a spot?"

"Sure don't!"

Then up with it. Ignore them. She liked the feel of the weights balancing above her. She moved her left hand over just a hair to get it right. Then the slow, deliberate motion—all the way down to her chest, then all the way back up again—ten times in all, not super heavy, really, but you could feel eighty pounds when your body weight was one forty. Three sets. Every rep was hotter and slower. Grow to burn, burn to grow.

At one hundred pounds she had to go a lot slower, but she got the ten. She heard the sweat tap-tapping to the plastic bench as she sat there breathing hard and deciding whether to max at one thirty-five or one forty.

She picked the lighter weight to look stronger in front of the men, a decision that angered her. She was ignoring them but aware of them in the mirrors, where she saw they were ignoring her but aware of her, too. They laughed suddenly then and two of them glanced over at her. Mike was looking down as if regretting something he'd just said. Merci wished she lived on a different planet. She thought again of Phil Kemp's ugly words and his touches and felt like all her strength was about to rush away.

Stay focused. Will away these things.

She heaved up on the bar and ground out five reps before she realized she wouldn't make ten. Six was a labor. Seven wasn't even up yet when she knew she'd had enough. The sweat popped off her lips as she exhaled. Kind of stuck, actually, not enough gumption to get it back up to safety on the stand, too much pride to set it down on her heaving chest and rest. Mike McNally now appeared in the north quadrant of her defocusing vision, looking down at her, a blond-haired Vikingesque once-upon-a-time boyfriend gritting "One more . . . one *more* . . . one *more, Merci*" at her until she felt the bar rise magically with his help. Her breathing was fast and short. She felt lungshot. Then she felt McNally ceding the weight back to her and down she let it come, all the way to her sternum, pause, then halfway up, then a little more than halfway, arms and bar wobbling like crazy now and Mike's lift helping her get it up then suddenly one side shot down and the other shot up and iron crashed with a clang and the bar smacked into her rib cage as the weights slid off and chimed to the floor beneath her head.

She was aware of three more bodies around her,

aware of Mike's cursing them away, telling them she was fine, aware of gripping his hand with hers and rising to a sitting position on the bench. Little lights circled her vision like the stars around a cartoon character hit with a hammer.

"You know the circuit court's going to hear the scent-box case," he was saying.

"That's great, Mike." Merci wasn't positive what century she was in.

"I know it's going to be accepted. I know that a hundred years from now they'll be using those boxes in court all the time. A good scent box and a good dog. That's my answer to high-tech crime solving. Plus we're going to patent the thing and make a million. I don't know what I'll name it. Mike's Truth Box or something."

"Hope you're right. Wow."

"Light in the head?"

"Um-hm."

"Lay back."

"No way."

"Well, pass out then."

"I'll lay back."

"Better?"

"Um."

She lay back down on the bench and felt her chest rising fast, her back pressing into the pads, the air rushing in and out. Mike was gone. Just her and the white ceiling and the mirrors in the periphery of her vision and the ringing in her ears. Lots of red.

When her heart rate settled Merci dozed a few minutes. She awoke to the sounds of weights, male voices, the harsh light of the gym in her eyes. She sat up, looked around and yawned. Her muscles felt enlarged and stupid. The pile of spilled weights was still next to her bench.

She worked herself up and collected the weights, walking them one at a time back to the rack and sliding them onto the pegs. Then she lumbered on heavy legs over to the stationary bike and climbed on, setting the resistance lower than the first time, but still pretty darned high.

For just a moment she thought about who she was, and about how strong she was. She remembered the most important thing she had learned in her life thus far: you are powerful and you can make things bend to your will *as long as you try hard enough.*

Your will is the power to move the world.

So she set the resistance even higher than the first time. Effort was how things got moved. Effort was pain. Pain was strength.

She looked at herself in the mirror as she stood on the pedals to get them going. Pale as a sidewalk, she thought, and about as good looking.

Merci thought of Hess to steady herself—how he might do this, his economy and focus. She liked the way he didn't waste anything. She couldn't forget the look on his face that morning when he'd seen the hood of Ronnie Stevens's car. It was the saddest, wisest face she'd ever seen. He looked like Lincoln. But he had been diminished by what he had seen. The Purse Snatcher had taken something from him, she thought, and that made her feel angry on Hess's behalf. *For him.* For someone not herself.

It was nice to admire someone you didn't want to be.

Thirty minutes on this bike should do it, she thought: burn the foolishness out of my brain and burn the strength into my muscles.

She picked up an ankle holster for her .40 cal derringer, got some takeout food and brought it home. Home was a rambling house that used to belong to the owner of the large orange grove that surrounded it. But most of the grove was dozed years ago for housing tracts, all but a couple of acres around the house, which was now owned by a friend of her father and rented cheap. It was old and the faucets groaned and the fuses blew in heat waves and the garage was full of black widows. It sat back at the end of a long dirt drive that filled with potholes in winter and bred dust in summer.

The land was flat and you wouldn't even know the housing tracts surrounded the grove because the trees were healthy and high. It was like living inside a wall of green. Merci liked the cheap rent and the smell of the orange trees and blossoms and the fact that she had no neighbors to consider. She thought little of strolling around in nothing but her underwear, behind open windows and screen doors, stereo and Sheriff's band short wave turned up loud while the orange grove cats lounged in the sunshine on her porch, licking themselves incessantly, alert to the sound of the food bag. Once in a while she'd walk out through the rows and look at things. Not much to see, really, because the big citrus company that worked these acres did a meticulous job. The workers were quiet Mexicans who hid their cheerfulness when she was around.

She stared back at one of the cats as she unlocked the door, then picked up the fast food and holster and went inside. She loved many things about cats without loving any one cat in the least. The place got hot during the day so she opened all the windows and doors, then went to her bedroom and stripped down to undies and her sport shirt with the sleeves rolled up, working off her bra and tossing it on the floor. She set her holster and automatic beside the bed, which is where it stayed when it wasn't on her. She strapped on the new ankle rig and slid in the derringer—lots of play, but the strap was good and taut. Skivvies or not, it was good to have a gun on, or at least one in each room, positioned where she could get it quick if she needed to. One of her father's habits. She had no fear at home. This was more or less a game she played to keep her life interesting.

Again she pictured her partner's face that morning. In the same way that something was taken out of Hess, something was taken out of her, too, and this reminded her that nothing they did would make a difference in the long run. The short run was their stage, collar the creeps and maybe save a life or even two.

But a purse full of human guts sitting on a Chevy Malibu in the pretty Southern California sunshine put you in your place. It said: you might find the perpetrator of this, but there will be other perpetrators of even worse things to follow. More and more of them, following your own children down the years if you ever have any. Job security, she thought. It really was a shame. It wasn't a surprise, though. Her father had taught her early on that being a cop was just plugging the dike for a while. It didn't make the calling any less genuine, but it suggested something about what you should risk your life for and what you shouldn't.

Of course, her father was an ineffectual man who never risked one whisker for anything. A man who couldn't stand up to a crazy wife was doomed.

She listened to her messages. One from Joan Cash, just a hi, how are you. One from bumbling, lovable old Dad—Merci's mother wasn't feeling well and it made her father frantic with worry. And one from Mike, saying he hoped she was okay, quite a workout she had in the gym today, coffee sometime? He must have called right after she left the weight room. That was all. They all seemed to imply so much obligation and worry. Sometimes Merci really didn't want to know how other people were feeling. Not that she didn't understand or respect those feelings. It was just that she *didn't give a shit about them right that minute*.

She called Hess.

No answer, so she left a message—nothing urgent, just wanted to talk, call if you want. She wondered if he was out getting pounded at the Wedge or maybe having another treatment. What a strange feeling to be him, she thought, to have almost seven decades of your life gone and maybe one left if you were completely lucky, but to be unsure if you'd see another year.

She wondered how come he had gotten married and divorced so many times. Why he never had children. Why he came back to work on something like the Purse Snatcher. Hess was interesting to think about because he was so different from herself. It was funny that he'd told her she'd have to feel what others felt and think what others thought in order to get ahead in the department, in life itself. Maybe she could try to feel like him.

It probably wouldn't be that hard because Hess was so large and simple. Of course, Mike McNally was large and simple too, until you got to know him. Then he seemed to grow small and hectic as a five-year-old at his own birthday party: me, me, me. She actually missed Mike right now, missed some of the casual hours. A guy who talked all the time made the hours seem longer. That was good. She missed his profile and the blue light on his cheeks when he was watching TV. And all the sweaty athletics in bed, well, she missed them too, although they made her feel things she wasn't in favor of feeling.

But she wasn't about to talk to him every single night, be his current steady woman, baby-sit his resentful kid, get engaged or even *talk* about marriage. So, she broke it all off rather than just part of it—which part?—and that was enough to loose the dogs of hell on her. Mike's dogs. Mike's Truth Box. The hardest part of the whole miserable thing was the way Mike attacked her for being closed and cold and controlling, and apparently blabbing such things to everyone else, thus the remark in the cafeteria regarding her sexual preference. Just thinking about it made her face flush with anger.

The phone rang and it was Hess.

"I was thinking about you earlier," she said. "And I

wanted to know if . . . well, I wanted to know . . . how you're doing with this morning."

"I'm hoping for prints off the interior."

"Well, I am too. What I meant, though, was if you were doing okay now, after seeing that."

"It got me. I remembered cleaning deer up in Idaho. The way the guts kind of stick together and fall out in one big mass. Hardly any blood. And I thought that was one awful thing to do to that girl."

"Six, Hess. We're looking at six now."

"I know. I just . . . it really makes you wonder where these guys come from. It's just pure meanness."

"Where *do* they come from, Hess?"

"I think they're born evil. That's not a popular notion these days but I believe it."

"They say these monsters are created, not born."

"I'm just disagreeing is all. I don't understand a guy who kidnaps and kills a woman, keeps her carcass but takes the time to do what he did with that purse. Again and again. What do you call that, besides just plain evil?"

She thought. "It doesn't matter, really. For us."

"No, it doesn't."

"It's interesting to think about, though."

"Yeah. It raises some interesting questions for Corrections and Sacramento and police science classes."

"And for politicians," she added.

"Writers."

"Priests and evangelists."

"I'll say, Merci."

"I've always known that. Some guys are just born bad."

"Well. I usually don't trust things that seem simple, but in this case I just can't help seeing it that way. It's what I've gathered over the years, is all. You see what you see."

"Hey, Hess, what if I came over?"

There was just enough of a silence to make Merci wonder if she'd done something wrong.

"That would be great," he said. "Not much in the cupboards, though."

"I'll bring something to eat."

"There's a parking space behind the garage."

25

A quick shower and clean clothes, plus Merci wanted Hess to know that she liked him now, so she tossed the old fast food and stopped for some new. She over-bought, then wondered if a guy on chemo and radiation ate much of anything. Fries and shakes, hamburgers, tacos, onion rings, the works.

She was surprised to find his apartment neat and clean, the opposite of Mike's place in Anaheim. She suspected it was a furnished rental unit until Hess told her so and removed all doubt. They sat in the living room at either end of a blue plastic couch, with the white bags strewn on the coffee table in front of them. Hess left the TV on. The windows were open and the shades up and Merci could see a pale prairie of sand topped by a black ocean topped by a blacker sky alive with stars. Voices wavered up from the sidewalk, laughter, the hiss of roller skates. Then the distant thump of waves followed by a sound like a soft drink poured over ice.

She leaned forward and ate.

"So, where were we?" she asked.

"Evil, I think."

"I never think about evil. I just think you should be punished for what you do. God, these hamburgers are good."

She looked across and saw that Hess was eating, too.

"They really are."

"Do you eat healthy?"

"I have since the operation. Before, anything went."

"How come you aren't fat? Alcohol is really high in calories, you know."

"Metabolism."

"Yeah, and thirty years of cigarettes."

"Fifty-five."

"You really are old."

He chuckled but that was all.

"I've got a terrible diet," she confessed. "I actually like cooking, but not for just me. So it's stuff like this half the time, decent stuff the other half."

"You work it off, though."

"I'm in the gym all the time. God, don't we sound like a couple of real Californians now, talking about what we eat and what we do with our muscles? I spend my vacation every year in Maine. Kittery, Maine. Dad took me out there when I was little so I still go. Anyway, they don't live like we do back there. You start talking *lifestyle* and they roll their eyes."

"I always hated that word."

"Me too. And anything with *cyber* in it. I promised myself I'd never use it, now I just did."

"Same with *virtual*."

"Yeah. Virtual sucks. It's all just bullshit to get you thinking you're missing something new. So you'll go buy things. Makes me want to puke. Vanilla or chocolate on the shake?"

"Chocolate."

"Good. I got two of them."

"And no vanilla."

"Not a one." Merci heard herself giggle, then giggled at the sound of it. "I thought that was funny when Izma asked me if I wanted ice water, then, when I bit, he said he didn't have any ice or any water. That's one large creepy dude, Hess."

"He was holding a frozen cat when I busted him. When he opened the door, I mean."

"What did he do with it?"

"He dropped it. It sounded like a rock on the floor."

"God, what a hoot."

"I was scared. I pistol-whipped him real hard to take him down. He hit the floor like a bag of nails, but after that, he was always real nice to me."

"I noticed you got his attention. Do you like beating people up? Someone who really deserves it?"

Hess was nodding. "When I was young I enjoyed it. Trouble is, it's hardly ever a fair fight, with batons and sidearms. You know?"

"If you're a woman it's fair. I mean, if you're up against a guy you need all the help you can get."

"I doubt you beat many up for the fun of it."

She looked at him. "True. You'd think I'd do it a lot, given my bad temper and what a misanthrope I am."

She thought of Lee LaLonde. "I actually didn't get that much enjoyment dunking the thief out in Elsinore. I mean, besides the thrill you get dominating someone physically. Just to know you can do it. But I got lots of enjoyment out of the results, though."

"You got them."

"Do you think I was wrong?"

"No. You might have saved lives."

"End justifies the means?"

"That's another one of those simple statements that sort of bug me. But with LaLonde you did what was right."

"How come you got married so many times? Wasn't it like, three or four?"

He was about to take a bite of his hamburger. He closed his mouth and stared at her a long beat.

"Three."

"Well, why three? Wasn't once horrible enough?"

"Stupidity."

"Whose?"

"Mostly mine."

"You mean you gave up a good one or two?"

"All three, really."

"How come you never had children?"

"Kept waiting. Waited too long. Some bad luck, too. Back when I was in my forties I wanted some. Never worked out."

Merci thought about this.

"I don't believe in luck. I think you're directly responsible for what happens to you."

"I used to think that."

"How else could it be?"

"I don't think you can lay what happened on Ronnie Stevens, for instance. I think she crossed paths with someone much stronger and more cunning and vicious than she ever was. Within the limits of what we'd call reasonable, it wasn't her fault."

"That's all this victimization bullshit you see on TV."

252

"The TV's all the extremes."

"Then why does everybody watch?"

"It comforts them to think everything's out of control."

"Bunch of goddamned whiners, if you ask me."

Hess studied her. He had a way of looking disapproving and tolerant at the same time. Maybe she was making it up.

"Power," she said. "Everything comes from the power you have inside yourself. Your will."

That look again.

"You've got this look, like you think two things at once."

"I guess I do."

"Well, what are they?"

More of the same look. "Can I just say that I admire you a lot? Your youth and everything it implies. I like the way you wear it, what you're doing with it."

"Even when I screw up?"

"Yeah."

She considered. "You're still thinking two things about me at the same time—things that don't go together except that you're making them."

"I'm wondering how you can be so bright and so dull at the same time. How you'll either do really well for yourself or you'll fail big. Just notions."

"Hey, I'm your commanding officer."

"You asked."

"I'm happy with this. This burger is great and it's nice to just sit here and talk about being a cop and a human being. Mike talked a lot but I don't think he

253

listened to my side very much. Then it was either TV or bed."

Hess said nothing.

"Can you still, Hess?"

"Still what?"

"You know. *It*. Make love."

His face went red and he looked at her again with that double-thoughts kind of expression.

"I mean, when you're close to seventy, can you?"

"Of course you can."

A slight edge to his voice as he looked at the TV and the light from the screen played off his face. She couldn't tell if it was still red or not.

"I wonder if my mom and dad still do it. They're your age."

"You could ask *them*."

"They're kind of sensitive."

She was truly surprised to see him laugh. She realized she'd never seen him do that before and it changed everything about his face: lines backing into shape over his eyes and around his mouth, actual dimples on his cheeks. A happy light.

Kind of amazing, really, how laughter could change a man. She realized she was looking at him with a kind of dumb astonishment.

He really let go, then. Eyes wet, big chest and shoulders moving and the goofiest look on a face that had held no goofiness she'd ever imagined until now.

"Good God, young lady. You're funny."

She wasn't sure how to feel about this. "Well . . . really?"

254

"Really."

She felt confusion about what she'd said, and some embarrassment along with it, and some shame, too. She wasn't a zoo chimp who'd done something cute. She thought of how heavy and tired he'd felt when she helped him out of the chair on Friday evening and thought he owed her more for that than just this sudden amusement.

"Merci, I'm sorry. It's just that I haven't laughed in so goddamned long. I was *not* trying to make you feel bad."

"Not at all," she said.

"Really."

"I know. Did you know we both use blue note-books?" Anything to dampen the comedy.

"Yeah, I did notice that. Hey, would you like to take a walk?"

"Why?"

"Well, it's a warm summer night and the ocean's right there and you can digest your meal and feed your soul."

"Yeah, okay."

Something had gone out of her—the lightness, she thought, the freedom to say what you want to say. She felt tired and miles from home. She tried to think of something to cheer herself up.

"Hess, don't you wish it was raining and we had one of those upside-down umbrellas to collect the rainwater?"

"God, those were great."

"I would have bought one, but I was too busy being a hardass."

"You ate him alive, Merci."

"Sure did, didn't I?"

They took the boardwalk north toward the pier, staying to the pedestrian side while skaters and bikers whizzed by them. Merci looked out to the water and watched the waves crashing in. She thought of Hess actually out riding those monsters at the Wedge. She'd gone down there with Mike once to see the bodysurfers and couldn't believe that they'd take such chances. For what? She'd dreamed about big waves in a black ocean since she was small. She'd never questioned where the dream came from because its message was so clear: stay out of the water and save yourself. Easy enough. You didn't have to be Old Testament to interpret that one.

The pier was hopping on this summer Sunday—lovers and skateboarders, white punks and gangster-style Mexicans, college kids and bikers, bums and cops and glum Asian fishermen with their lines in the water and an occasional mackerel flap-flapping on the wet cement.

Merci walked just a half step behind Hess and watched him more than occasionally. She was waiting for something from him but she didn't know what. She thought it might come from his face rather than his mouth, plus, she just liked the way his head looked, battered but still noble, like a horse that had done great things. She wondered if that was where they got the term *war-horse*. She had this oddball desire to see what his hair felt like—that straight-up, almost jarhead, white wave in the front cut that made him look like a general from some war that was filmed in black and white.

He may think I've got the manners of a zoo monkey, she thought: but I know enough to keep my hands to myself. But if I could *distract* him for a second . . .

They had a drink at the Beach Ball and another at Scotty's and another at the Rex. These were her idea. It seemed to Merci that you got closer to people when you were high on alcohol, so long as they were high, too. Like taking a little trip together. She had never considered herself a drinker, but here she was two nights of the weekend, knocking back some pretty stiff stuff. You couldn't even tell with Hess. He was the same whether he had none or three. It surprised her he could drink his way through chemotherapy and radiation. Maybe it helped. For herself, the drinks made her feel hazy and warm and a little passive, which was good because she usually felt sharp and cool and prepared to kick serious butt. It was nice to get a glow you knew would be gone in a few hours, in the company of somebody you like. Temporary insanity.

But outside the Rex there was a scuffle on the sidewalk and Hess pulled Merci back from it just as two NBPD bike blues jumped in and broke it up.

Her anger just cut right up through the alcohol, sharper than it was when she was sober, and she felt her spirits rise then rankle in unfamiliar ways. Maybe that's why they *called* it spirits. Scotch was kind of spooky stuff.

She looked back and saw the bike cops handcuffing

a skinny wino to a parking meter. His opponent, a muscle type with a goatee, had a stream of blood running down his forehead.

"I feel like I have to do something in a situation like that."

"Let it go. You're a homicide investigator, not a beat cop."

"I hate to see that kind of crap going down. Two meatballs, two perfectly good heads. Makes me want to bang them together."

"It's over. Relax."

"Yeah, yeah, yeah. Let's go down to the water."

She trudged across the sand. The Scotch and the receding adrenaline left her legs heavy and her mind light. When they got to the berm near the waterline they stopped. Merci watched the faintly luminescent suds swoosh up toward them then fade back down. Small birds darted across the shiny slope before the brine soaked in.

"You're a good partner, Hess."

"You are, too."

"We're a decent team, aren't we?"

"We're doing okay, so far."

"I know Brighton wants me to fail. I know the lawsuit makes him look bad. I know you're supposed to watch me for him. Probably keep a record of it."

"I'm supposed to watch out for you. Like you are for me."

"That's the first bullshit I've heard from you, Tim. I know the score and it's more than you say it is. You can tell him what you want. I'm going to keep doing my job the way I think it needs to be done. Doesn't mean I won't mess up sometimes. What I'm not going to do is back off because of you, or Brighton, or anybody else. I'm going to find the Purse Snatcher and blow the brains out of his sick head and sleep good that night. All the rest of you can sweep up behind me, pick up the pieces, do what you have to do.

"This is the deal with me and Phil Kemp. Phil Kemp has been talking dirt to me since I got off jail duty my first two years. I mean real lowdown body parts and what he'd like to do. He's rubbed his crotch on my ass and brushed my tits and said stuff you wouldn't believe. I guess I didn't react right when I was young. I didn't know what to do. I thought that's how it went, thought that meant being one of the boys. Then I started warning him off. He thought it was cute. Couple of weeks ago he was waiting in the parking structure, late, talking shit about Mike and what I really needed. He was leaning on my car. He took ahold of my arm, pretty hard, pretty rough. I got the nine between his eyes and I told him he could let go or get shot. He let go. Tried to laugh it off. So I hired a good lawyer. *Because I'm sick of him getting away with it.* I never wanted to play that game. It's boring and it's trite and it's demeaning. Kemp's a waste of a human being but he's tight with Brighton. That's why Brighton's so eager for me to screw up. That would make it look like I'm suing because I can't cut it."

They walked south with the black water at their feet.

"What do you want, Merci? Out of this lawsuit? You want Kemp fired? Jail? A settlement? What?"

259

"I want Kemp to goddamned apologize to me and stop. It's that simple."

"That's all?"

She thought about this. She wondered how clean she could come with Hess. Maybe it was the scotch or maybe it was just her instincts, but she thought she could trust him with this.

"Truth, Hess? What I want most is to go back in time and *not file the goddamned thing.* I'm already sorry I did it."

She hoped he wouldn't say just drop it, and he didn't.

"But I'm not going to drop it, Hess. I'll chase Kemp all the way to court if I have to. He's gonna stop and he's gonna apologize or I'll ruin him. Guaranteed. And if fifteen other broads want to join in and wreck him with me, then they've got the right. They can do what they want. But I wish they'd quit treating me like some kind of leader. I got ten e-mails over the last three days, thanking me for stepping forward. For being courageous enough to stand up to the system. What they don't get is I *love* the system. I'm part of it. I'm going to run the whole thing someday. Put money on that. And it really infuriates me to have to file a suit to get this guy to stop asking me to suck his miserable dick. But what I want to say to everybody else is, stay off my side."

Merci heard a nightbird cry behind her, up close, like it was zooming past her ear. Then she could see it, just a blip of a shadow on the night, vanishing.

"You're doing the right thing," said Hess.

"That's right. I'm doing it. Tell Brighton if you want

260

to, since he doesn't have the nuts to ask me himself."

"This thing caught him by surprise."

"That's right. I never ratted Kemp out. Not until I talked to him. Then warned him. Then stuck a gun in his face. He's getting what he deserves, Hess. I'm sorry if it upsets Brighton's happiness, but it's sure as hell upset mine."

They ended up back at Hess's apartment around eleven. Merci fell asleep on the couch and when she woke up at midnight Hess had made coffee.

He was lying back in a cheap recliner by the window with a glass of something on the sill, moonlight on his face, snoring. Merci stood over him and felt a strong urge to touch his hair while he wouldn't know it.

She reached out, but stopped.

26

The Department of Mortuary Science of the health sciences division of Cypress College waits behind a heavy blue door next to a snack area with a view of the campus.

It was Monday morning. Hess went through and waited in the small lobby. The lobby was poorly lit and gave off a feeling of a decade long past—the 1950s, perhaps. On the walls were pictures of the school in the old days, when it was still located near downtown Los Angeles. Important mortuary science directors of the past, and some graduating classes, were also featured. A glass bookshelf held antiquated embalming texts, among them the seven-volume *Humane Embalming.*

The director came from the inner building and offered his hand. "Allen Bobb," he said. "Detective Hess?"

Bobb was middle aged with a wide, pleasant face. His hair was thinning and his smile both open and wily at the same time. In Bobb's crampéd office Hess was offered a small chair on rollers that both men chuckled at.

Hess thought of all the chemicals they filled you with when you died and all the chemicals raging through his own blood right then and wished he was twenty-two again, bombing through giant waves at the Wedge, functionally immortal.

"I'll cut to the chase," said Hess.

"Shoot."

He explained the circumstances: the missing women, the purses, the remains, the blood and trace formalin discovered in the soil by the lab.

Bobb nodded along like he'd heard it before. "He's not embalming them, then. Not in the standard American way. Not if he's removing organs and intestines. We leave those in. Are you familiar with the embalming process, Detective? Its goals and purpose, its limitations?"

"No."

"Historically, the purpose was to discourage the spread of disease. Biologically speaking, there's nothing more dangerous than a dead human body. Secondly, there were the cosmetic considerations—making the body presentable and natural for viewing before burial. The modern method was born in the Civil War, when thousands of bodies were shipped home for burial."

"How long are they, uh, good for?"

"The bodies? Three to five days is our goal. Longer, if there are family circumstances that will delay interment."

"Can you go weeks? Months?"

Bobb raised his eyebrows and shrugged. "Weeks, maybe. Detective, if you underembalm, the corpse decomposes too quickly. If you overembalm, it becomes discolored and hard almost immediately."

Hess scribbled down the questions in his own

shorthand. His fingers seemed clunky again this morning, with patches of cold numbness on the tips. He lifted his pen hand and rubbed it with his thumb. The radio played an old Elvis song now, one that Hess remembered listening to at the beach many years ago.

He pulled a copy of Merci's sketch from his pocket and handed it to the director. Bobb studied it with apparent patience, then gave it back. "No. I don't think so, Detective. I've got a good memory for faces. I mean, this one's pretty distinctive, with the long hair and mustache."

"Former student, maybe someone who dropped out?"

Bobb pursed his lips and shook his head. "Sorry. Wish I could just say I know him."

"Your graduates? You keep their records here?"

Bobb nodded. "And yes, there's a student photograph with each file. I won't offer to let you see them. But I won't disallow a request."

"I understand. If I could see the last ten years of graduates, that would be good."

Bobb picked up his phone and spoke to someone about graduate records for the last ten years.

"It will take about fifteen minutes to have them ready, Detective. Would you like to see the procedure? We've got three student embalmings going on right now."

"That might be helpful."

On the door of the embalming room was a framed copy of the California Health & Safety Code forbidding anyone but family, police, doctors, nurses, mortuary personnel and students from being in the room during an embalming.

Hess followed the Director in. The lights were bright against the tile and the sweet smell of aldehyde compounds was strong.

The tables were laid out in the center of the room, with the corpses' heads toward the far wall. Hess heard the metallic ping of instruments hitting pans, low voices and a heavy, rhythmic *chunka-thunk, chunka-thunk*. Bobb guided Hess past the first three tables.

"Here's one just starting, Detective. The features have been set and the corpse has been disinfected and bathed. The student, Bonnie, has chosen a fluid she believes is right for the decedent—based on age, condition, cause of death, medications, et cetera. In this case she's chosen a formalin solution called PSX. It's made by Champion. It's one of my favorites. Did you know that good cosmetic results come from *inside* the body and not *outside*?"

"I did not."

"Sometimes you don't even need makeup."

Hess joined Bobb beside the last table, where an old man lay stretched on the aluminum. He looked to be about Hess's age, and he was surprised how bad this made him feel. He glanced at the Case Report Record: Age—69, Cause of Death—cirrhosis of the liver. The sonofabitch is two whole years older than me, he thought, and that's a lifetime of a difference.

Hess had always assumed, for no particular reasons, that he would live to be seventy-five. It was a good number, a number with bulk and character, a number that always seemed far off in the future. This assumption had sat well with him until the diagnosis. At that moment he'd resolved to get those seventy-five years no matter what it took. The last eight were his and he was going to live them to the fullest. Sometimes he told himself it was a matter of principle. Other times, he admitted he was just plain scared to death and didn't want to leave yet.

The smell of the aldehydes started to sicken him. He hadn't gotten queasy at an autopsy for forty years. He looked at the student across the corpse from him and saw that she was early twenties, tall, wholesome and probably beautiful. A surgical mask covered her nose and mouth. She looked at him and her eyes smiled, but there was concern in her expression, too.

"Stand back just a little for this, Detective. Okay, Bonnie, locate the main right carotid and make your incision above the clavicle. Oh, this is Detective Hess. He's interested in what we do."

"Hi," said Bonnie.

"Morning," said Hess.

"Not going to tip over, are you?"

"I'll stay up."

Her eyes conveyed the powerful smile of youth and she picked up a surgical scalpel to make her cut. Hess watched her.

"Good, Bonnie. Not too deep. Now use the aneurysm hook to lift out the artery. Good. Do your ligatures now, and not so hard this time. You don't want to—"

"—I *know.*"

"Bonnie overdid her ligatures last time, and the artery burst."

"I *am* capable of learning, Al."

"Make me look good."

Her fingers were nimble. "There."

"Very good. Go ahead with the insertion tube now."

"Roger."

Hess watched her slide the two smaller ends of a metal joint into the cut of the artery and connect the tube to a black hose coming from a machine. It was like setting up a drip irrigator for your tomatoes. Bonnie flipped a switch on the machine. A moment later it was *chunka-thunking*.

Hess noted that the machine was a Porti-Boy. It looked kind of like a giant blender. The clear canister on the top held the embalming fluid that Bonnie had chosen. There were controls and indicators for flow and pressure. Bonnie looked at the dials, then down at the body, setting one gloved hand on his thigh, the other on his shoulder.

"I'd like to start a little early on the massage, Al. I want this to be the best embalming in the history of Western civilization."

"Go ahead, then."

Hess watched as Bonnie squeezed something onto her left palm, added some water from the counter faucet, then rubbed her hands together and applied them to the dead man's right breast. Palms down and fingers together, she began kneading the tissue. She started in a tight circle and spread slowly outward, glancing up every few seconds to check the Porti-Boy.

"Detective, what Bonnie's doing now is helping the PSX work in. The pressure of the machine pushes the fluid through the entire arterial system—right down to the level of the capillaries. Then, of course, it backs into the veinous system and eventually moves into the large veins. What we're looking for are distribution and diffusion. Massage helps the fluid proceed evenly and easily. It overcomes clots and obstructions. It's an overlooked aspect of good embalming. We know we're ready for the next step when the veins in the forehead start to swell, the eyelids engorge, and a natural color begins returning to the face. It's almost like they're coming alive again."

"Boy, I wish," said Bonnie. "I'd make a fortune."

Bobb took Hess into a small back room that was lined on three sides with shelves. The shelves held scores of bottles, all labeled. There were cases stacked against the other wall.

"These are the solutions," he said. "Most are formaldehyde based, but there are others. Glutaraldehyde is becoming popular these days. They're mixed with humectants in most cases, then diluted. There's an embalming fluid for almost every circumstance. For instance, this one."

Bobb handed Hess a dark plastic bottle of Specialist Embalming Fluid. The label said it was "specially formulated for 'floaters,' burned, decomposed, frozen or refrigerated bodies." He set the bottle back on the shelf and read more labels: Champion, Embalmers' Supply, Dodge, Naturo.

Back at Bonnie's station, she was massaging the old man's face, both hands up on his cheeks. It looked like she was imploring him. Hess could see the temporal veins starting to fill.

"The color is beginning to come to the face," said Bobb. "That means he's filled with so much blood and solution that he's basically full. So you're ready to start draining, Bon. Find that jugular and open her right up."

Bonnie gave him a remonstrative glance over her mask. She looked at Hess and winked. He watched her take up the scalpel again, open the neck, deftly pull out the jugular with the hook. With one hand she pulled and "v"-ed the vein toward the table drain. With the other she cut it in half with a pair of scissors. She controlled the flow with finger pressure.

"You'll see the pressure inside release almost immediately," said Bobb. "Right now, the solution is pushing the blood out. The draining process should take around ten minutes in normal temperatures. A good embalmer will continue the massage, in order to move the fluid further in."

Bonnie was already at work again with her hands, rubbing them over the lifeless gray flesh in opposing circles. The man's head and feet rocked and his thin white hair lifted in the breeze from the air conditioner.

The color returned to his face. Hess didn't notice it by the degrees by which it surely had come, but rather he saw it all at once: the gray skin turned natural again, the stony complexion become flushed and natural, the lips swelling with color. It was like a switch had been thrown.

"Oh," said Bonnie. "There we are." She worked the hollows of his cheeks and his temples, his forehead and chin, under the eyes, his ears and nose and mouth. Then down the neck to the shoulders and arms and chest.

Hess stared. He was suddenly dizzy. It was easy to see Janet Kane or Lael Jillson in front of him now, easy to imagine that Bonnie was the Purse Snatcher and a beautiful young woman was coming to life beneath his patient and expert hands. Then Hess blinked, and the body before him was simply a dead old man's. But a second later it was Lael Jillson. He looked at Bonnie and she was a handsome man with long blond hair and a mustache and remorseful eyes. Then she was Bonnie again and Hess suddenly felt something very strong for her, a desire to defend and enhance and help her in a sometimes violent world. He wanted to see her triumph. It was a surprisingly powerful feeling. He knew it was absolutely inappropriate but there it was anyhow, filling his body like something pumped in. It made his heart beat fast and his muscles feel strong and urgent. It had as much to do with Bonnie and his impulse to love as it had to do with the Purse Snatcher and the old man supine in front of him and his own certain but unscheduled death. When he looked down at the man again it was Merci Rayborn and he was doing Bonnie's job, with caring, desiring hands. Her dark nipples rose after his fingers passed over them.

"I'm going outside," he said.

"I'll go with you," said Bobb.

"Don't bother."

"Let me show you where the door is . . ."

Outside Hess bent in the shade of a big pepper tree, his hands on his knees and his head up like an umpire but breathing hard and sweating coldly. His shirt felt wet under his sport coat and his shoulder strap slid on the damp fabric. He looked back at the campus buildings shimmering as if in a heat wave, outlined in a blue light that grew brighter until he blinked, then got brighter until he blinked again. He closed them and thought of where he had just come from and saw this time that the lifeless body back there was his and the hands bringing him back from the dead belonged to Merci.

He felt the air going in and out of his lung and a third, filling them up and purging fully, but it was like he wasn't getting the right thing, like the air was mixed wrong, or maybe there just wasn't enough of it getting in. He asked himself what he expected from fifty fucking years of smoking like there was no tomorrow. Help me get through this, he thought: just help me beat this thing and I'll be good forever. Forever. I honestly do swear I'll do whatever you want.

He opened his eyes and looked down at the grass but there were naked gray bodies upon it. He saw Lael and Janet and Ronnie and Merci and Bonnie and himself. And the old man and his father and Barbara and Lottie and Joanna. There was a kid in a cowboy shirt standing beside them with a blank look on his face: Tim Hess, age eight. Lightning cracked blue and rain splattered down on them all with drops bright and heavy as mercury. Young Tim had a green garden hose in his hand, gushing water. He rinsed everybody off then gave the hose to himself fifty-nine years later and the old once-dead Hess rose and drank from it and said he was going to give everyone else a drink, too.

Then Hess saw nothing but the green Bermuda grass beneath the tree and the pink pepper hulls lying by the trunk and his own bent shadow leaning away from the sun. His heart was way up in his throat somewhere and he could feel hot drops of something running down his cheeks and see them splat against the pepper shells where they fell. He heard himself panting. He felt an erection in his briefs, something that seemed no more related to this moment than the north rim of the Grand Canyon or UFOs. He smelled himself—a blend of man, chemicals, death and terror of death that he'd never smelled before.

"Detective? Mr. Hess? Al told me to come out and check on you. You okay? It's the chemicals. One time I was setting features on this lady and then I was just lying there looking up at the lights. You okay?"

"Sure I am."

"You're white and trembling."

"Breakfast. Skipped it, I mean."

"Ah, come on. Quit being such a tough guy. Here, sit down in the shade. Just breathe even and keep your eyes up on the horizon. Think about your wife or your grandkids or someone you love."

Hess took a knee. His eyes were burning still but he couldn't let himself wipe them. He was confused by his arousal and ashamed of it and happy to hide it from the girl. Bonnie squatted across from him.

"Don't," Hess heard himself say.

"Don't what?"

"Don't *ever*."

"Ever *what*?"

"Let anything bad happen to you."

272

27

Two hours later Hess was still in the Department of Mortuary Science, setting aside the last file. He was exhausted and his neck felt like cold metal and the words he had been reading sometimes blurred and jumped off the pages. He thought to pick a word off the desk and put it back on the paper before he understood how spent he was.

For two hours Hess had looked at every photograph and name of every Department of Mortuary Science student graduated from Cypress College in the last decade. Four hundred and fourteen.

Based on age and appearance Hess came up with eighteen maybes, but nothing hot. None of the maybes wore long hair and a mustache. Bobb explained that they had a professional dress code the students had to follow when they were here. And few homes would hire an embalmer with a less than conventional appearance. Hess gathered that the college had screened all students for felony records before admission, so he knew his chances of stubbing his toe on a creep who'd been looking to learn a trade weren't great. But, he thought, cracks were there to be slipped through.

Bobb was also kind enough to call a friend at the state Morticians' Licensing Board, who agreed to supply Hess with a complete listing of Southern California undertakers. It would be on Hess's fax machine by the end of the workday. If he wanted faces, he'd have to come up to Sacramento—the black-and-white two-by-twos didn't transmit well at all.

The DMV 1028 list was on his desk when Hess got in that afternoon. He checked the names against their possibles from the Sex Offenders Registry, the department graduates and the outstanding warrants listing kept by the Sheriff's Department.

Nothing added up. He wondered if he could get a list of embalming machine buyers, tick them off against the van owners, maybe get a hit.

What he had for sure was 312 panel vans registered in Orange County. This didn't include the commercial ones. He circled the males, which left 224. If he could get Brighton to cut loose twenty-two deputies to run down ten vans each and check the tires, they could have it nailed in two shifts if they went fast—three if it went slowly.

Brighton's secretary said he'd be in a meeting for the next hour.

Hess phoned Southern California Embalming Supply Company, the regional dealer for the Porti-Boy, Sawyer and several other embalming machines. In fact, they carried every major brand and some minor ones. He asked the president for a list of embalming machine buyers in the last year in Southern California. He explained that he wanted to run the names against the state board licensees.

The president was a pleasant sounding man who seemed to listen carefully to what Hess was saying. His name was Bart Young. He very politely refused Hess's request for a customer list reaching back one year. Young said it would be a violation of trust. In the end all Hess could do was press his home and office phone numbers upon the fellow, and ask to have Young's home number in return. If you framed the request right, giving a home phone became a small atonement for not giving something better. Hess believed in home phones because he did some of his best thinking at night, and he wasn't afraid to intrude so long as he had a reason. He made a note on his desk calendar to call Young every day until he gave up the names.

An hour later Brighton approved the manpower shift and got an assistant to make the assignments. The first shift of tire checkers would hit the streets in four hours.

It was almost five o'clock when Bobb's friend at the state Morticians' Licensing Board faxed over the current list of Southern California embalmers. Hess settled down with it, his eyes tired and his vision blurring, long enough to find no matches at all with panel van owners, registered sex offenders or hotsheet fugitives.

He got his second dose of chest radiation after work. The doctor took some blood before the treatment, said he wanted to check the white cell level—it could rise or fall during chemotherapy and radiation—and it was important to keep an eye on things. He seemed surprised that Hess was working but said it was probably good. His tone of voice suggested to Hess that it mattered not one bit whether he was working or not because the outcome of all this was determined and unchangeable. He could be training for a marathon for all the radiation specialist cared. Hess thought of the oncologist's statement that the average life span of a human being with a small cell cancer in the lung was nine weeks, but reminded himself that his was caught early, his was relatively small, his was surgically removed, his scans and X rays since the surgery had come up clean.

Lying on the table Hess imagined a target of black concentric circles on his chest, with his beating red heart as the bull's eye.

The evening news carried a brief story about a suspect in the so-called Purse Snatcher abductions. Wallace Houston, the sheriff's Press Information officer, showed the sketch and explained that this man was seen at an Orange County shopping mall "concurrent with the abduction of Janet Kane," and was wanted for questioning. Hess thought the sketch looked good on TV—it came across clearly, and was specific rather than general, as many artists' sketches seemed to be. Wallace held back the silver panel van with the mismatched tires, per Merci's request. In keeping with Kamala Petersen's observation, Wallace noted that this suspect might be wearing a vest and long coat, and was likely to be found at shopping malls.

It was only upon direct questioning from Lauren

Diamond that Wallace admitted they were now looking at five, possibly six victims.

Hess ate a TV dinner.

An hour later he was floating face up out in the black Pacific, watching clouds made red by sunset. It seemed imperative to get the death off him, the sight of Ronnie Stevens's purse overflowing onto the hood of her car, the formaldehyde and injection tubes and the pulsing machines and the temporal veins swelling with false life. When he came out he wrapped a big towel around himself and followed his own dark footprints across the sand to his apartment.

The phone was ringing. It was Kamala Petersen. She told Hess she'd called him because if she called Merci Rayborn, Merci would kill her.

"She about killed me when I told her I'd been drinking that night, and wasn't sure about the pictures she showed me."

"I'm glad she didn't. How can I help you?"

"Well . . . this is the deal. I hope you don't want to kill me, too. But I was watching CNB and they got that guy on a twenty-four-hour watch now, the sex offender? Like every time he sticks his head out the door or goes to the window, they go live and show him? Anyway, I think it could have been him at the mall that night. You know, with a blond wig and a fake mustache to make him look like a rock star from the seventies. Or that guy Paul Newman played in *Buffalo Bill and the Indians*."

Hess wondered how Kamala Petersen could so blithely make a face ten days after the fact, a face on TV no less, through a wig and a fake mustache.

277

"You think the guy on TV *could* be him."

"Right. I wouldn't swear it was him, like Merci wanted me to with those pictures. But I will swear it *could* be him. See, both times I saw him on TV I was like totally awake. So my unconscience wasn't working? But then after the second time I dreamed I was back in the mall and it looked like the guy on TV. The same eyes. You know, kind of sad and thinking something's funny. Both at once."

"So, are you making the man at the mall from the TV image, or from your dream?"

"From the dream."

"Oh."

Hess got the remote and found CNB. There was something on about a fire in Trabuco Canyon, no castrated sex offender peeking out from behind his blinds. He turned off the sound.

"Kamala? The problem here is that the sex offender in Irvine—his name is Colesceau, I believe—has short dark hair. The man you saw at the mall had long blond hair and a mustache. We've got no reason to believe he was wearing a wig. I mean, the hair samples we've got here are human, not synthetic."

"There are plenty of human hair wigs out there."

"There are some."

Kamala sighed. "I know. I know you and Merci think I'm a complete ditz, but I'm not. It just takes a while for things to settle in my head sometimes."

He wondered if three margaritas could be argued as an asset, too, something to loosen up Kamala Petersen's "unconscience," but he didn't wonder very long.

Intoxicated, hooked on fashion mags, old movies and TV. Thinks everybody looks like somebody famous she's seen a picture of.

Our witness, rendered uncallable in court by hypnosis.

"Kamala, when you saw this guy up at the Brea Mall, then down in Laguna Hills, did you ever think, hey—that's a wig?"

"No."

"But that's your business, isn't it—appearance, beauty, fashion?"

"Maybe that's how good it was. My specialty is cosmetics, really. But I can tell you from my work that a good wig is hard to see. If you do the feathering right, and have a good cut to start with, it's almost impossible, especially from a distance, or if you're not really looking for it."

True, thought Hess. And also true that her description had led to a sketch good enough to be recognized by the OCTA bus driver, the clerk at Arnie's and Lee LaLonde. In fact, Hess himself had thought at first that there was something of Kamala's man in Colesceau's eyes.

But if it was Colesceau, why hadn't the mug from his jacket clicked for her? Or the newspaper shots?

Hess wondered about a lineup. It seemed reasonable that a convicted violent sex offender disguised and seen in the vicinity of a sexual abduction might be considered suspect. It was a good way to turn up the heat on a guy. He imagined getting this Colesceau fellow outfitted with blond hair and a mustache.

The bad news was that an ID of a suspect *in a*

disguise would probably be laughed at by any DA's office in the country.

The good news was Colesceau had no search and seizure rights as a sex crime parolee: he and Merci could question him and check out his house any time they wanted until Wednesday, the day after tomorrow, when he completed his parole and his chemical castration program ended. If he was stashing a wig of golden human hair, a Deer Sleigh'R and a Porti-Boy, they could pretty much just walk in and look for them.

Hess watched a silent Mercedes commercial, a radiant blonde in a red convertible. Women in cars, he thought: secure, confident, protected. No word from LaLonde on the Purse Snatcher's dysfunctional alarm override.

"Kamala, one more thing—did Merci give you the number here?"

"In case she wasn't available. Oh well, let her kill me. I want to do the right thing."

"You have."

"They say on the TV that the guy's been castrated. Then these doctors come on and say rape is a crime of anger."

"That's the current thinking."

And if you'd ever seen what a bottle or a club or a gun barrel did to a woman who'd been raped with one, you'd probably agree. But he didn't say that.

"They didn't show very much of him," Kamala said. "Mostly, the good video is from when they first surprised him a couple of days ago. The last time they showed him live, he was looking out from behind the door. It's his eyes that give him away, Mr. Hess. Wet. Sad. Like Omar Sharif in *Dr. Zhivago* or Lon Chaney's in *Wolfman*. Before he turns into the wolf. On TV he looks scared, like an animal."

"He's behaved like an animal."

"To those women."

"And those are the ones we know about."

"It makes me want to never trust a man again."

"Be careful who you trust."

"I will. Well, thanks."

He hung up and called Merci.

28

The next morning Colesceau watched the cops come to his door on TV because it was easier than getting up to look through the blinds.

The Purse Snatcher duo, he thought, recognizing them from the papers. Not that you'd have any trouble telling what these kind of people were. Hess, the fascist general, and Rayborn, his Doberman bitch helper. He imagined their offspring with black feathers, four legs and grotesque genitalia.

Colesceau's heartbeat upped its rate. He felt a cold prickling sensation on the skin of his face. Then he saw himself sitting there, waiting for whatever they had in mind. What could they possibly want with him?

He was physically and emotionally exhausted by the crowd and by what Grant Major had pulled on him. It made him want to give up and blow his brains out.

Just remember who you are, he reminded himself: Colesceau the innocent, Colesceau the wronged, Colesceau the castrated and contrite.

MAKE OUR NEIGHBORHOOD
SAFE for the CHILDREN!

He thought about murdering some local kids just to add some relevance to this irritating chant. Stake their

282

heads on the push-arms of some FOR SALE signs. The trouble was he kind of liked most of the kids he noticed these days—so happy and spoiled and obsessed with their own selfish little schemes. It would probably just be a waste of time.

Then he saw the old cop ring his doorbell on TV and heard his actual doorbell ring at exactly the same time. There were so many reasons to be awed by America.

He decided not to answer for a minute so he could watch them react. Surely Trudy Powers would vouch for his whereabouts. The whole mob would. That, in fact, was the very proof of his innocence—these fine neighbors always knowing where he was. His witnesses. He'd never expected such convenience to develop from such humiliation.

The Doberman bitch turned to look at the crowd. She wore sunglasses like a fighter pilot and her hair was wavy and dark. A big one, he saw: a strong-legged, proud-assed, heavy-breasted dog. He pictured her in something revealing, sitting beside him in Pratt's yellow Cobra doing ninety. Maybe. He preferred a more delicate, feminine woman, though he could see her features were strong and far from unattractive. She probably had yellow teeth. He could easily imagine doing her out of pure meanness, as a way of repaying her for what she was.

She reached out and the doorbell rang again.

"I am coming!" he shouted.

Funny, how on the TV screen he could see them fix their attention on the door like it had just spoken to them. Really quite amusing.

283

He went to the front door, opened it two inches and peered out. "Yes?"

Out came two badges—Sheriff's Department somethings. Behind the badges were two sets of sunglasses and two frowns.

"Mr. Colesceau, I'm Sergeant Rayborn and this is Lieutenant Hess of the Orange County Sheriff-Coroner Department. We'd like to come in and have a word with you."

He opened the door. The chant got louder.

"Welcome to my home."

The bitch pushed in first, then the fascist. Colesceau looked out at Trudy. She was at the forefront per usual, her picket sign in hand, her face lovely. She looked directly back at him. He saw that the higher calling was still in her, that she was still tasked by her God to deal with the human excrement Colesceau. He saw mercy and understanding and dignity on that face.

He shut the door and locked it. They stood there looking at him, hands on their hips. Both sets of sunglasses were gone.

"You can come in and have a seat if you want."

"Thanks," said the male.

The bitch stood her ground and watched him pass by her, as he followed the old one into his living room.

"Would you like something to drink?"

"No," said the bitch.

"No, thank you," said the other.

Neither of them sat.

"I have no rights that I am aware of," he said. "I will

284

answer any questions you ask. You may search this apartment all you like. I ask that you don't break anything more than necessary. I'll be happy to show you where things are located, if this will make your job easier."

"You give me a pay raise, too?"

The bitch, of course.

"I would give myself a job first," Colesceau answered. "My old boss, Mr. Pratt, has given me two weeks of pay, but the work is gone. There was a mob outside there, too."

"My eyes are misting over," she said.

"I worked there for two years, at five-fifty an hour. No benefits. No vacation. I only missed one day. That was when an accidental overdose of female hormone made me vomit for six hours without relief."

"What are these things?" she asked, ignoring his woes. She was standing in front of one of his display cabinets, facing his mother's artistry.

"Eggs."

"You paint them up like this? Put on the lace and glitter?"

"My mother does this. Egg painting is a respected Romanian folk art. She is considered accomplished."

"Isn't that where the vampires and werewolves live, Romania?"

"They only live in the imagination, I believe."

"What kind of name is Matamoros? I mean, it's a city in Mexico but you're Romanian."

Colesceau was slightly surprised to hear her say this. She was correct, but it was rare when an American knew anything about Mexico, their closest neighbors to the south, let alone the city of Mata-moros. In fact, there were *two* cities of Matamoros in Mexico. Colesceau decided long ago that he was named after the larger and more important of them.

He realized he had an odd feeling inside.

"My mother fell in love with a picture of Mexico when she was a young woman. For her it represented a paradise far away from the frigid Carpathians. She never went there until we came to live in America. She chose the name out of a book. And she gave it to me."

Doberman: "Hmf. I like this giant blue one with the yellow feather boa around it. It looks like a pregnant stripper."

"Cassowary. I think it's garish and obscene."

"You're sensitive for a three-time granny raper."

She turned and looked at him. The odd feeling was still inside him, slightly stronger.

No, he thought.

"But that was a long time ago," he continued, "and I am a different man. Please, sit down. You can watch the crowd outside on the TV, or you can open the blinds and watch them in reality. You can do both. I usually just watch on the TV because I can turn it off. Of course I can't turn off the crowd outside. But it's a comfort."

"Do you get out much?" asked the Doberman. She was still standing in front of the display case. The old general was on the other side of the room so that Colesceau couldn't see them both at the same time.

"I used to, occasionally. Now, it's not possible."

She looked toward the door. "Got you surrounded."

286

"Like Custer in American history."

"Custer thought he was a military genius. What kind of genius do you think you are?"

"None at all, I'm afraid. But I'm surrounded just the same."

"Sit."

Colesceau sat. He was suddenly outside himself again, watching himself sit. From this dislocated vantage point he could look down on the old guy's bristly head, the Doberman's wavy locks and his own thinning dark hair. When the bitch's coat fell open he saw the holster up under her arm, saw the snap was loose, wondered if she kept it that way for quick kills.

And the strangest thing had begun to happen—his shrunken, hormone-battered sex organ was starting to stir.

"So, where did you used to go, when you could get out?" Sergeant Rayborn asked him.

Sergeant Rayborn.

"Movies, Sergeant. Inexpensive restaurants. The library."

Yes, it was growing. Why now?

"When? What time of day?"

"After work, Sergeant. Evenings. Generally not on weekends because of the crowds."

"Ever go to malls?"

"Yes. I like malls."

"Why?" She was looking at him sharply now. And he was looking down at himself, at the beginning of a lump in his pants. He crossed his legs and locked his fingers over his knees.

287

What was going on?

"Variety," he said. "Food, entertainment, merchandise. A nice environment. If you grew up where I did, an American mall is a wonderful place."

"Ever go there to look at the women?"

"Never. I have had no interest in women for three years. I have no desire to look at them or touch them. Occasionally I want to talk to a female person, because females can have such a refreshing way of seeing things. Then, I can call my mother, or perhaps my psychologist, Dr. Carla Fontana. But so far as striking up conversations with unfamiliar women—I don't do that. Very occasionally, one will strike up a conversation with me."

"What do you do then, run?"

"I'm a good listener," he said. He wondered if he was laying it on a little thick, because this Merci Rayborn was no typical American airhead. He had the feeling she was seeing right into him. He pressed his legs together to apply pressure to his shrunken testicles, in hopes of discouraging his excitement. *What is it about talking to her that does this to me?*

"I'll bet you are," she said. "Gives you a chance to think about them, watch them."

"This is what conversation is, no?"

"Not when you're figuring out a way to rape them it isn't."

"That is never what I do."

"Stay where you are."

He felt his excitement rise a notch.

"Don't move."

"Yes, Sergeant. Whatever you demand."

Another notch. Something to do with her commanding voice, he thought: her authority and conviction. It was like she wore an invisible uniform. And not some indecisive American law enforcement costume, but the actual power-emanating uniform of the Romanian state police.

Merci thought that Colesceau was one of the weirdest guys she'd ever laid eyes on. The weirdness was too vague and vast to identify yet but she felt it anyway, like the first breeze before a massive storm. She shook her head and walked over to Hess, who was now looking at the eggs.

"Take your tour," she said. "I'm going to stay on him."

Hess looked over her shoulder, toward Colesceau, then back to the display case. "Keep him in front of you. He used an ice pick on those dogs."

"I'd like to see him try one on me."

"Beware a weak man's rage."

"Yes, master."

She left Hess at the case and went back to Colesceau. He was right where she had left him, legs crossed and fingers locked over one knee. He looked pudgy and soft and she thought she could see mounds of breasts under his shirt. A track light from the ceiling lit the back of his slightly balding head. It was hard to imagine this man doing what was done on the Ortega, or at the construction site off Main. But he was compact enough to fit into the floor space behind the front seat of a car. So were half a million other men in the county.

"I've got some dates I want to ask you about," she said.

He looked at her and smiled. "From a woman as attractive as you, I would say yes to all dates."

She gave him her drop dead look, heartfelt. "Let's get something straight, worm. One more comment about my appearance, I'll book you for verbal assault. I'll have your ass back in slam before you can form your next thought."

He squirmed a little on the couch, nodding with apparent sincerity. He almost looked repentant.

"You clear on that, Jack?"

"Absolutely, Sergeant."

His eyes, when I got up close, looked wet and sad . . .

A good description of this shitbird, thought Merci.

"Saturday night, fourteen August. Three nights ago."

He looked at her with his regretful eyes and sighed. "I sat here and listened to my neighbors chant. I would like to state right now that I love children and have never harmed one. Anyway, I watched TV. I saw myself interviewed by a man who presented himself as an American Civil Liberties lawyer. He was in fact a reporter with a hidden camera. I confronted the crowd at approximately six, to see if they would be a little less loud. And again at nine-thirty, because they had not yet set a time to discontinue the noise. So, Sergeant, you can go outside and speak to them. They are my witnesses."

"I'll do that. All right, three August—two Tuesday evenings ago."

"I need my calendar. It's on the counter over there, by the phone."

"I'll get it. You'll stay put."

He was smiling again, an expression that seemed to hold a thousand messages but contain no clear meaning that Rayborn was familiar with. He recrossed his legs and fingers. "Thank you, Sergeant."

Hess started in the kitchen. He could hear their voices as he stood in the middle of it and took in the generalities: neat, clean, used. He slid out the drawers and looked at the flatware, the oven mitts, the utensils, the plastic wrap and foil. No ice pick. The inside of the oven was clean. So was the stovetop. He turned on the sink faucet and let the water run a minute, turned it off and listened to it gurgling down the garbage disposal U. He looked in the cabinet under the sink: wastebasket, pots and pans, dishwasher soap, glass cleaner, rags, brushes. The dishwasher was half-loaded. No lidless canning jars. The refrigerator was lightly stocked with ordinary staples and condiments. The freezer had boxes of vegetables, ice cream and a package of hamburger.

The small downstairs bathroom looked rarely used. The fixtures were dusty and dry and the toilet bowl had a pale stain just above the water level.

Hess climbed the stairs and went into the main bedroom. Colesceau slept on a small twin that was neatly made: brown cotton bedspread, white sheets and pillow. On the wall above the bed was a poster of a bright yellow Shelby Cobra with its hood open to reveal a big highly chromed engine. Hess recognized the coveted Holly carbs of his youth. The print at the bottom said "Pratt Automotive—Classic Automobile Restoration," which Hess remembered as Colesceau's recent employer.

Eggs with their insides altered, made decorative.

Cars with their insides altered, made custom.

Bodies with their insides altered, made ... what?

The closet held a few shirts and trousers on hangers; underclothes folded and stacked on a shelf; shoes toe to toe in a plastic sleeve hung from the ceiling. Like Janet Kane's, he thought. No wig—human hair or otherwise.

Where would you hide the driver's licenses? Flat and small enough to fit into a million different places.

Where would you hide *them*?

He bent down and looked under the bed: an aluminum baseball bat, a short rod and spinning reel, a Daisy spring action BB pistol cast to look like a six-gun.

When Hess stood back up he felt the blood rushing to his head, then a ringing lightness. The walls bowed convex then back flat again. Two of them were empty but the one opposite the bed had a framed poster of a castle looming atop a jagged mountaintop. He walked up close but there was no title or description. Against one wall was a dresser, which held sport shirts, shorts and more underwear. On top of it, Hess found some change, paper clips, a pen and stubs from three computer-generated movie tickets dated over the last three months. He wrote down the dates, times, titles and locations of the theaters, and put them back. One of them was for the night Janet Kane disappeared from the mall at Laguna Hills. The theater issuing the ticket was in Irvine, just a few miles away.

In the bathroom he scraped one of his credit cards down the bath towel hanging over the shower door, using a sheet of toilet paper to catch the fallout. With his head angled to the light he pulled several hairs out of the cotton terry and set them on the toilet paper too. He added more from the hairbrush in the top drawer, then folded the paper and slid it into his coat pocket. There was nothing of interest in the wastebasket, the cabinets or the toilet tank, from which he removed the top for a look. Someone had set bricks in each corner of the tank to save water.

Save water, Hess thought.

Save eggshells.

Save cars.

Save things in canning jars.

Save bodies.

The spare bedroom was really quite small—just a bed, a dresser with a lamp on it and a closet. It felt larger than it was because the closet doors and the back wall were mirrored. In the closet were four boxes of books, most of them in Romanian. Some extra blankets and pillows, a collection of men's clothing that looked faded and rarely worn. A TV. The dresser held heavy sweaters, coats and socks. On the mirrored wall opposite the bed hung a black plastic crucifix that struck Hess as the loneliest depiction of Jesus he'd ever seen.

It seemed to Hess like a waste of a room. Why

bother to pay for a two-bedroom unit? Hard to imagine overnight guests in the home of Matamoros Colesceau.

29

". . . I would say that the most drastic part of my treatment was the terrible feelings I experienced internally. It was explained to me that the hormone treatment would make me feel like I was constantly having premenstrual syndrome, but this description did not mean much to me because I was male. Am male. But it is a very bad feeling, as you know. Only in my case it lasted for three years instead of three days."

"Constant or intermittent?"

Colesceau was still outside himself, looking down on the authoritatively seductive Merci Rayborn and his own rather hapless body. But he was having a good time talking to her, telling her about how the Depo-Provera murdered his sex drive and turned him into a peace-loving, nonsexual lamb of a man. His stimulation made him feel mentally sharp and physically lithe. It was like a spark being fanned.

"Three years seems very constant to me."

The sergeant fostered confidence and energy in him and Colesceau was thankful for it. It surprised him. He wondered if he was changing.

Her dry, unloving voice again: "Did your imagination continue to work when you felt that way?"

"Regarding what?"

"Regarding things you'd like to do. Things you could do before and couldn't do then? Could you picture things you'd like to do?"

Colesceau sighed deeply. He looked down at his own expression and thought it deserved some kind of award. He could be no more convincing than this. "For me, no. I lost my dreams along with my desire."

"I'll bet."

"You would then win the bet. You cannot imagine what the death of that feeling is. The instinct to love and mate and extend the human race. Without it, you are nothing but a shell. Empty, like one of these eggs my mother decorates."

"No sexual desire at all?"

"None."

"Then how come you used your silver van to pin Ronnie Stevens's car three nights back at the Main Place Mall?"

He was intrigued by this information. He felt his lips part and his face go slack. But from the outside, this had a positive effect: he looked bewildered and hapless. He looked innocent. And just a little bit insulted.

The neighbors started up their chanting again. He wished he could machine-gun every last one of them.

"I do not know Ronnie Stevens. I have never met him. I drive a red Datsun pickup truck from 1970. I haven't been to the Main Place Mall in several months. Sergeant, remember one thing about me. About my behavior. This is it—never once did I deny my disease or my crimes of the past. I fully confessed to my acts. I am many things, Sergeant Rayborn, not all of them good. But one of the things I am, that I

296

have never been able to change, is that I am honest. To a fault, perhaps."

He watched her study him with her cold brown Doberman eyes. She looked dispassionate but unimpressed. It was the cop's fundamental expression, he thought, and this Merci Rayborn looked like she was born with it on her face. He was sure now that she wore the holster strap unsnapped so she could get her gun quick and shoot fast.

"Okay, honest shitbird. Tell me where you were on Saturday night."

"I was right here, as I explained earlier. I was even on TV, I believe. I'm sure the stations must keep video records."

Hess went back down the stairs, through the kitchen and into the garage. It was nice to be able to get into the garage from inside the house, and Hess wished his apartment at 15th had the same feature. He turned on a light and looked at the decrepit little pickup truck. It was so old they were called Datsuns back then. Seventy, maybe, seventy-two? The doors were unlocked and the windows down. The registration and insurance were current. The odometer said 00000. The tires were in good shape and matched. Hess looked at the bed: lightly rusted and dented, no chemical or solvent stains. The glove box had the usual: tire pressure gauge, maps, pencils, cassette tapes. Hess pulled out three and read the titles: *Eternal Health Through Yoga*, by Sri Ram-Hara; *TravelAudio #35— Destination Romania; Deadwood*, a novel by Pete Dexter.

Hess looked at the picture on the novel cassette: a

long-haired, mustachioed gunslinger he recognized as Wild Bill Hickok.

. . . *or that guy Paul Newman played in* Buffalo Bill and the Indians.

Wrong Bill, right hair, thought Hess. He sat down in the passenger's side and put back the tapes. He examined the headrest of the driver's seat for hair. Same with the floorboards and the transmission hump. Nothing.

Outside the crowd started up again:

> MAKE OUR NEIGHBorhood
> SAFE for the CHILdren!

Hess was sure there were no crimes against children in Colesceau's jacket, but told himself to check again. He was a little surprised by the volume of the chant, the way the combined voices reverberated through the thin plywood of the garage door. The voice of fear, he thought. The papers said the vigil had been twenty-four hours a day for four days now, and that the neighbors had vowed to continue it until Colesceau got into his miserable little Datsun and left forever. The mob had set its own noise curfew at 9 P.M. so as not to interfere with work, school and sleep. Hess also read the people were driving in from other cities of the county to join the protest and that CNB had cameras set up round the clock, going to them live when Colesceau was visible or during slow periods during the news day.

He got out of the truck and looked around the garage. It was small, with two cabinets against the wall, which contained nothing of interest to him. No

Deer Sleigh'R, no gambrels or ropes, no big game cleaning implements, no Porti-Boy embalming machines or fluids. No blond wigs made of genuine human hair. No canning jars with missing lids. No chloroform.

Clean, Hess thought.

If he does it, he doesn't do it here.

Merci joined Hess in the small downstairs bathroom. She leaned against the sink, and could see Colesceau still sitting in his living room. She couldn't tell by Hess's look whether he'd scored big, small or not at all. His eyes sparkled in the bright bathroom lights and she wondered what he was thinking.

"No silver van with mismatched tires, I take it."

"Not one."

"Well?"

"He'd take them somewhere else."

"He says the crowd outside saw him here at least twice on Saturday night, when Ronnie got it. Says he was at the movies on the Kane date, and may have a ticket stub to corroborate. The Jillson night, he was having dinner here, with his—get this—his *mom.*"

"He's got a Tuesday night ticket stub upstairs. One of several."

"It doesn't mean much."

"I know that."

"Did he say anything about the second bedroom?"

"It's for his beloved mother, of course. She comes to dinner often and stays over."

Hess nodded and the vertical lines between his eyes deepened.

"I vote no, Hess. Much as I'd like to pinch his

vicious little head right this instant. He's supposed to be chemically castrated—until Wednesday, anyway. He's weird. He raped helpless old women, not strong young ones. He's got a spare bedroom for his mommy. Everything physical about him is wrong except for those eyes that Kamala dingbat Petersen fell in love with. She saw his face on TV, for Chrissakes. Or was it a dream? Nobody's said anything about our golden-haired boy talking with an accent—not LaLonde, not the Arnie's guy, nobody. This place is clean. He sure as hell didn't walk in and out of here Saturday night without the lynch mob seeing him—that's for sure. I'd love to pop him for something—*anything*—but I think we ought to keep turning over rocks for our main man. Let's put a loose surveillance on this nutcase and forget about him. Give him line. If he swims anywhere pertinent we'll yank him aboard and see what he's been nibbling."

"All right."

She looked into Hess's eyes in the hard light. The fact that she couldn't determine his thoughts irritated her because he was the only person whose thoughts she wanted to determine.

"Do you agree?" she asked.

"You're the boss."

"God*damnit,* that's not what I asked."

"I agree. But I get a bad feeling here."

Merci tried to think it through. What she kept seeing was an elaborate waste of precious time. One thing about Hess was sometimes he acted like they had all the time in the world. When, theoretically, he had less than most people.

She said, "My fear is, he speeds up, now that he's got the hang of it. And while we're firing down on this nutless, teary-eyed little creep, the real guy's out there looking for number four. I think we'd be better off with ten lady cops, dressed to kill, hair up, planted at ten malls."

"That's a real possibility, Merci."

She looked out at the back of Colesceau's head. He sat motionless where she had left him. She could see the shine of his scalp below the thinning black hair.

"Hess, I mean, look at that guy. Look at the back of his *head*. He's crawling with progesterone and he's got the muscle tone of a bean bag. He's beyond pathetic and disgusting. He's like a bug that's already been stepped on."

"There is that about him."

"I think we're after someone with a higher octane rating."

"There's something about him I don't get."

"Maybe you should be thankful for that. Look, if he so much as shows his face, those people start blowing gaskets. It's about time we got some help from the spoiled middle-class fatheads we serve and protect."

"Well said."

Outside, several of the protesting neighbors said they saw Colesceau not once but twice on Saturday night, Ronnie Stevens's last. They concurred that Colesceau had come out once around six and once later—around nine or nine-thirty. The rest of the time he watched TV. They described what he said to them and what he was wearing, and Hess took notes. He discovered that before Colesceau's cover was blown, none of these neighbors paid him much attention at all. They'd see the little faded truck come and go, and that was about it.

One of the organizers was a woman named Trudy Powers, whom Hess remembered from a newspaper article. She said that she received from the "damaged man" a hollow decorated egg—a promise of his good behavior until finding a more suitable place to live. She said she believed he was looking for a new apartment because he had promised her he would. Trudy Powers implied an understanding and relationship with Colesceau that she seemed proud—or somehow obligated—to not explain. Hess wondered about her. She had enough qualities in common with Lael Jillson and Janet Kane to make him genuinely uneasy. But how could he tell her that? What he did do was look her straight in the eye and tell her to be careful. She seemed to pity him, but Hess couldn't tell if it was because of what he said or how he looked.

A young man with a camera case hanging from his shoulder said he saw Colesceau not twice but several times Saturday night because he crept up close and looked through a crack in the blinds. He did this around seven-fifteen, eight-thirty, and again around ten-thirty, before he left for home. Colesceau was watching TV. The neighbor said it was the news, then a police drama, then a movie.

Hess asked if Colesceau saw him peering in.

"No. The TV in there faces the street, so all I saw was the back of his head."

"How come you kept checking in on him?"

The young man shrugged and looked away. "I took some pictures. But the film's still in the camera."

"I want that film," Hess said.

"I thought you might. Three left." He unslung the case, took out the camera and shot one picture of Hess and one of Merci and one of them together. He rewound the film and smiled with an odd expression of pride as he handed it over to Hess.

"I'm glad to help. Can I have them back when you're done?"

Hess got his name, address and phone number.

Rick Hjorth of Fullerton, ten miles north.

The County News Bureau reporter assigned to "Rape Watch, Irvine," was a tense blonde who fell into step with them and introduced herself as Lauren Diamond. Her video shooter trailed behind with a heavy-looking rig over his shoulder. She proffered a microphone to Hess, who kept walking. Hess remembered Merci's early orders to leave all public relations to her. Merci didn't break stride either.

"Why were you inside with convicted rapist Matamoros Colesceau?" Lauren asked Hess.

"No comment," said Merci.

Still to Hess: "You're heading up the Purse Snatcher investigation. Any connection to the Purse Snatcher?"

"*I'm* heading up the Purse Snatcher investigation, lady, and it's still no comment."

Hess shook his head, mostly to himself. He saw the shooter getting all this down, wondered if Merci was even aware of him.

"Then what *is* it in connection with?"

Hess could feel the heat emanating from right

beside him. It was like walking next to a solar panel. She was about to speak but he beat her to it.

"Routine parole stuff, Lauren," said Hess. "That's all."

"Is Colesceau a suspect?"

Hess fixed a look on her, hooked his thumb back toward the crowd. "Pretty good alibi."

"Miss Rayborn, can you tell us something about your sexual harassment suit?"

"Absolutely not."

"Lieutenant Kemp has denied all the charges."

"Wouldn't you?"

"Five other female deputies have come forward since you did. Phil Kemp is a twenty-five-year employee of the department with a clean record. Why all of this, so suddenly?"

Merci whirled and pressed her face into that of Lauren Diamond. "Buzz off, lady."

Lauren Diamond slowed, then stopped, but the shooter kept up behind them. Hess turned, gave him a little wave, tried to make things look casual, and kept going. Merci was half a step ahead of him now as they headed toward the car.

"Thanks," she said.

"You're welcome."

"Do *not* tell me I should have felt what she was feeling, or thought what she was thinking."

"Oh hell, no. She's just an ambitious young reporter who might be happy to help you someday. It would have taken about thirty seconds of your time to be civil."

"So I screwed up again."

"Why be a bitch all the time?"

"I'll get the hang of good manners sooner or later."

"I'm starting to think you don't want to."

"Now you're thinking what *I'm* thinking."

When they got into the car Merci exhaled and looked at Hess.

"I'll tell you something, partner—bringing that suit was the dumbest goddamned thing I've ever done in my life. How can I get out of it now, after I've started all *this*?"

30

Hess lied to his partner then, excusing himself for an oncologist appointment. He was puzzled by this Colesceau, no matter what Merci thought, and he was going to ride that feeling for a couple more hours, before they headed up to Sacramento and the state Morticians' Licensing Board. He was tiring of watching Rayborn start fights wherever she went. He felt like a nanny for the neighborhood bully.

First he went by Pratt Automotive and had a talk with Marvis Pratt, his wife, Lydia, and an employee named Garry Leonard. They told him Colesceau did his job okay, though Pratt didn't trust him as far as he could throw him. He hired guys like Colesceau because he thought people deserved a second chance, and because Holtz was a friend.

They showed him through the place—the front shop and office area, the high bay in back with the beautiful yellow-and-black Shelby Cobra that Hess just stood and stared at. It was the most beautiful car he had ever seen.

"Four hundred fifty horse," said Pratt.

"That's a car and a half."

"We've done a lot of restorations. They come here dogs and leave here dolls."

"How much?"

"One eighty. Firm."

"Colesceau ever drive a different vehicle to work here, not that old red Datsun?"

"No, just the truck."

Hess looked at the expansive bay, the clean racks, the orderly tools, the rafters catching the late morning light through high windows. In dogs and out dolls, he thought. Paradise, for a car nut.

They went back to the office. "Does he call in sick, miss work, spend time on the phone?"

"No. He's good about being here. It's easy work. Mainly what he does is sits on that stool, helps some customers and wiggles his tits around every once in a while."

"They *hurt*, Pratt," said Lydia.

"Whatever. I gave him his walking papers. I can't have a crowd demonstrating outside the place. Jesus, it's hard enough to make a living anymore."

Hess knew from LaLonde's statement that "Bill" had computer printout sheets containing nine different car manufacturers' specs on the alarm system frequencies. He noted the computer and monitor on the office desk, and a similar one behind the counter in the front store.

"The computers replace those old catalogs?"

Pratt said they did that, but lots more: he got daily updates, changes, recalls and corrections right from the factories. They'd get information on new models coming out, incentives going to dealers, even newsletters from different plants around the world.

Hess asked him to print out repair/replacement data on the 1998 Infiniti Q45 and 1999 BMW 525 antitheft systems. Lydia sat down and two minutes later Hess had eight pages of specs and exploded drawings.

"You can go on and on with this stuff," she said.

"Colesceau know how to work the computer?"

"Sure. That's part of his job," said Lydia. She looked at Hess with a dark expression, then away. "I think it's lousy what you guys did to him. Getting his neighbors all riled up for nothing. He's a lamb, really. Mixed up, but a lamb."

"I hope you're right," he answered mildly.

Hess then showed them the drawing of the Purse Snatcher and gave all three his work and pager numbers. Per usual, he got a home number from them, just in case. You never know.

In the office of Quail Creek Apartment Homes, the middle-aged and overweight supervisor, Art Ledbetter, told Hess that Colesceau had never complained or been the subject of a complaint until now. He assumed Colesceau paid his rent on time, but rent checks went to corporate up in Newport. Ledbetter did light security and scheduled maintenance work, took applications, fielded questions and complaints. But they had no choice but to evict. Thirty-day notice already served. What could you do with protesters camped out around the clock?

Hess stood and looked at a model of the complex, which hung from one wall. The aerial view was interesting. He saw that the complex was actually an enormous circle, and the quadrants of apartments were designed in perfect symmetry with each other. He noted the way that the developers were packing them in these days: each snaking row of units had a front facing one street and a front facing another, but shared a common rear wall. Thus, the illusion of privacy without real privacy at all.

"Ever see any unusual activity around his unit?"

"None at all. No complaints, like I said."

"What about his hours? Come and go all the time, late at night, maybe?"

"I ride that little golf cart around 'til ten some nights. I've never seen him out and about at that hour. But, you know, one of the nice things here is you can use the remote, open your garage door and drive in without hardly disturbing anyone. Walk right into your unit from the garage. That's the idea, keep things quiet, private."

"Do you know most of the tenants?"

Ledbetter shook his head. "Some. There's a batch of ghost people I never see. Maybe they work nights and sleep all day, never use the pool, I don't know. Some fly in for business, stay a month, fly back out. But they pay rent every month, or corporate would serve them."

"How about visitors to Colesceau's?"

"His mother. And a couple—man and a woman. Twice, maybe. Not often."

Hess asked him to describe them and he did: Holtz and Fontana, right down to Holtz's Corrections Ford. Ledbetter was good with cars, like a lot of men are.

Hess looked down at the map of the complex that Ledbetter had given him. Colesceau's was an end unit apparently no different than any other two-bedroom end unit.

"What about his immediate neighbor, to the left?"

"Nice young lady, works nights."

"What about the unit behind his?"

"Old lady, never see her. One of the ghost people."

"Ever seen a silver panel van at Colesceau's?"

Ledbetter frowned. "Silver panel van. Well, yeah, a few months back I *did* see a silver van pulling out of the complex. One of those fancy conversion things with the running boards and the riser on top. But who knows what unit it came from. Driver could have been lost for all I know."

Hess made his notes, gave Ledbetter a card and thanked him. "Would you mind giving me your home number, just in case?"

"Not a problem."

Hess did a brief door-to-door after that, but six of the neighbors he called on were gone, and the other three had nothing of note to say about Matamoros Colesceau except that he should get the hell out of their city.

He got the Lifestyler's address from the phone book—the closest wig shop to Colesceau. It was in a little shopping center by the freeway, between a community newspaper office and a walk-in clinic.

A young Chinese woman stepped up to greet him while an elderly woman who looked like her mother regarded him placidly from behind the counter. The walls were high, with long shelves full of white heads wearing all styles and colors of wigs.

Hess felt like a thousand faceless women were staring at him. He also felt the walls waver in and out just a little, like they were leaning in for a closer look.

He identified himself and gathered what he could about human hair wigs: they were available, typically 10 to 20 percent more expensive than synthetics, the upside was they looked good, the downside was that you had to shampoo, condition and set them just like you would your own hair—often.

He asked if they'd ever sold a long, blond, human hair wig to a man. The two women consulted in their native tongue, and the young one told Hess yes, several over the years. Sometimes, she said, men will buy for their wives. Sometimes for themselves. She exchanged glances with her mother and smiled very demurely at Hess.

The old woman stood and took up a long wooden pole with a metal V at the end. She shuffled along the wall behind the counter, stopped, reached and hooked a head off its platform. The hair was blond and wavy.

"Human hair," the old woman said. "Eighty-nine. You try."

"It's not for me."

"Okay. Sit. You try."

The younger held open a little swinging door and Hess stepped behind the counter. He sat in the styling chair, facing a mirror surrounded by lights. The older woman displayed the wig for his inspection, then lifted it and snapped it over his head. Hess was surprised how tight it was. She snugged it into place, brought up a wide-toothed plastic brush and started picking the hairline locks down over Hess's forehead.

311

Thirty seconds later he looked like a signer of the Declaration.

He looked at the women behind him in the mirror in front of him.

"Good," said the older. "Human hair. Eighty-nine."

Somewhat amazingly to Hess, it *was* good. It looked like it could be his hair. If he just squinted a little and glanced at himself—as he did just now—he could believe this image in front of him was a man with long, wavy blond hair. Absurd, yes, but still . . . unified, credible.

He sat there for a moment in the wig, offering a deal with the younger: eighty-nine for the wig, copies of all receipts for blond human hair wigs sold to men for as far back as they had them, and a home phone number for each woman.

The old woman listened, then nodded and smiled cagily at Hess, who smiled and blushed.

"This isn't for me," he said.

Both women were smiling and nodding.

Old one: "Deal. Receipts come later."

He used a pay phone to call Brighton's direct number. The sheriff picked up himself.

"She wants an apology and she wants Kemp to stop," said Hess. "She's sorry she brought the suit."

Brighton was silent for a moment. "Why couldn't she tell me that herself?"

"She didn't want to rat out a friend of yours. You're her boss, Bright. She wanted to be a stand-up deputy."

More silence. Then, "Thanks."

Hess and Merci caught the one-fifty flight from Orange County to Sacramento. They rented a car at the airport and Hess drove them toward the city. The afternoon was bright and ferociously hot, with the rice fields wavering in the sunlight.

Hess felt light-headed and he watched the shimmering mirage of interstate before him with particular attention. A bird hit the windshield and he flinched. All it left was a clear patch of something wet and a ring of small gray feathers. Hess looked through it but didn't look at it: part of him was still in Matamoros Colesceau's apartment.

He used Merci's cell phone to call Bart Young, the president of the Southern California Embalming Supply Company, again, hoping to pry loose the list of recent buyers. The pleasant sounding president was hesitant at first, then firm again in his decision not to give Hess the list. Hess could tell he felt bad.

He thanked him and hung up. "He's close. Maybe if you called him back and said something about the victims, he'd cave in. He's a decent sort, but he doesn't want to betray his customers. Why don't you try him? Get him to feel bad about the women? Men have a harder time saying no to women sometimes."

Five minutes later Merci was castigating the man for his noncooperation and gutless mercantile behavior. Apparently he hung up because Merci pushed a button, cursed and slapped the mouthpiece back over the keypad.

"I've never once been able to sweet-talk anybody in my life," she said. When Hess looked over she was actually scowling. Her hair was pulled back and her ears were red. "I'm the wrong one to get guilt or sympathy out of anybody. I made Mike cry once. And the way I look at it is, if he won't cough up the names, then this embalming machine pusher'll get a hotter place in hell for himself. It's out of my hands. I wash 'em."

Hess used the phone to run a records check on Rick Hjorth of Fullerton. He was intrigued that Hjorth was so eager to help. It was a fact of life that a high percentage of thrill killers liked to get close to the investigation of their crimes and Hess had detected something of morbid interest in the photographer's attitude.

Hjorth came back clean.

Hess called Undersheriff Claycamp for an update on the panel vans: seventy-five done, nothing yet, another team ready for 5 P.M.

The Morticians' Licensing Board was housed in a stately building near the capitol grounds. They were given an unused office, two chairs, a table and a pot of coffee. Two maintenance men wheeled in the file cabinets on dollies. Hess worked for a straight hour, then went to the men's room and vomited. It was the twelfth time in the last three days, and Hess had no idea why he was counting. He brushed his teeth with a travel brush that had a small tube of toothpaste in the handle, purchased after his first round of chemo, just in case. He looked at himself in the mirror and thought he saw shadows under his skin.

Three hours later they sat on the return flight, leafing again through the fifty-seven mugs they'd printed.

314

Bernal, Butkis, Carnahan . . . no Colesceau . . .

"The more I think about what he does, the more I think he's off the grid," said Hess. "He's not a professional. Undertakers don't even remove the things he's removing."

"Then why is he?"

"So they'll last longer, is my guess."

She looked at him. "But if he's doing what we think he's doing, he learned the skills somewhere."

"I wish we could get a list of all the people who took mortuary science and flunked out. But junior colleges don't keep records of who flunks, drops or fades out. They're too big, too busy, too disorganized."

Hess noted a woman across the aisle looking his way, then quickly somewhere else.

"Well, dream on, Hess. I'm starting to think he just keeps them in the freezer, or down in the basement. Here, I'm going to try that supply guy again."

Drascia, Dumont, Eberle, Eccle, Edmondson . . .

She pulled out the phone from the seat back in front of her and read the directions. Hess shook his head, blinked, tried to concentrate on copies of the mug shots. The Licensing Board had let them use a good-quality copier/enlarger, but the reproductions were one more step removed from reality. And when you figured a guy might be wearing a wig and fake mustaches it took the sharpness out of your eye. It could be just about any of them. The sky was the limit.

"Hi, Mr. Young, this is Sergeant Rayborn again, from the Orange County Sheriffs? Look, I really want to apologize for what I said earlier—I'm just really

315

involved in this case, the sheriff is leaning on me hard, my partner's screaming at me all the time, I'm at thirty-three thousand feet with no leg room and I'm just . . . *frustrated*."

She looked at Hess with an exaggerated grin. She was nodding and holding up her free hand, yapping with her fingers and thumb.

"I know . . . I really do understand. It's just that these women—well, he got another one Saturday night. She was nineteen years old and living with her mom and just a heck of a great gal from what I've gathered. Her name was Ronnie. I never met her. In fact, all I ever saw of her was a couple of pictures and a pile of her intestines and organs on the hood of her car . . . I'm serious, that's what this guy's doing. Plus, we've got two more assumed victims from a couple of years ago, possibly three. Uh-huh, yeah . . . well, sure, I can wait."

Hess looked out the window. Below was a vivid grid of green and yellow stretching all the way to the tan hills in the east. Clouds whisked by, torn by the jet. He watched the engine housing vibrate. *Colesceau came out of his apartment Saturday at six and nine, or nine-thirty. Gilliam said the heart in the purse stopped beating between 7 and 11 P.M. Indications are she was abducted after work. But what if he got her later? After the snooping photographer took his last shot? What if Hjorth or Gilliam are both off a half hour each way? That would give Colesceau an hour and a half to do what he did to Ronnie Stevens. Possible. Not probable . . . How would he get out of the apartment without anyone seeing?*

No Pule . . . no Eichrod . . .

He closed his eyes and saw the layout of the place again: the living room, kitchen and downstairs bath; the upstairs bedrooms and bathroom. Colesceau's place was an end unit, so there were downstairs windows on the south wall, which was the kitchen. Ditto the west, which faced the street. Hess remembered the kitchen: a small cooking area and an alcove with a dinette in it, pushed up near the windows. Salt and pepper shakers on the dinette table, a stack of newspapers. He pictured the alcove and remembered green outside, with some color in it—bougainvillea maybe. Could you see the kitchen windows from the street, at night?

But how does he get the truck past the crowd without them knowing? It's impossible. Then . . . another vehicle. Out of the apartment, on foot to another car . . . silver van, mismatched tires . . . no . . .

He made a note to canvas Colesceau's neighborhood for the silver van, check Colesceau's DMV records for a second vehicle registration, ditto his employers at Pratt Automotive—maybe they loaned him a vehicle to get him through the hard times. Also, get back to the apartment for a look at the south window by the kitchen, and talk to more of the neighbors. He wondered if there was any space under the structure, a crawl area for electrical conduit or vents, something he could wriggle into and out of without being seen.

Hess pondered the time line and it held up: Colesceau had been released from Atascadero on the castration protocol three years ago. Six months later, the first woman disappeared.

"—Okay. All right. Well, I sure thank you, Mr. Young. Bart, I mean. You're doing the right thing."

Merci hung up and looked at Hess. "I did it. Young's going to fax us the customer list of all the embalming machines sold in Southern California in the last two years. By noon tomorrow."

Hess could see the mixture of pride and surprise in Merci Rayborn's face.

"Nice work."

"It was hard. I feel lucky now. See what's popped at headquarters."

So she called her work phone for messages. Hess watched her shrug, then hang up.

"Well?"

"Nothing. But the Western Region rep for Bianchi sent me a pigskin shoulder rig. Free for 'select law enforcement individuals.' You know, the cops on the beat see I'm using a Bianchi, then make head of homicide by forty, they all buy one, too."

"I'd rush right out myself."

"I *should* have bought a Bianchi in the first place, because the snap on this one keeps popping off. I enjoy talking about weapons and gear. Do you?"

31

The developed exposures from Rick Hjorth's film were on Hess's desk when he got back that evening. They were printed four by six and most of them were in focus. The ones taken after dark weren't very good because the automatic flash was too weak for much distance. Hess was pleased that Hjorth had used the date/time feature on the camera, which marked each print in the upper right corner. He slid the pictures of him and Merci into his coat pocket.

Hess looked at the image of Colesceau's apartment with the mob outside, picket signs and candles, even though it was still daylight—5:01 P.M., August 14. Saturday. And Colesceau looking through the cracked door—6:11 P.M. Colesceau on his porch—6:12 P.M. Then Colesceau and the pretty neighbor, Trudy, apparently exchanging something near his porch—6:14 P.M. A close-up of Trudy Powers after, smiling dreamily into Rick Hjorth's lens—6:22 P.M. Next, a picture of a young man holding a sign that said NEXT TIME CUT THE DAMNED THINGS OFF and flipping off the photographer while he smiled at the camera—6:25 P.M.

And so on.

"Anything good?" Merci called over. She was at her desk with the phone pressed to one ear and a notepad open in front of her. Hess knew she was hassling Bart

319

Young of the Embalming Supply Company once again, trying to get him to hurry the customer list. Hess had to hand it to her: she was obsessive enough to be a good investigator someday. Head of homicide? Maybe. Sheriff by fifty-eight? We'll see, he thought. On the plus side, she's got twenty-five years to figure it out.

"Nothing yet," he called back.

Next time cut the damned things off.

He looked at the picture of the smiling flipper-offer, then sat back. It helped to laugh when you could, but sometimes there wasn't a chuckle anywhere in your heart.

Hess looked out at the near-empty investigations room—it was almost seven o'clock—and wondered about the behavior of his own species. He was done being shocked by it at twenty-two. He was finished being disgusted by it at thirty. It was too grim and hopeless to be amusing and too amusing to be grim and hopeless. It made him want to be somewhere people didn't murder and gut one another for thrills, where you didn't carry around a sign calling for your neighbor's nuts on a platter, where people had other things to do than stand around taking pictures of each other. Hess had spent too many of his sixty-seven years contemplating the grimace of his race, and he knew it. You could end up looking just like it. That was why when he made love to a woman he always made it last as long as he could because when he was doing that he wasn't quite himself anymore, he was just a little better, a notch above the bullshit, temporarily upgraded.

Make it last, he thought. Make it last just a little longer.

Hess looked at the pictures that Rick Hjorth had snapped through a crack in the blinds of Matamoros Colesceau's apartment.

They were taken from the same general angle as the view that Hess had of Colesceau that morning while he conferred with Merci in the downstairs bathroom. The couch, the wall opposite the front window, the TV. They were dark and the image small—reduced by distance as well as the top and bottom of the crack through which it was shot. Hess held the picture away and squinted at what looked like the back of Colesceau's head. It was just visible above the back of the couch. Thinning hair over the dull patina of a scalp. It was *somebody's* head, Hess concluded. Past it, the TV screen held the blurred picture of an actor walking down the hallway of a hospital set. The snapshot said, August 14, 8:12 P.M.

The time Ronnie Stevens's heart was being removed, thought Hess. But Colesceau's watching TV.

He got a loupe from the desk drawer and bent down for a better look. The image got bigger but more blurred. He breathed deeply and fogged the loupe. For a second it was like watching Colesceau through a window in a snowstorm. Sure, he thought, the TV watcher could really be a pillow or a stuffed bag or a doll or a cantaloupe on a stick with Magic Marker hair drawn on. It could be a holographic projection, swamp gas, or Lael Jillson's severed head with the hair cropped short. He tossed the loupe back in the drawer and flipped the photograph toward the stack.

321

The back of Colesceau's head is the back of Colesceau's fucking head and he was sitting there watching TV while someone bled and gutted Veronica Stevens in the Main Street construction site.

Deal with it.

The photographs proved it. And they also proved that nobody could crawl out of the kitchen alcove window and not be seen. The angle was wrong. The neighbor's porch light shone upon the glass. It would be as obvious as someone pinned on concertina wire with a searchlight bearing down him.

Using the date/time numbers, he arranged all the shots in chronological order. Everything was so clear, right there in living color. But something wasn't quite right. He stared, unfocused his vision a little, rearranged them according to subject: Colesceau, crowd, whole apartment, lower story, upper story. It wouldn't come to him. It was like getting brushed by the wing of a bird you never saw. He asked Merci to come over for a look.

She stood beside his desk, hands on her hips, lips pursed. "I don't see it."

"Something touched me, then it left."

She gave him a look. "Let me try the loupe."

She bent, taking her time. "The only thing I can think of is, when he watches TV, doesn't he even move? I mean, it's like he's frozen. Mike's kid is like that, though. He gets in front of the tube and goes hypnotic."

"Well."

"No?"

"That's true, what you said, but it's something

322

about the exteriors, I think. Not Colesceau himself."

"Time and date are right there. I'm not seeing it, Hess. I don't see the problem."

He looked at the pictures again. "Right now, I don't sense anything odd there at all. It's gone."

"Goddamned creep is what he is, though."

Hess sighed and flipped the pictures over. Try again later. "Colesceau can get that car alarm stuff at work, you know."

"Any idiot with a computer can get car alarm stuff."

Hess called Undersheriff Claycamp for an update on the search for the panel van, and to change the assignments just a little. Nothing had popped and Hess needed a little something for himself.

Then he told Merci goodnight and headed down to his car.

He drove to the medical center with his mind back in the haunted oaks of the Ortega. Then in the high bay of Pratt Automotive, seeing that black-and-yellow Shelby Cobra again. Then Allen Bobb's mortuary sciences class. Then it was in Matamoros Colesceau's garage, where he found nothing he'd hoped to find. Big waves kept shouldering their way into his thoughts, too, but he banished them as distractions. He allowed himself to be inside just one, however, speeding and swaddled in the cold blue Pacific, happy as a bullet in a barrel.

During his radiation treatment Hess suddenly broke out in a scalding sweat. It evaporated off his skin immediately and left him feeling as if he'd been purged by fire. He lay there wondering if they'd turned up the rads too high. Maybe it was punishment for having to stay open late for him on a Tuesday. Dr. Ramsinghani told him "the heavy sweat is an occasional side effect," and smiled at him like he'd just bought a fine casket for himself.

He buttoned his shirt over his newly purified skin and walked back out to the waiting room.

Merci looked up from a magazine. "I tailed you."

"I got four of the panel vans to check myself."

"I heard you stealing them from Claycamp. Figured you might need your partner for it. Plus there's goddamned reporters waiting for me at work. I'll drive."

"Then let's get out of here."

"You've got a nice glow to you, Hess."

"Funny."

"No, I *meant* it . . . you look . . . oh, hell. Okay. All *right*. That's the stupidest thing I've ever said. Ever."

She looked at him with a guilty acquiescence on her face—but it was really only a minor guilt—and Hess smiled. Her slow shrug said sorry, this is what you get, don't expect me to improve all that much, I'll try.

"And Hess, they say if you laugh a lot you live longer."

He just looked at her.

"I give up," she said. "Put me out of my misery."

"Put me out of mine?"

"Deal. I feel lucky tonight. Where's that first van?"

Hess was thankful that Merci kept the Sheriff radio down low. It was a quiet night so far, calls for disturbing the peace, drunk in public, a car theft in Santa

324

Ana. A bank thermometer read 81 degrees and the sun set through a bank of smog that spread the light into a red blanket low in the west.

They checked two vans in an hour—one in Mission Viejo and one in San Clemente. The registered owners had come up clean on records checks and all the tires were matched. None were new. Hess figured if the Purse Snatcher had caught on to his own identifying flaw, it would be a new right front, maybe a new set all around.

Vern Jackson, the third van owner, wasn't home. He came up with assault and concealed weapon raps in '79 and '85. The vehicle wasn't parked in the driveway or the street, so Hess stood watch while Merci went through a side gate. A few minutes later she was back out again, shaking her head.

The last van was registered to Brian Castor of Anaheim. He came back clean on the record check. The van sat in the driveway of an older tract home with a neat yard and a mailbox in the shape of a shark. It was red. They drove past, U-turned and parked along the curb in front.

The front door of the house was a dutch door with the top open. A large man with long blond hair stood just inside, watching them get out. Hess waved and pointed at the van.

Castor met them next to it, his hands on his hips, his "Gone Fishin'" T-shirt tight over his chest and arms.

"What's up?"

"We're checking a few vehicles—part of an ongoing investigation. Do you mind if we look at the outside?"

"Why mine?"

"Panel vans in the county."

"Go ahead."

But Merci had already gone ahead. She rounded the front of the van behind Castor, walked past him to check the right rear. She shook her head. Hess could see that the two right-side tires were not new.

"We need a look inside," said Merci.

"Nice to meet you, too," said Castor. "Go for it. It's unlocked."

Hess looked at the fisherman while Merci swung open the back door. A moment later she slammed it shut.

"Nix."

Hess thanked Castor and apologized for interrupting his evening.

"Whatever, man. See you later, sweetheart."

"Dream on, fish eyes," said Merci, already moving toward the car.

Castor looked at Hess and smiled. "Spicy."

A few minutes later Hess heard the words that he had learned to dread when he was twenty-two years old, just starting off, and had dreaded more with every passing year.

"Deputy down, eighteen-twelve Orangewood, El Modena off Chapman! *Deputy down and it's bad. Suspect down, too. Need paramedics and need 'em now.*"

The words shot through Hess's body like electricity. He realized they were half a mile away, told Merci the quickest way in.

32

She gunned the big four-door down the avenue and
made the right onto Warren, another onto Hale, then
a quick skidding left at Orangewood. The back tires let
go, the car swung sideways into the curb and Hess felt
his head rattle. Up ahead he saw the flashing lights of
a Sheriff's unit and a group of people gathered to one
side of it. Then he saw a silver van parked in a driveway and he thought, good God we got him. He
fingered open his holster catch and jumped out as
soon as Merci had braked the car to a stop beside the
prowl car.

He looked at the faces in the flashing light and saw
their stunned resentment. He walked toward the van,
toward the lit garage, the lights slapping red and blue
and yellow against the scene: a uniformed deputy face
up on the driveway between the van and the garage,
another uniform bent over him with his arms stiff and
hands locked pumping at his chest. And past them,
lying in the garage doorway leading to the house, a
big man not moving but a young woman screaming
and shaking him. Halfway between the two down
men was a stainless automatic handgun that Hess
picked up by the barrel and moved away from the
screaming woman, who had just begun crawling over
the prostrate man on her way to the gun.

"No," he ordered her. "Go back to him."

Hess set the gun high up on a shelf and went to the big man in the doorway. He could hear Merci behind him, outside the patrol car, talking on the radio, then the rising pitch of distant sirens. He knelt. The guy looked fifty, maybe, balding and powerfully built. Jeans and boots, no shirt. Black tattoos up both arms, one of the central county gangs Hess recognized. He had two holes in his bare chest, close together at the heart. Hess felt the neck for a pulse and when the girl saw his expression she attacked, coming over the body at him, her nails raking at his face. He moved sideways and used her motion to take her lengthwise onto the garage floor and get her wrists back. He snugged the plastic tie tight and walked her at arm's length to Merci's car with one hand on her arm and one in her hair while she snapped her head back trying to bite him.

Merci pumped at the deputy and Hess got the look he didn't want: chest covered with blood and a pool of it under him, his head nodding back and forth with Merci's efforts, eyes open and feet splayed as only dead feet splay. Merci was talking while she did the chest compressions, demanding that the deputy respond, refusing to let him check out.

"You hang *in* here with us, Jerry," Hess heard her say, not much more than a hoarse whisper. "You stay *here* with *me* . . . you just keep breathing . . . I'm giving you the power to do that, so do that . . . just *do* it, Jerry . . ."

The kid looked about twenty-five. His gun was still in his holster. His partner was maybe forty, blood on him as he leaned down and kept talking to the kid, *we're with you now, Jerold, come on Jerry, we gotta get you back to Cathy in good shape or she's gonna have my hide . . . come on, Jerry, I'm gonna keep talking and you just keep listening, we're going to get you out of this, partner, don't you fade on me now, kid, I need you here . . .*

Merci kept pumping but she looked up at Hess with a devastated expression and shook her head. Her forearms were heavy with blood and she was kneeling in a pool of it. Hess checked the van tires—an older but uniform set—then looked over at the crowd. He saw their fear of him. It was one of those moments—Hess had experienced them before—when the killing was done and lives suddenly gone and all you could do was nothing at all.

He went back to Merci.

"I can take over there," he said to her.

"I got him, man, move over," said the partner. His name plate said Dunbar. *"All right, Jerry, I'm back now . . . "*

The sirens whooped and stopped behind him. Two city units and one Sheriff, Hess saw. The paramedic van came tilting around the corner where Merci had almost lost it. The sound and the new flashing lights and the slamming doors and weapons-drawn officers all seemed to reanimate the tragedy, or to make possible a new one. Dunbar was blubbering and pumping too fast. Merci walked slowly toward the arriving troops, her hands out from her sides, as if unsure of how to carry them or herself.

Hess opened the back van doors and looked in. It was carpeted and had a small table and two bench chairs instead of seats. On the table was a freezer bag half filled with light brown powder. A pound at the most, probably less. Hess poked it with his finger— heroin—Mexican by the color. There was a scale, a box of smaller plastic bags, a couple of teaspoons, two open beers and a bag of some kind of powder to plump up the smack and create profit.

They had walked straight into the cutting and packaging, he thought. Like stepping on a scorpion in the dark. Jerry's life for a pound of poppy dust. The Purse Snatcher's seventh victim.

He made sure the arriving crime scene investigators knew where the stainless automatic was stashed.

Then he walked the inside of the house, touching nothing, just looking. It was predictable and soulless, heavy on black leather, chrome and electronics. A new computer in boxes. Plenty of guns. He came into the kitchen just as Merci turned from the sink with her hands clean and wet, looking for a paper towel. Finding none, she dried her hands on a cotton one folded on the countertop.

"Jerry Kirby's dead," she said quietly, "and so's the creep. Let's get the bitch out of my car and get out of here."

She tossed the towel into the sink and walked out.

They sat in silence outside Colesceau's apartment on 12 Meadowlark. Hess leaned back in the seat and peered out between heavy eyelids. He could feel the blood surging inside him and it felt hot. The rads? His brain felt sluggish.

It was after ten and he counted only six protesters. The CNB van was still there—'round the clock coverage for "Rape Watch, Irvine"—but Lauren Diamond was nowhere to be seen. The neighbors sat in lawn chairs with their signs on the ground and votive candles burning in holders beside them. Hess looked at the south-facing kitchen window and knew with certainty that nobody could get in and out of it without being seen.

"It was worth checking," he said. "But there's no way he could get in and out of that window. None whatsoever."

"I told you."

"I needed to see it."

"Tim, this pathetic little troll isn't our guy. He looks wrong, the parole officers have been on him for three years, his own neighbors won't let him fart without taking his picture. I mean, we've got actual photographs of him at home taken while Ronnie Stevens bought it. It just isn't him. But I respect your instincts. I absolutely do."

"I don't care about my instincts. I care about getting this guy before he takes another girl."

"That's why we need to run with what we've got. The artist's sketch with the hair is the one that's popping for us, Hess. Kamala guided it, LaLonde endorsed it, the bus driver and store clerk recognized it. Sure, it could be a wig, but what are the chances? Nobody sees him do what he does, right? So why go to all that trouble, parade around in a well-lit mall with somebody else's hair on? It's real. It's his. We're looking for a long-haired, blond, beach-god type. A guy good-looking enough to catch Kamala Petersen's eye. So we've got to get the sketch out there more, get it *seen*. Maybe do a billboard like we did on that Horridus guy last year. Maybe get Lauren Diamond to put it on the TV more. Maybe circulate them by hand at the malls. We could get some rookies or cadets to do the canvas. Hell, we could do it ourselves if Brighton won't authorize the manpower, which he probably won't."

He nodded, wishing he could get his head clear. It was harder to keep everything straight later in the night. He just wanted things to add up. He listened to his voice.

"We've got the graduates of the Cypress College program," he said. "We've got all the licensed under-takers in Southern California. We've got 224 owners of panel vans. We've got a mailing list from Arnie's Outdoors—the biggest hunting/fishing chain in the county. We need the connection, Merci. If we could just find one name on two lists we'd be onto something. Until then, things are spreading, getting bigger but not tighter."

"And don't forget the embalming machine purchasers, as of tomorrow morning."

In fact, he had forgotten them.

"Right, and them."

"How many vans left?"

"We'd done ninety-four when I talked to Claycamp this evening. The night shift is going to be real slow after what just happened. But they ought to make that one twenty or thirty by morning. Those tires are our best physical evidence. If we find the van, we find the Purse Snatcher. When we're down to ten, I'd say start in on the ones registered to females, maybe do the commercial ones."

"What about road blocks or checkpoints?"

Hess was positive that he had covered this angle, but it took him just a second to recall how. When he did, he felt more relieved than he should have.

"I did a radius plot from the abduction sites to the dump sites, tried to narrow down his home base. But it didn't tell me much. The Ortega screws up the parameters because it's the only way to get to where Jillson and Kane were. That means his point of departure could be anywhere this side of the mountains. What I'm saying is, we'd need checkpoints all over the county for a decent shot at intercepting that van."

"Brighton won't approve that kind of manpower. Not on one of my cases, he won't."

Hess suspected she was right, but said nothing. He could feel his blood boiling again.

"Say it, Hess, I don't care."

"He's prepared to see you fail," he answered.

"You going to help me do that? Or just submit the paperwork when it happens?"

"Neither, I hope."

"I'm just a goddamned woman, not the antichrist. I don't see what makes all you guys so afraid."

Hess looked out the window, felt his vision blurring.

"Well, what is it, Hess? How come we make you guys so afraid?"

"We're old."

"No, it's more than that. It's because we're women."

"We think you want to bottle our seed and kill us all."

She laughed. "Sounds good to me."

"Then there you have it."

"I wasn't serious. But, to be serious, why? Why would we want to do that?"

"Maybe that's what we'd do if we were you."

"No, you like our bodies too much. Just the pleasure of them."

"You're right. What we're afraid of is that you'd run the world in your favor if you could. I mean, we run it in ours."

"You're right, we would. I would, anyway."

"Well, Brighton knows that."

Merci was quiet for a long while then, and Hess was aware of her looking out the window toward Colesceau's apartment. A couple of new faces arrived by car for the vigil—a young couple with a cooler and an electric lantern. The CNB news crew shot video of the arriving couple, then turned their lenses toward 12 Meadowlark.

Hess watched as two of the protesters stood and walked off with their arms around each other. The guy carried his sign at his side, no audience for him now. A middle-aged couple with a conscience and an evening to kill, Hess thought. Probably protested the war in college for reasons similar. He could hear their voices in the warm night but not their words. It was nice to see that it wasn't all battlefield between human beings, that a man and a woman could choose to be together and make a go of it.

334

But his mind eddied back to the task at hand and the task lay in darker waters.

"I think he's saving them, customizing them. Their bodies. Because, like you said, there's pleasure in them. But he's afraid of the life inside them. He's afraid you're going to bottle his seed and kill him. That's why I thought Colesceau was a good bet, at first. The physical evidence? Wrong. The situation he lives in? Wrong, too. I know that. But I felt something I didn't understand, in there, with him. I wish I could know what it was. We're looking for a guy whose insides are a lot like Colesceau's. I mean, imagine what comes into his nightmares after he's injected with female hormone, once a week. Can you imagine what he dreams?"

"No. Can you?"

"I've tried. And it keeps coming back, *fury*."

"Keep talking."

"One, we know he translates rage into lust. He's probably done it all his life, or most of his life. He rapes. Two, rage equals erection equals blunt instrument that gives pleasure to him and pain to another."

"Okay."

"So when he gets caught and castrated, we're taking away his expression of those things—rage and lust. But we're not taking away the basic feelings themselves. Rage now equals no erection, no blunt instrument, no pleasure to himself, no pain to another."

He watched her consider. "He needs new ways to express."

"I assumed so at first. But what if he just wants the old ways back? And he can't have them right now. All

335

he can have now is something . . . ready. So, why not just kill them and keep them for the day when he's ready to express the lust again?"

"Okay. It makes sense." Hess caught an odd tone in her voice, like she was trying to hurry him past this part of things.

"Now, in those pictures, the back of Colesceau's head doesn't convince me," he said. "I want Gilliam to enhance them for us. And I think we should bring him in and hit him hard. Tell him it's *his* print on the fuse. Line the purses up right where he can see them. Tell him we've got a witness. Really get inside his head and throw knives."

She was quiet again, then her voice seemed to come from far away, soft but urgent.

She held his sleeve, and what she said surprised him. "Tim, it isn't *him*. We've got photographs of him watching TV when it happened. We've got dozens of witnesses. We've got videotape. He can't get out of there without the world knowing it. You know? Tim? *It . . . isn't . . . him.*"

She looked at him and he saw the disappointment in her face. He also saw some of the devastation that had filled her expression as she pumped away on the deceased young Jerry Kirby. But this was different. Back in the garage in El Modena there was outrage and fury in her, too. Now, the outrage and fury were gone. And in their place was a sympathy that Hess found intolerable because he knew he was the target. She turned away and looked out the window toward the crowd. Hess could see her eyes in profile, focused down toward the steering wheel.

He knew that someday his reason would leave him and he had hoped it wouldn't get someone killed. He always knew it was going to feel bad. He had imagined looking foolish and old and useless and spent in front of his partner and himself. But he would manage this because it would mean one part of his life was over and he could feel good about that. It would just mean he was too old, was all. He had imagined that this would be the day he'd turn in his badge and gun, head out to the acreage in Idaho or Oregon with his wife, start fishing, let the grandkids visit and stay as long as they wanted. Yes, he had told himself, he was going to feel okay about it all when he finally slowed down.

But that moment was here right now, and what he felt was shame. He was thankful for the darkness that hid his face from her.

"Okay, blow up the pictures, Tim. But wait on the interrogation. That's a half-day setup and a half day of bracing him and I don't want to spend that kind of time right now. I got the art people to meet with Kamala Petersen today so they could colorize the sketch. Let's hope it came out well. We'll hit the county with it tomorrow, plaster it everywhere there's a space, shove it into every face at every mall he's struck and every one he hasn't. We'll say our prayers tonight that Bart Young's list will hit a match for us. Or the tire-kickers find a mismatched set of tires on a silver panel van and don't lose another kid's life."

"Okay. Solid."

She set a hand on his shoulder. "Help me find him, Hess. I need you to help me find him."

337

"I'm doing everything I can."

"I know you are."

Colesceau came to his porch. Hess watched him, bathed in the yellow bug light to his right, looking passively out at the crowd of six. He was wearing a green robe and a pair of white socks, and he held a tray of steaming mugs in front of him.

The protesters got to their feet and the signs came up. The CNB shooter moved in.

"We ought to pop him just for being such a dweeb," said Merci. "What's he got, hot chocolate?"

Hess watched as Colesceau walked toward his tormentors, set the tray down before them, then straightened and looked at them. He looked over their heads toward Merci's car but Hess saw no recognition in the dark. The cameraman stayed low and tight for a good shot of his subject.

Colesceau spoke with his neighbors but Hess couldn't hear a word of it. Then the small dark-haired man gave the crowd a little bow and walked slowly back into his apartment.

A while later the downstairs lights went off and an upstairs light went on. Hess could see through the half-drawn curtain upstairs the faintest of figures, the shadow of a shadow, moving on the ceiling. For a brief second someone looked out.

Then the upstairs window darkened and the living room blinds were illuminated again by the blue light of a TV screen.

"He watches TV all the goddamn time," said Merci. "What a life. Hess, don't do what I think you're going to do."

But he pushed out the door and plodded across the street to the living room window. The evening had cooled and there was a faint smell of citrus and smog in the air. His legs felt wrong. For Jerry Kirby, he thought.

He looked through a crack in the blinds and saw what Rick Hjorth's camera had seen the night before. Colesceau was slumped down in the couch, his back to Hess, just his head visible, tuned into CNB's "Rape Watch: Irvine," which showed a live shot of the front of Colesceau's apartment, a real-time clock running in the lower right corner and Hess at the window.

He watched Colesceau turn just a little and look over his shoulder, then again to the TV. On his way back Hess waved to the camera then stopped at the little crowd and asked them what Colesceau had said to them.

"He said, tell Tim and Merci they can have some hot cider, too. There it is, if that's who you are."

33

Eight minutes later Big Bill Wayne backed the silver van out of the garage and accelerated crisply down the street. He was breathing fast and perspiring heavily. This was a record time for getting out. What a help, to watch the cops come and go at Colesceau's, live on TV!

He drove steadily and within the speed limit. He hit the serene darkness of the Ortega and followed the moonlit highway through the hills. He thought of his favorite poem. *The road was a ribbon of moonlight over the purple moor/and the highwayman came riding, riding, riding/The highwayman came riding/Up to the old inn door.*

He found LaLonde's place. It was what you'd expect for an ex-con inventor with no job—a commercial space, rented cheap. Someone began raising the door after three knocks. Up it went, like it was letting him into a castle. Except the door was blue steel and Lee LaLonde was no nobleman. Bill stood there in his black suit and western tie and his golden hair, with Pandora's Box in his shopping bag, sniffing the inside of LaLonde's cave for danger or opportunity.

"Hi, Bill," said Lee LaLonde.

"Fix this, partner."

The toothy young man nodded and smiled. Bill could tell he'd been asleep. So he swept in without an invitation, turned on his boot heels and stared at LaLonde.

"It failed. I figured you'd know why."

"Okay, sure. Wanna beer or something?"

"Nope. I'm in a hurry."

"Not a problem. I'll check it out."

Bill gave the kid the bag and watched him go to one of his workbenches. LaLonde pulled the string and an overhead fluorescent light flickered on.

"You can sit down if you want. I wondered if I'd see you again. How's it hanging?"

"How's what hanging?"

Bill didn't like the furtive look that LaLonde gave him, or the seemingly genial talk. He didn't feel like sitting on LaLonde's couch.

He snapped on a pair of latex gloves and toured the place: meaningless inventions, organized tools, posters of girls. Beautiful women, made in America. Before him was a shoebox of identical metal rings, ten of them, maybe, big enough to fit around the wrist of a small woman. From each ring protruded a thin arm. Each arm widened into a flat, thin, shiny leaf of metal about the size of a quarter. They looked to Bill like they could be used for scooping something out of something else.

"What are these?" Bill demanded, slapping the back of the box with his hand.

"Flashlight Friends."

"For what?"

"You put the ring around the end of your flashlight and adjust the deflector end into the beam. It sends some of the light to your feet. That's if you're aiming

341

the light straight ahead, I mean. So you can see where you're walking but see what you're looking at, too."

"Shoots the light to your feet while you walk in the dark?"

"Uh-huh."

"Do they work?"

"Not really. I don't think you can divide light that way. Or not enough of it, maybe. The second beam's too weak. But, you know, three bucks is all I wanted."

Bill liked the idea. Some of the things he'd seen at LaLonde's table at the Lake Elsinore Marina swap meet had been better, though. And, of course, the electronic alarm override he'd commissioned was the best thing he could imagine, short of a device you could turn on a person to make them just do whatever you said from then out. Like a gun, but unthreatening and legal. Something small and secret, they couldn't even see. Maybe someday.

But on to more practical matters, Bill wondered if LaLonde could devise some kind of display stand for his driver's license collection. Something to show them off. Something expandable.

"What's this?"

It was two pieces of plastic about the size of counter tiles, connected at right angles. One side was backed by a large suction cup. From the bottom extended a three-foot tube that ended in some kind of coupling, from the other a short nozzle of some kind.

"It didn't work, either."

"I asked what it is, partner."

"The Shower Power Coffee Caddie. It's a coffee warmer for the shower. You know, for those cold mornings when you want to take a shower but you want your coffee, too? The suction holds it to the shower wall. Put your cup on the plate. That hose takes water from the hot water pipe and circulates it through coils. The cooler water comes out the nozzle to make more room for more hot."

Bill set the Coffee Caddie back on the bench.

"What's the problem with that device of mine?"

"I'm looking, I'm looking."

Bill could hear LaLonde tinkering at the bench. He viewed the tools and projects on the other benches, glanced at the kitchenette/sitting area, looked into the bathroom. There was a Formica table near the refrigerator. On it were cardboard salt and pepper shakers, some magazines about inventing and a letter holder made of wire that displayed the envelopes upright and in fanned layers, like the tail of a peacock. The tail pivoted on its base. Bill spun it once, then again. No squeak. The little bastard did good work when he wanted to. A tan-colored business card with black writing and a gold badge toppled out when he spun the holder again.

Orange County Sheriff-Coroner Department
Sergeant Merci Rayborn
Homicide Detail

Bill turned over the card and smiled to himself: her home phone, written in a woman's slanting print. He slid it into the pocket of his duster. When, he wondered. When had they been here, and how did they know?

"What's the problem?" he asked.

343

"It's just the fuse. I'm putting in a new one and it should work."

Bill wondered where the old one had fallen out. The device had quit working after Janet, and La-Londe's prints might be on the fuse. If it had fallen out near her car . . .

"There," said LaLonde.

Bill looked over at him: dumb smile, hair all funny from being asleep, his jeans falling off his slender hips and bunching up over his boots.

"Yeah, see, the circuit's fixed now and the charge is running. I'll put in a couple of new nine volts to top it off."

So merry, thought Bill. Guilty. Watch his face now. "When did you talk to Sergeant Rayborn?"

"Who's that?"

"The dark-haired police gal who was here, partner."

A heavy burned smell wafted through the shop.

"Oh, *her*. Couple of weeks back—they were asking questions about this guy in the slam with me. They think he's heisting again, thought I might know about him. I don't. Wouldn't tell those pigs anything if I did."

"Of course. And the older man, Hess? Was he here, too?"

"Old fart? Yeah. Hey, this thing's working now. Looking good, Bill."

"Demonstrate."

"Well, I can't, unless your car has an electronic alarm."

"No alarm."

"Mine neither, piece of junk. This is fixed. It was

344

just the fuse. It must have fallen out somehow. I soldered a piece of wire to hold it in."

LaLonde held out the little box. Bill walked over and took it, examining the new fuse and the soldered restraint. The solder gun lay on the bench with its tip over a tin ashtray, smoke wobbling upward toward the light.

Bill picked it up. "Smells like burning bones."

"I wouldn't know about that, Bill."

"I burned a woman once, but she was already dead."

"Jesus. I've wanted to a few times. You know, get real mad at one or something."

"I'll need two extra fuses."

LaLonde nodded and picked out a plastic box from the bench top. He rummaged through its compartments, chose a tin of fuses and offered it.

"Thank you. Here is payment for what you've done."

Bill felt in his pocket.

"You really don't—"

Bill pulled out the derringer and blasted the inventor in the forehead with it. LaLonde hit the floor like someone had yanked it from under him. He was jerking and the blood pouring out of his head was deep red on the concrete. Bill shot him in the nose.

Bill mused on how some people would worry about doing something like this, whether it was right or wrong.

Then the traitor went stiff, the orgasm of his life, thought Bill.

345

He got $32 out of LaLonde's wallet, then threw the worn-out canvas thing on the floor.

Fifty-five minutes later Colesceau came downstairs in the blue TV darkness to watch some more CNB.

The station was running old news of the day because it wasn't prosperous enough to program fresh news all the time. Hence "Rape Watch: Irvine" and Colesceau's continuing torment at the hands of the video shooters and Lauren Diamond.

He went to the door and opened it. There they were, the after-ten crowd: two couples sitting on lawn chairs in a semicircle facing his front door. They were playing cards. One couple was dressed for tennis. The guy had a towel around his neck. The hot cider looked untouched. The video shooter heaved himself out of the CNB van and came his way with the camera down, not shooting, and a cigarette in his mouth. Colesceau had overheard his name, Mark, and rather liked his sloppy look and sleeplessness.

"Well, Mark, our law enforcement people didn't want the cider."

"Guess not," said Mark, fiddling with his microphone. "They left about half hour ago."

"Hmmm."

He padded across the porch and lawn in his robe and white socks, bent over and collected his tray.

The protesters stared at him, cards still in their hands. Tennis man stood up.

"Don't you ever go to sleep, shitface?"

"I'm about to."

346

"You can dream about all the old persons you molested."

"I raped them, actually. And I've never dreamed of them, not once."

"You're disgusting," said Miss Tennis.

"You ever give me half a chance," said Tennis Man, "I'll beat the living shit out of you."

"I know you would. Give my regards, please, to the reasonable and decent Trudy Powers."

"She thinks you're a bag of shit."

Colesceau sighed. He glanced at Mark, who was right up close by now, gunning away, then back to the Tennis Couple.

"I have paid my debt and I am rehabilitated. Harmless. So why are you so frightened?"

"If it was up to me I'd just cut them off."

"Why? To make earrings for your wife?"

Words of disgust, then, from all of them, and Mark in close.

He headed back inside. On his porch he turned, balanced the tray with one hand and waved.

347

34

Merci pulled up beside Hess's car in the medical center parking lot. The sedan had collected dew in the cooling night and some comet-shaped leaves from a eucalyptus. She thought, what a lousy place to have to visit after working your ass off all day. And all night. Hess hadn't said much since the shooting. She knew he was embarrassed for the Colesceau idea. Or maybe just pissed off, because she wouldn't buy in. But it wasn't the smart way to go and she knew it. She'd thought it through.

More to the point, Jerry Kirby's death had spread through her spirits, spread through the night like an infection. She knew it had contaminated Hess too.

"I'm only about twenty minutes from here," she said. "Come over and eat?"

"It's almost eleven."

"I know what time it is."

"I'd like that, then."

"It's in the middle of an orange grove. Follow me."

She waited while Hess got out and into his car. He looked uncertain opening the door, as if he didn't know how much strength it might take and he used a little too much.

At home she opened the windows and turned on the TV and made two Scotch and sodas. She'd bought a big bottle of each because she'd enjoyed it that night at the beach with him. She changed out of her bloody pants and showered. She listened to the messages— Mike McNally, *again*, hoping she hadn't "busted a gut" in the gym. Then the Bianchi rep saying they'd shipped the holster Federal Airborne, their compliments, no obligation whatsoever, hoped she'd use it. They'd sent it to her home because the offer was, again, only for "select law enforcement individuals."

"Select, my ass," she muttered. "Just send it."

Then she searched her cupboards for something to heat up—it was either beef stew or noodles in a Styrofoam cup so she went with the stew. There were some crackers that weren't quite stale. She tried to arrange them artfully on a fancy serving plate but they kept sliding down to the middle. There were always oranges, so she cut up two fat ones. Just two gulps of that drink and it went to her head.

Hess was watching CNB when she brought the plate in. She could smell the orange groves like they were growing through the screens. Hess looked at her, a cat on one of his thighs and another with its head on his lap. She shooed them away and put the plate on the coffee table. The cat on Hess's leg was standing up but not gone, tail jumping defiantly, so Merci held an orange hunk out and shot it in the face with the juice. The cat fled.

"It's okay," Hess said.

"Vermin."

"Why do you have so many, then?"

"I like them."

They ate some crackers and oranges. They clinked

349

their glasses together and drank but neither made a toast. There wasn't anything to say if you were thinking about what happened to Jerry Kirby and there was nothing else to think about. She could see him, youthful and dead on the concrete. Merci called upon her inner power to banish thoughts of it from her mind right now. And the thoughts obeyed, hovering outside her mind, though she knew they'd have to get back in sometime.

There hadn't been many times in her life that she had applied all of her considerable will to the task at hand and come up empty. Jerry Kirby was one of them, and it made Merci doubt herself, made her wonder if she wasn't as strong as she believed. She'd done everything in her power to make him live and he had died. What was important now was to put it out of her mind so she could come back to it fresh, maybe see what she'd done wrong, how to do it right the next time.

So she sipped the drink and let the alcohol lead her away.

"It's either canned stew or Styro noodles."

"I like stew. It reminds me of hunting trips to Idaho. Look, Colesceau again."

"The TV makes him look bigger."

She watched him on his ten-fifteen appearance, padding around in his socks and robe, collecting the tray, talking to the tennis people. She took another couple of sips of her cocktail. When Colesceau suggested his testicles might make good earrings for Tennis Man's wife, Merci scoffed, "I'd like to see those."

Hess said nothing.

Then the CNB anchor said they'd be back in just a moment, with traffic, weather and the breaking story of a murder in nearby Lake Elsinore.

"Maybe the Purse Snatcher killed LaLonde because his device broke down," said Hess.

It surprised her, that Hess would make a jump like that, so quick, no reason at all for it.

Then Merci realized that if by some stretch of the imagination the Purse Snatcher *had* killed LaLonde, it well might have happened while they were sitting there outside Colesceau's apartment an hour or so ago. Or maybe just after they'd left. Either way, CNB had Colesceau, on video, *at home*, not in Lake Elsinore.

Maybe Hess would believe his own eyes, since he wouldn't believe her.

And then it came. Just like Hess had willed it to. Just like he'd seen the picture before it got to the screen.

She sat there with a buzz of excitement running along with the Scotch as the CNB anchor reported the murder of "amateur inventor and convicted car thief" Lee LaLonde in his Lake Elsinore workshop. He was apparently killed by an unidentified intruder "earlier tonight." Riverside Sheriffs said robbery was apparently the motive.

Merci looked at the video footage of the shop, its door open and crime scene tape flapping, the deputies trying to do their jobs.

Hess was already on the phone. He left a message and her number, clicked off and put the handset on the arm of the couch beside him. Then he pulled the small notepad from his pocket, flipped through and wrote something.

The phone rang less than a minute later and Hess, to her irritation, answered it. He listened for a moment, asked what time, listened again. He thanked someone and clicked off without saying good-bye.

"Nine, nine-thirty. Some other tenants saw the door halfway up, then the body. Gunshot to the head. They're saying botched robbery."

"Well, it wasn't our man Colesceau."

"No, it wasn't."

He looked at her and she could see the exhaustion and indecision in his eyes. He sat forward with effort, then stood. "We might be able to help, out there."

"Riverside Sheriffs don't need us tonight, Hess."

"I know. But we could just . . ."

"Yeah, I know, too."

She put her hand on his chest, lightly, and eased him back down to the couch. He didn't resist, which she found sad and exciting.

They ate in near silence in front of the TV. Merci flipped to a sit-com rerun, one of those that bred so many future stars. Fun to see them with long hair. Hess didn't seem to be looking at it, but he didn't look at her, either. Most of the time he seemed to be staring out the dark open windows of the house. He kept his sport coat on, even though the night was warm.

She wondered if old people took tragedy harder—things like Ronnie Stevens or Jerry Kirby, things like being wrong about the suspect in an investigation.

She continued to will Jerry Kirby out of her mind. And she willed Hess to feel better. She wondered if he was just sickened by what had gone down and had run out of things to say.

After dinner they walked the orange grove around the house. It was Merci's idea to lift Hess's spirits. She got fresh drinks and a couple of big flashlights they didn't really need in the moonlight. She wanted Hess to smell an orange grove from the inside. And she wanted him to see something.

Now she stood astride a soft chocolate furrow and heard herself telling Hess to take a deep breath, a *deeeep* breath and see if he could feel the oranges going inside him.

"No, not exactly."

"Try again."

And he did, taking a long deep breath that made her wonder how much of his lung was gone—had he said half or two-thirds?—then she banished *that* thought from her mind too because it didn't fit what she was trying to accomplish with regard to smells, oranges, being inside of things and improving the spirits of Hess.

"They'll take up root inside you," she said.

"I used to imagine that about ocean water. If it made you part ocean inside. Because sweat is salty."

"That's exactly what I wanted you to realize." It really was exciting to educate an older person, if only a little.

"Mission accomplished, then."

They came to one side of the grove, where it ended

353

at a culvert. Merci could see the outline of the irrigation gate against the weeds. Past the culvert was a flood control channel lined with concrete. Overhead the moon was smudged by clouds. And just beyond the channel rose the tan stucco townhomes of some recent development, their backsides tall and flat and almost windowless. They reminded her of stuck-up people at a party, huddled together, looking away. When she came out of the trees the buildings always surprised her, how tall they were and unexpected, even when you knew they were coming.

"It's like they can't look at the grove behind them," Merci said. "Because they're too good."

"The developers?"

"No, the buildings. Hardly any windows, like they don't want to see. But that would go for developers, too, right? Not wanting to look behind, like at history and stuff."

"Why look backward, when you're driving to the bank?"

"All's they do is pack in more people."

"I never had much problem with that. People need places to live. I think if people don't like it they should just leave."

"Why not preserve some things? I never thought of that until I moved in here. And I only moved here because Dad knows the owner and the rent's cheap. But some stuff, you just ought to save. Hess, check *this.*"

She led the way down the side of the culvert, shining her flashlight back every few steps to make sure he didn't stumble. Then she cut diagonally across the grove, aiming toward the back of her house. The ice in her Scotch glass clinked and she heard Hess's clink behind her and she drank more. Her ears felt warm but her lips tingled and there was a cool patch on her forehead.

"Okay back there?"

"Just plodding along."

Approaching the last three rows Merci could see the back end of her house, the driveway that curved all the way around it, the ring of porch light active with cats, and the rat-happy garage dark against the trees.

She came out of the grove and started across the overgrown back lawn. The toes of her tennis shoes got damp. Hess had fallen back a few steps so she waited for him to catch up. When he did she heard the sharpness of his breathing and wondered if the chemo and radiation were getting it all. She banished that thought from her mind immediately. She rebanished Jerry Kirby from her mind, too. She felt strong again, in control. Probably the Scotch, she thought. So she turned and shined the flashlight at Hess's chin—not quite into his eyes—laughed, and turned it off.

"Funny," he said.

"*Had* to."

"What's the big attraction?"

"Over here."

Behind the garage was a bare quarter acre of land that Merci had decided was once a vegetable garden. She had made the discovery digging there, trying to save money when the septic tank needed pumping. She was actually trying to sweat out a ferocious anger at Mike McNally and his diabolical little son for letting themselves in, eating her food, leaving the dishes unrinsed and letting the bloodhounds shit tremendously upon the lawn. For about the hundredth time.

She thought the digging might help. According to the owner's drawing the tank lay about twenty yards south of the garage. The drawing was off by ten feet at least because she never did find the tank, or even a leach line. But the soil was soft and her anger diminished as her blisters grew. And she found what she found, proving to Merci that a will to locate the known could result in discovering the unknown. Her mother would call it serendipity, but she also called a vase a *vawz*.

She shined her light down through the dead tumbleweeds, saw the plywood. She'd secured the plywood with scrap cinder block, and tied the tumbleweeds to the wood with dental floss. The last thing she wanted was neighborhood kids or dogs into her discovery, or some eggheads from the university.

Hess was standing beside her now. She could hear the short precision of his breathing. He looked slightly forlorn as he stood there in his sport coat with his general's haircut and stared down into the beam of his flashlight. But there was a good shine to his eyes when he looked at her.

"Nice tumbleweeds," he said.

"Check it out."

She set down her glass and flashlight and carried off the cinder blocks with both hands. The edges were sharp and dug into her fingers. She got under the plywood and slid it away. She pulled out the wadded newspapers.

Then she stood and aimed her light in.

"Meet Francisco. He's real."

He looked the same as last time, she thought, which was probably the same as he'd looked for about four centuries. The rusted, upswept horn of his conquistador helmet protruded out from the recessed skull like the prow of a ship. The bones were brown and, to Merci, disturbingly small. The skull still had some skin attached, which was black and thin as paper. The beauty of him was the way his old brown bones were still encased in the armor—the helmet and chest plate and belt buckle. He seemed to her a tiny man caught in the hard, oversized diapers of history. His sword with its deeply eroded blade lay to his side. It was the only part of him or his gear that didn't seem small. In fact, it was gigantic compared to the frail, chest-crossed hands that had once wielded it.

"Is he cool or what?"

Hess was leaning forward at the waist, looking in, the light held out in front of him.

"I think he could have been some kind of law enforcement, but they took his harquebus because it was valuable."

"No badge."

"Maybe it rusted away."

"Hmmm."

"But he was probably just a soldier. Either way, four hundred years ago he came about halfway around the world and died right here in my back-yard."

She looked down at the small brown bones and pitted armature, feeling what she always felt when

357

she looked at Francisco: that he was here on a mission far more perilous and important than any she would undertake, that there were many more important moments per year back then than there were now, that people had more courage. And they didn't live very long, either.

Hess continued to stare in. "He looks awful . . . alone down there."

"Not so alone, since I found him."

"Well, whatever, Merci. He looks goddamned alone to me. Have you told anyone?"

"Who? *Who* are you going to trust with him? A scientist would take him. The health department would take him. A relative would probably say leave him right where he is, but where's a relative?"

Hess had brought his hand to his face but was still looking down, thinking.

"I like everything about him," said Merci. "Look at that helmet. And his hands, the way they fold over his ribs. And look at the way those ribs connect up around the back. I never knew the rib cage was so graceful. Plus, his teeth? Look how big and sharp they are, like he was used to eating wild animals."

"Out here he probably did."

"And check the belt buckle. I mean, that must have been one big belt he wore. I wish he had some boots on, but I'll bet you he died with new ones and they took those along with the gun."

"You've given this some thought."

Merci didn't answer for a long time. She just looked down at Francisco and tried to let her mind retreat through the centuries. The things about him that

358

really bugged her were height and weight, what color his hair and eyes had been, if he'd had a beard or not—the kind of stuff you'd need for a solid suspect description. Sometimes she wished she could think different than a cop, just once in a while.

"You find a conquistador in your backyard and you'd think about him, too."

35

Back inside she turned on the TV and went to make new drinks. Standing against the yellow tile of the kitchen counter Merci got hit hard again by Jerry Kirby. Then the word *six*. She couldn't stop the thoughts. Her pants were in the hamper in the bedroom, drenched in his blood. She could smell it and feel it warm on her forearms. She tried to think of something humorous or diverting but all she could think was *if you're so goddamned powerful why couldn't you make him live?* The kitchen clock said midnight and she felt worse. She snuck a gulp of the Scotch and forced it down. Bad stuff—it made your feelings big and blurry, with ledges in them you didn't see. Easy to fall off one.

She sat across the sofa from Hess and tried to let the smell of the orange grove inhabit her. It didn't.

She watched him looking at the TV, saw the way the blue light played on his face, then realized he wasn't right. His skin was pale from more than just the cathode rays. His eyes were closed but the lids quivered like he was trying to open them from a dream.

"Hess?"

"Yes."

"What's happening?"

"Something. It feels like the world's tilting back and I'm gonna slide off."

In fact he was gripping the arm of the sofa with one hand, the other was raised off the seat, ready. Like he was going to have to catch himself. His whole body shook once, then started to tremble. His face had gone white.

"I think I'm just tired."

His voice wasn't right, either, like the cords making the words were freezing up.

"Don't move. It's more than just tired."

She went over and knelt in front of him. She could see his eyes moving behind the closed lids and the odd look of anticipation on his face.

"Open your eyes," she said.

He did, and Merci could see the confusion in them. But it only lasted a moment. She watched as he returned to inhabit them again.

"Breathe deeply. Slow."

He took a deep breath. Then another.

"Count these."

She held up three fingers and he said three.

"Whoa. Strange," he added. His head tilted back, then corrected, like a kid nodding off.

"What do you feel, right now?"

"Like a big hand held me back. Kept me from falling. Whoa. There."

"Continue to breathe. All right, Tim."

Merci realized that she had her hands open on Hess's legs and she moved them to the couch. But she stayed on her knees in front of him, studying the details of his face. Not right, she thought: not yet.

"I have a can of chicken soup."

"No. I'm just going to sit a minute. I'm fine."

But the color still wasn't back in his face. He looked pale and silver, like someone caught by a flash strobe. He was breathing fast and slumped within the sport coat, both arms down. She could smell his breath and it didn't smell like cancer or chemo or rads to her, but like an old man's—human, alive, a little meaty.

"Here," she said. "Take off that coat."

He leaned forward as if to take off the coat but neither of his arms moved. So Merci leaned into him and took a cuff while Hess withdrew one arm, then the other. She felt the heat of him as she set the coat aside and placed her open hands on his shoulders. He seemed heavy and hard as wood.

"Sit back, now."

"Oh, boy."

"Look, Tim—your color's coming back."

"Tell me about it."

"First white, then silver, now kind of peach colored, with pink on the cheeks. No more sweat on the forehead. And the pupils of your eyes are the right size again. How are you seeing?"

"Good now. I'm fine, Merci. Really."

"Be still. I'm going to loosen your tie some more."

Not being familiar with the half-Windsor, she succeeded in doing little but yanking Hess's head forward. Power, she thought: *will*.

"One side slides," he said. "My left. Your right."

"Got it."

She slid the silk down the silk. Hess fumbled with

his top button, but Merci got it open. His big hands felt leathery as she brushed them out of the way.

She set her hands on Hess's cheeks and let her fingers rest against his skin. *I want to make you well.* A low but strong current issued up into her wrists and arms. At first she thought the energy was coming from him—all his years and experience and strength —but when she moved her hands off him they were still buzzing and she understood it was all coming from inside herself.

Power.

"I want to touch your hair."

She was surprised to hear herself say it, but once it was out it was okay. God knows, she'd wanted to do it for long enough.

"Why in the world?"

"I don't know. I always thought you had the nicest hair. And I've wanted to touch it."

"My head always feels hot. I think it's . . . I don't know what it is."

"I'll scratch it."

"Well, okay."

She set the tips of all her fingers gently on his forehead and told him to close his eyes. She ran her hands together along the top of his head, then, rising on her knees and pulling him just a little closer, continued down the back to where the hair ended at his strong warm neck.

It was pure contradiction, as she suspected it would be. Soft but thick. Firm but pliable. Bristly but smooth. She had never been able to imagine its actual texture.

"Hess, that's just absolutely wonderful stuff."

"Thanks."

"I'm going to do it again like that, then start scratching."

So she combed her fingers back through his brush of hair, then she did it again, pausing to touch the white wave in front with her index finger.

What a delight.

She realized the wave was the softest of all his hair, rather than the stiffest, which was what she had predicted. She realized the color of it actually started on the top of his head, behind the crest, so to speak, appearing like spots of ocean suds then condensing gradually toward the peak.

More importantly, she realized that the white wave, and the rest of Hess's hair, was now reacting strangely and sticking to her fingers.

But just a few unruly hairs, she told herself, the kind that might expire when a fellow deputy falls in the line of duty. So she ran her fingers along his head again just to make sure everything was okay now. More hairs jumped off.

A lot more.

She couldn't believe it. She watched Hess's hair abandon his scalp, then climb onto her fingers like it was being rescued.

"That does feel good," he said.

So she ran her hands through again while she wondered what to do and the forest of hair thinned and clung statically to her fingers and began to sprinkle down on Hess's ears and shirt front and shoulders and bunch up on the backs of her hands like the little nests that ended up on her smock at her hairdresser's.

No, she thought. *If I summon my will the hair will not fall out.* And Merci summoned her will, all the deep power of it, all the blinding light of it and she closed her eyes and focused its beam directly at Hess's head.

"Ummm."

And she pressed her nails in a little deeper, applied a little more strength. Went a little faster, because she knew when she opened her eyes the hair would not be falling out. But it was. And Hess, eyes still closed, was groaning like a dog. Merci looked at him and smiled, as if her smile might mitigate his disappointment when he realized what was happening. She rose up and leaned into him a little more because Hess in his relaxation had melted back into the sofa. She rested lightly against him, feeling the great weight of failure in her heart beating against the particular hardness of Lieutenant Timothy Hess. She was too surprised to move away. She didn't. And a moment later, when her surprise was gone, she didn't want to.

This, she understood, was something that her will could *not* fail. She could take him, all of him, all his years and his exhaustion and his disease, all his desire and his dreams, and she could accommodate them. She could absorb and absolve. She could take in and transform. She could will the death right out, and the life right into him.

Power.

"Merci."

"Keep your eyes closed."

"It's falling out, isn't it?"

"Yeah."

365

She reached over and turned off the lamp.

"Come on," she said. "Follow me."

At four in the morning Hess awoke to the sound of cats screeching somewhere out in the grove. Merci breathed deeply and didn't move.

He lay still and remembered: fishing with his uncles, his dad making pancakes on Sunday mornings, the creases on the back of his mother's blouse as she walked, Barbara's expression as she came down the aisle in the church where they were married, his first dog, what the world looked like from the tail gunner's position of a B-29 thirty thousand feet above Korea. He had no idea why he thought of these particular things. It felt like they were lining themselves up for his inspection. *This is what we were.*

Eight more years, he thought. *Seventy-five years.*

He set a hand on Merci's back. He thought of standing in front of her bathroom mirror a few hours ago, looking at his new head. He remembered her hands kneading his scalp and the hair falling lightly onto his face, and later, the shower they took together when she shampooed it away by the handful.

It was a strange moment as he stood there, naked and still wet, newly bald and thoroughly exhausted, with Merci naked herself under a towel, this large and quite lovely woman who had just made love to him, dark moles on creamy skin, the strands of black wet hair on her shoulders, crowded right up close in the steamy little bathroom to look in the mirror with him. She had actually smiled. He had felt the heat of her on his skin, through the towel. They had shaved off the remnants. Eyebrows gone, too. He looked like a giant baby.

Hair or not, it seemed too good a thing for him to be here now, still alive in the world, still touching and touched by it all. And he was thankful for it in a way he could not express.

He got up and walked through the warm old house, looking through the windows to the dark groves and the moonless sky littered with stars. The floorboards creaked under his feet and a clock ticked echoes across the living room at him.

He sat for a while and wondered how he could use the rest of his life in the best way possible. He had no specific ideas, but the general concept of using his years to live well was a good place to start. It was certainly a new concept, that much was for certain. *Use the years to live well.*

He made coffee and took a cup back to the bedroom. He stood beside the bed and looked down at Merci Rayborn as she slept. Her hair was tangled with shadows and her face was pale as cream against the darkness. He saw the rise of her hip under the sheet, the way her fists came together at her chin. He wondered what might have happened if he could have met her forty years ago.

In the kitchen he turned on the light over the stove, got out his blue notepad and pen and wrote Merci a letter about what he was feeling at four-thirty in the morning in her house in the orange grove. Hess considered himself a clear but dull writer, and as he composed the letter to her he read it quietly to himself. It was clear and dull. That was okay, he thought: the purpose wasn't to entertain or divert. The purpose was just to tell her how much she meant to him and how she had inspired him enough to write her about it. It came off sounding like a thank-you card, but he was thankful. So what?

Dear Merci,
I wish we'd have met when we were both young.
But you weren't born then and I would probably have
been too witless to do you right anyway. I feel happy
now and blessed by the years, by circumstance and
by you.

Sincerely,
Tim H.

He left it on the kitchen table with one of the snapshots Hjorth had taken of them together, to use up his roll of film. The picture caught Hess attentive and Merci scowling at the camera. A few minutes later he was dressed and looking down at her again. Her face was lost in hair and pillow and she was snoring lightly, the sheet halfway down her back.

He locked the door on his way out and walked across the driveway toward his car. Cats scattered in fractional starlight. Sunrise was still an hour away and Hess wondered why it always seemed darkest just before dawn.

36

Colesceau parked outside the old Santa Ana Court-house. You could park two hours for free, and he liked the imposing old building with its heavy stone archi-tecture because it reminded him of torture and exe-cutions. It was early Wedneday afternoon and the smoggy heat hung over the county like the mist along the Olt. Thick enough to hide your thoughts in, Colesceau thought, but not quite thick enough to hide your body.

Too bad about that, he thought, seeing them from a block away. They were gathered outside the entrance to the Parole Board building with their cameras and cables and lights and vans. The pushy, preening re-porters. The shooters. The techs. The Grant Majors of the universe. And more folkish demonstrators with their signs and placards and candles. Lots of them. Some of them were from his neighborhood, some were new converts. He looked for Trudy Powers but couldn't find her.

You can't even serve out your sentence without a TV show about it, he thought. America really is crazy.

He sidled down a busy side street and found a pay phone behind the old courthouse, called the Sheriffs and asked for Merci Rayborn. She answered. He used his American accent to introduce himself as John Marshall over at Federal Airborne in Santa Ana with a package for her they couldn't deliver. Similar to the accent he gave to the Bianchi promotions fellow, but a bit of a Texas twang to it.

"Parcel got damp back east, address smudged up in transit," he explained. "Your phone numbers were still on the sticker."

"Who the hell's it from?"

"Let's see here . . . Bianchi International in—"

"—What's your number there?"

He heard the rudeness in her voice, the reflexive caution, the automatic defense.

He sighed and read her the number off the phone. "You're going to need the parcel number."

He gave it to her and she hung up. Thirty seconds later she called.

"Federal Airborne, Marshall."

"Merci Rayborn again."

"What do you want us to do with this—"

She interrupted and gave him her home address, hung up.

Colesceau smiled, slid the pen back into his pocket, firmed his clip-on necktie around his neck and tried to put some resolve into his step. In the glass of a building front he saw himself: dark Kmart slacks, short-sleeve white shirt, plump and unremarkable body. He looked hunched and harried. He carried a brown paper grocery bag in his right hand and a vinyl briefcase in his left. The bag had gifts for Holtz and Carla Fontana, and the briefcase just a few pencils and paper clips. He brought it because it made him feel as if he had something meaningful in reserve.

They spotted him crossing the street and they bristled with readiness. He was barely onto the sidewalk when they were upon him, the reporters with their mikes brandished and their questions popping, the shooters gunning him in silence, the protesters yapping at him like toy breed dogs you could impale beautifully on a hat pin.

He stopped and looked at them and tried to compose himself.

How does it feel to be taking your last injection?

"I am pleased. It is an unhappy experience."

How long until the effects of this last injection wear off?

"I'm told it will be months. It will take my body many months to recover its former health." And when it does, he thought, I'd like to pay a call to every last one of you . . .

Where are you going to live next?

"Somewhere I can be forgotten."

Will you date women?

"I have no desire for the company of human beings."

What about employment—what kind of work will you be looking for?

"I would be good as a lighthouse watchman, but there aren't any lighthouses left."

What will you do when your sexual desire returns? Will you turn violent toward older women again?

"I have not had sexual or violent thoughts for many years. I never intended violence, even as a confused young man. I will never harm another person as long as I live. This is both a fact and a promise to all of you."

Al Holtz barged outside, waving his arms and shouting as he ushered Colesceau through the throng and into the building. "Sonsofbitches have no respect at all," he said as soon as they got through the door. He clapped a heavy hand onto Colesceau's shoulders. "How you holding up?"

"With difficulty, Al."

"I'm so goddamned sorry it came down this way."

"I'm sure you tried your best to avoid it."

"Just between you and me, I wasn't the only vote."

"I expected no mercy from the women."

"It's old news now, Moros. But there's good news for you, too. You're ten minutes away from being a free man."

Psychologist Carla Fontana and Sgt. Paul Arnett, a deputy from the Sheriff's SONAR program, were waiting in Holtz's little office. Carla extended her tanned and freckled arm, gave him her 200-watt smile. She smelled like skin cream. Arnett shook his hand and looked him steady in the eye.

On the desk were a small round cake with frosting and a six-pack of root beer. Red napkins and white forks. The cake said GOOD LUCK MOROS in a script so inept Colesceau knew it could only belong to Holtz himself.

Holtz arranged the seats, still jabbering about the media outside, then started cutting the cake with a plastic knife. Colesceau wondered for the hundredth time how the PA saw anything out of his grimy glasses, which slid down his nose as he peered at the cake. Carla poured the root beer and the sergeant sat back against one wall with his arms folded over his chest.

Colesceau looked around the office—neat and small, that of an inconsequential bureaucrat—and was happy to think he was seeing it for the last time. It was actually kind of pleasant to sit here and realize he was finished. Except for the imminent visit from the nurse—a large flabby matron who smelled of sterile dressings and worked the needle into his vein each week with endless deliberation and satisfaction—it was exciting to him to be sitting here, being processed out of the system. He half expected an erection to begin, but none did.

"I have gifts for you, and for you, Carla," he said. "Sergeant Arnett, I had no idea you would be attending."

"Carry on."

He brought out a yellow turkey egg for Holtz and a pink goose egg for Carla. The yellow egg had small checkerboard flags on toothpicks protruding from each side near the top. It wore a snug muslin vest trimmed in gold piping and festooned with gold sequins. Thus a rococo high-performance racing egg or something. He shuddered at what his mother must have been thinking when she did it. She made it for him right after he got the job at Pratt. It was astonishing in its ugliness, and Colesceau had happily chosen it for Al Holtz. Fontana's was hung with tiny strips of dangling frill, giving it the look of a rotund, headless flapper from the '20s. Tiny silver slippers were affixed to its bottom. Pure Carla.

He presented them one at a time. Holtz's eyes actually became misty behind his filthy glasses. Carla Fontana smiled at him with a smile so pitying and genuine that Colesceau wished he could smash her teeth out with a brick and make her swallow them.

He shook Holtz's hand and then Carla's. Sergeant Arnett nodded to him.

"Well," said Holtz. "All I can say is you've been a good man to me, Moros. You've abided by the rules and maintained a sense of good humor and cooperation about it all. Especially this last part. Good luck. And, I arranged with Corrections to send you out of here today without that last injection. It's up to the Board physicians and they took my advice. After three years of it you don't need any more. And if you do, one more's not going to do you any good at all. So, to you, my friend. Cheers, salud and godspeed."

He lifted his root beer cup for a toast. Colesceau raised his own and drank.

"Drink up and have some cake," said Holtz. "When you're done we'll sign the papers and sneak you out the back."

37

Tim Hess sat in the mournful hush of the detective's pen. He watched the fax machine print out Bart Young's list of embalming machine buyers in Southern California over the last two years. It was arranged by date of purchase. The addresses and phone numbers and signing purchaser were conveniently listed, too. Mostly funeral homes and, presumably, their owners or managers: Marv Locklear of Locklear Mortuary . . . Burton Browd of Maywood Park . . . Peg Chester, Orange Tree Memorial Park and Cemetery . . .

Allen Bobb was on the list, signing for the Cypress College Department of Mortuary Science. Most of the sales were in Los Angeles County. There were nineteen in Orange, sixteen in San Diego county, fourteen each in Riverside and San Bernardino.

Lots of dead people to take care of, thought Hess. He was hoping for a match with the registered panel van owners or the customer list from Arnie's Outdoors, one of which he flipped through with each hand as the fax rolled out its own list. His head moved back and forth as he went from one to the other.

He could feel the draft on the back of his head whenever someone walked behind him. The air conditioner coming on was like a freezer being opened.

He was curious what the back of his head looked like without hair in a way he was never curious when his head was covered by it. At home, before coming in, he'd tried on half a dozen hats. They called attention to what he was hiding, but he decided on an old felt fedora that had been his rain hat for a couple of decades. He hadn't figured on every little draft once he took it off indoors, however, or on the stares of the other deputies who worked around him. He could actually feel their eyes on his newborn skin. After an hour or two, he was getting a little irritated by them.

. . . D.C. Simmons of Simmons Family Funeral Home . . . Barbara Braun at Sylvan Glen . . . William Wayne of Rose Garden Home in Lake Elsinore . . .

Lake Elsinore, again, thought Hess. The Ortega. Lael Jillson and Janet Kane. Murdered LaLonde. The buyer of an electronic car alarm override, calling himself Bill. A Porti-Boy embalming machine delivered November of last year, three months before Lael Jillson, one month before the Deer Sleigh'R and rope purchased with cash at Arnie's by a man who looked like the one described by Kamala Petersen.

But William Wayne wasn't on the other lists. And no one else on Bart Young's list was either.

Too easy, Hess thought, though easy things broke cases all the time. In fact, a surprising number of high-profile murder investigations turned on something like this—something simple and direct. Hess thought of the dead man sitting next to Randy Kraft in his car; the Atlanta child killer tossing a body off the bridge in view of the FBI; the bloody chainsaw returned to the rental yard by a killer whose name Hess could not at the moment remember. But that kind of good luck wasn't something you expected. And it only seemed to come late in the game, when the casualties were high, when everything else you'd tried hadn't worked.

... Vance Latham at Trask Family Mortuary ... Fran Devine for Willowbrook Memorial Park ... Mark Goldberg at Woodbridge Mortuary ...

Claycamp came by to tell him they were down to twenty-two panel vans registered to Orange County males. Gilliam came by with the now moot blowups picturing Matamoros Colesceau as he watched TV, courtesy of concerned citizen Rick Hjorth. Hess looked at them anyway. They were less definite than the originals, as he knew they would be. He shook his head and slipped them into his side coat pocket. Maybe see them later, in a different light.

Ray Dunbar, Jerry Kirby's partner, stopped to thank Hess for being there the night before, for doing what he'd done, for trying what he'd tried to do.

Brighton came over for a casual debriefing on the Jerry Kirby aftermath. The sheriff set a hand on Hess's shoulder, thanked him, then walked away. Hess had always hated hands on his shoulders—condescension, pride of ownership, false assurance. Brighton's hand made his skin start burning again. And his heart sank a little when he finally realized that word of his new head had leaked out, and his friendly visitors were coming to see it for themselves.

"Nice head," said Merci, passing him for the first time at work, acting her part. She had a thick stack of papers in one hand. Hess saw Phil Kemp look over at her, then away. "When did you shave it?"

"Last night."

He was aware of the other homicide detectives, all men, watching him.

She appeared to study his new hairstyle for the first time. "I like it," she said with a smile. "It shows off your face."

She had said the same thing the night before, as Hess dried himself after the shower. He couldn't remember the last time he'd taken a shower with a woman just because he wanted to be close to her some more. Or the last time he had held for a long while and really *looked* at his lover after they were done. It had been decades since he'd been with someone Merci's age and this made him feel as if he were somehow not himself. Like he'd gone back in time.

Merci looked down at him. There was a brightness in her eyes. She was wearing a different scent than usual. She took hold of the still lengthening fax transmission. "Bart?"

Hess nodded.

"Anything good?" she asked.

"There's an Elsinore buyer. William Wayne of the Rose Garden Home."

"William as in Bill? LaLonde's customer? It's worth the call. After that, we drench the three malls one more time with these."

She held up the papers—color copies of Kamala Petersen's Purse Snatcher. Hess was disappointed because he thought that TV and newspapers were a better way to broadcast a suspect sketch than walking malls, giving them away hand to hand. Deputies had already done it. This felt like they were going backward.

But, as if she had read his mind, Merci continued, "Look, I called that Lauren Diamond and said I'd talk to her about the Purse Snatcher case. I even kind of apologized a little. Anyway, she's down here at the Corrections building anyway for that Colesceau thing, so she's squeezing us in. She's just doing a *bullet* on our progress, she said, not a news *feature*."

"Good work."

She looked down at him with a gently bemused expression, but said nothing.

A moment later he pivoted in his chair to see her before she was out of the pen, acting like he was checking the wall clock.

Claycamp came through just then, almost bumping into her. He said something to Merci, then at Hess he flashed his right-hand fingers, three times.

Down to fifteen, thought Hess: the panel vans with mismatched tires are going to be a bust.

He sold it.

He stole it.

He got new tires.

His girlfriend, wife, sister, mother, company, church holds the paper on it. Run the women.

It cost Jerry Kirby his life to find that out.

He dialed the Rose Garden Home in Lake Elsinore and got a recording that said it was open during regular business hours, but failed to say what those were. The voice was a man's, a clear baritone that spoke of sympathy and efficiency. Hess entered the address, the purchase order information and William Wayne's name to his blue notepad.

His fax machine came alive again. He read the transmission upside down: a list of male buyers of blond, human hair wigs from Lifestylers of Irvine:

Burt Coombs
Lance Jahrner
Roger Rampling

There were three other buyers, the fax stated, who paid with cash.

He ran them past the other lists and came up with nothing.

Bald Hess, trudging the storefronts in his fedora, offered the color sketch of the Purse Snatcher to hundreds of shoppers at all three target malls.

Most were indifferent, hadn't heard that much about the Purse Snatcher. Some were frightened of Hess and his pale, sharp, old face. The kids on summer break were wiseasses as usual. And although Hess and Merci had tried four days ago to make sure that every employee of every store in all three of the malls had a copy of the drawing, it was made difficult by unresponsive personnel departments and sluggish mall security companies. So he went to all the first floor stores again. Merci took the ones on the second story. They divided up the big department stores that took up both.

In an electronics showroom he watched one of ten big screens with stereo that were tuned to CNB. He saw the recorded news bulletin featuring Merci, recorded outside the Sheriff's Department. She looked larger but quite beautiful on the TV and Hess felt an irrational pride. She told Lauren Diamond that the Purse Snatcher investigation was "progressing well on several fronts," but she wasn't free to discuss details at this time. She couldn't predict an arrest. She couldn't say when they expected an arrest. She did say they *expected* an arrest. Yes, Veronica Stevens was considered a victim. And the two missing women whose purses had been found along I-5 were considered victims, too, with a possible sixth unconfirmed at this time. Merci emphasized the word *sixth*. Hess could tell she was getting angry—Merci could go from zero to pissed off in about three seconds. She called the Purse Snatcher "an animal and a coward" for the way he chose only unarmed, defenseless, unsuspecting women. Hess shook his head when she said "creeps like this aren't usually too bright," because it was just the kind of statement that could motivate the Purse Snatcher. Which was what Merci intended. Lauren Diamond nodded along intently, like she was getting directions.

A moment later Lauren was live outside the Corrections building, at a demonstration outside the Parole Department. Colesceau's last injection, thought Hess. The crowd was big and the stereo broadcast was faithful to its volume and emotion. It was like the protesters were all around you, Hess thought. Like you were Colesceau. He watched the strange, round little man make his way toward the crowd with a resolve that Hess found admirable. He could tell by looking at him that Colesceau was anxious, perhaps afraid. Hess recognized the parole agent, Holtz, when he came through the door with an angry expression on his face and tried to usher his charge through the crowd.

Lauren Diamond got a mike into Colesceau's face but Holtz pushed it away. The front door of the building shut with a flash of reflected sunlight and Colesceau was gone.

Hess watched for a while, listened to the protesters, then went back out and gave away another fifty sketches.

Nothing.

Half an hour later he was back in the electronics store. On the ten identical screens Holtz was hustling Colesceau out a back door of the building—Hess recognized it immediately because he had used it himself. They'd ditched the demonstrators but Lauren Diamond's CNB shooters were waiting. Colesceau turned to Holtz after he came through the door. "What a fine idea, Al. Send me through the looking glass again." He raised his eyebrows and smiled and nodded his head in an exaggerated way.

"Something like that," said Holtz, shrugging with fake modesty.

Colesceau complimenting Holtz on his cleverness, thought Hess. Why bother? They must have used that back door more than once before.

In Hess's mind, Colesceau was like a shadow that never quite faded. Hess drew a deep breath into his lung and a third and wondered if fixation was a sign of senescence. He was pretty sure it was.

Hess found a bench, took out the blowups and

looked at them in the oddly bright but unrevealing mall light. Colesceau's head, larger and less clear with the pixels loosened to expand the image, looked neither more nor less convincing than before. The ambient light was still poor. Colesceau's TV screen still hogged the autofocus. The shadows were still large and indistinct. The crack in the blinds still framed the shot with horizontal bands of black. What appeared above the back of the couch could be a mannequin's head—something like Ed Izma would have in his closet.

Or, the head could be Colesceau's as he watched TV.

Send me through the looking glass again.

Hess knew the hardest time to trust your instincts was when you needed them most.

They sat in the food court, on purple plastic chairs around a green table. The foods of several nations were offered from kitchens around the perimeter of the room, each trying to lure customers with free samples and dazzlingly uniformed employees. Hess was hungry and everything smelled good mixed together like it was.

Merci studied him. "Do we need to get some things straight about last night?"

"If you want to."

"Like what?" She blushed.

He smiled. "Well, that would be up to you."

"Okay. It happened. It was what it was. It doesn't mean anything except what it means."

"A-okay, Merci."

They said nothing for a long moment. Hess committed himself to Nikki's Tandoori Express.

"I really do like you, Hess."

"I absolutely love you, Merci."

Her breath caught slightly. "That's what I meant. I love you, too."

Hess smiled and touched her hand.

She gulped, exhaled loudly, then laughed. "Goddamned glad *that's* out of the way."

He laughed, too, and it felt like something he hadn't done in centuries. "Thank you," he said.

"And Hess? Live forever. Direct orders. Please?"

"I'm going to."

Hess looked at her and thought again that she really did have a lovely face, just about any way you cut it.

Merci, still flushed, stirred her coffee. Hess could see her retreating from the moment, leaving well enough alone, which was all right with him.

"Gilliam pulled three latents off the purses—one CalTrans sweeper and two CHP officers. He's working the hair and fiber, but none of it's pointing at our creep. I'm disappointed about Bart Young's list. All my charm and patience on Bart for nothing."

"There's the funeral home out in Elsinore—the Rose Garden. Owner or manager is one William Wayne. Elsinore puts us close to the Ortega, close to Janet Kane and Lael Jillson. Close to Lee LaLonde, the security system override, the swap meet at the marina. It's an outside shot, but I think we should look at it. I called—a man's voice, just a recording."

Merci considered. "It really frosted my butt when I had to admit we're not that close. *On TV.* We're not that close to him yet, Hess. And I had to tell the county that. And six. You know how hard it was to say he's killed six women on my watch?"

Hess nodded but said nothing. He knew you weren't always close just because you thought you were close, weren't always far just because it felt that way. Cases had their own secret length, their own surprise endings. But you could only see them when they were over.

"Tim, I called Claycamp a few minutes ago and we're down to eight vans. I took four of them. I'm starting to feel lucky again. Man, I can feel it," she said. Then, as a consolation she tried to sound enthused about: "And after that, we can hit the Rose Garden Home in Elsinore, if you want to."

Hess's heart sank a little: his own partner was throwing him a bone. "All right."

"These unmatched tires still smell right."

"That's good enough for me, Merci. What if we run the women on the DMV list? The women with late-model panel vans?"

Merci looked at him sharply. "That's a lot of man-hours if you—"

"—No, just run the names against the other lists. Maybe the Purse Snatcher's got someone who loves him, too. Like Colesceau. A relative. A girlfriend. Maybe she's got money. Maybe she's old and he can use her as a front and she doesn't know it. It's worth looking at."

She studied him for a moment. She looked at the TV screen. She nodded and took the cell phone out of her pocket. "I'll get Claycamp on that," she said,

385

dialing. "Maybe he can get someone to run the lists while we hit the last four vans and Lake Elsinore."

It took them almost three hours to find the vehicles, with all the traffic, driving from one end of the smog-choked county to the other, wrecks all over the place. One of the vans wasn't operable; one had been stolen the day before. The other two were family vehicles. None of them was silver, or had mismatched tires or embalming machines hooked up to generators in the back.

Midway through the fruitless expedition they stopped to get coffee and for Hess to get his radiation treatment.

He came out with a strange feeling in his face. Like it was numb and cold, packed in mint. The back of his hand hurt because the nurse took five stabs to find his "shy" vein when she took blood. Dr. Ramsinghani said yesterday's white cell count was very low, and he might need a transfusion if it hadn't come back up by today. He was borderline anemic. They'd know tomorrow. Until then, get plenty of rest. Eat well. Lots of water. Relaxation, meditation. Don't even consider going to work.

38

To his authentic horror, Matamoros Colesceau glanced at the TV in his living room to see his mother making her way through the crowd toward his door.

He watched her barrel through the demonstrators. She threw one arm up to cover her face and peered over it like a leper from a cave. The mob parted for her.

MAKE OUR NEIGHBORHOOD
SAFE FOR THE CHILDREN!

She was dressed, as always, in her long loose black skirt and black v-necked shawl. The lapels of the shawl were embroidered with white crosses of her own design, but the effect was far more pagan than Christian. From any kind of distance the crosses looked like rows of teeth closing in on her throat. She was a strong woman, thick as a lumberjack. Her face was round and white. Her mouth was open even when she wasn't speaking, the heavy, dry lips parted over posts of misshapen teeth that were separated by spaces suggesting violence. She wore the thick oval sunglasses favored by dictators and a black knit babushka over her head. Even to Colesceau she looked like the witch in some fairy tale illustrated with woodcuts. He opened the door and let her in.

"Moros, I am saddened and furious."

"I am, too, Mother."

She looked at him. Even after twenty-six years his first instinct on being close to his mother was to run.

She took his wrists and pulled him down so he could kiss her. He did. He could smell the breath from her never-closed mouth: a red American mouthwash she used by the gallon.

"Why didn't you tell me sooner?"

"I was ashamed."

"They are the ones who should be ashamed."

"They're not ashamed of anything. That's why I've become so important to them. What could you have done?"

"Done? I could have helped the only blood I have left on earth. Why, the television, it says you have no job, and no place to live in just a few weeks. And still, you don't call or write me?"

Colesceau stepped back a little and sighed. "Thanks for coming."

"How do you live with that noise outside?"

"It stops at nine."

"They would crucify you if they had the courage."

"And the hammers."

"Make me some tea. I'm going to sit here where it's cool and think about this situation. There must be a way we can overcome it."

Colesceau made the tea. He brought it out to her.

Helena was watching "Rape Watch: Irvine."

"Are you on the TV all day?"

"They broadcast live when I go outside for any

388

reason. Or when someone visits. Yesterday, law enforcement. Now you."

"What are they saying about the children?"

"They're demanding a safe neighborhood for them."

"But you love children."

"True."

"And if you had ever shown interest in a Romanian girl, she would have given children to you, like I gave you to your father."

References to his mother in childbirth disgusted him. His father was weak, womanly and traitorous. Matamoros was ashamed to be sired by him. Which was why he had taken his mother's maiden name when he came to the states. He tried to think of something pleasant, always difficult in the presence of Helena. "You've told me that a thousand times, Mother."

"Instead of the French or Italian girls in Bucharest. Instead of the German girls in the magazines. Instead of the American girls in California."

"I know your opinions." Certainly, he did. She'd been opining about his prospective mate for twenty years or so. Her words had always made him sad and edgy and angry. At first it was because he didn't really understand them. Later, because he knew she was right.

"You will never attract an American woman like you desire."

"This isn't the time to discuss it."

"It's the reason for all that's happened. Your *own* type, Moros. Your *own* level. What is similar and harmonious. A hummingbird for a hummingbird. A sow for a hog. Beautiful and educated American women for beautiful and educated American men. For you, a simple Romanian peasant girl. Someone like me."

"You horrify me, Mother," he said softly. "I love you, but you always have."

When she forced him to sleep in her bed after the death of his father, Colesceau had begun to truly understand why his mother so adamantly choked his desires for other women. He began to understand this while he lay in her bed the very night his father was shot to death by the state police, lay still and silent and in considerable pain as she sobbed and worked the cooling herbal poultice over the stitched fang holes that the attack dogs had left all over his body. Her desire was easy for him to feel. It entered him through her fingers, arcing down into him like electricity in slow motion. It never left. He could never really make it leave.

Now, years later, he considered killing her just to stop her damning words, but there was the money she gave him, the rent she paid, the vehicles she financed for him, the savings and checking accounts she helped him maintain, the lawyers and doctors she hired and fired like maids.

"I believe I have a solution for our immediate problems, Moros. You will move in with me. We can transport you in a private way, and no one will know you are with me."

He just looked at her, the brown and broken teeth rising from her gums.

"What do you think of that, Moros?"

"No."

"Do you have a better solution?"

"I'll be all right here, Mother. I'll finish out my lease here, that's twenty-five days. Then I'll find another place to live. It's not impossible. It's a free country."

"Not for sexual perverts, it isn't."

"I'm not a sexual pervert. And I'm not moving in with you. I'm not going anywhere. This is my home."

"Then *I'll* move in here. And I will hear no argument about that, if you expect to continue your allowances. No arguments from you, Moros. But, more tea. And turn up the TV."

He picked up the remote and pressed the button. As the "Volume" bar rose up one side of the screen, hatred rose up in his heart. It was like water jumping to a boil. But it was a soft, compromised hatred, not one that would ever spur him to action. It frustrated him so much that he couldn't just shut her up and get it all over with. Then start to rebuild his life from the ground up, clean slate, American Dream and all that: no Depo-Provera, no shrill neighbors, no Helena to tell him he should aspire only to women as ugly as her.

"Who is this woman on the screen, Moros?"

He looked. "I don't know."

His mother turned her white round face toward him and Colesceau knew she was studying him through her sunglasses.

"Yet she is a neighbor?"

"You see her there, staring at my front door—what else could she be?"

391

"You desire her."

"No, not really."

"They say her name is Trudy Powers. You know her, don't you?"

"She's lived here longer than I have."

Colesceau took Helena's cup back to the kitchen, poured some fresh tea. What he hated most about her was the way she knew what he was thinking when it came to women. She always knew the ones he'd like, ever since he was just a boy. He looked out to the living room at her, his black-shrouded harridan of a mother with the dictator's sunglasses, the babushka and brown, broken teeth. His heart was pounding heavy and hard, like an idling Harley. But his muscles felt loose and strong, better than they'd felt in years.

Over one week without a hormone injection, he thought. *After three years of it you don't need any more. And if you do, one more's not going to do you any good at all.*

Here I am, he thought, caught in another drastic moment. But it felt like he was getting stronger every minute.

Then the doorbell rang. He looked to the TV screen to identify his new torment. He could feel the soft hatred still inside, the swirl of it through his blood and nerves. But instead of more cops, or reporters or something wretched like his mother, there was something wonderful now standing on his porch, asking that her ring be answered. She had her purse slung over her shoulder and something flat and heavy in one hand.

392

Trudy rang the doorbell again and Colesceau smiled, turning toward the entryway.

But Helena was already there, swinging open the door. Colesceau looked past the black-shawled shoulder of his mother to see the look of genuine fright on Trudy's face as she smiled at Helena. Tried to smile, was more like it.

"May I come in for just a moment?"

"Only for just a moment."

"You must be Mrs. Colesceau. I absolutely love the eggs you decorate."

Helena turned to look back at him, and Colesceau knew she was trying to understand how Trudy Powers knew about her eggs. Colesceau knew that behind the black plastic of her sunglasses her little pig eyes were narrow, suspicious and uncertain.

She turned away from him and back to Trudy Powers. "It is an art I have practiced for many years. I've never felt worthy of its tradition."

"I'm no expert on the tradition, Mrs. Colesceau, but the eggs are beautiful."

Colesceau smiled and bowed to Trudy very slightly. In the afternoon light that came through the still-open door Trudy Powers looked like a goddess. She was radiant, beautiful and filled with power. The dust rising in the sunlight around her was gold. Her skin and her hair and her thoughts were gold. Beside her, Helena seemed like one of those black holes they always talked about on the Discovery Channel, a place of hungry nothingness that ate solar systems like appetizers.

"Miss Powers," he said, bowing again.

"I'm concerned that they did the wrong thing in demonstrating at the Parole Board building today. I'm really sorry they did that, and I advised them it was wrong. I apologize for what they've done. I made you a pie."

Helena turned away and waddled into the living room. Colesceau extended his arm toward the kitchen, encouraging Trudy to go in ahead of him.

She smiled on her way past him, a nervous smile. "Can I set it here on the counter?"

"That's fine. It was kind of you."

She put the pie on the counter, then looked at him. She was nervous but she didn't back away. He could tell it took resolve. But she seemed convinced that she was animated, or at least endorsed, by a higher power than herself. God's little errand girl, he thought, placating the evil monster.

"How nice to have your mother here."

"Oh, very." Colesceau felt a swirl of things just then: hatred, attraction, frustration, power. And a light, fizzing sensation down in the fleshy end of himself.

"Mine died when I was young."

"But you still are young."

"I'm thirty-four. You're just twenty-six, aren't you?"

"Miss Powers, I feel a hundred. At least."

"After all you've gone through, it's understandable."

"I've sinned. But it was a long time ago. And I have honored the promise I made you. My behavior has been excellent in all ways."

394

Colesceau thought he heard his mother grunt from the living room, but it could have just been the TV, or the blood rushing against his eardrums.

"It's good you can acknowledge your sins."

"It's easy when they're as large as mine."

"Paul was the great sinner, until his conversion. The farther you have fallen, the higher you can rise."

He pursed his lips and looked down. It was a look of contrition he'd practiced for years on Holtz. "What's inside the pie?"

"Apples. Organic apples. I hope you like apple pie."

"Oh, powerfully."

"Mr. Col . . . *Moros*. I brought you something else. I hope you don't think it's presumptuous or something, but I just thought, from some of the things you've said, that you'd understand it."

"I understand your kindness."

"It's about a kindness far greater than my own."

She opened the flap of the purse, leaving it over her shoulder. Out came the black book he fully expected to see. He could see a sheet of folded paper marking a place about halfway through. Trudy set the Bible on the counter next to the pie.

"It's yours to keep."

"I feel it could ignite in my hands."

"Don't underestimate the power of forgiveness."

He stepped forward and set his hand on the cover. He smiled at her, then looked down again.

"Well, I should go. Maybe we can talk again."

"I would like that very much."

She smiled—all of life and goodness was contained

in that smile—and hiked up the purse strap. He could see her breasts move under the blouse. Soft and large, still fairly high. She walked by him, then stopped behind Helena.

"Mrs. Colesceau, it was nice to meet you."

"Moros does not need the company of American women. You confuse him. You cost him his testicles."

She pronounced it with a long "e" at the end, so it sounded like a Greek philosopher. Testi*clese*. Colesceau winced. Even though Trudy Powers knew what he had gone through, knew the rough outlines of it, anyway, when his mother said that word it brought a fresh sense of shame to him.

"God can give them back," said Trudy.

"And he hates apples."

"Then give the pie to someone who doesn't."

Trudy looked at Colesceau and walked out.

He read the note left in the Bible by Trudy Powers. It was written in graceful, feminine script, with the eyes dotted by circles that looked like happy balloons:

Dear Matamóros,
My husband and I will pray with you any time you
need God, any time of the day or night. Just call if you
need us! We could meet at a chapel or park or down at
the ocean, allow you to get away from the crowd for a
while. Please do call. 555-1212.

With Jesus' Love
Trudy and Jonathan Powers

Helena went out for dinner groceries around six, promising him a good meal. She came back with cube steaks—the kind with the gristle like rubber bands, frozen peas, a coconut custard pie with a clear plastic lid and two half gallons of generic vodka. He watched her approach his apartment home on TV again, shopping bags in one hand and the other held in front of her like a battering ram as the neighbors and reporters converged.

Dinner was a tribulation he thought would never end, and through it Colesceau could feel his shame turning into anger, his anger into rage, his rage into calm, his calm into hatred.

"Moros, it hurts me when a woman like that neighbor steps into your home. The home I pay for."

It was after dinner, time for dessert but still before nine, so the chanting outside was going strong. Some of the Parole Board demonstrators had joined the neighborhood demonstrators, so it looked like twice as many of them. The increased numbers had brought more media, too—there were three network vans outside, plus some local L.A. stations, and some whose call letters Colesceau didn't even recognize. Where was WJKN, anyway?

Helena drank deeply from her tumbler. Colesceau heard her slurp. He took another long draw from his own glass—the generic vodka smelled just like the swabs that Holtz's fat nurse used to wipe his arm before she plunged the needle in.

"It was the first time Trudy Powers has ever been in here," he said.

On screen he saw Lauren Diamond and Sergeant Merci Rayborn, lead Sheriff's investigator in the Purse

Snatcher investigation. He'd forgotten about her in all of this.

But at the sound of his own voice saying Trudy's name—or was it at the sight of Merci on his TV—Colesceau felt his desire stir. Actually felt a nudge against the forearm lying across his lap. He breathed deeply.

. . . the Purse Snatcher investigation is moving ahead on a number of fronts right now . . .

"She's an impudent, self-righteous whore."

"She means well."

We were considering Veronica Stevens of Santa Ana to be the Purse Snatcher's third victim until we discovered . . .

Helena sighed hugely. She sat her bulk back into the couch and sighed again. She slurped down some more vodka. "Do you miss Romania, Moros?"

"Not at all."

"I love America, too. But sometimes I remember the good things about home. I miss them."

"Name me one good thing about home, Mother."

"Oh, I remember the springtime in Tirgu Ocna. The sunrise over the Danube. The beach at Constanta in August."

"They mean nothing to me."

. . . we try not to make predictions like that . . .

"More vodka, Moros."

In the kitchen Colesceau poured his mother fresh vodka. He'd heard her nostalgic blubbering before. Another drink or two and she'd tell him about her beautiful lover from Matamoros, Mexico, a slender Mexican idealist, poet and photographer who had seduced her as a young woman. Colesceau's namesake. The whole story sickened him.

398

After putting a handful of ice into her glass, he popped the roll of paper towels off its holder and tilted out the ice pick. Cold. He put it in his right front trouser pocket, tip up.

Back in the living room he gave Helena the glass, looking at her through the periphery of his vision because it was too much to look directly at her. He felt the bile rise in his guts. He sat down and saw Merci Rayborn still on the TV.

. . . he's an animal and a coward, picking on unarmed, defenseless, unsuspecting women . . .

She looks better on TV than in person, thought Colesceau. Just a little heavier. Softer in the eyes and face. His penis felt like it was crawling.

"I miss Voronet," said Helena. "The outdoor frescoes. You know, Moros, the ones they painted on the outside walls of the churches, because the poor people were considered too unclean to enter the church. It was like TV for the poor, although the pictures didn't move."

"I remember the frescoes. They're one of the few things about Romania I liked."

"Moros, remember 'Soul Taking' at the Moldovita church? What an unforgettable thing, to see that fresco, to actually feel what the artist felt. People were closer to God in those days. There is no doubt about this."

He glanced at her. He'd seen the fresco "Soul Taking" that she talked about. It was a bunch of gray demons with claws, wings, and tails who tore the souls from both the living and the dead. It was a grotesque carnival of pain and torment that had always made

399

Colesceau giggle, even as a child. He thought his mother was psychologically misshapen, to get passion out of something that frightful and comedic.

. . . the rules of common sense. Always lock your car. Always park in a well-lit place. Always check your car before getting in—especially the backseat . . .

He looked at Merci Rayborn's mouth as she spoke, then at Helena's. He liked to compare his mother's features with the features of women he might possess someday. Merci Rayborn had even white teeth. Helena had tusks. He pressed down with his forearm just a little, but the resistance was gone. For the millionth time in the last three years it simply evaporated, like a drop of spring rain on a warm sidewalk. It was the single most infuriating feeling he had ever known.

. . . why will we get him? Because creeps like this aren't usually too bright, that's why we'll get him . . .

CNB went back to "Rape Watch: Irvine" and Trudy appeared on the screen. Helena grabbed the remote and turned down the sound.

"It is time to put your mother to bed, Moros."

"Of course."

He tucked his mother into his own bed. It flattered her to get his bed—though she also seemed to feel entitled to it—and he favored the arrangement for other reasons. He felt the tip of the ice pick in the darkness to make sure it was there.

He took off her babushka and stroked her hair, which was wispy white with brown on top, like meringue. He listened to her ramble. He knew she'd

400

be stubbornly unconscious in a matter of minutes. He pulled up the covers so they were just covering her breasts, tucking them in nice and snug around her, just as she liked it, just as she'd taught him to do.

"You are the good son, Moros."

"You are the good mother."

Her mouth approximated a smile and he bent to kiss her. He felt the tip of the pick against his hip and he knew this was the time. His arms were trembling like he'd just lifted a car off the ground.

He thought so often about it. Not so much the beneficial results, but the pleasure the act would give him. But he could never do it. He had had a thousand chances in two different countries on two different continents over two decades, and he had still never been able to do it. He hated himself for this failure. The hatred of himself was his bedrock, the foundation on which everything else inside him was built. There was no escaping it when she was near him.

And now she was threatening to move in.

Helpless to stop her. Helpless to end her. The hatred made thin, red outlines like halos around everything he looked at.

. . . because creeps like this aren't usually too bright, that's why we'll get him . . .

Colesceau shut the door on his already snoring mother, went downstairs and poured a giant cocktail of pure vodka. Then he went back upstairs and into the spare bedroom, locking the door behind him. He was weeping though he wasn't sad, and he could feel the cool tears on his cheeks.

401

It had been like this for three years. His body did one thing, and his mind did another. No connection. No unity. It was strange to feel rage and anger, but to have no erection; to feel furious and frustrated, but to have tears running down his face.

He stripped down to his underwear and stood in front of the mirrored wall. He set the tumbler on the floor beside him. He wanted to see himself now that the hormone treatments were stopped. He unbuttoned the shirt, realizing with a sense of dread that this was the worst he would look, that the effects were as bad now as they would get.

This is what they have made of me. Manhood shot through with womanhood and the result is neither.

So he dropped the shirt, pulled off his underwear and looked at himself in the glass. He saw that his general shape was suggestive of the human female rather than the human male. He saw the deep pocks the dog teeth had left, and the jagged suture scars guaranteed by disinterested government doctors. Before the police dogs his skin had been pale and clear and taut. He saw his flabby midsection, the valiant little breasts trying so hard not to become what they were not intended to be. Before the hormone treatments they had been flat, efficient ministers of strength. He saw the loose nest of hair and skin between his legs. Before all of this they had been his precious cock and balls, they had always been there for him, they had *been* him when he needed them to be—his expression of hate, desire, rage. Now they were an image of pure defeat. And no matter what he imagined, he couldn't get even the faintest stirring of desire to register down there. For now, as it was so often in the last three years, his organ was nothing more than a phantom.

He stooped and got his vodka, draining it down to the last cold drop.

Then everything hit him. The hatred and rage, the desire and impotence, the frustration and weakness. All of it stewed in the vodka and progesterone, all of it mixed together into a toxic blend.

Colesceau opened his mouth and bared his teeth. He trapped the scream far down in his throat and didn't let it out. His head rang with pain. He could feel his own hot damp breath all around his face and see the steam it formed in the air-conditioned room. Like he was breathing smoke.

He looked at himself again and saw the thing he had become. He drew another breath and choked down another soundless scream. The glass broke in his hand and he felt the ice landing around his toes.

And he had the vision—while his head roared with a silent bellow of despair—of what he would do next.

To establish himself again. To better himself.

To show his mother and the miserable world that he could rise above what they had made of him.

He thought it through and he thought it through again. He watched his face, still a grimace of tears and a frozen scream. So much to do now, and so little time.

Trudy's number was still in the Bible in his living room, and he'd need to leave a little something for his mother.

Work to do.

39

By sunset that evening Hess was driving with Merci back out the Ortega, along the swales shadowed by oaks, up the grades of sunlit stone, past the shimmering cottonwood and spring-fed grass. He looked out at the stand of trees where purses and blood belonging to Janet Kane and Lael Jillson had been found. Just darkness now, locked in by the shadows of sycamores and oaks. He thought of how cold that blood had been in the ground out there, already returning into elements by the time they'd found it. He could feel his own blood again now, hot and somehow foreign, apparently borderline anemic, but fortified by rads and noxious chemicals, antacids, antiemetics, painkillers, vitamins and the lingering narcotic of desire. It felt to him like the blood itself was polluted. But he was glad to have it. He noticed his eyes were blurring just a little again now, not so much blurring as failing to focus as well as they could. But that had come and gone, since the chemo.

"Kemp apologized to me this morning. He actually seemed to mean it. More to the point, he said he'd keep his mouth shut and his hands off me."

"Good. That's how it should be."

"It's not a victory. It's just basic human respect I'm after."

"Phil's a tough one to get that from. You more than earned it."

"Tomorrow he's going to make a statement to the press. He's going to apologize without admitting he did anything wrong. A misunderstanding or some such thing. I talked to Brighton afterward, and just between you and me, Kemp's headed for an Admin desk."

"Funny way to get promoted."

"At least they'll be able to watch him better. So, I'm thinking about the suit. I can drop it now without feeling like I backed off. That'll probably get me more publicity than bringing it. Now they'll say I'm abandoning the other women. But I don't care. I've just got to get onto other things. Case closed, as far as I'm concerned."

Hess looked over at her but Merci just stared out the window.

The Rose Garden Home sat at the base of the mountains, west of the lake. There was a gate across the driveway entrance, and a gate closer to the house, but both were unlocked. Merci stood in the dust and slid the gates back on steel wheels while Hess watched her in the headlights.

The house was mostly dark—three rooms lit inside, and a porch light throwing a glow above the front door. The grounds were lit well, with halogen patio lights on stands. Hess could see that it was a large wood-sided home that had once been blue. The garage door was up, no cars inside. On the dead brown grass sat a wheeled sign with a big red arrow above a message board. The letters were black against the faded yellow background, and not very straight:

Rose Garden Home
Respect and Care
You Are Welcome

Hess stepped out of the car and into the heat. He wiped his forehead with his coat sleeve. Low nineties, he figured, maybe higher. The house loomed before him. He looked up at the slouching porch, the crooked stairs, the old sofas against the wall, the wrought-iron grates over the windows, the empty bird feeders hung from the awnings, the onyx wind chimes motionless in the heat.

He could hear voices inside the house but they were overlapping and faint and could have been from the TV or a radio.

"This is one fucked-up looking funeral home," said Merci. "What's that owner's name again?"

"William Wayne."

"Jesus, look at this place."

"Listen."

Through the heat came a moan, a long, unhurried and oddly painless moan from the second floor. A moment later Hess heard laughter downstairs—a young woman.

Merci shook her head. "What's he do, pickle them before they're dead?"

"Be careful."

Hess looked at her, reached under his coat and loosened the strap on his shoulder rig. Merci did the same. Hess stumbled on the slanting stairs, recovered across the porch and got himself left of the door. Merci backed up against the wall on the right, her

H&K out now and at her side, tucked back behind the leg of her trousers.

Hess reached out with his right hand and knocked. The door was thin and he could hear the report on the other side. The moan started up again but the laughing stopped. He could feel his heart beating too fast in his chest, more rpm than horsepower, an engine with gears that weren't quite meshing. It wasn't something he could do much about.

He tried the knob but it was locked. He looked at Merci. She stood relaxed but alert, arms at her sides, boots apart, back to the house. She shrugged and Hess knocked again, harder and longer.

Still nothing. Just the moaning.

"Here goes," said Hess, holstering his sidearm. He stepped back, lowered his shoulder and charged the door. It took him two tries, but the doorjamb splintered on the second and he stepped aside and let Merci push through.

Hess drew and followed. The anteroom was hot and the smell was strong. There was no mistaking that smell. He noticed the hornets buzzing lazily in the dark heavy air of the stairwell. There were two hallways leading off, one left and one right.

A young man with long blond hair stepped into the dull light of the hallway, looked at them in fear, dropped a tray of something and whipped around the other way.

Hess and Merci yelled at the same time, a chorus of threat that echoed up into the stairwell and bounced off the walls. And the moaning still, plaintive and caged.

Hess pounded down the hall, jamming the gun into his holster. The guy cut left, out of sight. Hess didn't hesitate. Into a kitchen, bright, a big butcher block and a table with chairs. Three steps and Hess jumped and caught him at a far doorway of the kitchen, bear-hugging the guy's arms tight to his body, using his weight to crash them to the floor. Hess rolled and forced the face against the linoleum and he could feel Merci behind him, nullifying the strength of one arm, then the other.

"He's bagged, Hess! Roll off clean, watch the teeth! Watch the teeth! *Don't move, you sonofaBITCH!*"

Hess pushed, then rolled away and saw her above him, sidearm aimed down at their prize. He righted himself, held the guy's neck down with one hand and body-searched him with the other. He got a janitor's key chain off one belt loop, a pocketknife, some kind of laminated ID card. Then he turned the man over onto his back and stood. He was breathing hard, short little gasps that didn't seem to get enough air in. It was quiet all of a sudden, no moaning, no cop screams.

"Good," Hess said. "Work."

The guy looked early twenties. His hair was long and wavy, he had a thin mustache and dark, frightened eyes. Skinny and pale. He wore a filthy T-shirt, dark jeans, red tennis shoes with no socks. He looked at Hess as if he was about to be devoured. Then at Merci. His chin was quivering and he still hadn't said a word.

"Name, shithead."

Eyes on Hess again, then to Merci. Dark and haunted and maybe even remorseful, thought Hess.

No struggle at all now, just belly up and lying on his arms, stranded like a tortoise.

"What's your name, young man?" he asked.

"Billy."

"Billy what?"

"Billy Wayne."

Hess looked down at the plastic-covered card. "William J. Wayne," he said. "Number 113."

"I didn't do it. And I want my lawyer."

"Exactly what didn't you do?"

"Whatever it is. I live here. I'm the man in charge when we're alone."

"In charge of *what*?"

William J. Wayne looked at each of them again, suspicion, genuine fear. "All of us. When the doctor goes, I'm in charge."

Hess looked at Merci and Merci looked back. The moaning started up again from above them somewhere.

"You got a lot of goddamned explaining to do, Bill. I'm going to let you stand up, walk over and sit you in a chair here. Then you're going to tell me what I want to know. You try to fight me and I'll kick your balls all the way to the lake. Got that?"

"I want my lawyer and I didn't do it."

"Yeah, yeah, now stand up real slow and get your ass into this chair. Tim, maybe you should secure this haunted house before Billy tells us everything he hasn't done."

Hess, with the janitor's key ring in one hand, started with the left hallway. The place smelled like a

409

portable outhouse that has been out in the sun a long time. The hornets droned. He came to a door on his right and looked through the window. He could see the wrought-iron grating that protected the glass from the inside. Beyond the grating was a small room lit by a fluorescent shop lamp affixed high on one wall. A small twisted person lay upon the bed, half covered in the sheets. Sharp bones and skin, weak light and shadow. Mouth open, no sound. The person blinked. Hess saw the excrement on the floor around a hole cut directly into the wood. A clipboard hung from a nail outside the door listed the patient as J. Orsino. The hornets buzzed in and out, clung to the walls, pivoted on the light fixture.

The next room down held a young woman laughing. All Hess could see of her was her backside, the honey-colored hair and the arms of the gray straitjacket criss-crossed around her waist. Her bed was pulled into the middle of the room and she sat on the far side of it, facing the wall, her head bowed like she was crying or thinking. Laughing. There was an upturned pot on the floor beside her bed, food stuck to the bottom and sides, hornets flickering on the red enamel. Beside that a kitchen tub that appeared half full of water.

The last room off this hallway held a man who lay atop his bed and stared at the ceiling. The chart said B. Schuster.

Hess tried to breathe deeply but it was hard to inhale the foul air without tasting it all the way down. He retraced his steps to the entry room and went down the hallway to his right. In one room was a disfigured boy; the other was empty.

Upstairs. The unemphatic moaning was an adolescent girl who looked out at Hess from under the covers of her bed. When she saw him she stopped and smiled.

Upstairs on the third level Hess found a spacious room that served as an office. It was well lit. An air conditioner groaned steadily, cutting the temperature and the stench. There was a desk along one wall, one chair and six tall file cabinets. There was one framed picture on the desk—a young couple with a small boy—one of the small black-and-whites popular in the fifties, from which era Hess had several of himself. He recognized neither the people nor the landscape.

He found the business license and county permit for the Rose Garden Home—"an intensive care and hospice" facility. The owner operator was a woman—Helena Spurlea. She'd been in business for eleven years. The small photograph on her county permit showed a stubborn-faced woman with dark bangs and unhappy eyes. She looked like the woman in the little black-and-white, forty years older.

They both looked at him when he walked in. Merci had pulled up two chairs to face Wayne, backs forward. She sat with her arms on the wood, and a mildly amused expression on her face.

"Billy's decided he doesn't need his lawyer right now. We're going to have a little chat, let him go if that's what seems right. Sound good?"

Hess got the cue. "I wouldn't let that sonofabitch go if I had a gun to my head."

411

Merci sighed, looked at William Wayne. "This is Tim, by the way. He eats chicken heads for breakfast, but he's an okay guy."

Hess opened his mouth and slowly bit down on his thumb.

Wayne stared at him from what looked to be a wholly exclusive universe. Then he turned to Merci again. "Maybe I could just talk to you."

"That mean Tim can look around a little?"

"It's the doctor's place."

"But you're in charge."

"I am in charge."

"Let him look around, and we can get this over with. Get all of us back to what we were doing."

"I was feeding 227. I'm in charge when she's gone."

"I want to hear about that. Tim, maybe you should take a tour."

Hess studied William Wayne as he backed out of the room.

"Okay, Billy," said Merci. "Now what's the deal with the Porti-Boy?"

Billy giggled. "What's that?"

The file cabinets in the upstairs office contained patient records. William J. Wayne was a twenty-three-year old native of Riverside, born to an alcohol- and methedrine-dependent mother. He was born with "substantial" mental retardation and his developmental age was estimated to be eleven. Hess noted that he was capable of writing his name, which looked like something a first grader might produce, the letters put together one line at a time. There was no mention of

412

any crime in Wayne's file, sexual or otherwise. Parents long divorced, mother in Beaumont, father's LKA Grant's Pass, Oregon. Wayne's mother apparently signed over her state checks to the Rose Garden Home, in return for the care her son received: $388 per month. Hess made notes.

He got Bart Young's home phone number out of his blue notebook and used the desk phone to dial it. Young told him that the method of payment on William Wayne's Porti-Boy was a money order, if he remembered correctly. He could confirm in the morning. He also said they usually used UPS for deliveries in the western states. Hess then called Brighton at home, who said he could get UPS Security at this hour. Five minutes later the phone on Helena Spurlea's desk rang. Hess spent the next minutes explaining his needs to the UPS regional security director, who said he would fax a signed delivery receipt to the Sheriff Department first thing in the morning. Hess thanked him and hung up.

He called for a law enforcement DMV run on Helena Spurlea: 1992 Cadillac Seville and 1996 Chevy panel van. Three points on her driving record. He wrote down the plate numbers. Her CDL was current and a fax of it and her record was on its way to the Sheriff's Department Homicide Detail, attention Tim Hess. The van, he thought: where is it?

He pulled out the bottom file cabinet drawer and fingered his way through the folders. Cancelled checks. Invoices. Receipts for expenses. Handwritten notes. He pulled one at random: the expected payments for mortgage and utilities, staples and medications, vehicle maintenance, repairs of appliances, labor costs for landscape, painting, cleaning. Some unexpected expenses, too: $956 for H. Spurlea, round trip travel from LAX to Dallas to Brownsville, Texas, in the fall of 1998; payment of $370 to New West Farms in nearby Temecula for "ostrich and emu products" in 1997; regular monthly payments of $875 to the Schaff Management Group of Newport Beach for "storage" and $585 to one Wheeler Greenfield of Lake Elsinore for "rent." There was a $1,235 payment to Inland Glass for "wall glass installation" back in 1997, which Hess found odd because he'd not seen a single mirrored wall in the Rose Garden Home so far.

Lots of outlay, thought Hess. She makes some money in this hellhole. Enough to buy "emu and ostrich products" to feed her patients. And why so much for "storage"? What's she storing—cows?

More scribbles into his blue notebook, Hess's fingers feeling thick and unwilling, his sense of disgust growing.

In the receivable files, Hess found a dizzying labyrinth of private payments, insurance reimbursements, and state, county and federal payouts. Some were payable to individual patients, some to family, some to Helena Spurlea, some to the Rose Garden Home. Between the discharged, the transferred, the institutionalized and the deceased it was impossible for Hess to account for the income per patient. Even his cursory inspection revealed that one A. Bohanan had expired in March of 1996 and received monthly medical insurance payments of $588 through September of the same year, payable to the Rose Garden Home. A similar benefits-for-the-dead history for M.A. Salott.

It was profane.

The file for January of this year contained nothing at all related to the purchase of an embalming machine by William Wayne.

Hess inspected the house, the garage and the grounds, finding no trace of the Porti-Boy and no documents relating to the purchase of such a thing. No mirrored walls, no ostrich or emu meat in the freezer. No van, no Seville. Just a junked old truck, up on blocks, half of it missing. No tracks on the old asphalt of the drive-way. When it was light they could check the road.

Merci was standing across the room from Wayne when Hess came back into the kitchen. Her arms were crossed and she had one hand up, fingers rubbing her chin.

"William is kind of forgetful about things, Tim. Foggy."

"Let's throw him in jail and see if he clears up."

"He's in charge here. Doesn't want the other patients to get hungry. The doctor, he says, she cuts out two or three days in a row, sometimes. Stay put, William. Tim, come with me?"

Standing in the stinking hallway, Hess heard the moaning again. Merci's face looked pale in the bad light. He stood so he could see part of Wayne's feet through the door.

"He's too stupid," said Merci.

"That can be faked."

"I'm convinced."

415

"I am, too. No record. No driver's license. He probably doesn't even know how to drive a car."

"He says he doesn't know anything about an embalming machine. Had to tell him what one was. Says he thought people went to heaven when they died. Says he doesn't know where the Ortega Highway is. Never heard of Jillson, Kane or Stevens. Can't remember the doctor here—Spurlee, or Surplia or Slurpia—something in that area. Christ."

"Why'd he run?"

"Saw the guns."

Hess thought. "We can get hair and prints."

"I already did. Offered him water in a clean glass. He pulled out the hair himself—even got some skin on the end for DNA. It's in a paper towel inside the glass."

"We can hold him forty-eight on the resisting. Keep the questions coming, get Kamala Petersen in for a look, see if his head clears up."

"It's hard to clear up a skull full of lint."

"I think you're right. I also think someone used his name to order a Porti-Boy, signed for the delivery, maybe used his money to pay for it. He never saw the damned thing. Maybe he's covering someone. Maybe someone's using him. Spurlea owns a panel van."

Merci leaned back against the wall, looked up. "What's the rest of this place look like? How come it stinks so bad? What's all that moaning about?"

"Take five and see for yourself."

She came back down the stairs a few minutes later. Hess looked at her and saw the desperation on her face, like when she was working Jerry Kirby's dead heart. Her voice was low, wavering just a little.

"I'm calling the cops, shutting this place down. I'm going to get the Health Department as soon as they open in the morning. We'll take Wayne for resisting, see if anything pops, see what Kamala thinks of him. If he's covering for someone on the Porti-Boy, maybe he'll tell us who. I'll get him a protective cell, make sure the creeps don't hurt him."

"Good." He looked in at William Wayne's feet again. Then at Merci, whose eyes were cold and dark.

"He really is in charge of this hellhole, Hess. That goddamned Dr. Slurpee is who I want. I really can't believe what I just saw."

"I couldn't either."

Merci turned and kicked a hole in the wall. "Steel toes. I'm just a little bit pissed off right now. Call Riverside Sheriffs."

Back out the Ortega the sky was dark and the hills were darker. The road was just a black ribbon with a yellow line through it that kept snaking out of his headlights, then out of Hess's focus. He stared at it, the only line on earth.

Finally, Merci cut loose.

"The worst part of it is none of those people did anything wrong. They probably *never* did anything wrong. William Wayne probably didn't. And the scum we deal with every day, this Purse Snatcher puke we're after? All they *do* is bad things. They've got good minds and good bodies and all they do is bring the hurt down on other people. But you get unlucky enough to be born like those people back there, you end up in the Rose Garden Home in Lake Elsinore. That isn't right, Hess. You keep trying to tell me to feel what other people feel and think what other people think and all that? Well, I never could, until I looked at the people in the rooms back there. That's the first time I could really feel—and smell, and see and think —just *exactly* what other people felt and smelled and saw and thought. And it made me ashamed to be a human being and it made me furious. I'm always furious, though. That's a different story."

She leaned across the seat and Hess thought she was going to hit him. Instead, she drove a stiff index finger into his shoulder and leaned toward him.

"Those people aren't ever going to get better. And they never did anything bad to anybody. That pisses me off and I intend to stay pissed off about it just as long as I can. I wish Dr. Slurpee had a jacket. I wish she was looking at some time."

Hess nodded. "She might get some. You did the right thing, calling the police."

"I should have waited for that bitch and blown her heart out."

"Save your shells for the Purse Snatcher."

"I got plenty for whoever needs them. We just wasted three hours, Hess. Maybe that's what pisses me off most."

Merci stared out at the darkness and the stars as they dropped back down into Orange County. So much sky, she thought, and so little time. Her fury had cooled down to a simmer but she could feel it eager to boil up and over again. That was fine; it was what kept her going.

But her heart felt wrong. It was all mixed up, not unanimous like it always was. It felt heavy with her failure to save Jerry Kirby. It was tender at the sudden and powerful empathy she had felt for the people at the Rose Garden Home. It was still coiling with her own indigenous anger. And there was something else inside her, too, something underlying it all like a small blue flame warming a pot, and this had to do with Hess.

He pulled up next to her car in the Sheriff Department lot, left the engine running. She looked at her watch: pushing midnight.

"Come over?"

"Sure."

She shooed some cats out of the way and made drinks. Her big toe hurt. In the living room she sat across the sofa from Hess and tried to let the smell of the orange grove inhabit her. That didn't work.

Hess stared at the tube but didn't touch his drink.

"Stay tonight?" she said.

"No. I'm going to go in a minute."

"Why'd you come over in the first place, then?"

"To make sure you were okay. Didn't want you to kick all the walls in."

She thought about this. "I'm okay. Look, it's good if you go. I'm better off alone when I'm like this."

"I know."

419

40

Hess parked and walked across the sand to the life-guard stand at 15th Street. He could feel the damp-ness on his cheeks and in his ankles. He climbed the stand and sat on the platform with his back against the house and watched the silver-black Pacific ripple under a sky shot with stars.

He began a prayer but fell asleep. He woke from a dream in which a huge bird crashed through a mirror and emerged on the other side as a Porti-Boy embalming machine. His watch said 4:54 A.M.

He made coffee, paced his apartment, looked at his new head in the bathroom medicine cabinet mirror. Left side. Right side. Front. Pretty different, really. The smoothness looked okay but the color was bad, kind of a yellow, like there wasn't enough blood behind it, or the blood had turned clear. Borderline anemic. Bonnie the beauty would have to embalm me with plenty of flesh tone, he thought. He kept looking at his pale, hairless reflection.

The mirror glass was old and thin at the edges but it gave a true likeness, Hess thought. He opened the door and tried to read the name of the maker inside, but the ink on the sticker had succumbed to the decades.

Mirrors, he thought: mirrors in dreams, mirrors for

baldness, mirrored walls not installed, steamed mirrors in Merci's bathroom, and what was it Colesceau had said, *Send me through the looking glass again?*

It was the again part that bothered Hess. Why *again?*

Because Holtz had taken him out the back door before.

But why? The mob hadn't been there before.

Goddamned *Colesceau* again, he thought. Inside my brain like a tumor that won't stop growing. Age. Repetition. Senescence.

He turned the TV to local news. For a moment he considered the screen, how it looked kind of like a mirror but had its own images inside.

Unless you turn it off. Then you could do whatever you wanted in front of the dark gray screen, and see yourself doing it.

He turned it off and looked at himself. With the living room lamp behind him, the reflection was surprisingly good: a bald old man with a sharp face. He could even see the wig on its faceless foam stand in the background, $89, human hair.

An idea. He got Rick Hjorth's pictures from his briefcase and the enlargements that Gilliam's people had produced. He found the Saturday, August 14, 8:12 P.M. shot that showed Colesceau downstairs in front of the TV, and set it aside. What he wanted was a picture of Colesceau watching TV with no picture on.

But no luck. Probably not enough light, Hess thought: and why would Colesceau sit in front of the tube without turning it on?

He looked through the pictures again. They showed him now what they had shown him before: that Colesceau sat watching TV in his apartment while Ronnie Stevens was slaughtered at a construction site on Main Street in Santa Ana.

Enough, he thought. *It's . . . not . . . him.*

Hess sighed and shook his head. It was 5:10 now. Without real purpose, he dealt the photographs onto the yellow dinette tabletop, like cards in a game of solitaire. He turned them up one at a time, studying each. Then he grouped them by subject: the interior shots of Colesceau, taken through the crack in the blinds; exterior shots of Colesceau on his porch; exterior shots of the apartment, taken from the street to show both the lower and upper floors; the protesters; law enforcement; media. He'd done all this before and learned little.

Hess looked out the window again. *The years have become minutes and this is what we do with our lives.* As a protest against the passage of time, Hess rearranged the pictures according to sequence: an act of small order in a world of grand chaos.

Of course, he'd done this before and learned little, too. The date/time feature was a help but it couldn't show what wasn't there.

But now, as he gazed over the time line again for no better reason than to be doing what was apparently useful, something caught his attention. Something he'd seen but not thought about, looked at but not noticed. Just an oddity, really, a question. He could feel the gears starting to mesh now, the teeth coming together, the wheels starting to turn.

The 8:21 P.M. exterior shot showed both the downstairs and upstairs lights were off.

The 8:22 interior shot, taken through a crack in the blinds, showed Colesceau watching TV.

So far, so good, thought Hess.

Then an 8:25 exterior showed the upstairs light on.

Okay, he either went upstairs or used a convenience switch downstairs. Simple enough.

Another 8:25 exterior showed the upstairs light *off again.*

Still all right.

But the next interior shot, taken at 8:25, showed Colesceau watching TV.

Why hadn't Hjorth taken a picture as Colesceau came back to the couch? Every shooter's prize: a picture of his subject's face? Why had he waited until Colesceau turned his back to him and sat back down? He'd already shot the back of Colesceau's head, at 8:22. Why again?

He flipped his blue notebook open to Rick Hjorth's number, and dialed it.

He got an answering machine, but identified himself and waited. Sure enough, Hjorth picked up.

"Man, it's early, Detective."

"It's quarter to six."

"Did my pictures help?"

"Maybe. I want to know why you don't have a picture of Colesceau's face. I mean, after he turned off the upstairs lights and came back to the couch to watch TV. You let him turn his back, sit down and get settled. I know you got to the window fast because

423

both of your outside shots *and* the Colesceau shot were all taken at 8:25. You were fast."

"Well, not fast enough. See, I can't tell you the times but the light upstairs was pretty much off all night. Then it went on and I thought I'd document it. And I liked the way the lit window showed up against the sky. Then the light went off real fast—it was only on for a second, like he just wanted to check his watch or something—so I figured he was done upstairs and he'd come down to the TV again. And I realized I could get a face shot. So I *ran* to the window, to shoot through the crack. But he was already sitting there. I was totally bummed. It was like he never even moved."

Like he never even moved, thought Hess.

Like someone other than Colesceau had turned the light on and off again.

Like someone upstairs had made a mistake with the light, caught himself, switched it back off in a hurry while Colesceau watched TV.

"Thank you," he said, and hung up. He checked his watch against the softening darkness beyond the window glass. It was 5:48.

Hess stood then, his heart chugging a little faster, his mind alert. He looked at the wig, touched it. He went to the window and looked toward the ocean but what he saw was the inside of Colesceau's house: the beige carpet, the white walls, the rough acoustic ceiling, lawyer's bookshelves filled with painted eggs, the TV, the stairway leading up. Then, upstairs, Hess pictured the main bedroom on the left: Colesceau's narrow bed neatly made with its brown spread, the bright yellow

424

Shelby Cobra poster from Pratt Automotive on the wall, the dresser top littered with change and movie ticket stubs, the framed poster of the castle on the mountaintop. Next Hess pictured the spare bedroom, the lonely black plastic crucifix hanging on the wall opposite the bed with the Jesus who, facing his own image in mirrored glass, had struck Hess as the loneliest savior he'd ever seen.

Mirrored walls. Jesus in glass. Lonely and black.

Who's in there with Colesceau? Who turned out the lights for him? Maybe this friend plays the role of Colesceau so Colesceau can go out. Idiot Billy Wayne?

But how could Colesceau go out, or anyone get in, with the crowd right there?

Something that Hess had just seen drew him back to his own bathroom. He looked at himself in the medicine cabinet mirror again. He opened the door and looked at the manufacturer's sticker. He closed the cabinet door and watched his face reappear. He opened it and watched it vanish into a shelf of shave gear and medicine bottles.

Glass. Glass, a hole in the world.

Sending me through the looking glass again.

Again.

Hess felt a funny little rush in his head and got his blue notebook. He found the home phone number for Quail Creek Apartment Homes manager Art Ledbetter and dialed it while he looked out the window. He answered on the second ring. Hess told him who he was and told Ledbetter he had a simple question.

"All right, Detective."

"Do any of the smaller bedrooms in the Quail Creek apartments have mirrored walls?"

"No, sir. None of the Quail Creek units do. We don't use glass on the closet doors, either. It's too expensive."

"So a tenant would have to put up mirrored walls at his own expense?"

"We wouldn't allow it. But it would be easy enough to do without us knowing."

Hess considered. He thought of his dream, a huge bird crashing through a mirror, then changing into something else on the other side. A Porti-Boy. *Was the bird an ostrich? Hold that thought.*

"Can you give me the name and phone number of the tenant who lives directly behind 12 Meadowlark? That address would be . . . I have that complex map in my file here . . ."

"It's 28 Covey Run. And the tenant is one of the ghost people I hardly ever see—I told you about her— a single woman. Anyway, I'd have to call you from the office with her name and number. I don't have it here."

Hess asked Art to call both his office and home numbers as soon as he had them.

Next he dialed New West Farms, hoping that someone might be there an hour before the start of business. Farmers could be like that, he thought; up before the sun. But he got a recording and left a message, identifying himself and saying a return call was important.

What was it about the big bird breaking through the mirror?

What was it about Spurlea buying ostrich and emu meat?

Hess was hot now and he knew it, and he knew the luck was with him and he thought—for the first time in days—that he should trust his instincts again.

He was starting to understand. He saw the picture: a big bird crashing through the mirror, a big bird hatching from a big egg.

Hold that thought.

He called the station and got the watch commander to have someone check his fax machine. A moment later the watch commander called back.

"Hess, you've got some document with a signature on it. A UPS delivery receipt, I think."

"Who took the delivery?"

"Looks like William Wayne."

"No doubt?"

"The writing's good and clear."

"Look like an eleven-year-old did it?"

"No. I'd guess man's writing, slant forward, low, heavy, kind of rushed. A grown-up."

"Put it in the top drawer of my desk, will you?"

"Okay. Anything else?"

"That's all."

"How you feeling these days?"

"Better by the second."

Hess hung up and went to the window again. Dawn was breaking behind him, to the east, and the first faint line of the horizon was coalescing above the gray ocean.

The phone rang.

The owner of New West Farms told him that

Helena Spurlea had never bought so much as one ounce of ostrich meat from him.

Hess understood why.

"She only buys the eggs, correct?"

"That's right. She doesn't eat the goddamned things. She *paints* them."

"Can you give me the delivery address?"

The owner was happy to.

It was Wheeler Greenfield's place in Lake Elsinore, just like Hess knew it would be. Of course, she rents from him . . .

Hold that thought.

Spurlea is Colesceau's mother.

Hold that thought.

He called Art Ledbetter again.

"Just heading out the door, Detective."

"Is the woman who rents 28 Covey Run named Helena Spurlea?"

Ledbetter was quiet for a beat. "I don't know. Like I said before, I don't collect the rent—I just oversee maintenance and sec—"

Hess exhaled and felt his heart thumping in his throat. "Where do the rent checks go?"

"Schaff Property Management in Newport Beach."

Monthly checks of $875 for storage to Schaff . . .

Hess hung up and dug into his miscellany file, where he had kept the documents relating to Matamoros Colesceau. At the bottom of the second page of Colesceau's protocol agreement with the State of California, the document specifying the terms of his parole and his chemical castration, was Colesceau's signature.

428

It was slant forward, low and heavy.

Mother and son, he thought.

He got Judge Ernest Alvarez's home number from his black book and dialed.

Ten minutes later he was granted phone warrants to search the apartments of Matamoros Colesceau and Helena Spurlea for a Porti-Boy embalming machine, formaldehyde-based solution, a homemade car alarm override, a Deer Sleigh'R, chloroform and a blond wig.

41

In the grainy half light preceding dawn, Big Bill Wayne sat in his van and sipped a Bloody Mary from a mason jar. He wondered where the top had gotten to, probably out in the Ortega somewhere. No worries. He stared as Trudy Powers and her husband got out of their Volvo wagon, shut the doors, joined hands and walked together slowly across the park toward the rise. It was 5:14.

Trudy had a Bible in her right hand and the same purse slung over her shoulder as the day before. She was wearing a white dress and sandals. To Big Bill's satisfaction, her hair was up. Her husband, Jonathan, tall and bearded and stork-like, wore shorts and a T-shirt and a baseball cap. He looked like something that would propagate only in wetlands.

Colesceau had said that Trudy Powers would be good to her word, and she had been. He had thanked her for the pie, arranged to pray early the next morning in the park just east of the Quail Creek Apartment Homes. Colesceau had told her the sunrise was beautiful from there—that he'd often gotten up early and gone alone there to see it and pray. Bill hoped she'd honor her commitment.

In fact, Colesceau had never prayed from the park, but Bill had been there twice before, unable to sleep and looking for a place he could dump Lael or Janet if they got to be too much of a problem. He'd covered half the county looking into places for occasions like that. Which was how he found the hanging trees in Ortega. And how the bodies of his first three completely botched preservation attempts had ended up deep in the bottom of Black Star Canyon, in a forgotten mine shaft half a mile beyond the DO NOT ENTER BY ORDER OF THE FIRE MARSHAL sign. It was so deep he never heard them hit.

Bill felt his heart speed up. He checked himself in the mirror, then got out, locked up and walked into the park. Looking ahead he saw Trudy and her husband disappear over a gentle rise. It was an ideal place because the condos all around were hidden by trees to give park users the illusion of privacy. And in this near-dark, no one could see much anyway.

He walked down the swale and started up the rise. The park was empty and he could feel his things in the pockets of his long denim coat. One for Stork and one for Trudy.

He was really surprised that he was this close. Colesceau had been fantasizing about this for months, he knew. Bill had always liked the idea but hadn't seen a reasonable way to implement it. But when it became clear to him what he needed to do, it also became clear how it could be done. And Trudy's invitation to pray with Colesceau, slipped into the Psalms of her Revised Standard Version of the Holy Bible, was the opening Bill needed.

Coming over the hillock he looked down across the next gentle swale: a picnic table with attached benches, a built-in barbecue nearby, a Norfolk Island pine alone in a sea of Bermuda grass and a couple standing arm in arm in the grass looking toward the lightening eastern sky.

He breathed in deeply and exhaled fully. He lowered his voice as far as it would comfortably go. "Gonna be beautiful this morning, isn't it?"

They both turned. They had to disengage each other to do it. Stork smiled and looked back toward the sunrise.

Trudy looked at him. "I'm sure it will be. God's new morning."

"So true."

She turned away. Bill watched a pair of doves whisk by on squeaky wings. The sky beyond them was tinged with orange now. His heart was beating fast but steady and his body felt young and strong, especially his hands and his eyes.

He breathed in deeply and exhaled fully again, then started down the hillock toward them. The grass was damp and soft under his boots and he could smell it. The sky registered another octave of light, an orange glow that seemed warm and fertile and unhurried.

"Is that the Bible you've got there?"

Trudy turned back again but Stork kept looking east. "We were going to pray with a friend but he didn't make it. Care to join us?"

She was just ten feet away now. He could see her watching him, see the back of her husband's capped head in the middle of the brightening sky. She had the same sense of holy mandate about her that

Colesceau had described, but also a trace of uncertainty in her face.

"Wherever three are gathered in my name," he said. "Isn't that how it goes?"

She took her husband's arm. "Honey, Jonathan? This guy would like to pray with us."

"Fine," said the Stork. He turned to face Bill and Bill smiled at him. "What's your name?"

"Big Bill Wayne."

Stork offered his hand. Big Bill brought the ice pick from his pocket and slammed it into Stork's chest. Bill used every bit of strength he had, starting down in his legs. The crack of bone, then instant depth. He hung on it with both hands for a split second. Then he let go.

Stork arched skyward like he was yanked by wires. He rose up on his tiptoes with his arms out and the handle profiled against the gray-orange sky. Trying to fly, thought Bill. His beak was wide open but nothing came out but a brief dry gasp. Bill could tell by his eyes he wasn't seeing anything. Stork dropped to the grass with a *hmmfff*.

Trudy had stopped in place, her hands out toward her husband but suddenly frozen midair, the Bible already on the ground at her feet.

It seemed to Bill he had waited a lifetime to see the expression on her face: helplessness, powerlessness, fear. Worth the wait.

There was a sudden eruption from Stork, a sound like a cough and a sneeze and a retch all put together. It had the ring of the final. Trudy's white dress caught red mist. Bill waved to clear the air in front of him, like shooing off a fly.

433

Then he pulled out the derringer and put it to Trudy Powers's temple.

"Just me and you now, little darlin'."

Merci clambered up through incomprehensible morning dreams and got the phone. It was 6:22 A.M., she saw, and Hess's urgent voice startled her from the other end.

"Helena Spurlea is Colesceau's mother," she heard him say. "Colesceau used Billy Wayne as a front to buy the machine. She's renting the apartment behind her son's. That's where we'll find it, and God knows what else."

It took her maybe two seconds to process the information.

"We'll need warrants for the Porti-Boy. Alvarez might be willing—"

"—I've already got them."

"Wait for me, Hess. I'll be there as fast as I can."

"I'm already waiting."

Merci turned up both radios full blast, slapped on a T-shirt and her body armor, a loose blouse and sport coat, pants and duty boots. She strapped the ankle cannon over her sock, then the shoulder rig with the loose snap and the H&K nine. Where was that "select law enforcement" freebie, anyway? Hair up, then on with a Sheriff's Department cap. She grabbed the charging cell phone off the bathroom counter and put it in her purse, making sure the cheap stiletto was still there, too.

She glanced at Hess's note on the kitchen table, still there from the morning before. Sonofabitch was right about Colesceau! Her heart was beating hard and strong as she trotted across the drive toward her car.

She got in and turned the key just as the smell hit her, then something cold and wet locked over her face.

At first she was baffled; then she understood.

She jammed her boots against the pedals and slammed her body and head back. She threw her elbows and twisted at the waist, first one way, then the other, then back again. She told herself not to inhale one drop of anything but he'd caught her somehow on the exhale and she was starved for air even as she realized she'd better not breathe.

And through all of that she kept thinking she'd break the guy's grip on her face but she couldn't. His hands, and the smell she couldn't get away from, just rode her thrashing head like a rodeo cowboy on a bull.

She willed the man's grip to give. She focused all of her power on making his arms relax. *His arms are weak now* . . .

Then she noticed the roof liner of the Impala was a very interesting smoke gray color.

Hess waited in his car at the entrance to the Quail Creek Apartment Homes for Merci's Chevy to come charging down the street, but by seven o'clock she still wasn't there.

He drove over and parked across from Colesceau's apartment at 7:05. He didn't want to tip their plan but Colesceau wasn't going anywhere now, with Hess watching. He noted the plates on the black Caddy

435

parked in front of him and checked the numbers against the ones in his blue notebook: Helena Spurlea's. He radioed Dispatch, told them to get Rayborn to Quail Creek ASAP but Dispatch said she wasn't responding to the call.

Hess got out of the car and approached the crowd. He adjusted his hat to cover as much of his face as he could. There were only half a dozen protesters this early. They were sharing a box of donuts and coffee from a couple of thermoses. The CNB shooter was there, but the big networks had packed up and left. He talked one of the coffee drinkers into letting him use his cell phone. He called Merci direct and got plenty of ringing but no answer. Not at home, he thought. Not at headquarters. Not en route to headquarters. Not on the cell either, and she carried the damned cell everywhere.

He went to the apartment window and looked through the crack in the blinds. The TV was on, but he couldn't see anyone watching it. He went back to his car and tried Dispatch again but Dispatch couldn't raise Merci Rayborn any more than Hess could calm the worry starting to work itself into him. It made his nerves feel brittle and jumpy. Things felt wrong. It was 7:11, and he gave her four more minutes to show.

Then another three.

Then he lumbered across the street again, past the little crowd of demonstrators, and asked the CNB shooter to come with him, please.

He was a young man of maybe twenty-five, Hess guessed, sleepy after a long night's vigil and probably disappointed that his shift had yielded nothing compared to yesterday's circus at the Corrections Building. Mark. Hess got him away from the others and laid it out: don't shoot the next five minutes for CNB and Hess would make sure he got into the house first, ahead of the other cameras. If he didn't want first access then he'd get none at all, and he could explain that to his bosses however he wanted.

Mark said fine and Hess shook his hand and looked him in the eye while he did it. Whatever threat Hess was trying to convey seemed to hit home, because the guy looked away, nodding quickly.

He went to the porch and knocked. No answer. He tried the door but it was locked. He looked back at Mark, who was standing with the protesters, his camera at his side.

Hess stepped back, turned his left shoulder to the door and summoned the strength of his legs. It wasn't a stout door but it took him three assaults to get the thing open. That was the most any door had ever taken, he thought, as he pushed it back and stepped inside. He was breathing hard and his thighs were shaking. He looked back at the CNB shooter, who was still with the protesters, watching him, good to his word. The neighbors stood still and silent.

Hess closed the door behind him and stopped in the short entryway, waiting. No sounds from upstairs, no response from a heavy sleeper awakened by a splintering door. There was a faint smell of cooking in the air and he could see the dishes and pots and skillet from last night's dinner piled into the left sink. Enough for two, he noted. The refrigerator cycled on with a hum. He checked the living room and the little bathroom downstairs. He drew his .45, chambered a round and started up.

On the landing he stopped and listened to the silence. He tried not to think about how heavy his legs felt, how short of breath a little stairway had made him.

Helena Spurlea was lying on the floor in Colesceau's bedroom, her legs twisted in covers. She'd fought. Her nightshirt was a bloody rag. She was on her back with her eyes open and her mouth agape. Hess had never seen more stab wounds on a corpse, not even a satanic ritual murder he'd been called out on back in '69, where three people had gone at it. Sixty or eighty, he guessed, hard to say because they were so small. Colesceau and his ice pick.

He moved back out, then across the hallway to the guest room. The bed was neatly made: no Colesceau, no body, nothing he hadn't seen here a week ago when something inside him knew that things here weren't adding up.

Except that one entire panel of mirror on one wall was removed, neatly propped to the side to reveal the framing. Stuck to the glass were two devices with thick handles and black rubber suctions the size of salad plates. *Wood's Power Grips*, Hess read. Behind the glass a big rectangle of insulation had been cut away, making a passageway through to the other side.

Resting on one of the exposed horizontal studs of the wall frame were two Styrofoam heads. They were facing him. One was bald, the other had some dark hair attached, eyebrows, too. A hit of adrenaline shot through Hess: one to hold a human hair wig, and the other to watch TV? Through the opening he could see into the apartment behind. A faint bad smell wafted through to him and Hess understood now what he had come so close to understanding before.

He stepped through. The cold hit him first and he could hear the hiss of the air conditioner. The room was empty except for a change of clothes—pants, shirt, shoes—arranged neatly on the floor of the closet.

He heard the faint mutter of a TV and followed it. With his sidearm up and ready he turned into the second upstairs bedroom and stared past the sights. What had once been Lael Jillson reclined in the bed wearing provocative lingerie, facing a morning talk show. Hess recognized her by her hair and by the general shape of her skull and face. Her skin was rippled and gray and looked rigid. She wore sunglasses, like she was hiding a bruise.

Downstairs he met Janet Kane, who was seated at the breakfast bar with a book in her hands, wearing a white blouse, a short black skirt, nylons and black high heels. Her legs were crossed. She dangled one shoe from her toes, as women will sometimes do. Her hair was up. Again, the general shape of her head and face was enough like her photographs for Hess to tell who she was. Her skin wasn't as dark as Lael Jillson's, but it had the same hard rippling, like swells on an ocean frozen solid. Sunglasses, too.

Veronica Stevens lay on her front on the living room couch, head resting on her hands, looking into the room. She wore red lingerie. One calf was raised at the knee, like a forties pinup girl. In the half light of the draped living room she looked almost alive.

Hess stood among the women with his gun at his side, his hat covering his naked head, looking down. His shame matched his anger but he still couldn't quite believe what he had seen.

For no real reason he walked across to the front windows, moved the drapes and looked out: suburban Orange County, citizens on their ways to work, the lazy hot haze of summer already rising up from the earth. Nothing special. Nothing different. Business as usual.

Business as usual for Colesceau, he thought.

He checked the garage for the van but there was no vehicle. No Porti-Boy. He lifted the sheet off a waist-high object to reveal an aluminum table with blood gutters and drains at each end.

He used the kitchen phone to request deputies to 12 Meadowlark, 28 Covey Run and to Merci Rayborn's home in the orange grove. Then an APB on Spurlea's van. He read the plate numbers slowly and clearly but he could feel his heart racing.

Back in the garage he pressed the automatic door opener and waited. When it was up he pressed it again, ducked under the lowering door and ran back to his car. The protesters and the cameraman watched as he turned the key, yanked the shifter into drive and gunned it hard.

He skidded up Merci's circular drive and stopped short of her Impala. The driver's side door was swung open and he half expected to see her but there was no

Merci, no body, no nothing but the squelch of the radio and the cats lounging in the morning sunlight on the porch. He slammed through the front door and ran through the house but it was empty as he knew it would be. So was the garage.

Except for a disappearing rat and the body of a young woman, naked and hung by her ankles from one of the rafter beams. Arms loose and fingers nearly touching the floor. Hair down, filled with golden light admitted by the garage window, glittering and ornamental in her slow rotation.

Hess moved in closer to see the shiny stainless steel object stuck up against her clavicle. He recognized it from the mortuary science department, an insertion tube for tying off one end of a severed jugular and pumping fluid into the open other. The floor was a pond of red-black blood and the woman—Hess thought she looked like the protester spokeswoman he'd seen on CNB—appeared blanched and lifeless in the dusty morning light. Her purse sat in the middle of the gruesome lake.

Hess tried to think and to think clearly. He left her unfinished, he thought, he did all the work and left her for us to see. Because he's got Merci, and two are too many to handle. He traded this one for Merci, and he's going to start in on her next.

Where?

He needs privacy. He needs somewhere to hang her. He needs electricity to run the Porti-Boy.

Back in his car he got Dispatch to patch him through to Brighton. When he got the sheriff he requested a helicopter search of the Ortega Highway for the silver panel van or a man on foot; Riverside County units to the Rose Garden Home and Lee LaLonde's old address in Lake Elsinore; and the coroner to Merci Rayborn's home.

"Christ, Tim. We've got another homicide in Irvine, just came in. Goddamn county park."

"Look, can we get Mike McNally and the dogs out here to Rayborn's house? It's a long shot but the scent's fresh."

"They can't track someone in a vehicle."

"They can't track someone in a *kennel*. It's worth a try."

"You've got it."

He sat there in his car for a moment, the morning heat coming through the windows at him. He lifted the hat, wiped the sweat off his head. Through the dusty garage window he could see the pale shape of Trudy Powers suspended in the air.

Somewhere to hang her. Privacy. Electricity.

The Ortega was too obvious, no outlets, and covered. The Rose Garden Home was covered. LaLonde's place was covered. Colesceau had figured someone would look here for Merci, so he left in a hurry.

Somewhere close. Somewhere private. Somewhere familiar.

He thought of the high bay at Pratt's, where the old cars *come here dogs and leave here dolls,* and started up the car at the same time.

The heavy sedan fishtailed around the driveway, straightening out on the dirt road leading to the street. The ruts crunched the shocks and threw the tires up. Hess clamped the wheel like a captain in a storm.

442

He was calling Dispatch for a Costa Mesa PD assist when he got the Chevy airborne over a rise, landed hard and cranked a turn onto the asphalt.

42

She saw the room through pressure and pain. It was an upside-down world of chrome wheels, spray guns and canisters, the walls lined with Peg Board and hung with hand tools and posters of women, a concrete floor—directly below her, just out of reach of her fingertips—stained with layers of paint and oil and fluid. It was all flushed in red.

When she turned to her right she could see the grill and headlights and tires of a silver panel van. She was too far away to see the tread patterns. Near the van was a gleaming yellow-and-black convertible of some kind. If she tightened her stomach and neck muscles and strained into a sit-up she could see her legs all the way up to her boots, which were lashed together with orange rope and tied to a platform that was elevated high off the ground. Merci had heard Ike in the impound yard call such a platform a "rack."

The pain was excruciating and inescapable. It was like having your head pumped with molten lead. The swollen flesh of her face pushed against the tape that was cinched over her mouth. She could feel it cutting in. If she folded up at the waist and got her head level the pressure would stop growing for as long as she could hold it. But that wasn't long. And it sapped her strength, with the five pounds of body armor choking off her breath and sending the sweat running in a steady stream off her chest and down into her eyes. The muscles in her armpits were burning and stretched. Her wrists were locked together with tape and her fingers, dangling almost to the floor, felt like they'd been scorched and split and rubbed with salt. Her ankles throbbed with the pain of constant strangulation. She felt nothing in her feet at all.

And through it all she smelled the gagging sweet smell of chloroform, which she remembered from chemistry class was a simple $CHCl_3$ chain once popular as an anesthetic. So far the bastard had hit her twice with it while she dangled here, plus at least once in her car and God knew how many times while they were in transit.

Her H&K was gone—she'd seen him handling it over by one of the workbenches. Her ankle cannon was gone, too. He had laughed at it, then put the tiny thing in his pocket. Her only undiscovered secret was the Chinese-made Italian stiletto, which was in the bottom of her purse. And her phone. But her purse remained just out of the reach of her outstretched hands, purposefully placed on the floor like some ideal, something she could strive after for the rest of her life and never quite get. She wondered if she could get herself swinging like a pendulum the arc might bring her within reach of it.

"Time's a running short," he said. His voice was calm, accented lightly in a strangely indefinable American manner—kind of western but southern, too, a hint of Texas and maybe Arkansas and even California. There was another influence floating around in his voice and Merci assumed it was the Romanian inflection learned early in life by Matamoros Colesceau.

"I don't like to work fast," he said. "Because you know, honey, it's the process that's important."

Merci had no voice. The tape choked off her words and left her with only grunts and growls. And there was the damned roaring of blood in her head. It was like standing next to a waterfall or a jet.

What she thought was, important for who, shitbird? But even her own thoughts sounded feeble and far away.

"So I am going to have to move things along. Don't want the owners getting here at nine, and us still around."

Merci looked at him: a short, chubby man in boots and tight jeans, a boldly striped country-singer shirt and black leather vest. And flowing blond hair and a thick blond mustache that she knew to be fake, though in spite of her knowledge looked undeniably authentic. But under it all she recognized Colesceau, even upside-down like he was, something in his posture, the shoulders hunched to hide the budding breasts, the sad, untrusting eyes. Yes, this was the man she had talked to just a few days before.

The one she'd bullied and disrespected and dismissed. Called stupid on TV.

The one Hess understood but couldn't explain to her. Or even to himself.

More disturbing than his appearance was the gleaming contraption over which he stood: an embalming machine, likely the one delivered to the Rose

Garden Home. She wondered if the mother was in on all this.

She tried to get herself swinging in the direction of the purse. She might be able to grasp it with her blood-bloated fingers, get to the knife and . . . what? At first she hoped to be covert about it, but soon understood that just getting some momentum took a lot of work. She flexed her legs, bent at the stomach, swung her aching head. When she felt the first small kinetic glide of energy kick in, she turned her head to look at him. He had one of the embalming machine tubes in his hand, but he was watching her.

She watched him back and kept pumping with her shoulders and hands, and tightening her calves to create sway. It was amazing how much effort you could put into something for so small a result. He dropped the end of the tube and picked up a half-gallon bottle of something and began pouring it into the canister on the machine.

She had to slow him down long enough to let someone in the world find her, but it was hard to imagine someone finding you when you had no idea where you were.

A shiver of fear broke over her. It was like drowning—no oxygen and a need to scream. She told herself to be calm. Calm but alert. She estimated how far her body was swinging now, in each direction away from center. It seemed to be about four feet. The purse was still at least a yard away from her hands. Through the red panic and a sudden clutch of nausea Merci tried to counsel herself: I *will* you to stay calm. I *will* you to overcome this situation. I *will* you to prevail.

But it was extremely hard to draw extra breath with your mouth taped shut.

"That's funny," he said. "Hold on now, honey. I'm gonna hit the brakes."

He came around behind her and Merci felt the rope stiffen, breaking her momentum and slowing her. Something inside her panicked, then broke.

She flailed blindly with her bound wrists, in hope of catching any part of him. What she wanted most right then was just to make him hurt somehow.

She heard fluid splashing into fluid. She turned her head—God, it was just a throbbing ball of pain—and watched Colesceau swing into view. He plugged an orange extension cord into the wall. He carried the contraption toward her, setting it down on the stained concrete floor.

Merci felt her body settling into a little circular orbit now. The dregs of her energy were all that was left. As she swung slowly on the rope she tried to think of how to best stall Colesceau, give him something to worry about, give her companions in law enforcement time to find her.

She watched him approach her, upside-down, blond waves on his shoulders, boots shining, vest taut.

"Nice try," he said. He steadied the rope. "I don't see anything else you could have done, little woman."

Then he reached out his hand. He seemed to be offering her one of those faded red shop rags sold in bunches of fifty. It was folded neatly and cupped in his palm.

She felt his boots press her fingers against the floor.

She knew if he put all his weight on them she'd lose a knuckle or two, maybe more. But the smell of the CHCl₃ hit her and she couldn't help herself. All the panic rose inside her and it put up a ferocious struggle to get out. She tried to pull her hands free of his weight but it was useless. She screamed against the tape. She felt him grab her hair hard and press the cloth up tight to her face. For the first time in her life Merci thought of heaven as a place with a door, and the door would not open.

And back she fell into the soft black nowhere.

Colesceau unfolded one of the big gray blankets used to protect newly chromed or painted automobile parts, and laid it down over the stained floor. Then he lowered the unconscious Merci to the blanket. He cut away her blouse. He unfastened the heavy bulletproof vest and cut her bra off and set them aside. He ran his fingers lightly over her pale skin and kissed each nipple and was pleased to feel them harden between his teeth. Then off with her boots and pants and undies. He was efficient but not hurried. He arranged her hair up, a crown of dark lavish curls.

He stood and looked down at her. She was more beautiful than he'd thought she'd be: large, well proportioned, strong but smooth, like a mare. Powerful legs, but shaped well. Not very hairy, considering that dark-haired women often had extra. Big knockers, as the Americans liked to say. The way her beauty marks contrasted with her skin was exhilarating.

He regretted that he'd have to drain and preserve her simultaneously—standard operating procedure taught at mortician school—but for Colesceau a hurrying of what should be a calm, meditative and often erotic procedure. Still, an hour and a half should be plenty of time. If push came to shove he could load her into the yellow-and-black Shelby Cobra, squeeze the Porti-Boy into the trunk and check into a motel somewhere to finish his saving. A little TV volume would be enough to disguise the chugging of his machine. Maybe he could find an old western on.

He touched the red ligature marks around her ankles. They would restore easily. Same with the tape marks on her wrists, but it wasn't prudent to cut that tape away just yet. Or the mouth tape, for that matter. He moved the Porti-Boy up close and hit the "on" button just to test it. The motor whirred assuringly and he turned it off.

Well, he thought: cut in, hook out the carotid and install the insertion tube. When everything was up and running he could start massaging the life out of her and the preserving fluid in. Inject her with eternity.

He took the blade from his instrument book and started pushing his fingertips down into the gristle around her clavicle. And there it was, lovely carotid, throbbing against his finger like a snake.

What a weird thing to be doing, he thought, going to so much trouble to preserve a cop.

43

Hess made a left on Palmetto, gunning the Chevy through the light industrial zone of Costa Mesa, past a boatyard and a liquid propane distributor and a wrecking yard for German imports and a surfboard maker and a custom motorcycle shop. At intervals, large dogs regarded him through chain link. Then the brick and windows of Pratt Automotive. He cranked a hard right at the next corner and came around the backside behind the bay.

There it was, sheltered behind two metal doors that opened from the ground up. Into each big slider was built a man-sized convenience door. No van in sight. Hess planted his sedan to block the use of either doorway, then cut the engine and called his position into Dispatch. Hess said there wasn't a Costa Mesa prowl car in sight and Dispatch told him there was a 211, armed robbery, going down on the east side, all area units requested. But the real news was Sheriff's deputies had pulled over a panel van eastbound on the Ortega Highway, stand by.

He got out, put on his hat and walked toward the doors. That set off the guard dogs, a whole pack of them from the sound of it, their voices shrieking all around Hess in the warm summer air. He could hear the clink and rattle of the fences. The convenience doors wouldn't move. Neither would the big sliders. Locked from the inside, as he'd expected.

And if there was anyone inside, they'd heard him.

He went around the building to the front. No van. There were five spaces in front of the store, a patch of brown grass and ivy up by the windows, a break area with some patio furniture on it. He was breathing hard by the time he rounded the corner and he wished his heart would just settle down but it was thumping away. It felt like something was slipping in there. Hess told himself not to worry about it. When was the last time his heart did something he asked it to, anyway?

Up close to the building and bent low under the windows, he crept along. The chipped letters spelling out Pratt Automotive went past over his head. The ivy he stepped on was threadbare and almost leafless. He squeezed behind a rusted wrought-iron bench surrounded by cigarette butts. His back hurt and it was hard to ignore the pain when he was bent over like that. The front doors were mesh-reinforced glass and they were locked, too. He cupped his hands to the dirty scarred glass and saw the dark wood paneling of the front office, the counter with the computer on it, the rows of shelves. At the end of one row Hess could see a door with a square window.

The front of the shop sat in darkness but light showed through the window to the high bay. An orange rope swayed very slightly, hung in the cavernous bay beyond the glass.

His vision went sharp and his heart kicked in strong and fast. He ran over to the wrought-iron chair and dragged it away from the building. The legs caught on the moribund ivy, leaving furrows in the hard dry earth.

It took him two tries to get it up and balanced over his head. He swayed, feet planted in the cigarette butts.

The window exploded just under "Pratt," carrying most of the name with it. Jagged triangles rimmed the frame. Hess pulled his .45 and knocked some of them out with the butt. Then he swung one foot onto the bottom of the window frame and hauled the rest of himself up. He crunched heavily to the floor inside, slicing open his left finger on the way down. Swaying in the broken glass, Hess tried to keep his balance. He found the hatch in the counter and slammed it up and open.

Then he was running the aisle between the high stacked shelves, left arm reaching for the high bay door, the window getting bigger as he approached.

He grabbed the door handle, jerked down and pushed through. The sound of the door closing behind him echoed faintly in the high ceiling.

Over his gun sights now: a silver van. Yellow race car. Orange rope. Merci curled on the floor below the rope, naked but moving. She lifted her head and shook it when she saw him. Her face was taped and Hess could hear her scream against it.

Then a small long-haired man popped up from behind the race car and shot him in the stomach.

Hess fired fractionally later and the man blew backward against the van. He looked like Kamala Petersen's guy, and he wore a thick black vest over a bright shirt. Hess's next two shots seemed to pin his target to the metal. But two more blasts quickly came back at him. Hess ducked into a shooter's crouch, hearing the bullets careening around the bay. When he went to fire again he saw nothing but silver vehicle. He looked to the floor by the van, unable to believe that there was no body lying on it. Then one of the bay doors flew open and the sunlight charged in and the little man charged out.

He was back to Merci in five steps. Her eyes were clear and focused and her neck muscles strained against the tape. She was still trying to speak.

"It's okay," he said. His voice didn't sound believable to him. "Here."

He used his pocketknife to cut the tape from her wrists. It was hard to get the blade out because both his hands were covered with blood. He'd told himself not to look at the hole and not to touch it, but apparently he'd done just that. So he glanced down at his abdomen as he slid the knife back into his pocket, not seeing much but a bloody shirt and belt. A bullet made no bigger hole going in than a sharp pencil, but going out was different.

Right now it felt like someone had swung an oar into his gut, maybe an oar with a big nail in it. And it felt like his body was trying to gather around where that nail had gone in and out again, trying to fill the gap. His flesh was confused. He popped the little .32 from his ankle holster and held it up to her, then set it on the blanket.

Seconds later Hess was in the sunlight behind Pratt Automotive, surrounded by the barking of dogs, looking down the alley to his left where the Purse Snatcher ran with his long blond hair shining in the sun. He had a hundred yards. No more. A cold shiver of nausea went up through Hess, even as the warm blood drenched his underwear and ran down into his shoes.

He ran.

Hess's legs pumped in rhythm with his lungs. He could feel his body trying to writhe away from what had gone in him—or through him, more likely.

He wished he hadn't worn his black wingtips, wished he could trade them for a set of body armor. But he'd had that opportunity before he left home this morning, deciding against it, looking for the damned fedora instead.

Dogs bounced off the fences on either side of him. He was close enough to hear their teeth snap. Hess tried to keep his legs working on the same beat as his lungs but he was gulping and spitting out air twice per step now and that funny red outline had come back and it made him feel like he was dreaming.

The important thing was to keep the legs moving, keep those wingtips aimed at the Purse Snatcher and keep him in sight. Keep him *in sight*. Hess was only sixty yards back. Sixty yards back and closing. Half of that, and he could try to take him out. Half of *that* and he could take him out with certainty, aim for his butt, below the armor. The pain in his gut made him squint.

So Hess squinted ahead through the red world and kept his vision riveted on his prey. His footfalls were the sound of wet socks in wet shoes. The Colt was slick and heavy and he thought he might change hands but he also thought he might drop it. He thought he must be slowing down because Colesceau seemed further out. So he really dug in and tried to get his knees up, get some better speed going.

The Purse Snatcher vanished right. Hess followed seconds later. Through a yard of hay bales with archery targets tacked to them, no archers in sight at this early hour, then around a yellow stucco clubhouse of some kind. Hess could just make out the bright shirt and flowing hair turning the corner away from him.

Then across an empty street and into the grounds of a commercial nursery. Hess saw a stout Japanese man staring first at Colesceau then at him with set, stoic eyes. He held a flat of flowers.

Beyond the nursery was the slough of the Santa Ana River, a thicket of bamboo and weeds inhabited by feral cats and human beings too poor to afford a place to sleep. Hess watched Colesceau scamper between the deep rows of five-gallon trees and potting soil, look back just once, then climb the chain-link fence and drop over. He seemed about a mile away by now, but Hess figured it was just the pain that made his eyes tight, made things look farther out.

Then his legs faltered. His balance began to abandon him and he had to put both hands out like a tightrope walker to keep himself steady, but the gun was heavy and this threw him off even more. Still, he didn't fall. He realized with disappointment that his hat was still on: how fast was he really moving, anyway?

Colesceau was headed for the jungle, a hundred yards away.

Then Hess sensed something behind him and Merci stretched past. She seemed to be eating up the ground ten feet at a time and there was something small and silver in her hand.

On her way by she said, "I got him."

And there she went.

Hess felt his feet slow down, felt the big trunk of his body swaying for balance as it tried to slow down too, then saw the ground coming up at him and turned his face to the side so he wouldn't break his nose.

This he accomplished. With his head in the dirt he looked toward the river in time to see Merci's body pitch over the chain-link fence.

Hess was pleased to see his hat had finally fallen off. He was pleased to see that he still had control of the big automatic .45 in his right hand. Forty-plus years and he'd never lost his sidearm to anyone.

He worked himself up to his knees, gathered his hat and stood. He holstered the gun, which in the nursery seemed to be an absurd, almost shameful possession. He looked for a place to sit and found a wooden bench beside the path by the potted roses. There were a million of them, it seemed, reds and yellows and whites and purples and even a fountain with a dolphin spraying water from its blowhole.

The bench had a back and he leaned against it. He put on the hat and adjusted the brim. He didn't even bother to look down at himself. It felt like someone had burned a hole through his middle with a cigarette the size of a fire log.

457

He was still breathing fast and shallow. Couldn't get quite enough air. Just not enough to go around.

He could see the Japanese man coming toward him down the pathway, with the flat of flowers still in his hands.

Hess didn't really feel like talking. But he knew he should have something to say, some accounting of himself. After all, he was armed and trespassing and taking up space on a perfectly good bench. He could hear the slow pitter-patter of liquid hitting the ground below that bench, like night fog spilling off an eave.

Hess straightened himself and looked up. He folded his hands in his lap and it was like putting them into a pan of something hot and wet. He tried to figure out what he should say. But his thoughts came slow like thoughts in a dream, and he couldn't tell if they were really good or not.

Hello. I'm Tim Hess . . .

It seemed to him that the nurseryman was studying him from a rather long distance. His lips moved. No sound. Earnestly, Hess tried to read them. Then he remembered that there were words, too. Always words. You just had to wait for them.

"Are you the good guy or the bad guy?"

Very slowly, because he could not do it any other way, Hess removed his hat. Something here demanded manners. He set it on his lap and looked at the nurseryman. It took a long time and a lot of strength to formulate his reply. He wanted to get it right. And in the end he got it out in what he hoped was a strong and resonant voice.

"I'm an Orange County Sheriff Department . . .

detective. You put the creeps away. They come back again. Over and over. I've done small. Things. Only a small number of people . . . care about. A few people will remember me. I wish I had children to . . . give things to. I did save three lives. Three. Those are sure saves. Maybe a few by . . . accident. So those . . . three lives are my best contribution to. Things. What I wanted to be was. Useful. In a way you could. See. Like a trash man or a bricklayer. Or a doctor. That's all I have to say."

The nurseryman hovered above a mirage on a distant horizon. His flat of flowers threw colored beams of light into the sky.

"Sounds like you do all right, old man."

"I guess I'm ready."

"Don't talk. I'll call someone."

44

The trail led through the tall bamboo and she could only see him in flashes, out ahead, in the small clearings, looking back over his shoulder before vanishing back into the pale yellow thickness. Cats slithered through the stalks. In an opening she leapt over a small campfire surrounded by three stupefied men in rags who just stared at her, mouths hung in dirty beards, wordless as she flew past.

She wasn't fully aware of how she had gotten here. The haze of the chloroform hadn't fully cleared when she saw Hess, tried to warn him off, heard the shots boom, then saw the sunshine flood through the door as Colesceau made his escape.

Her instincts had made her pull on her clothes and take Hess's backup gun, upend her purse, then stumble into the bright summer morning. She saw Hess lumbering down the alley and the Purse Snatcher skittering out ahead. And she willed her legs to carry her where she needed to go. While she ran she tore the tape from around her face, unreeling it in big rasping circles that left her skin burning but free.

Now she was deep in the thicket and Colesceau was thirty yards away. She felt the air piercing deep into her lungs and every step seemed to push more of the poisonous gas out of her. If he stopped and hid and waited, he could shoot her on her way by. She knew this and tried to watch the bamboo in front. And every time she saw him she thought of Hess and dug deeper and tried to close the distance. He looked wobbly. She wished she had her nine.

Colesceau heaved himself toward the trail. He wasn't sure if his hormone-depleted legs could carry him much further and he knew the jungle would give way to the wide, dry riverbed soon and when it did he'd be out of cover. Then he'd have to start shooting. He had the fancy police gun but really no skill with it at all. His shot at the old bastard was pure luck, but from the *whap* sound of it, he'd hit him good.

The vest was heavy as steel around his chest and it pressed tightly against his breasts. But it had saved him from the ugly Hess. Now he wished he could just shed it and gain a little speed. He looked back again and saw Merci twisting her way through the towering bamboo. She was gaining fast and he knew how determined an angry woman could be. And weren't they always angry about something?

So close, he thought, so close to getting what I wanted. Another ten seconds and he'd have had that carotid hooked and out and cut, and the insertion tube in place and the Porti-Boy churning and Merci Rayborn would be immortal right now. But the second he heard the car pull up outside, then heard someone trying at the doors, he knew it was the old man who was her partner. The tank captain. It made better sense to get on the vest and slaughter Hess than it did to start the preservation. Then he'd have had almost an hour before Pratt and Lydia and Garry arrived. Seconds, he thought. Just seconds from giving her all the fluids necessary for eternity.

He thought of his mother and how free and light he'd felt when he was done. Why had he waited so long? He thought of Trudy Powers and how satisfying it was to see her face when Stork went down. He thought of Lael and Janet and Ronnie and how liberating it was to be rid of them, their demands, their petty games, their selfish power.

Through the thicket ahead he could see the sandy expanse of the riverbed and he knew it was time to make his move. Rounding the next curve in the trail he saw a small pocket of space in the stalks. He stopped, turned and ran back to it. He got there and backed in and with both hands raised the big automatic up to his chest.

When he glanced down at the barrel it was like staring into a big dark pit.

Merci saw the riverbed through the bamboo and she went fast into the curve. She looked far up the trail before her and saw nothing. She looked right out in front of her and saw an elbow tip protruding from the foliage.

She slid like a base runner. Feet out in front, plowing her boots into the mulch. Made sure she had the .32 ready, left arm up to protect her face. The momentum of her body brought her upright, three feet from the blond man hiding in the stalks.

She fired twice and he flinched.

My body armor.

462

He pointed something at her.

She shot a snap kick, standard academy issue, not pretty but her boot caught his wrist and the gun barrel jumped. She ducked, dropped Hess's gun, then came up fast and with both hands swept the stiletto across the top of the vest. A hiss. Colesceau's eyes went wide. His head tilted back, and a gap yawning open under his chin. She changed her grip on the knife and brought it back higher, point first, planting it hard in his temple. She let go and brought both her fists down on his hands. The H&K went off with a crack and flew onto the trail.

Colesceau sank to his knees, hands at his neck.

He looked up at her with eyes that seemed sad. The wig had slid up on his head.

"Tha . . . you," he gurgled.

"You're welcome," she answered. She could barely hear her own voice, though the world was silent.

Colesceau looked down toward the H&K so she kicked him in the forehead and he went over backward.

She got her gun and stood over him with the barrel pointed down.

"Tha . . . oo."

"You're welcome."

She pulled the trigger and his face jerked and his skull lost its shape but his eyes were still on her.

"Tha . . . "

She heard the half syllable and she shot him again.

Hess was sitting on a bench by the roses when she got back to him. His hat was on his lap and his head hung comfortably like a man in siesta. She saw the red all over his shirt and the little shiny puddle of it under the bench.

She knelt down in front of him. He was looking down toward the ground. His expression was hopeful and gentle and he was seeing nothing. The lines of his face had softened and he looked like he did that night when he fell asleep in the chair by the window and she had wanted so badly to touch his hair.

Merci touched his cheek. Then she saw motion to her left and she stood. A man was coming her way with a blanket in his arms. She recognized him as the same man she'd run past a few minutes ago, but then he'd been carrying a flat of flowers.

He stopped when he saw her, a large woman with blood on her and a big gun in her hand.

"He's a detective," said the nurseryman. "No one is going to remember him. He saved three lives."

She looked at him. "It was four and you don't know squat. Give me that blanket. Please."

45

In the spring, Merci bundled up the infant and drove
to the Wedge. It was late, a cool and blustery night
following an unseasonable May storm.

The baby bawled almost the whole way there, but
this was no surprise. It was an inconsolable thing,
always hungry, miserable or asleep. It wasn't much to
look at, either: big and lean, hardly any fat, a head of
wispy black hair. Its lungs and voice box seemed
unnaturally, unbelievably, strong. It suckled greedily
and cried for hours without a comma. All this, delivered in twelve hours of agony she had never imagined
possible. When she saw the thing all she could do was
weep.

For Merci, the last nine months had been the most
miserable of her life. Burying Hess was like losing half
of herself, the half she liked. Burying her mother six
months later was worse. She hadn't expected it to
make her feel so bad, but it made her think of a million things she'd wanted to say but hadn't. Trying to
console her father was impossible because he clung to
Merci with a desperation she never knew was in him.
Had her mother put up with that for forty years?
Well, now it was all hers. He was all hers. He was
asking to move in.

Then came her request for the maternity leave. As

she talked about it with Brighton she felt like she was handing over her career. No more head of detail by forty, no more sheriff by fifty-eight. No more sixty-hour weeks for a while, maybe not ever. He had nodded, leaned forward on his elbows and tried to look glum. She could read his thoughts. She knew her ovaries had accomplished what no amount of political maneuvering on the part of Chuck Brighton could accomplish: she was soon to be a single mom and her career was shot. Maybe not fatally wounded, but shot just the same. Nature had put the little woman in her place.

Merci parked and gathered up the baby and walked down to the sand. The moon was three-quarters and she could see the jetty rocks jutting out into the ocean in a straight line. The waves were no longer high from the storm but she could still see them building along the rocks until they got in close, then rising in the moonlight and breaking on the beach.

The ocean at night could be a frightening thing. Not as frightening as Colesceau hiding in the bamboo with her H&K in his hands and murder in his eyes.

As she climbed onto the jetty Merci could feel the power of the waves vibrating into her legs. Good thing she'd worn the trekking shoes, she thought, the ones with the lug soles and solid grip.

She looked out at the black, horizonless night and forced herself to think of all the good things that had happened these last few months, the worst of her life: the Deputy's Valorous Conduct award back in January, all sorts of PR about courageously chasing down the Purse Snatcher, getting bumped up a pay grade in the rank. A series of private talks with Chuck Brighton, who wanted to leave her in Homicide. No problem there.

She knew that some of these good things came in return for dropping the suit. The trade was understood and unspoken, though clearly engineered by Brighton. It was a time for healing. For forgetting and moving on. And most of all, for the saving of face. She was glad to have the lawsuit gone. It wasn't her battle anymore. The other five plaintiffs were holding tough and Kemp wasn't out of the woods yet. Fine with her.

There was no mention in the media of what was for Merci the worst of all that had happened: that her gun had killed Hess. No mention whose life was laid down to save whose. No mention that the suspect Sergeant Rayborn had earlier rejected was the very one who had three corpses stashed in the apartment behind his own, was the very one who had shot her partner. No. The Grand Jury's criminal justice committee, investigating the shooting of Colesceau, had gone easy on her.

There was plenty of public ignorance, but Merci knew how it had gone down, and so did most people in the department.

She would carry that knowledge to her grave.

It had not occurred to her that she had done pretty much the right thing, given the circumstances. Given the fact that nobody was always right, always smart, always fast. She felt too bad about Hess to entertain such a notion.

He wouldn't let her.

*   *   *

She walked further out on the rocks. She could feel the breeze sharp against her face. It didn't seem that strong back on shore. She could see the jetty out in front of her, the moon and its silver wobble of moonlight beyond the rocks, the waves growing higher as they approached, the infinite black Pacific all around her. Hess's ocean, she thought.

"Here it is, Tim," she said. "What your father loved."

Odd. Odd to say that name now, privately, just to herself and her baby. There was something truthful and unbreakable and sacred in it. It meant something different now, but what it had meant before was still true.

She stood there and looked at the dark water. The swells heaved and shifted. She was surprised how big they were, given that the storm was over. The horizon was impossible to see, as impossible to see as tomorrow. She looked to her right just as an advancing mountain of water clipped along the rocks toward her. The big wave passed in front of the moon, the moonlight caught the water as it lumbered past, then rode the back of the swell as it went by. It was like nothing she had ever seen before on earth.

The tears exploded out of her. For Hess, for herself, for the baby. For Jerry Kirby. For Colesceau's dead, the Rose Garden Home patients, even for weird, misused LaLonde. For everybody who was touched by it.

Most of all for Hess, because she'd felt like he was accusing her from the other side of death's river every waking moment of every day: *you, you, you.*

"Let me go, Hess."

The waves didn't answer. Tim had gone quiet and she could see the twinkle in his eyes, a galaxy of two, deep down in the blanket.

"Just let me go. I loved you and I lost you and I killed you. I'll never forget I killed you. That what you want? Want me to say it, Hess? *I'm so fucking sorry I killed you."*

She sobbed and looked at the water right below her.

I could just step off the rock and get lost in it, she thought: let Hess's ocean take care of everything.

No, I'm better than that.

I couldn't save your dad, Tim, she thought. I tried so hard to do everything right. Everything I knew.

And with this thought something inside her broke away—Hess, perhaps, or what she believed about Hess—separated and moved from her, out over the water and into the night. There was sadness in watching it go, and more tears. Then even those were gone.

She started back, choosing her steps carefully, hugging Tim tightly to her body. She could feel his grip on the collar of her coat.

She wanted to look again at the waves, Hess's beloved waves, the waves over which something inside her had just glided away forever.

But the spray turned her face away so she never saw the thing that pulled her in.

It was like being grabbed. For the second time in her life, she was taken from behind by a monster she had not known was there. Merci could think of only one thing: keep Tim alive.

She knew she had to reach the surface or he would die quick, but the wave had taken her upside-down and headfirst and with the roar of the water around her and the ocean pounding her down and down and down and then dragging her one way then another she couldn't know where she was. No up. No down. And when she willed her eyes open all she saw was a shapeless dull black world and she realized she was almost out of breath. She thought if she could just be still, she would rise to the surface, back to air, back to life.

So she called on all her powers to do this. And in the great calm of will, she rose. She broke the surface, holding Tim high in both hands. She kicked for their lives. Tim bellowed for his.

Then Merci felt herself being picked up from behind, felt her body lifting. Higher. Higher again. Higher still. Her stomach dropped. The world withdrew. She looked down at the terrible trough of blackness and she held Tim tight and surrendered.

She closed her eyes in the fall but she held her son tight. That much she could do, and she could do it well and she would do it forever. She apologized for letting him die like this, her fault entirely, stupid and cowardly and self-obsessed. But she did not let go. Nothing was strong enough, not even this wave and this ocean, to make her let go of him now.

When she hit the bottom the wave crushed them down and pounded them forward. Over once. Over twice. Direction gone now, ears roaring, a scream of red inside her eyeballs.

Then she was sliding on her back up the slick wet

beach and her eyes were burning and Tim was tight in her arms screaming with his fists still locked on her coat.

She looked up at the stars. She heard the rush of water receding around her, sliding back down the beach to join the sea.

What's next?

Tell us the name of an author you love

Jefferson Parker   Go ▶

and we'll find your next great book.